A MOST GRIEVOUS FAULT
A Mystery

KATHRYN A. IMLER

FOREST PARK PRESS
Fort Wayne, IN

To

SME, SMS, and KEZ.

Wouldn't have, couldn't have, done it without you.

Chapter One

The body was there at nine o'clock. Not the body they would find later.

This one they were prepared for.

Father Henry Felger shoved open the heavy oak door at the main entrance of St. Hedwig's Catholic Church and motioned to the men with the casket.

Father Felger hated funerals. Not as much as weddings.

He despised weddings.

With weddings, there was too much time for the family to change its mind. To add a string quartet. To work in a solo by a cousin. Maybe put an archway over the center aisle.

Not funerals. Funerals generally had a short window for planning; and no matter how long the illness, how old the deceased, death was always a surprise, making grief—or even disinterest—trump everything else. Occasionally the family knew they wanted "Amazing Grace," but often it was "You pick whatever you need for the service, Father."

Easy.

Father Henry would select the Scripture readings that matched his favorite funeral homily, then he'd tell the organist or cantor to choose hymns they knew he liked.

Father Henry's prayers had been answered in this regard: St. Hedwig's was an old parish with old parishioners. A parish without a school fostered a half dozen weddings a year at best, but an old parish, with old parishioners, could put the number of funerals to thirty or beyond, yielding monthly, sometimes weekly, affairs. Now in their eighties and nineties, the descendants of the sturdy German stock that built the church, regardless of where their lives and spouses had taken them, wanted to come home to St. Hedwig's to be buried.

"Morning, Father." Don Fleck brushed at the shoulders of his black overcoat. He smiled genially; his soft, round face practiced at expressing sympathy. The double doors were pushed open, letting wind rush in as if it had been wait6ing, like the casket, outside at the top of the church steps.

"Spitting some mean stuff out there," he said, wiping his forehead with the palm of his hand and drawing his fingers along his thinning hairline to smooth what the wind had disturbed. "Could use a little salt on those steps."

Father Henry held his own thick, gray hair in place. "I'll see what I can do." He dodged a large floral display coming toward them. "Inside?"

"Too late probably. But they'll have a tent over the gravesite up for us."

"I'll be brief."

Don Fleck winked. "You always are."

Father Henry smiled and headed down the long, ivory marble aisle. He was dressed simply in black slacks and shirt, a burgundy cardigan.

The hundred-year-old church was not yet warm, but it was a cavernous building to heat in January. Five huge pillars stationed every twenty feet on each side rose up past stained-glass windows from the Motherland and splayed into arches that supported the cathedral ceiling. Only the sound of the crew from the funeral home discreetly opening the casket, setting out prayer cards, and positioning flowers; along with the icy sleet pelting outside, met the echo of Father Henry's footsteps.

Almost over, thought Father.

At seventy-two, Father Henry Felger was a tall man, muscular even, owing whatever fitness he possessed at this stage more to family genes than to any exercise program. His mother had lived to be ninety-six. He wasn't hoping for that many genes.

Father Henry was tired. All the time now, it seemed. What he really wanted was his routine uninterrupted: up at five thirty a.m. to shower, dress, feed and brush the cats while reruns of his favorite sitcoms brightened the dark mornings. If everything went well, his table by the window at Sunrise Cafe would be waiting for him, along with Geneva, the ancient waitress who knew his order without asking (two eggs over easy; bacon, meaty not crisp; and whole-wheat toast with strawberry jam); kept pleasantries to a minimum; and had coffee, freshly brewed, strong and black, next to the morning paper when he arrived. All this before prayers and Mass at eight a.m.

Father Henry found it irritating when any of these elements was off. Not a disaster. Just enough to throw a glitch in the day, make it seem as if anything could go wrong.

Of course, a funeral. That could kill a good day right off the bat.

Nearing the large center altar at the front of church, Father Henry's foot snagged a phantom step. His hand caught the carved arch at the end of the closest pew and, while waiting for the tingling in his lower leg to subside, he noted the spot: directly parallel with the ornate confessional boxes to his right and left.

Fifth row back.

+ + +

Fifth row back. Because I was tall. And we had a big class—sixty kids. Boys on one side in front of St. Joseph's altar. Girls on the other side by the Blessed Virgin Mary. Boys in pressed white shirts, white ties. Which my father tied four times. Bodies and souls scrubbed as clean as second graders could get.

I suppose I felt holy. That's what Sister Mary Elizabeth had aimed for.

But when the actual day came, the church packed with parents and grandparents ... oh, that procession. So grand! Two-by-two, all of us carrying lit First Communion candles, all that sweet incense, the organ playing full blast. I can still see Monsignor Koenig in his heavy gold chasuble with his entourage of servers in cassocks and lacy surplices gliding up into the sanctuary. All I could think of was a picture I'd seen in one of my father's history books: "Charlemagne

Ascending the Throne." Yes, grand.

+ + +

By the end of the long aisle of pews, Father Henry could see that Wayne had not, again, set out the hymnals for the funeral. Father Henry couldn't care less, but Libby and Bernie would both remark on it. Be irritated.

Father Henry didn't need any more irritation in his life today.

"Good morning, Henry."

"Good morning, Bernard."

Although physically he leaned toward the slender, his thin hair already white, there was a wiry stamina about Bernie Fruehauf. For over forty years, he had played the large three-manual pipe organ at St. Hedwig's; fifteen years prior, the one at St. Pius X, setting a diocesan record. Pipe organs and organists who stayed put were becoming rare in these days of smaller churches with part-time musicians trained in the more practical piano accompaniment, leading contemporary praise bands. After so many years, seventy-six-year-old Bernie was grateful he could continue doing something he loved. Playing the organ was steady employment: a Saturday evening and Sunday morning Mass, and bonus pay for extra services. Like weddings and funerals. Having brought over 1,500 brides down the aisle in his day, and accompanying almost as many cousins' solos, Bernie, like Father Henry, disliked weddings. He gritted his teeth to play for most, but if they smacked the least of a big production, he might, especially as he aged, arrange for another organist to take it.

Funerals were another matter. Not nearly the fuss and they were quick, easy money.

Bernie sat now in the chilly church sacristy to the left of the main altar at a large oak table, room for eight to sit comfortably at a Parish Council meeting, with his music satchel and winter cap in front of him.

The organist and priest had been friends for a long time, starting with a pilgrimage to the Holy Land where they'd met years ago. Bernie had been delighted at the chance to work with Father Henry when the priest was assigned to St. Hedwig's, Father Henry's home parish, the parish of his youth.

It had worked well. Bernie was old-school and deferential to all clergy, so almost anything Father Henry did that might bother him, Bernie let pass on priestly privilege. Father Henry, too, enjoyed their comfortable relationship. Bernie could be touchy and overly sensitive at times, but he was easygoing compared to many in Father Henry's pastoral experience.

"Is Wayne here?" Bernie asked.

Father Henry dropped into a chair on the other side of the table. "Somewhere."

Bernie's long, bony fingers picked at his cap. "Do you want me to put the hymnals out?"

Father Henry shrugged. "Suit yourself."

The sound of the wind outside vied with the wheeze of the furnace's blowers struggling to heat the small room.

Bernie's voice was tentative. Cautious. "I was just thinking that if I'm going to play, it would be nice if people had songbooks."

"He said he had some plumbing issues over at the Hall this morning."

"I don't want to step on Wayne's toes. Or get him in trouble, but …"

"Believe me, Bernie, if there was an abundance of maintenance men to pick from at this salary, it would be different." Father Henry lifted his hands in frustration. "I don't know. Maybe I shouldn't have hired him. And trust me. I've got more than hymnbook issues to fire him for."

He turned away and began to thumb through the sheer, tissue-paper-like pages of his breviary lying open on the table. "This is when I think priests should not be administrators," he mumbled. "I hate firing people."

Bernie's curiosity overrode his caution. He tried to sound discreet. "Are you firing Wayne?"

Father Henry concentrated on turning each delicate page. "I shouldn't have said anything. Shouldn't have implied it was him."

"Someone else?" Bernie pressed.

It wasn't that Father Henry wouldn't tell Bernie, but unpleasant subjects often got short shrift in their discussions. Avoidance was the norm.

As tantalized as Bernie was, he knew when to move on. "Are you going to the visitation for Jonny Kwan's son this afternoon?"

"No."

"The Pastor not doing well this morning?"

"The Pastor would rather be home reading. Are the roads bad?"

More gusts rattled the sacristy windows, peppering them with sleet. "Icier than I like."

"We should all move to Florida," suggested Father Henry dryly.

"You don't like Florida," Bernie reminded him.

"I might today."

"I could pick you up. Take you to the funeral home."

"If I make it through this funeral, I'm taking to my bed.

Bernie recognized this particular tone of Father Henry's. It included an edge of levity, weariness, and a strong undercurrent of let's-drop-the-subject.

Chapter Two

Fifty-two-year-old Libby Kinder glanced at the ice scraper on the passenger seat. Between the slush already collecting on the windshield and the prediction that temperatures would be falling during the day, she knew she would need it when she returned to her car an hour or so later. The motor was off, the heat dissipating quickly. She had warmed up her voice with a string of favorite Beatles songs and, although the music had stopped, the assertion that money can't buy me love continued to repeat itself in Libby's head.

Since childhood, melodies, complete songs, refrains, a measure or two snatched from a TV commercial, or a classical piece on the radio would often get stuck in Libby's head and could linger deliciously, in a hum or full-throated rendition, for hours or days. Cold, dark, winter mornings did not thrill Libby, but singing for funerals—that was something else.

"Hey, lady!"

Libby slipped the strap of her music bag over her shoulder and waved to the compact, middle-aged man on the porch across the street from the small parking lot in the rear of the church. "Hey, Antonio! Get in out of this cold!"

Antonio Silva was part of the new wave of immigrants. Replacing the original German settlers was a flood of Burmese, Vietnamese, and Hispanics drawn to the family homes surrounding St. Hedwig's. Like many inner-city neighborhoods, this one had struggled through the "white flight" to the suburbs, decay, and dismantling. With a combination of city funding and a genuine rebirth of interest in the charming, historical residences that surrounded the church square, the area had begun to stabilize and come alive.

Antonio lived next door to the two-story, ninety-year-old, brick rectory. In the summer he sat on his porch with friends, and every Sunday morning before Mass, had a teasing exchange with Libby. The exchange was much shorter on wintry days.

"What you doin' here on Monday?" Antonio called. "Somebody dead today?"

"Yeah," Libby shouted back, against the wind and freezing rain. "Somebody dead. Funeral."

"Okay. Sing good, lady!"

Libby gripped the slippery railing and picked her way up the half dozen steps to a small landing where she unlocked the two back doors of the church and let herself in. With the funeral visitation underway, the alarm had been disengaged. She carefully locked the inner door behind her. Inner-city church rule number one: church doors remain locked at all times, especially the back ones, even if you are inside. Front doors open only if services are occurring. And so, everything safe and secure, Libby entered what everyone referred to as the bride-side sacristy, distinguishing it from a matching room on the opposite side of the church. The two areas were connected by a narrow inner hallway that ran along the backside of the church, all behind the three front altars—the large main altar in the center, and a slightly smaller one for St. Joseph to one side and one dedicated to the Blessed Virgin Mary on the other.

For weddings, this initial room was filled with dresses and flowers and shoes and snacks. Brides and attendants shed jeans and gym shoes to don gowns and spiked heels. To reflect the transformations, a full-length mirror hung on the restroom door; another ran horizontally over a countertop with cabinets above and below. Tall closets for acolyte and server outfits were topped with oversized seasonal decorations, and even at that, nothing reached the twenty-foot ceiling.

But today, the room was quiet. Solemn. A round, Formica table that would be filled with nosegays and jewelry on more joyful days was instead laid out with funeral items: the folded pall for the casket, a small crucifix, the aspergillum to sprinkle holy water, and the ornate thurible set with charcoal briquettes, ready to be lit then plied with incense for the impending ceremony.

Libby removed her mittens and hung up her coat, traded snow boots for black heels. Collecting her music bag, she proceeded to the passageway that curved behind the main altar, a dim, eerie walk past a gallery of stern-looking former pastors, sepia-toned portraits dating to the 1800s when German-speaking immigrants had built the church.

If Libby was a cradle Catholic, St. Hedwig's had been that cradle. She had been raised in a time and place of black-and-white beliefs that made childhood choices certain and secure. Then there was the added proud pleasure of believing she belonged to the One religion that had all the answers. It was perhaps a measure of how firmly her faith was rooted that the doubts, when they came, so shook her soul—and yet would not let her just pull up and leave.

Not only did her Church not seem to have all the answers, but she was questioning whether the ones it did have were valid. No, it was not going to be an easy break, not a clear and quick upheaval followed by a swift severing and falling away as many in her generation experienced. More like the break in Millay's sonnet, as with "dull shears / Meeting not neatly, chewing at the threads."

Libby emerged on the opposite side into a brighter, lit room, the priest-side sacristy, similar in size to the bride-side but with more cupboards and tall closets. A wall of glass-front cases displayed reliquaries, bells, gold chalices, and vestments from other eras. She wondered what Father Henry's mood might be this morning, knowing how he felt about funerals.

Father Henry could be grumpy. Not surly, but short. Like lots of old men. And old women. He could be self-involved. Like lots of priests. Spoiled into the state by mothers who revered them, parishioners who brought them food, and people in the community who gave them the use of their condos for vacations. And a hierarchical Church that told them they could walk on water.

But he also had a droll sense of humor that Libby appreciated, gave intelligent homilies, and was often found reading prayers from a worn breviary in the calm before services. He was easy. If people did their jobs, he left them alone. He didn't call a lot of meetings, get flustered or demanding if last-minute changes had to be made for Mass.

As Libby entered the room, Father Henry rose and carried a

plastic shopping bag to the small refrigerator in the corner that housed bottles of cold water and open bottles of sacramental wine.

Bernie rubbed his hands in delight. "What tasty morsel did the Good Pastor receive today?"

"Soup," replied Father Henry, with a pleased lift of his eyebrows. "From Mrs. McGrew."

"Lucky you," said Libby as she approached the long, oak table.

Father Henry looked up, still pleased. "See you got here."

"I did."

"Hello, Miss Libby." Bernie shifted to make room for her at the table. "Ready to wow this crowd?"

Libby turned to Father Henry. "Yikes. Is it a big funeral?"

She quickly reviewed her lineup. Were there enough verses in the hymns she'd selected to bring a large cortege down the long aisle? Enough to cover if they all went to Communion? Was there …

"No," Father Henry said. He rolled his eyes toward Bernie. "You know he won't do big funerals. Will you, Bernie?"

The organist laughed. "I'll do big funerals. Not big weddings. Not small weddings either. But any size funeral is fine. Long as I get paid." He gave Libby an impish smile. "Just kidding. Either way, I'm sure you'll sing as beautiful as you always do."

She swung her music bag onto the table and took a seat.

"Only the best for St. Hedwig's."

Bernie gave a self-deprecating snort. "Don't let it get too deep in here." He then added, as he always did, "You know I like playing for you better than anyone else."

"And you know the feeling is mutual."

And it was. The exchange was corny, but sincere. Libby had been the primary cantor, singing at most weekend Masses, for the better part of fifteen years. Her day job as grant writer for St. Bonaventure University, a small local college, supplemented by freelance editing and tutoring, made her available to sing for funerals during the week as well. Through all those years, Bernie Fruehauf, almost twenty years her senior, had become both friend and musical partner.

Many people misjudged Bernie. He was old-school polite to women, reverential to any priest. He had a string-bean build and a goofy laugh that belied a great talent for not just playing the pipe organ, but also for accompanying a religious service. Some organists just played what was in front of them, disconnected from the events taking place on the altar or insensitive to the congregation or the cantor. Bernie always paid attention and pounded out a melody if a singer got lost, improvised if a procession went longer or shorter than planned, and accommodated the musical idiosyncrasies of each celebrant.

"Webber. That's an old parish family," said Libby. "Lots of kids, if I remember."

"Do you think Stanley will be here?" Father Henry asked.

Bernie looked down sheepishly. "Oh. My. I hope not."

"Who's Stanley?" asked Libby, pulling out her music for the morning.

The priest laid out his wireless microphone. "Somebody Bernie slapped silly one time."

"I did not. Slap him silly," Bernie said defensively. Then added, "I may have wanted to."

Libby was nonplussed. "Bernie? You slapped someone?"

The organist rose up slightly in his chair. He was flushed with embarrassment. "It was over thirty years ago. He was in my choir. Stanley Webber. One of those boys who was always messing around. You know how a bunch of sixth grade boys can be?"

"Yes," said Libby, then getting her dig in, "because we all know girls were not allowed in the choir."

Father Henry sighed. "That was Monsignor Koenig. Don't get her started, Bernie. Stick to Stanley Webber."

"I must have told him twenty-five times to quit fooling around. I finally went over to him, and there, he'd carved his name in the choir loft railing. I was so mad, I just slapped him right on the spot."

Father laughed out loud. The thought of mild-mannered Bernie swatting some rowdy trouble-making child got to Libby, too.

"That group called me Mr. Flew-off. From Fruehauf. Like 'flew off the handle.'"

Libby laughed again. "I've seen you get upset, but nothing like that."

Bernie picked at his hat. "I've come a long way."

"You could never get away with that now," said Father Henry.

"And rightfully so," declared Libby. She stifled another laugh and tried to sound serious. "I've never seen Stanley Webber's name in the choir loft railing."

"I made him sand it out," said Bernie. "The funny thing is, I went to apologize to him later, and Sister Esther Louise, who taught that sixth-grade class, said I'd have to wait because Stanley was in detention because he'd smarted off to her. Oh. My."

Muffled voices drifted in from the church proper. The windows continued to rattle and the heaters blow, contradicting the cold. Libby smiled to herself as she felt the air of the sacristy, warm by comparison to the wintry bluster outside. Her disillusionment with the Catholic Church in general did not always extend to St. Hedwig's in particular. And in particular, on a day like this, she was aware of the rarity of this present trio: the priest, the organist, the cantor. All in sync. They each arrived early, each competent and trusting the others to be prepared. There was little vanity or need for control as they laughed often and shared a cynical view of the world.

It wasn't the first time Libby wondered to herself just how long it all would last.

"We all set?" she asked, pulling the rest of her music sheets for the funeral from her bag. "I put the numbers up Sunday. Nothing unusual?"

After a slight pause, Bernie said, "We need to put out some hymnals."

Libby looked at Bernie. They were on the same page for this. Both thought the music was important. Both thought people should be able to sing if they wanted. Both were aggravated by someone not doing his job.

"Don't get me started." Father Henry tried to head off his cantor's annoyance. "No. Wayne did not put them out. And you know …"

"… people don't sing at funerals anyway," Libby finished.

Father Henry threw up his hands in mock seriousness. "Ex-actly."

Libby threw up her hands, still miffed but resigned. "As I said. Nothing unusual." Squaring the pile of music in front of her, she chatted on. "Crappy weather out there today. Supposed to get worse. What time are you guys going to the funeral home for Jonny Kwan's son?"

The hesitation was slight, but Libby caught it immediately. She looked out of the corner of her eyes at Bernie beside her.

"I'm going right at the beginning," he said. "I have a funeral in Latin at six." Bernie's eyes darted in a way Libby also recognized immediately. Discomfort. His voice dropped a fraction. "I don't believe Father's going."

Unlike Bernie, Libby was not known for her deference to clergy. "What do you mean, you're not going?" she said directly to the priest. "It's Jonny Kwan."

Father Henry corrected her. "It's Jonny Kwan's *son*. *He* left the Church. *He* became the Buddhist or Muslim or whatever."

"But you're not going for the son," she countered reasonably. "You're going for Jonny Kwan."

Father Henry did not respond.

Unlike Bernie, Libby was undeterred. "Jonny Kwan is your parishioner. He lost a twenty-three-year-old son who battled cancer for four years. Jonny Kwan has been a faithful servant forever; here at every function and holy hour and chili supper fundraiser this parish has thrown for the last thirty years."

"And his son became a Buddhist."

Libby tried to tease her friend and pastor from his stance. Sometimes he just needed a reality check. "A Buddhist today. A Jew tomorrow. And probably studying for the priesthood, had he lived, by the time he was twenty-five. You know how kids are about leaving the Church. For a while."

"I'd be glad to pick you up," Bernie offered tentatively. "So you don't have to drive in this weather."

Father Henry stood. He was not loud or in a huff. But he was adamant. "I am not going to the funeral home. He left the Church. The Church did not leave him." He pushed his chair in noiselessly and disappeared into the dark passageway to the other side sacristy.

Libby waited until the priest was out of earshot. "I can't believe he's not going to that visitation."

"I already asked him," said Bernie. "He told me no, too."

Libby and Bernie could hear Father Henry clicking the lighter to get the charcoal burning for the incense in the other room. None of the three liked this kind of confrontation. One of the reasons they survived working together was that once things were said and points of view stated, they usually respected each other's positions and moved on. Things didn't necessarily get resolved the way everyone wanted, but they moved on.

"Was he in a bad mood when you got here?" Libby asked.

"Nothing unusual."

Bernie regarded the distant clicking of the lighter and spoke with a note of intrigue. "Just between the two of us, I think he's going to fire someone."

"Really? Wayne?"

The organist tried to recall Father's exact words. "Maybe. But might be somebody else. It wasn't clear."

More people could be heard arriving for the early viewing at the back of church. Father Henry returned, the smell of charcoal hanging lightly about him as he began pulling his funeral vestments from the closet. He fastened the snap at the top of his long, white alb; kissed the embroidered cross on the stole that went around his neck; and looking up toward the sacristy doorway that led to the sanctuary and altar, suddenly said, "Uh-oh. Here comes trouble."

Bernie and Libby turned to see Lawrence Davis saunter in the small room.

"You've got that right." A deep baritone voice came at them from the tall, sharply dressed African American with a lean, basketball-player physique.

Bernie smiled broadly. "Good morning, Detective Davis."

"Hope I'm not butting in on anything."

"Wow," said Libby in a teasing swoon. "Aren't we looking snazzy today?"

Davis slid his thumb along the lapel of a finely tailored jacket. "Public appearance. Need to look good." He crossed his arms and casually leaned against the counter. "I'm lectoring."

Libby feigned awe. "Gosh. How does Mrs. Webber rate a big-shot police detective doing the readings at her funeral?"

"Old neighbor. Grew up with her son Jimmy over on Wabash Avenue. They came back for Mass once in a while. Knew I was a regular. Knew I could read."

"That's always helpful," said Father Henry.

Good humor returned to the sacristy. Libby Kinder liked the camaraderie. The men. The banter. They talked about their work, the Church, basketball. Rarely about her love life, which other people could be so curious about. These men were either happily married, like Lawrence Davis, or happily unmarried like bachelor Bernie and celibate Father Henry. An unattached woman, she was viewed as vibrant and normal, neither on the prowl nor aspiring to the convent.

In her fifty-plus years, Libby had actually been close to a wedding twice. Called off once by the guy and once by her. She had come to see the criticism of her best friend in college as a good thing. "You act like you're already taken care of," her friend had said. At the time, it was meant to indicate Libby was standoffish, overly particular, selective. Libby liked to think she'd softened the hard line on people she currently kept in her life without compromising her personal standards. Right now, being a single woman, moving on her own path, in her own direction—she was taken care of, and it suited her just fine.

Father Henry liked the congeniality, too. The banter. Libby Kinder could be teased. She was smart—a little too evident sometimes when she was argumentative or on her soapbox. As far as he could tell, she didn't hold a grudge or get easily offended. Not many women, or men, or priests for that matter, could make that claim. She'd accommodate if she could, do a favor if asked.

Father Henry didn't like everyone. His occupation was more a matter of tolerating people rather than truly liking them. Maybe it was because there were so many people in his life—all the various parishioners multiplied by all the various parishes—most of them just slid across the surface like stones across a slick frozen pond. Only a few stuck. Like Bernie. They'd been friends for a long time.

Father Henry started past Lawrence toward the sanctuary. "Do you want to go over the readings? The lectionary is already marked."

Lawrence caught Father Henry's arm and lowered his voice. "Not necessary. But as you guessed before, I do bring trouble."

"Oh?" The priest stepped back. "If you're arresting any of us, could it wait till we get Mrs. Webber in the ground?"

Lawrence spoke into the new hush of the sacristy, backed only by intermittent wind blasts and struggling heaters. "Jimmy's little brother's been in prison. Was granted special permission to come to his mother's funeral. I'm really also on duty so Stanley Webber doesn't …"

"Stanley Webber?!" Libby shot a glance at Bernie. "*The* Stanley Webber?"

"Today?" asked Father Henry.

"Here?" Bernie finally choked out.

Libby leaned forward and whispered, "What'd he get sent up for?"

Father Henry's head tilted down, but he looked up at her through the top of his eyebrows. "Don't you just know the jargon?"

Libby shrugged. "All those PBS mysteries." She swung around

to Lawrence. "So?"

"Armed robbery."

Libby was impressed. "You mean hands up, guns, bullets? That kind of armed robbery?"

Bernie shrank back, melting into his chair. "Oh. My."

"Maybe you should have slapped him more often," Father Henry calmly said. "Guess it's good we don't take up a collection at funerals.

Chapter Three

No, he won't be in shackles and handcuffs. Nor wearing stripes or an orange jumpsuit. Nothing that will stand out," Detective Lawrence Davis explained to Libby, whose imagination spilled over with everything from Dickens's convict on the moors to Jack the Ripper loose in London. Though he did assure her that Stanley Webber would be wearing a monitor.

Father Henry and Bernie pressed in behind Libby and Lawrence. The foursome huddled at the sacristy door, like neighborhood Peeping Toms, trying to get a look at the crowd milling around in the back by the coffin.

"Oh, dear," said Father Henry, only loud enough for the little group to hear. "I forgot to empty the Storm Relief Fund boxes yesterday."

The detective reassured him. "Trust me, Father, there are enough police here this morning to keep your donations safe."

"Good point." The priest leaned out farther and asked very softly, "Where will he sit?"

Lawrence indicated the pews to the right. "Probably up front here. That's where the family usually sits, isn't it?"

Father Henry nodded. "Family, yes; convicted felons, wherever they want."

He left the conclave to light candles on either side of the main altar in the sanctuary.

"Oh. My," repeated Bernie, barely audible. He took cover, walking next to Father Henry as far as the altar, then scurried off to his post in the organ loft.

Without warning, a child, unfamiliar with the proper decorum at such events, sent a jarring screech echoing into the cavernous church.

"Okay!" said a startled Libby. "That's a little unnerving."

Still standing next to her, Davis said, "Are you that jangled about this, or did I butt in on something earlier? Sounded like a bit of a conference when I walked into the sacristy."

Libby waved a hand. "Couple of … unpleasant issues. Jonny Kwan's son's funeral."

"Oh, yeah. Very sad," the detective agreed.

"And …" Libby hesitated as she was still trying to sort out who might be the person meant by the comment. "… apparently Father might be getting ready to fire someone."

"Oh. That does always shake a person. I wouldn't think there are many to pick from at St. Hedwig's."

Mourners were now arriving steadily at the back of church. They took off their wet coats splattered with icy rain and collected around Mrs. Webber's open casket. There were pockets of conversation as relatives reconnected, a few more shrieks from the errant child.

Detective Davis's eyes swept the large space before them. His professional training noted pillars to hide behind and pews to crawl under. Two enclosed confessionals with ornate latticework doors stood near the front of each side aisle, but otherwise the view was fairly unobstructed.

Father rejoined them at the sacristy doorway. Libby craned her neck to get a better look. The church was still dim and chilly on this dreary, midwinter morning. The familiar, friendly church, home to her soul since birth, now seemed ominous and foreboding.

A shiver ran up her spine. "Bernie gets to be safe upstairs. Will Stanley really be that close to where I'm singing downstairs?"

Davis turned and smiled down at her. She isn't a very big person, he thought. Healthy-looking, as if she jogs or swims. She always dresses nicely, like my wife: classic suits, tailored jackets, with a smart flair of color or jewelry to make the outfit interesting. And heels.

She always wears heels for services. She always looks good.

Today she looked vulnerable. "I don't think you have to worry." The detective turned and patted the priest's arm. "Father Henry is a much flashier target."

Not long after, Libby found herself sitting by the cantor's podium, to the left of the altar facing the body of the church. She could still see Father Henry, fully clothed in white funeral vestments, waiting at the sacristy doorway. Two grandchildren of the deceased, obviously more religiously inclined than their uncle, had come forward to be servers. They stood next to Father Henry, looking like miniature priests in black cassocks and white surplices, gently swinging the censer and sending up the familiar sweet smoke.

Upstairs in the choir loft, having sidestepped the Webber clan, Bernie began playing softly at the organ. The signal for him to stop playing was when Libby stood up at her microphone. She was able to see what he couldn't: the casket being closed, Father Henry and family in place for the procession, and all ready to start.

Until then, a modest crowd continued to assemble to send Mrs. Webber onto the next world. The wayward son, or so Libby guessed, was right where Lawrence had supposed he'd be. More defiant-looking than sad, the muscular man with the shaved head sat between two alert, dark-suited mourners. Libby was thinking that really, unless you knew one of them, all the mourners looked the same. As she discreetly scanned the pews, she realized that, in the distractions of the morning, she and Bernie had forgotten to set out the hymnbooks. Which Wayne had neglected to do to start with. She was annoyed all over again.

In front of Libby, on the top step by the communion rail, which had been left untouched in the renovations several years before, Don Fleck appeared and caused her to flinch, startled. The funeral director handed Libby two payment envelopes. "Sorry," he said. And just as stealthily as he'd come upon her, he glided back down the side aisle to the back of the church without another word.

Libby wasn't prone to being fearful. She was prone to being businesslike. Regardless of how much she liked to sing, she considered singing at a funeral a kind of job. She placed the envelopes on the podium shelf and turned her thoughts back to Wayne. There was not enough time to set the hymnals out by herself. That was not her job. But it affected her job. Again.

Custodian Wayne Nichols was a fly in the ointment at St.

Hedwig's. He was a weaselly kind of guy, and Libby had to work hard to be civil to him. While Bernie and Father Henry and she operated as a team, Wayne left candles unlit, songbooks on their shelves, chalices and bells not stored properly. He had a surly chip on his shoulder, an attitude that kept him in the shadows socially. Fittingly, he spent a lot of his professional time in the church basement workshop. Plumbing problem or not, he should have …

Libby stopped herself. She had been working on taming this uncharitable streak for a long time. Wayne was merely the latest to unleash it. Being critical just came naturally to her. She quieted her fingers, drumming along her skirt. Maybe Father was right. Nobody sings at funerals.

Father Henry, trailed by the servers carrying a tall gold cross on its pole and swinging the thurible of smoke, proceeded to the back of the church down a side aisle. Don Fleck corralled the mourners. The casket lid closed. Libby stood and Bernie's prelude drew to a close, the music replaced by the church bell bonging deep, solemn notes as icy rain splattered the roof and windows.

After reciting prayers to receive the body, Father Henry turned and led family, felon, and friends to the front pews during the processional hymn "How Great Thou Art."

Forty-five minutes later, the funeral Mass for Mrs. Webber was over.

Just like that. No bullets. No attempted escape by the monitored convict son.

Filing out the front door, mourners made a quick and orderly exit. The scraping of windshields gave background to shouts from people pairing up as passengers. Once arrangements were settled, cars, tagged with small flags, fell into one long line to wind through city streets out to the Catholic cemetery.

Activity in the sacristy was equally systematic and efficient. Father Henry changed out of his vestments and picked up his black topcoat from a hook as he passed along the corridor behind the main altar to the bride-side sacristy. There Bernie had laid his music satchel on the table next to the returned funeral paraphernalia and was buttoning his coat. Libby came through the door from the sanctuary, carrying the heavy brass hymn numbers, having taken them down from the board behind her podium on her way to exchange them for the new numbers for the upcoming weekend.

Into this choreographed routine, the back door pushed open and another head ducked into the warm room from the frigid outside.

"Wow! Am I too late for the party?" Daniel Giglia stepped inside and smiled broadly. Certainly one of his best features were his bright, strong teeth enhanced by flawless skin, which even in winter remained sun-kissed by his Sicilian heritage. He was of medium height, solidly built, and had sharp facial features, but that smile made for an immediately amiable presence.

"Hello, Daniel," Bernie greeted him pleasantly.

"Not a party," said Libby with a hint of mystery, "but an armed robber."

Daniel's eyes grew wide with concern. "We had a robbery?"

Father Henry's comeback was dry. "We had the robber," he said, pulling out a white silk scarf and sliding it around his neck. "We were not the robber-ee."

"Nice scarf," said Daniel.

"Thank you. The robbery was five years ago. The dead woman's son. They let him out for the funeral." Father Henry hunched into his topcoat. "Are you going to be around for a while? I'd like to talk to you."

"Turned out to be nothing," said Libby. "He came, sat through the funeral, and left. Kind of disconcerting, seeing how easily someone can blend right in. Is it still icy out?"

Daniel stuffed gloves into the pockets of his black leather coat. "Yes. Really slick," he said to Libby. "And yes, I'll be here for a while," he said to Father. "Water plants. Check the candles. Maybe start looking through stuff for Lent."

Don Fleck stuck his head in the sacristy doorway. "Ready whenever you are, Father."

The funeral home director's appearance reminded Bernie to thank Libby for bringing his check upstairs. "Can't forget that," he said, tucking it into his pocket. He adjusted his wool cap, looking, for all his German bones, as if he were off to an Irish pub. "Sure you don't want to ride to the cemetery?"

She shook her head. "I didn't know the family that well. Not like you, Bernie," she said, playfully jabbing. "And I'm not hanging around here for the luncheon."

"I'm already in the car line. Detective Davis said I was safe. Stanley doesn't get to stay for that. No reason to pass up a free meal.

Family said everyone was invited."

"As soon as I put these numbers up for the weekend Masses, I need to get home and get some work done on this Visual Arts grant."

"You're putting those numbers up this early?" Father Henry asked.

"It's only Monday," added Bernie.

Daniel looked puzzled.

Libby rolled her eyes. "It's Father's superstition."

"It's not my superstition. Priests aren't allowed to believe in superstitions. It's a fact."

"Father believes—" Libby corrected herself, "has a theory, that if I put the hymn numbers up too early there's time for someone to die. Then I have to change them all for the funeral. He has a theory that one thing might cause the other."

Daniel looked askance at Father Henry.

"It's true," the priest said with an air of confidence in the face of nonbelievers.

"I'll take my chances," said Libby.

Daniel looked down at the funeral accessories on the table. "Is Wayne around?"

"No." Libby and Bernie answered in unison.

Father Henry started toward the door with his funeral director escort. "He's with the plumber at the Parish Hall. Lock yourselves in if you're staying; set the alarm when you go. Wayne said he'd be back over to dump the ashes. I can't deal with it now. We'll talk later, Daniel."

It was not his parish. Just a part-time job. But there were several perks to taking care of the environment and decorations of St. Hedwig's Catholic Church. One was a welcomed outlet for his humble artistic talent. The other was access to this beautiful holy space. To get lost in. To be found in.

Changing candles was a meditative task for Daniel Giglia. As he began, his thoughts were unleashed, a rush of data downloading helter-skelter.

He crossed over to the side altar of the Blessed Virgin. How gentle the look on the face of her statue was. The faint smile. Her arms open to embrace. He came to focus on the single flame of a candle at her feet and tried to let the chatter of his thoughts become still.

He didn't set out to pray, just to move a bit outside himself. He never expected answers or great insight. The quiet was his reward. The connection to the Eternal One. Eventually, given enough time, he was usually flooded with gratitude. For all the good—the people, the love, the work, the beauty—in his life.

In the solitude, Daniel waited for the shift that would take his racing mind to a higher place.

Instead a sharp, unbidden pang of anger flared up.

The jarring distraction would not be tamped down.

It was too bright to ignore.

~ ~ ~

The dark windows above Libby's sink were opaque with the steam that filled her kitchen as onions and carrots sautéed in a pan on the stove. She was chopping fresh mushrooms and humming "How Great Thou Art," which had clung stubbornly to her vocal chords since the Webber funeral that morning.

The kitchen was warm. That warmth, plus the chance of food being dropped in their direction, kept her longhaired dachshund-terrier mix, Dash and her panther-sized black cat, BabyCakes, sitting patiently, expectantly, in the doorway; even though they'd both already been fed.

Dash was a handsome, mostly-root-beer-colored miniature, whose size was no indication of his loyalty or feistiness should it be called into action. BabyCakes, eighteen pounds of feline muscle, stealth, and radar, crossed every room as if it were the African veldt.

In most of the house, the frugally heated house, a sweater was mandatory, especially when sleet and dampness like today added to the chill. But the kitchen was cozy with pots and pans being moved about and the general commotion of dinner being fixed by one who likes to cook.

Libby had been unwittingly wise to have purchased a beautiful brick house, larger than she could afford at the time and more room than she would ever need. But the house at 1901 Apple Street had been converted into a duplex many years before, with an upstairs apartment above her own. The arrangement allowed her to have high ceilings, hardwood floors, the brick fireplace, and window-filled solarium of a grand old house, while giving her the bonus of renting out half of that grandiosity to cover some of the bills. Like heating.

Over the years, she had had many and various renters. Three years ago, Namita Green, in her late thirties, a Director of Reference and Technology at Caldwell Community College and first generation child of India had moved in. She came with a bit of a bohemian flair and an elegant rescue greyhound. Happily, Paki got along as well with Dash as Namita did with Libby.

Libby held the long high note on *great* before *thou art* brought her back down. The animals barely blinked. They were used to such outbursts. "You wouldn't have been so blasé in the presence of a convicted felon," she told them melodramatically.

Residual creepiness from that event made Libby jump when the phone rang. Although the mushrooms were poised to go into the pan, when she saw that the call was from Maggie Mueller, the church secretary, she set them aside, turned off the stir-frying vegetables, and answered on the next ring.

"What's up?" she asked cheerfully.

Maggie's voice was not cheerful. It came back distant. Chilling.

"Father Henry's dead.

Chapter Four

Maggie Mueller had married young. She'd given birth to a little girl; then her husband died in a car accident in that same youthful period. A single parent in her early twenties meant that higher education for Maggie consisted of on-the-job training as a bookkeeper. That, coupled with certain innate receptionist skills, had gotten her employed at St. Hedwig's rectory where, for the last seventeen years, she had managed people, payrolls, schedules and records; answered the door, the phone, emails; and, in general, handled all of the major and mundane business of an old parish with three hundred families.

Maggie worked alone in a downstairs office of the rectory, across the street from the church, while her priest/employer/boss counted everything else as his living space. At St. Hedwig's, this meant a public office for the pastor, living room, dining room, kitchen, and private quarters upstairs.

Maggie came to work at nine. At five, she locked up and went home.

Not that night.

"What do you mean, 'Father Henry's dead'?" Libby barely got the words out as she stumbled to a chair and sat at her small kitchen table.

In contrast, Maggie sounded calm. But then, she was used to unplanned tragedies in a job where people's most intimate and consequential life events crossed her desk on a regular basis.

"I didn't know who else to call."

"What happened?"

Maggie took a deep breath. "It was so icy when I left work. I leaned against my car to let some crazy driver go by. Something moved. One of those feral cats Father feeds darted over near the church. Scared the shit out of me. I saw this … thing at the bottom of the steps. A box. The closer I got, it looked like one of the Storm Relief Fund boxes. Kind of smashed."

She paused.

"And there he was. On the back church steps." Emotion finally crept into Maggie's voice. She cleared her throat. "I couldn't see well, but it looked like he'd fallen down the steps. It was so icy. I figured he hit his head. There were a couple of those Target gift cards from the fund box lying there. Otherwise nothing. Just him."

Libby was numb. "Oh, Maggie."

The secretary's voice rose up. Strengthened. "One minute that man is pissing me off with his petty ailments and excuses, and the next thing he's dead. I called 911. The EMS took him away."

Libby and Maggie were colleagues thrown together by church activities and concerns. In addition to Libby's job coordinating music for all manner of services, as a member of the Parish Council, she was involved with organizing chili suppers and other fundraisers that brought the two women together. They had other things in common: both were single, they held similar views on church issues, and they discreetly shared their thoughts on observing and dealing with clergy up close. Over the years they had become friends. Not confidants necessarily, but reliable and compatible cohorts.

"You should have called me," offered Libby.

"I should have called the Vicar. The Chancery beats that into your damn head: Always, always, call downtown first. Naturally, when the time comes, it all goes out the window."

"Where are you now?"

Maggie sighed audibly. "Still at the rectory." All the bravado disappeared from her voice. Instead, she sounded weary, shaky. "I didn't go with … the body. To the hospital."

Libby could hardly imagine the situation. Being alone in that big, old, empty rectory at night. Rain and sleet still coming down. And dealing with … "I'm so sorry, Maggie. Do you want me to come over?"

"No. I'm locking up and going home soon." Maggie took a minute to run through what else she might be required to do. "Once the EMS was on the way, I did call the Vicar. He decided to go straight to the hospital. I'm trying to think who else I should call. You know, so they don't find out through the grapevine first."

Libby tried to think who fell into the need-to-know category. Churches were odd organizations. It wasn't easy to draw the line between who was a legitimate family member and who was a parish family member. The threads could cross and knot and be pulled in many directions. That was certainly true for Father Henry, having been at St. Hedwig's for close to ten years.

"I suppose Father's two cousins," suggested Libby. "That's all he's got as far as blood relatives, isn't it?"

"The ones here at St. Hedwig's, yes, and then there are some out-of-town cousins. I think the Vicar will call them. Who though, like you, in the parish, should we be calling personally?"

Several people came to Libby's mind. "Bernie," she said at the same time as Maggie. "I can call Glen Watson, since he's Parish Council president. Maybe Sam and Edith Reith ..." Libby suddenly felt weary herself. "I don't know. Word will get out soon enough. It'll spread like wildfire."

Maggie gave a low moan. "Oh, God. Yes. Bird Hawkins. The town crier. Bernie will undoubtedly tell him. And he'll tell the world."

"Then your job is done. No need to call anyone else." The attempt at humor wasn't convincing to either woman. "Do you need a drink or something?" asked Libby.

"No," Maggie said flatly. "But thanks. I'm going to call those few people and then go home."

"Okay."

"Okay. Good night."

"Night." Libby's usual chatty self could think of nothing else to say, to ask, to offer.

But Libby was reluctant to hang up. To do so meant she could no longer distract herself by talking to Maggie. She'd have to start dealing with the fact that Father Henry was dead.

Maggie sat in her quiet rectory office. Father Henry's two cats had waited patiently during the chaotic events of the evening. Dunkirk, a hefty, dark-tortoise-shell Persian, was sprawled across abandoned paperwork on Maggie's desk. Calico Two, also a Persian and as long-haired as Dunkirk, but snowy white with butterscotch markings that helped name her, gave a plaintive mew at Maggie's feet.

Maggie scratched the top of Dunkirk's head absent-mindedly and let her hand ease down his furry back and out to the end of his thick, soft tail. "Oh, you poor dears. You don't know yet. And you're hungry."

She reached for her phone directory. "Let me make one or two calls. Then I'll feed you. And tell you all about it."

Bernie Fruehauf sat in one of the two brown-leather recliners his father had splurged on for his wife, Alice, to watch TV in after he retired. A globe lamp from Bernie's grandmother gave such a soft glow it did little to alleviate the deep darkness that enveloped the cold January evening.

The house had been without grandmother or parents for several years; so Bernie sat there, alone.

Taking in the news.

Since the phone call.

Bernie was not a man of great outward emotion; he had a sturdy, brick-like foundation, built from his strong faith in God. It wasn't that he didn't feel things deeply, but he was more of a fretter, nervous about immediate things, like being on time or making sure he had all of his music. Or getting paid.

People—they were in a different category all together.

Practically speaking, Bernie was an only child—a sister had died before he was born. Until working with Father Henry, Bernie had only two human constants in his life: his parents, Alice and Gus. Alice Fruehauf adored her son and took pride in his musical talent. Her support and encouragement made the timid child adore her in return.

But Alice could be volatile, raging at a neighbor's slight or household finances run short. Like his father, Bernie loved Alice when he could, stayed out of her way when he couldn't, and prayed to accept God's hand in it all.

Alice spent five years refusing to let go of life in a nursing home, where she slowly forgot who she was and went from being sad, to sullen, and finally angry.

Angry at God. Angry at her sweet-natured husband. Angry at Bernie, who, along with his father, visited her daily, even in the last difficult years. They slipped out of her small, hot room, the sound of her fury following them down the hall. "Dammit, Bernard, come back here and take me home!" Or worse, contrite, mournful pleas for the same. After Alice died, Gus shuffled along quietly for another decade until Bernie laid the last of his small family to rest.

Bernie had known Father Henry Felger for over forty years. They first met when Father Henry had been chaplain on a pilgrimage tracing the footsteps of St. Paul through Spain and Greece. A friendship arose. Back home, in a city small enough for clergy and organists' paths to cross, they saw each other at various ordinations, holy hours, and penance services, as well as meeting for an occasional lunch or movie. Almost ten years ago, when the time came to rotate pastors among the parishes, Bernie stormed Heaven with novenas to get Father Henry assigned to St. Hedwig's.

The novenas succeeded. The easy-to-work-with, good-sense-of-humor, holy, and respected Father Henry Felger was assigned to St. Hedwig's.

And now he was dead.

Outside Bernie's house, wind blew erratically, shaking everything.

The front room of Wayne Nichols's apartment was bright from the light of a large-screen TV in the corner. Generally unkempt of person, Wayne's surroundings were strikingly neat by comparison. His furnishings were Spartan, although not by Wayne's design or temperament. He had little, but wanted more. In town for less than two years, these meager rooms were still all he could afford. Even though his rambling life had equipped him with a variety of handyman skills, it was luck, not talent or initiative, that had gotten him the job at St. Hedwig's. He didn't really believe in luck, but rather that he deserved things—a job, money. A special girl.

Maggie Mueller, the church secretary, she was cute. A little shy for his tastes, but he wasn't opposed to the quiet ones. Now Libby Kinder, the singer, she was a pistol. Probably ten years older than he was, but still good-looking. Sassy. Always something smart to throw back at him when they talked. He couldn't tell if she was flirting or just flip.

Unless she was making fun of him. That would not sit well.

"He fell on the steps at the back of church." That's how Maggie had delivered the message—the message that Father Henry Felger was dead. Wayne lit another cigarette, leaned back on the worn, secondhand couch, and blew a hot huff of smoke toward the ceiling.

"Shit," he said out loud. "Icy steps."

He picked up the TV remote and, leaving the sound muted, surfed from channel to channel. Thinking. He stopped at the shopping channel. Men's gold signet rings. He could definitely see himself sporting one of those. Yes, when he had the money, there would be so many things he would buy. He liked the shopping channels, liked looking at expensive things. Somehow having them only a few feet away, if only on the TV screen, made them seem attainable. Practically his.

A cigarette and the shopping channel. He would chill. Not worry. An accident, that's what the church secretary had said.

"That means no police," he said out loud.

Smiling, he took another drag of his cigarette and wrote down the numbers on the screen for a really nice camera.

Dinner was ignored. Libby pulled an afghan up over her, wadding it under her chin for warmth. Next to her on the couch, Dash shifted and pressed closer against her thigh, reassuring her of his loyalty and comfort. Physically, Libby's body was clenched; her eyes stared, unfocused. Emotionally, she was afraid to move. For the moment, all her energy was diverted to her mind, which was active and engaged, as if a project had been assigned and different parts of her brain were taking charge, sorting information, filing, noting the impact, assessing the effects, the responses. One thought kept rising to the surface: This was real. Father Henry was dead.

Libby's reaction to bad news traveled down a certain path, usually starting with factual curiosity. How badly were they hurt? What kind of surgery? Treatment or rehab?

Because she was trained to be helpful and because church relationships spilled over into the family-and-friends category, those questions invariably gave way to: Do you need a ride? Is anyone bringing in supper?

And all the while, anxiety, dread, and sympathy stayed in the background, not forgotten, but held at bay.

The sequence tonight was off the mark; the questions different.

Dash stirred. BabyCakes was in a deep slumber behind Libby's head on the back of the couch. Libby glanced at the mantel clock and realized she'd been sitting there for almost an hour.

Dash sat up, ears at attention, tail in high gear. Now the one emotion that did show up consistently when Libby was under pressure—annoyance—made its appearance.

She didn't want to take Dash out, as predictable and anticipated and justifiable as his request was. It was slick out. Cold.

Pets were wonderful, essential to Libby, but they came with some unyielding obligations; and so, with annoyance, she put a sweater on the miniature Dash and snapped on his leash, then yanked on her own boots and coat and hat and gloves.

As was almost always the case, Dash was right. Not only about his own needs, but about Libby's. She needed to move, needed to do something physical, to pull her body out of its lethargy and her mind away from its stupor.

Outside the sleet had stopped, but it had covered everything over with a stiff, thick glaze, leaving the world temporarily frozen in place. Libby picked her way down the back steps and occasionally chose icy grass over icy sidewalk for better footing.

Because a person could fall.

A person could die.

Shoot! Someone with a dog was coming from the opposite direction. In the dark, she didn't recognize them. They weren't moving over. Not even paying attention. Dog Walking Etiquette 101. Courtesy of the road to yield the right of way. At least offer to move to the outer path.

Of course, she knew she was being irrational. To think that they and not she had to do the sidestepping—or that sidestepping was even required. Her stomach knotted; her eyes began to smart.

It was only Father Henry she told herself.

The slight detour took her and the quick-walking Dash to the opposite side of the slick street, past homes lit with a comfort that

Libby could not see, much less feel. Wet on wet, her glove swiped her cheek. Her shoulders hunched against the cold that chiseled its way into her body until those shoulders broke loose and great heaving sobs took over.

Over and over she muttered, "It wasn't supposed to happen like this."

+ + +

Easy day. Finally, cool fall temps.

Pulled up the tomato plants today. Walt S. helped clean up perennial beds and put tools away for the season. Think there's a new stray in town—cute, little orange tiger. Probably looking for winter quarters. Guess the feral we will always have with us.

Parish Council needs roof repair estimates. Dreading that. New servers—Josh B. and Jeremy H. Jonny Kwan got them outfitted. They drown in those surplices, had to duct tape cassock hems. So young. They've been playing "Mass" at home so think they already know how to do everything. Excited to be on the "real altar." Makes me wonder if this is how the Church really carries on, not through seminaries and rosaries but kids pretending until it seems real. Libby Kinder would say it was indoctrination. Don't get her started. Gave the boys an old lectionary for authentic readings at their homemade Masses.

Cats to the groomer's today. They hate it. I love it. So soft and clean and de-matted when they get back. Calico Two sits on my lap for hours afterward. Can't tell if she's sucking up to me so I'll never send her again (fat chance) or just so worn out and happy to be home that any port in the storm will do.

Shrimp for dinner. Really good. Crispy. Great night for high school football. Creamed the Lutherans.

+ + +

Maggie sat alone in the rectory office. At her desk. By the phone.

She was tired. Exhausted really. It was almost eight p.m. and she hadn't had dinner. After hours of running in high gear, things now descended into the nightmare at hand. Before she collected her coat and scarf, she straightened some of the papers in front of her, thinking that tomorrow would probably be worse. More to do. People would have heard and have questions.

She would be the first one they called.

She'd thought about Father Henry being dead before, but hadn't considered all the extra work that would fall to her. Dunkirk jumped and landed noiselessly, front and center, on the Parish Records Book. Maggie scratched his stubbly chin till a steady purr filled the office and brought his roommate, Calico Two, back to rubbing against her leg. They both began insistent mewing.

"Oh, golly. I never did feed you."

The rectory kitchen was inordinately quiet. Even the wind outside seemed muted. Distant. Maggie watched the cats, side by side, like two friends after work sitting at the counter of a bar. There will be no brushing tonight, she thought. No sitting all evening on the lap of the man who rescued you and cared for you.

The ringing phone sent Maggie back to the office. She didn't really want to answer it. But it might be the hospital. Might be the Vicar.

It was John Chapman. Parishioner. Worked as a security guard.

"No, Father Felger isn't here," she began. "He … Oh, hi, John. Yes, the Storm Relief gift cards were mostly from Target. Libby Kinder is in charge, but usually …" Maggie listened and responded to his brief questions.

"Yeah. He comes to St. Hedwig's sometimes ..."

The guard offered a description.

"Yes. That's him," she said.

She reached for a notepad.

"Maybe the cards really do belong to him …"

And a pen.

"Gosh, that is a lot …"

She wrote down the number he gave, but she was nearing the end of being polite.

"No, I know you can't cash them in. Apparently he did not, but …"

Finally he got to the point that roused her interest. "Well, yes. Maybe we did come up short. Today. I mean, one of the boxes was found …"

Maggie again sat down at her desk. "Go ahead and call the police,

John. I'd better call the Vicar."

The two cats wandered back in, always curious about parish matters. Dunkirk got to the rolodex directory first and laid a heavy paw across it.

"I know," Maggie admitted. "I don't want to call him either." She ran her thumb between the cat's eyes. "What kind of mess is this all going to be?"

The day had definitely not turned out the way she'd thought it would. As she punched in the Vicar's number, she sighed. Even in death, Father Henry Felger was going to be a lot of work.

Chapter Five

The wide windows in Libby's solarium framed a bleak morning. It was early; the day, gray. No sun meant the branches and bushes in her garden were still trapped in a layer of ice from the night before. It made for an eerie quiet as she sat in a chintz-covered loveseat with hot apple-spice tea and the newspaper.

Libby knew the daily newspaper was on its way out, that it was primitive and archaic. But she liked the physical feel of it. The largeness of it. After getting news this way all her life, she found it soothing to have it, tangible, in her hands. This morning, with the shock of Father Henry's death only hours old, it was reassuring just to hold it.

Loving the newspaper did not make Libby indiscriminate. She didn't spend hours lolling over every article or advertisement. It was an efficient read: headlines, a few select articles in depth, sports scores, the obituaries.

Obituaries.

When her parents passed away, the first really devastating deaths in her life, Libby had found it surprisingly comforting to be visited by their friends and acquaintances from the past, in addition to neighbors and friends from the present. It had been more meaningful than she had ever anticipated. These were people who had taken the time to come to the funeral home, tell stories, give evidence that her mom had mattered in the world, that her dad had been a kind and honest coworker. As a result, Libby tried to be vigilant about making contact with the bereaved, either in person or by note, when someone she knew appeared on the obituary page.

What Libby did linger over of a morning were the cryptogram and Sudoku puzzles. She knew she could get them online by the boatload, but this was just the right amount, one of each, every morning. It gave her great pleasure to crack the code of the cryptogram, letter by letter, word by word, like some undercover spy; or to solve, square by square, the placement of numbers.

Not this morning.

She hadn't slept well. This morning, she cupped her mug of tea in both hands, holding it just by her chin. She closed her eyes and let the spicy steam rise up warm and dampen her cheeks, as if she was in a tiny private sauna.

This morning, the newspaper lay open but untouched on the footstool next to the loveseat. When BabyCakes plopped his massive feline body across it, Libby leaned forward to stroke his soft, black coat. Her eyes caught the late-edition banner at the top of the paper:

PRIEST'S ACCIDENT TURNS SUSPICIOUS

The phone at the rectory was busy. No response on Maggie's personal cell.

Libby paced. She reread the paper.

And tried another number.

"Bird Hawkins called about five a.m." Bernie's voice was flat. From experience, Libby knew it was how he sounded when he hadn't slept well.

She rolled her eyes and reheated her tea a third time. She should have known Bird Hawkins, parish gossip and close friend of Bernie's, would know something before anyone else.

"He said it was bound to happen. In that neighborhood." Although Bernie was saying it, the undertone was all Bird's, the implication that the changing ethnic makeup of the families moving in around St. Hedwig's was the problem. "Is it in the newspaper already?"

Libby sat at the kitchen table where she'd lit during her pacing and read, again, the words she already knew by heart:

"What originally appeared to be an accidental fall on icy church steps by a local priest at a downtown parish last night is now under investigation as a possible robbery homicide."

"Bird said some kid was caught trying to cash in gift cards they think were stolen from Father Henry. You know, those cards from the Storm Relief boxes. Makes sense. He was so careful about not leaving them or the money in the church. Bernie's voice wobbled, "And here he is, taking them home to be safe ... and he ... Oh. My. Somebody sees him ... and takes those cards ... and ... kills him."

Picturing the scene brought out the same wobbly emotions in Libby. "Oh, Bernie. It's so awful."

"And then some detective just called to ask ... to ask when I last saw Father. I think he was at the rectory."

"That's probably why I'm not getting through."

"Bird said his police friends say they're treating the place like a crime scene."

"The rectory?"

"No. The church steps. Where Father ... fell. Or ... or was pushed."

The distress in Bernie's voice echoed her own. As with her, Father Henry Felger had been a friend to Bernie. And for so much longer. Libby also knew Bernie. Knew how fragile he could be emotionally. Not only would Father Henry's death throw him—but the police calling. Even worse.

"Are you okay, Bernie?"

"I'm just ... it just makes me nervous. Maybe I should ... I don't think I can handle all of it. Everything that's going to happen, that I'll have to do because of this ..."

Underneath we are so alike, thought Libby. Death, even the death of a person close to them, called Libby and Bernie, church musicians, to the practical. "Are you worried about playing for the funeral? Because, you know, we can get somebody else. I'm not sure I can sing for it."

"Oh. My." Bernie's sigh was heavy. "No. No, no," he added quickly. "I want to play. I ... oh, no ... I must play. For Henry. No. I hope I can do that. I want to do that."

Libby could hear that this was only more upsetting. "Let's not worry about that now. Maybe you should try to rest. Take a nap."

"If I could just get some sleep," replied a weary Bernie.

"Yes," Libby said, reheating her tea. "I know just how you feel."

By ten a.m. Maggie Mueller had redirected all manner of communication for the church, the rectory, and herself personally, to answering devices. She was exhausted from the evening before; the dark, dragging, fitful hours of the night; then the morning's flurry of phone calls and emails once the news was out about Father Henry. Everyone always assumed she knew everything, and usually she did. Having overheard the police declare "the situation was fluid," her brain, swimming with input and decisions, clung to that as an appropriate image.

She was used to hosting the hodgepodge of traffic coming through a parish rectory. This morning that included police searching every room in the house. They had been quick, quiet, and, she assumed, thorough.

Maggie was a petite woman, barely in her forties, not unattractive. She crossed her legs and wrapped a bulky white sweater across her thin chest, a move made more for warmth than unease at being questioned by the police.

The living room in the rectory was formally furnished and only formally used. It was really more of a parlor, its function left over from the days when visits in it were stiff and proper. The antique couch and chairs were not very comfortable from Maggie's point of view, but Detective Mark Grass, sitting in the armless Queen Anne's chair across from her, did not register unease at all. With his winter coat thrown open, a red Tartan scarf breaking the monotony of dark slacks and gray sweater, he asked questions like a new neighbor taking a recipe for a potluck dish. He was curious and factual, focused; friendly without being personal.

The detective scanned the page of a small notebook. "So. It was a busy morning yesterday. The maintenance man, Wayne Nichols, saw Father Felger first thing, then didn't see him after he left to meet with a plumber. Before this funeral. A problem in the Parish Hall?" He looked to Maggie for confirmation.

She nodded. "A toilet in the ladies' room."

"And where is that? The Parish Hall?"

"It's the building on the other side of the rectory garage."

Grass looked up and out the window to get his bearings. "Rectory, garage, Parish Hall on this side. Church across the street."

Maggie nodded again. "Yes."

"Bernard Fruehauf, the organist, saw the priest at the funeral, where he said there was this convict?"

"Mrs. Webber, the woman who died," Maggie explained, "had a son in prison who was given permission to come to her funeral. Lawrence Davis—he's a detective, and a parishioner here—he was overseeing that."

"Yes. I've spoken to Detective Davis." Grass pulled at his jacket to give himself a freer arm and flipped the page of his notebook. "Mr. Fruehauf says he went to the cemetery, then to the luncheon, where he saw Father Felger but went home after that. Does that sound typical?"

"For Bernie. Yes."

"What do you mean?"

"I mean it was freezing cold. I wouldn't have gone to the cemetery. But Bernie considers it part of the whole 'bury the dead' God's work of mercy. A sort of Catholic act of kindness."

"And, the luncheon?"

"I think he considers that his just reward; but yes, he usually goes if there's a free meal. Bernie doesn't make a lot of money playing for St. Hedwig's, and I don't think he's much for cooking." Maggie shrugged. "Feed the poor. Acts of kindness can go both ways."

"And Father Felger always went to the cemetery?"

"It's part of the service. There are a few prayers that Father says at the gravesite."

Detective Grass swatted his Tartan scarf out of the way, then finally just slid it from his neck and laid it across his lap. He went back to his notes. "Obviously, a lot of people saw Father Felger at the luncheon. A Mrs. McGrew said she thought he was going back over to church from there. That's about when Daniel Giglia—who does what? Waters the plants?"

"Church environment. Takes care of plants, real and fake; candles; seasonal decorations; keeping altar cloths clean and pressed; that sort of thing. "

"According to him, Father Felger did, in fact, return to church, supposedly after this luncheon. According to Giglia, the priest was still in the sacristy when he, Giglia, left for his regular job around one p.m." The detective looked up. "Did Father smoke?"

Maggie blinked twice. "No." It seemed an absurd question. She tried and failed to picture it.

"Did he drink?"

That was easier to imagine. "Only socially, as far as I know." She had worked for priests who drank much, much more; and she knew that, at least, was not one of Father Henry's vices. "Why?"

"Just routine questions, Ms. Mueller."

Detective Grass made some marks in his notebook. He gave a kind of summary sigh. "Is there anyone else, either from the funeral, the luncheon, or the parish who would have seen Father Felger yesterday? Been in the church for anything?"

Maggie didn't think long. "Libby Kinder."

The detective wrote and spoke at the same time. "And she is … ?"

"Our cantor. She sang for the funeral that morning. I have no idea if she went to the cemetery or the luncheon. But she has keys to the church and often either comes early or stays late, or both, to help set up her music or Mass things in general."

"Is she paid?"

"A tiny stipend from St. Hedwig's for helping with the weekend liturgies. She's paid separately by the funeral home or family for funerals. Weddings are separate pay, too."

"Does she work somewhere else?"

"Yes," said Maggie. "She writes grants for St. Bonaventure University. Does some of it at home. She has pretty flexible hours. Makes it easy to have her sing for funerals."

"Anyone else?"

"Not that I can think of."

"Do you have Libby Kinder's number?"

Maggie knew it by heart, and at the detective's request, put in a call to St. Hedwig's cantor.

Libby had foregone her tea and newspaper puzzles and gotten dressed. A thermal top was added under her shirt and sweater, for no matter how much she moved around or how much hot tea she drank, she could not get warm. One advantage of working from home meant comfort over style on winter days like this.

When the phone showed the call was from St. Hedwig's Catholic Church, she answered immediately. "Maggie? What's going on? I've been trying to get ahold of you all morning."

"I was so sick of answering people's questions," Maggie said, "I sent everything to voicemail."

Libby started with her own list of questions, but Maggie interrupted. "There's a detective here who wants to ask you a few things. Can you talk?"

Libby froze. Outside of Lawrence Davis, she'd never spoken to a police detective before. Unconsciously, she sat up straighter in the chair she now took by the kitchen window. She reached for a pen and began to doodle on the back of a used envelope, a habit she had when she sensed the need to be alert. It made her feel as if nothing said or thought would be missed or forgotten because she would trap it on that envelope.

She was ready. Her pen was ready.

"Hello. This is Detective Mark Grass. Libby Kinder?"

He sounded pretty normal, thought Libby. "Yes," she said, writing his name down.

"When did you last see Father Felger?"

Just like in the movies. Libby traced and retraced the G on Grass until it was large and black. "After the funeral yesterday morning. We were all in the sacristy. He left out the front of church, with the funeral home director, to go to the cemetery."

"Was anyone else there with you?"

"Bernie. Bernie Fruehauf. But he left to go to the cemetery, too. On his own, I think. And Daniel. Giglia. He'd come to dust off decorations or water plants or something. I don't know. I didn't stay."

"Did you go to the cemetery?"

"No. I went home. I had work to do here."

"How about the luncheon. Did you go to it?"

A row of circles gyrated around the G, threatening to engulf all the other letters in the detective's name. "No. I only sang. Well, we all talked a little bit afterward, then I went home. I didn't know the family well enough to stay and, as I said, I had work to do."

"So, you didn't see or talk to Father Felger again yesterday?"

"No."

The pause at the other end of the phone left Libby filling in her circles.

"Okay," he finally said. "Is this the best number to reach you at if I need to speak to you again?"

More movie dialogue. "Yes. This is good."

"Thank you for your cooperation, Ms. Kinder. I'll be in touch if there's anything else. Here's Ms. Mueller."

Once Maggie was on the phone, Libby rushed to get what information she could. "I know you can't talk. Are you there all alone with the detective?"

"No," said Maggie. "Julia's here. But she's going to work soon. I'm fine."

"How about if I stop over in a little bit?"

Maggie was used to not reflecting any particular emotion. Not relief or anxiety, just professional calm. "I'll be here. I'd better go."

Detective Grass found another section of his notebook. "Tell me again. You didn't see Father Felger anymore all afternoon? Was that unusual?"

As church secretary, Maggie was also used to fielding questions of all kinds, from all sorts of people, especially concerning Father Henry's whereabouts. "Not really," she said noncommittally.

"And you said there were no other appointments on his calendar?"

"No. Although he didn't always write everything down or tell me where he was going."

"Tell me about these gift cards. And the box they were in."

"Just small cardboard boxes. Maybe eighteen inches square. Covered in shiny red contact paper with large black letters that said STORM RELIEF FUND. St. Hedwig's occasionally adopts a parish after a disaster. This was for one of the parishes that was hit by the tornadoes in Missouri last spring. We ask people to donate gift cards from national stores, like Target and Home Depot. The gift cards are easier to handle than cash—although people often toss cash in, too. The cards are a breeze to mail."

"So there's what? A slit in the top of the box for the cards?" he asked.

"Yes. Because they're so easy to get into, Father was keen on emptying them every weekend. Usually after Sunday Mass, but if he got distracted by a baptism or some other obligation, he might not get to them till Monday. He'd dump everything in one box then bring it over here, to the rectory, to count."

"How many boxes are there?"

"We put out four. One at the head of each aisle. Where the ushers can keep an eye on them. In a socio-economically mixed neighborhood like this, once in a while we get somebody wandering in off the street looking for a handout or access to this very kind of collection."

More notetaking by the detective led to more questions.

"What kind of money normally shows up in these fundraiser boxes? In a neighborhood like this?"

Maggie tucked her hands into her sweater pockets. She thought for a moment. "Anywhere from ten dollars to five hundred."

"Wow. That's quite a range," remarked the detective.

"Charitable donations tend to run that way. There's no predicting. You'd think it depended on how much money people had, but at least here at St. Hedwig's, the giving comes out of a different place. Some people give, no matter what, just because they're asked. Others are moved by something they hear or see about a given disaster and practically empty their savings on the spot. Just depends."

Detective Grass nodded as he made a small notation. "So, this kid would never know how much was in the Storm Relief boxes. Could be nothing; could be the jackpot."

"That's right."

"Do you know him very well?"

Maggie shook her head. "No. I know he's registered here and what he looks like. I work at St. Hedwig's, but I don't belong to the parish."

The detective looked directly at Maggie. "So, you were here, all afternoon? Alone? No coming or going? By you or anyone else? Do I have that right?"

"Yes."

"No Father Felger, in or out? No calling. No checking in?"

"That's correct."

"Daniel Giglia last sees him at one p.m. Alive. You find him at five p.m. Dead.

His eyes did not leave her face.

Maggie's did not leave his. "Yes."

Detective Grass closed his notebook. "Looks like that's our window of opportunity."

With that, he stood. He dropped his notebook into the pocket of his coat, slipped on the red Tartan scarf, and crossed it over his chest before buttoning up. "Let's go see how Guillermo fits in."

As Maggie asserted the locks on the rectory's heavy outer storm door, then the one on the inner beveled glass door, she watched the detective take in the location, looking across the street to the church, to the small parking lot for six or eight cars, then to the left and right at the neighborhood houses, the rectory, the Parish Hall.

He waved at one squad car across the street and patted the door of another, acknowledging the officers inside the car directly in front of him.

He gave a quick glance back at the rectory.

Maggie shrank away from the door, out of view. Behind her, noiselessly, Julia, her twenty-year-old daughter had walked up. Julia whispered. "Is he gone?"

Maggie didn't move.

Julia waited until the detective was in his car and had driven away. She whispered again to her mother, "Do you think he believes you?"

Chapter Six

Yellow crime scene tape lifted and fretted in the cold as if it wanted to be anywhere else but cordoning off the back steps of St. Hedwig's Catholic Church. The red-brick building filled nearly half a city block. Straight sides interrupted by buttresses and indentations for tall windows turned and met at the back door. There, six cement steps, edged on both sides by a brick-thick ledge, mounted to a small landing where a black-grated storm door guarded the original massive oak one.

Libby Kinder, having driven by two squad cars stationed on the street in front of the Parish Hall, sat in her car in the small parking lot behind the church in her usual spot. And stared at the unusual sight. Yellow crime scene tape. Crime scene. Crime. Where Father Henry had died. Been killed. On steps Libby had gone up and down a million times.

The sun had come out and burned off the veneer of frost; a sharp-blue sky outlined the great building, its steeple and glittering gold cross. Bushes edging the parking lot obstructed part of her view, but Libby could clearly see the officers in one of the police cars drinking coffee and staying warm as they kept watch from the street.

Suddenly, there was frantic tapping at her window. Hastily, Libby swiped her glove across the steamed up glass and a watery blur took shape.

"Antonio?" she said, lowering the car window.

"Miss Libby! You gotta help." The stocky, normally affable man, was hunched next to the car with no coat on, frantic, and shaking. "Madre de Dios. You gotta help me!"

"Get in the car, Antonio! You'll freeze out there," she said, clicking open the locks and turning on the car for heat as he climbed into the passenger's side.

"You know me, Miss Libby …" he was talking before he even had the door closed. "You know my family. We're good people."

"Slow down, Antonio. I don't understand."

"My family. We love this church, you know? We love this priest." He shook his head adamantly. "Billy could not do this terrible thing."

Libby began to run through what she knew, what she'd read, what she'd heard. "What are you saying, Antonio?"

His body rocked with the cold, the fear. "They arrested my nephew Billy. They say he killed Father Henry."

It was not easy, but Libby calmed Antonio down enough to understand, putting together pieces of the story as he randomly spun them out. Antonio admitted that his nephew had taken gift cards from the Storm Relief Fund box. "Stupid. Muy stupid. I tell my boys not to park over here. Park in front of our own house. He tried to get money for those cards. The police guard at Target said, 'That's a lot of cards. You can't get money, you know? You have to buy with them.'"

"So, he did steal the cards?" asked Libby.

"Yes. Yes, yes, he took the cards."

"What about Father Henry?"

Antonio's defense of his nephew flared up. "He didn't kill the Father. Billy couldn't kill nobody. He saw the priest. On the steps. He didn't kill him. He heard somebody coming. He just grabbed the cards and ran. Said it happened so fast."

Antonio turned, wide-eyed with fear, pleading with Libby. "You have to help. Help my family. You know people. You know English better. You can tell them what happened."

Libby stared at the church steps. The yellow crime scene tape. The officers in the car. She looked at Antonio's worried face and tried to sort things out. "Why was your nephew here?" she asked.

Finally Antonio sat back. The lady was listening to him. She was asking him questions but not in a hard way. Not like the police. "He comes over to do homework with my boys. They are cousins. He is my sister's boy. They work on their high school project in the shed. Back of the house. Play games. I tell them not to park here. They're good kids. No drugs."

"What about the gift cards? What happened last night?"

Antonio hung his head. "He didn't come last night. My nephew, Billy, he usually gets off work and comes about five o'clock, five thirty. School, then work, then at my house to do homework with his cousins. With my boys."

Libby was rattled by the scene this presented. "He saw Father Henry lying there on the steps? Why didn't he call for help?"

Antonio's voice was frantic again. "He got scared. He said he heard some person coming. He just took the cards and ran. He didn't think nobody would believe him."

"Okay. Okay," Libby said, trying to keep the man from tipping into more panic. "What did he do then?"

Antonio stared out the window that was now completely fogged over. The lady was beginning to sound like the police. Like the answers were not good enough. Antonio recited what even he knew did not sound believable. "He took them to Target. He thought he could get money for them. He only had ten, maybe more. So stupid. Madre de Dios."

Libby was skeptical. She liked Antonio and didn't think he was lying, but she knew there were often a lot more gift cards in those boxes, especially after a weekend. And, she didn't know his nephew at all—except being one of the boys who sometimes sat with Antonio's family at Mass. And how could he just let Father Henry lie there? She tried to focus. The cards. Maybe the kid was holding onto more cards. Maybe he wasn't as good as Antonio thought he was.

"No," repeated the man shaking next to her. "My nephew said he had only ten or eleven cards. He wouldn't lie. They were just laying there. Like the Father."

Antonio looked out the steamed car window toward the church. Sadness deflated him. "I like Father Henry. He is always nice to me, you know? Calls hello to me when I mow the grass. Or shoveling the snow." He tucked his hands into his armpits, holding himself together.

"Madre de Dios," he said under his breath. "He is only

seventeen."

Lawrence Davis, *Detective* Lawrence Davis, climbed out of his warm car with a large hot coffee. He liked coffee dark-roasted and rich, black, the flavor not nullified by creamy foam, sugar, or seasonal additions. Just black coffee.

Carefully sipping from his cup, he walked toward the back steps of St. Hedwig's as the four officers waiting in their patrol cars joined him.

Libby watched them, pointing and talking, surveying the area. Even though she was parked fewer than twenty feet away, between the closed windows and the heater on high, she could not make out their words, which came in frozen streams of breath as if they were huddling outside for a quick smoke. The conversation did not last long; soon the officers were heading back to their heated cars.

Libby knew Lawrence had seen her sitting in her car in the small parking lot. So had the officers. They were discreet, but observant. As Lawrence parted from them, he took another sip of coffee and turned in her direction.

"Wait here, Antonio," she said, adjusting her hat and scarf. "I'll see what I can find out. What's your nephew's name?"

"Billy."

"Billy?"

"Guillermo. Guillermo Garza." He added with a half-smile and paternal air.

"But he likes Billy."

"I'm afraid you can't get into church this morning," said Detective Davis as Libby approached. "Limiting the traffic through here for now."

"I see. I heard." Standing so close to the church steps brought the whole disturbing event into immediate, disturbing focus. Unable to keep from doing so, Libby sent furtive glances in the direction of the back door. Where was the splotch of blood on the sidewalk? Were branches of the yew bush next to the steps drooping from a scuffle or from the freezing rain the night before? Where was TV's familiar chalk drawing of the body, lifeless arms akimbo?

"What happened?" she asked. "When I talked to Maggie Mueller last night, she said she'd found Father Henry. He'd fallen. An accident on the icy steps. Then, this morning, I read that now they think some kid might be involved. Trying to steal the Storm Relief gift cards or something."

"The security guard at Target is a guy who goes here. At least enough to know about the fundraiser boxes. He got suspicious when this kid tried to cash in a bunch of cards. Kid seemed nervous, a little shaky-sounding with his story. So the security guard called the rectory to see if Father Henry might have noticed any of them missing."

"Must have been after Father'd been taken to the hospital. After Maggie and I talked. What about this kid?" Libby asked. "I think he's a parishioner. Likely that he knew about the cards."

"Likely." The reply was not unfriendly, but succinct.

"Don't suppose he admitted anything else?" Libby tried to inch her way to more information. "Do people really spill their guts in situations like these?" She watched a smile twitch on Lawrence's lips until he thwarted it with a sip of coffee. She felt totally inept. Caught red-handed. Spill their guts. Does anyone really talk like that?

She tried again. "I suppose most people swear they didn't do anything."

"Yes. That is what most people swear."

"I see this kid at Mass, Lawrence. Out here tossing a football. I can't picture him as a hardened criminal. Is that how he seemed to you?"

Lawrence softened slightly. "Actually, he fell apart. Crying. Went through a whole pack of cigarettes to get him calmed down. Funny how many kids are smoking again. As if all that lung cancer information never happened."

"How many cards did he have?"

"I don't know. Eight or ten. Enough to raise suspicion."

Lawrence stomped his feet on the sidewalk. The move was contagious, and Libby joined him, as if they both knew some special dance. She looked at her feet then up at the detective. "Do you believe him?"

He squeezed his elbows in close to his ribs, keeping a steady hold on his coffee. "Not mine to believe or not."

"Just the facts, ma'am, eh?" Libby recalled the line from an old TV show.

Lawrence smiled. "I hope I'm more open than that, but facts are a good place to start. Keeping an open mind. They'll do an autopsy, then we'll know if we're looking for a murder weapon. If something besides icy concrete steps put that gash in Father Henry's head."

Libby winced at the thought. "How long will that take?"

"Normally a couple of weeks, if not more. But I heard this morning that's likely to be moved up." Lawrence gave Libby a knowing look over his brown Styrofoam coffee cup. "The Bishop's already weighed in, wouldn't you know? High profile cases get high profile clearance. And speed."

"Sounds typical for both Church and State."

Libby knew Lawrence Davis only as a parishioner, a lector at St. Hedwig's. She admired his style, his clothes, and would chat with him before services in the sanctuary. He was present on this cold morning in his professional capacity, the only other time being when he'd watched over Stanley Webber yesterday at his mother's funeral, and it brought a whole different tenor to their conversation.

Libby found herself following his lead to keep an open mind. It seemed professional, judicious. "What do you think happened? Factually?" She tried to sound more curious than probing. "I know you can't say stuff officially, but no harm in weighing some options."

Lawrence closed one eye and glanced around, pondering a possible scenario. "Unofficially," he stressed, "the kid could have seen Father Henry come out the back door of the church. Guess it's possible he knew Father's movements and it was premeditated."

"But it was Monday," interrupted Libby. "Father was only here because of the Webber funeral. I suppose the kid could have heard of that, but it was more likely Father would have emptied the Storm Relief Fund boxes on Sunday. After the last Mass. That was his usual routine. And yesterday, being Monday, this kid would have been in school, right?"

"Okay. That points to a crime of convenience, then. The kid just happens to be here when Father Henry comes out carrying one of those red relief boxes. Even in the dark, you can't miss them. Kid figures this is an easy hit. Either Father falls in the struggle. Steps are slippery. Hits his head. The kid takes the cards and runs. Or. He deliberately pushes Father. Or uses something he's either brought with him or picks up nearby. Could be a rock. That we'll find."

"Is it possible," Libby started slowly, reconstructing a less dramatic option, "that Father came out. Slipped. Hit his head. And died. The donation box is smooshed."

"That a technical term?"

"Of course. Factual description."

Lawrence sipped at his coffee. "Proceed."

"Suppose Billy ..."

The detective choked. "Billy?" Clearing his throat of the coffee that had gone down the wrong way, Lawrence asked, "Who's Billy?"

So much for sounding innocuously curious. Libby shifted her feet in the little dance. "Guillermo," she amended.

Lawrence arched an eyebrow. "And, you know this ... Guillermo?"

Libby sidestepped the question. "This kid happens along. After school. After the whole fall-and-head-hitting part. Sees a body on the steps. Goes to check it out. Realizes Father is dead. Freaks. Grabs a few cards because they're there, having spilled out of the smooshed box. Or he doesn't even have time to check the body because he hears a noise like ... like ..."

"Like the secretary coming out of the rectory after work."

"And runs."

"Just grabs the cards ..."

"And runs."

Lawrence cocked his head. "An option, I suppose."

"Plausible," added Libby.

The detective smirked. He nodded over Libby's head toward the parking lot. "Who's the gentleman in your car? He looks familiar."

Libby didn't flinch. "Antonio. Silva."

"Not Garza? As in Guillermo Garza?"

"No, not Garza."

"Antonio?"

Libby gave a sheepish smile. "Uncle. Antonio."

Lawrence sighed as he surveyed the neighborhood. "Uncle Antonio Silva. Who belongs to St. Hedwig's and lives across the street from the church. The uncle with boys—cousins—that Guillermo, a.k.a. Billy, was going to meet after work."

Libby rushed to add, "They're really a nice family. Good kids."

"Are you giving a character reference?"

Before Libby could answer, the detective's tone unexpectedly became serious. "How well do you know them?"

Libby caught the implication and reacted defensively. "As well as I know you. They're parishioners. They … I see the boys play basketball over there and they …"

As she fumbled for the words, Detective Lawrence Davis nimbly, casually, moved around her so that he was still facing her but his back was to Antonio in the car. He leaned down and said in a low, careful voice, smiling all the while. "Look, Libby. They may be a very nice family. With a very dangerous relative. If this Billy really did—and I use this word specifically—*kill* Father Henry, you do not want to get involved." He backed away slightly, the friendly smile remaining on his face. "Let us do our job. If the facts prove Antonio's nephew is innocent, we'll be glad to turn him loose."

He stomped his feet again. "Gee, it's cold. I'm going to go over and see how Maggie's doing at the rectory. You go tell Uncle Antonio we'll do the best we can. I'll go over to his house in a few minutes to reassure him. Then, Libby. Go. Home."

As they parted, Libby wondered if the facts, indeed, would lean in Billy's favor. Did she even want them to? If Billy killed Father Henry, where was the justice in that? Then again, the police don't always get it right. Whose side was she on? She realized she didn't know Lawrence Davis any better than she knew the pleasant man who called to her from his porch. Her mind whirled.

Lawrence undoubtedly had more information than she did. Could she trust him to take the time to find a seventeen-year-old inner-city kid—with everything plainly against him—innocent?

It was too late. Not only had Libby's sympathy for Antonio and his nephew been unleashed, but her puzzle-solving brain had been thrown into high gear. Even as she tried to encourage Antonio to leave the matter to the police, she peppered the leery uncle with questions: Where did Billy go to school? Where did he work? Are you sure he went to school on Monday? What time did the cousins expect him? What did Billy say he did between work and going to Target to cash in the gift cards?

Antonio's mantra was always the same. "Billy goes to school. He goes to work. Comes here for homework. They're good kids. He wouldn't kill nobody." And finally, "Please. You gotta help us."

Chapter Seven

*M*onsignor Schmall has a new secretary. Goes through them like water. Scotch, in his case. This one "dismissed herself" he said. I'll bet he's a trick to live with.

Secretaries can make or break you. They fuss about your diet and how much sleep you get—like a mother hen. Then smother you with cookies and pies. And advice.

I can't complain. Kitty R. at Holy Angels made a really good pork roast. Hildegarde at St. Francis, she'd do anything for you. Even before you knew you needed it done. Quiet, too. I've always had ... oh, yeah. Forgot Evelyn P. Spiteful, old thing. Territorial. I think she worked for the CIA. Knew everybody's dirty little secret and never missed a chance to use it. Lied to me, then badmouthed the parishioners who really did the work. Finally caught on to her.
Maggie M. came with St. Hedwig's. Could have moved Hildegarde over here. Lots of priests do. Don't think she would have left. Besides, it's always nice to have someone who already knows the place, the situation, who to call when the furnace goes out, etc. Maggie can be moody. Takes things the wrong way sometimes. If she ate more, she wouldn't be so cold all the time. Might improve her disposition. Single mom. Has to be rough. Never enough money for what her kid needs. She can be very funny. Makes me laugh. Efficient. Great bookkeeper. And she's good to my cats. Drives me crazy sometimes. Suppose I do the same to her.

+   +   +

Libby waited in her warm car until she saw Lawrence Davis leave the rectory and disappear into Antonio's house.

"Still got company?" she asked as she followed Maggie to her office. The room was large enough to contain file cabinets, a desk, cupboards filled with work supplies, a computer and printer, and also an area with several homey chairs, a couple floor lamps, and an end table so visitors could be comfortable when planning weddings; or for a volunteer or two to help stuff fliers in the church bulletins.

"Everybody's gone," said Maggie, dropping into the swivel chair behind   the   huge   crescent-shaped   desk,   which   looked uncharacteristically cluttered today. From this center spot, as everyone knew, Maggie held the parish together.

"Detective Grass—gone. Detective Davis—gone. Julia—gone to work." Maggie grinned. "All alone and loving it!" The phone rang. Through the smile she sarcastically added, "Alone. Just me and the whole outside world wanting to know all the gory details."

She took the call, putting on her most pleasant voice, and politely gave brief and well-rehearsed answers to the inquisitor on the line.

Maggie Mueller had fine, sharp features. Libby always considered her neat and nice looking, though a bit plain. Since Maggie's husband was deceased and she hadn't remarried, she probably had no one to dress up for. And church salaries hardly allowed for extravagant wardrobes. But today, Maggie looked better than Libby had expected.

She was, as usual, draped in that ratty, oversized sweater she wore to stave off the chill in the rectory. The blouse underneath was nice. Purple. A good color for her, but nothing …

"Did you get your hair cut?" Libby asked as soon as the secretary finished on the phone.

Maggie poked at the pixie cut. It enhanced her size and features in a way that made her look younger than her forty-one years; the color picking up more blonde highlights that were striking in the sunlight that slanted through the tall east windows of the office.

"I, oh, I just … Julia thought it was time. For something different." As flip as Maggie could be, compliments made her self-conscious. She tucked a non-existent curl behind her ear and looked for something on her desk.

As Parish Council member, cantor, and just plain parishioner, Libby crossed paths with Maggie often. They got along. They shared similar views on church matters, whether local politics or Vatican-inspired dictates. As independent, intelligent women, they both chafed at the patriarchal bias they encountered in their religion.

Libby generally got along well with men, but ground her teeth over the good ol' boys who had risen to power and position in the Church. Or aspired to. For Maggie, working with priests, even those with genial characteristics like Father Henry, kept a certain frustration simmering.

The phone rang again. Libby sat and watched Maggie handle, with the same polite demeanor, what were obviously similar questions. Answered through the same wide smile. Was she giddy from exhaustion? Or was she perky? Libby wondered if it was possible that Maggie was relieved not to have Father Henry around.

"Frankly, I was glad he was gone yesterday," Maggie said plainly, without apology. "He can be, could be, so annoying. Sitting right here but not willing to take phone calls. All huffy if I asked him to handle the man about the sound system or to call back some lady who wanted his advice about divorcing her husband. It wasn't all that strange for him to be gone all afternoon. I wasn't really paying attention."

Libby shifted in her chair and arranged her mittens, one by one, on top of her hat, gauging the propriety of her question.

"Was it … creepy … finding him?" she ventured. Then quickly added, "Or don't you want to talk about it?" Unsure if she, herself, wanted to.

From habit, Maggie automatically began tidying the notes and papers on her desk. "I'm okay. Parts of it were creepy. I mean, he was dead. Cold and dead. But mostly it just seemed … unreal. I mean, I locked up at the usual time. Five o'clock. It was really icy out. Temperature had dropped. Plus more traffic at that time with people driving home from work."

She suspended the tidying to look up and out the window in recall. "Like I told you before, I was standing with my back against my car, facing the church, as someone drove by slowly, because of the ice. I thought I saw something move near the bushes by the parking lot across the street. Figured it was one of those outdoor cats Father always feeds. The more I looked, though, I thought I saw something by the church steps. On the ground. That light over the door is so dim, I couldn't really tell. I went over. The closer I got, I could see it was one of the red Storm Relief Fund boxes. All wet and broken. Then I saw his arm! That was creepy. I jumped. Maybe I shrieked. Funny how if nobody's around you don't carry on, you don't get hysterical. What's the point?"

Setting some papers aside, Maggie began to fidget with a pile of paperclips on the desk as she continued. "I knew it was him. His body was sprawled across the steps behind the brick ledge, so I couldn't tell much until I got close. His head was at the bottom. Next to his arm was the storm box; a couple of gift cards had fallen out. Oh. And a glass jar. I almost forgot! I kicked it accidentally. Funny it didn't break. Must have been cushioned by the box. Or his body. Maybe the grass. That good minestrone Mrs. McGrew makes."

"Hmm, yes," said Libby absentmindedly. "I think Father was putting it in the sacristy refrigerator when I came in before the funeral." But her mind was mostly picturing what Maggie described. With every sentence, every distressing detail, Libby had unknowingly pulled away, distancing herself from the awful images. She didn't realize she had shrunk back into the chair until, with this last comment, she bolted upright. "How could you tell it was minestrone?"

Maggie was now setting the paperclips in a row, end to end. She let out a snort of laughter. "Because I had it for dinner!"

Libby wasn't sure how to react to this revelation, but Maggie's amusement was obvious.

"It was so damn cold," Maggie said, squaring her shoulders, "and I was standing there, freezing, waiting for the EMS. There it was. Frozen solid. Nothing wrong with it. I'd seen those jars of soup a million times in the refrigerator." Maggie snickered. It was both impish and defiant. "Henry sure as hell wasn't going to eat it."

The absurdity made Libby laugh as well. And it made her bolder.

"Was there a lot of blood?" she asked gingerly, not sure she really wanted to hear the answer but helpless not to ask; like watching a car race and waiting for an accident, wanting to see a crash for the thrill but appalled and horrified if one actually happened.

"Not much. I could see some dark stuff, blood I figured, on the side of his head, by his ear. Like where he must have hit the cement or the edge of the steps when he fell."

"In the movies there are always big puddles of it. The blood."

Maggie shook her head. "Not even when the paramedics moved him. There was mostly dirt matted in his grayish hair."

The phone rang and Libby started.

She was jumpier than she'd realized. Maggie, used to its incessant ringing, hardly noticed. She waved a dismissive hand. "Let it go to voicemail."

Libby collected herself and tried to bring Antonio's nephew's story in line with Maggie's. "You didn't see anybody? Like someone running away?"

"You sound like Detective Grass. He seems kind of sure it was the kid who took the gift cards."

"Grass? The guy who called me?"

"Un-huh."

"Then, how does Lawrence Davis fit in?"

Maggie shrugged her shoulders. "I'm not sure who's in charge. Maybe Lawrence just has a personal interest. Being a parishioner and all. They've both been here this morning and both asked a lot of the same questions."

"The Grass guy didn't ask me much this morning. Did you get the third degree?"

"Routine stuff, like 'Did Father Henry drink or smoke?'" Maggie looked away from her paperclip train and considered. "I suppose he might have been drunk and fallen down the steps, à la the infamous Monsignor Schmall at St. Michael's." She returned to the clips. "Then, particular questions about his schedule, his calendar, things like that."

"You know that kid is Antonio Silva's nephew?"

Maggie sat back in her chair, a look of understanding dawning on her. "Oh, that's the connection. I knew he was … Antonio next door? Of course. And the boys."

"Antonio's a wreck," said Libby, telling Maggie of her conversation in the car. "He asked me to help."

"What can you do?"

Just then a plump Dunkirk lumbered in without acknowledging Libby or Maggie and went straight to the windowsill, wide enough and sunny enough to suit him. Shortly behind him, Calico Two made an appearance and was more hospitable to Libby. "I don't know what I can do," she said, stroking the cat circling her legs. "Antonio is worried Billy won't get a fair shake."

"He may be right," said Maggie. "Now that you mention it, Detective Grass did seem only mildly curious. Just asking the basic questions to cover the bases. Maybe he has more evidence than he's letting out. If he really believes Billy did it, he might not look much further. Easy. Quick. Case closed. Of course," she said, reaching down and lifting Calico Two onto her lap, "for all we know, Billy did do it."

The eyes of the two police officers in the squad car parked by the Parish Hall just down from the rectory were glued to Libby as she left Maggie and crossed to her own car in the church back parking lot.

She knew they were there. And she did not like the feeling of being intimidated it gave her. To combat that, she turned on her car and the heater, sitting longer than was reasonable to remove the frost from the windows.

It was a stupid and meaningless gesture. She knew that.

What was she doing? A man she barely knew—okay, a nice man. Scared. But a man she barely knew. He had asked her to help get his nephew, whom she did not know at all, off the hook for possibly killing, intentionally or not, her pastor. She had no skills in this area, except those inspired by watching too many movies and reading too many mysteries. She had a grant deadline clamoring for her attention. Which is why, when the blower began to send out warm rather than frigid air, she put the car in gear and resolutely quit the parking lot.

But Libby also knew herself. And so, she was not surprised when she found herself, at the first stoplight, scrambling for a pen and scrap of paper to scribble down questions about a timeline for Guillermo.

Billy.

Just in case.

Eighty-year-old Carl Baker called to his wife from their den.

"What?" she asked, unhappy to be pulled away from the pork chops she was frying on the stove. They'd dry out if she let them sit too long.

He summarized the online news before him. "Says that priest over here—the one who feeds all those stray cats—got killed last night. Behind the church."

His wife folded her arms, scarcely interested. "No kidding?

Maybe we'll get our yard back. All that poop and caterwauling."

"Says he was mugged."

"Serves him right." She gave an indignant hoot. "Between feeding all those cats and indigent people. Lined up for handouts while we keep up our property and take care of ourselves. Guess he didn't give 'em enough to satisfy 'em."

Chapter Eight

Privacy matters.

The front office at Lafayette West High School was polite but unable to answer any of Libby's questions about whether a certain student had been in school on a certain day. The most they could give her was that school was dismissed at two twenty p.m.

She had doggedly tried to put her grant-writing nose to the grindstone, but not without the worried face of Antonio constantly popping up in her mind's eye. By Tuesday afternoon, the scribbles on the scraps of paper she'd brought in from the car that morning would not be ignored. They were stuck to her conscience as sure as sticky notes on the refrigerator.

She would allow herself two hours.

She'd already clocked the drive times for a typical day in Billy's life: school to work, work to Antonio's.

Or: (skip school) go straight to church for robbery, then church to work.

Or: go to school, go to church for robbery, then to work (or skip work).

If Billy had been where he was supposed to be throughout the day on Monday, even if he drove like a reckless teenager, he could hardly have had time to commit the crime any earlier than when he said he arrived around five o'clock that evening. The slippery roads would surely have slowed down his driving.

Things could quite possibly have happened the way Billy claimed: a spur-of-the-moment, unthinking grab of gift cards lying next to an already dead body. Or he could have easily done Father Henry in at that time and trotted off to Target with his booty.

On her mission to tracking times and routes, Libby stopped to check on Billy's work alibi. No privacy concerns at House of Hunan. As Libby stood by a counter holding pastel mints and menus, the manager, wearing a crisp, white shirt; black bow-tie; and an air of determined helpfulness, reported that yes, Billy had worked Monday, but called in sick today. Very sick. Probably out the rest of the week.

At least that's what the man who had also asked such questions about Billy had told the manager.

Of course the police have been here, thought Libby, as she watched the orange-and-gold fish glide effortlessly in the large aquarium at the center of the small dining area. Without being asked, the manager went on to verify that their only teen employee punched in at two forty-five p.m.—a little late, but bad weather that day. He worked in back, doing dishes, and punched out at four thirty p.m. "Yes, a short shift on Mondays. ... No, Billy did not seem upset or in a hurry. ... Very dependable. ... Hope he will be back soon."

At two twenty p.m., as the Lafayette West Bulldogs poured out of the school building, Libby scanned the swarm for older-looking students. Billy was seventeen, a junior or senior by her estimation.

Midway down the parking lot, Libby leaned against the outside of her car as if waiting for someone. Clapping mittened hands together for warmth, she thought how the rush of kids, like horses running from a barn on fire, had such a universal feel. Separated by so many years from this part of youth, she did not feel separated from the experience. The clothes of these kids were different, their ethnic makeup more diverse, but below the surface of forced bravado and flirty confidence, Libby was pretty sure there lurked the same teen uncertainty; the same loneliness and confusion.

Here and there among the students an outburst of anger flared, an anger foreign to Libby's memory of those years. Maybe it had been there and she'd missed it. Being over-fifty—just over—also made her aware, as she had never been in high school, that the homes many kids came and went from could be vastly different from her own modest, but safe and nurturing, family environment. Having met plenty of adults since then, adults with stories of physical and psychological oppression and neglect far more damaging to kids than any lack of food her peers might have experienced. She knew this, too, was sadly universal.

Not far from Libby's car, a potential group of students milled around a beat-up van.

"Who wants to know?" Only one spoke as they all eyed Libby closely. The suspicious question was a step above the sullen silence she received when she asked if they knew Billy Garza.

"I'm from his church. His Uncle Antonio asked me to help. He's afraid the police might not get all the evidence they need to let Billy go. They're good, but they might not talk to the right people—to get the whole story."

"You got that right, lady," blurted a girl with an in-your-face sneer. She was not tall, more attractively round than plump; with a beautiful, long, ebony ponytail. "They shoulda ask us. We could tell them that Billy wouldn't do such a nasty, despicable thing.

"He's a good guy. Good student. Smart," the ponytail finished off.

With modern technology they, of course, knew everything.

A boy with the first fuzzy attempts at a mustache contradicted his friend. "He took those money cards, didn't he?"

The round girl with the ponytail sent a sneer in his direction. "He wouldn't just take money. That's stealing. He's a good guy."

The boy held his own and twisted his face back at her. "If the money was a-vail-a-ble, he would take it. Maybe to pay for his tattoo."

A boy in the back of the group, soft-spoken, disagreed. "His mother'll never let him get a tattoo."

Everyone had an opinion about the tattoo, and expressed it vociferously, until Libby broke in on the debate. "Apparently, Billy did take the gift cards," she said.

A girl off to the side, athletic and serious-looking, said under her breath, under the squabbling, "He might have been smokin'."

Libby heard her. And she remembered Lawrence Davis saying that Billy had gone through a pack of cigarettes the night he was arrested. But Libby had a feeling that wasn't what this girl meant.

She addressed the girl simply. And as softly. "Do you think Billy was high?"

The quiet girl's voice remained low, but it had an undercurrent of assuredness. "He didn't smoke to get high. And usually only on the weekends. At Paco and Raymond's."

"His cousins," Libby confirmed, recognizing the names of Antonio's two sons.

"It's really their hookah," admitted the fuzzy mustache, now that the squabbling had ended and attention had returned to the lady asking questions. "Sometimes Billy borrows it. It goes back and forth. The cousins have an old shed in the backyard where they go. Antonio, he's a good guy. He never looks there. They just dump the ashes on the garden."

"Ashes?" Libby's knowledge of hookahs was strictly based on movies she'd seen of Alice and the Cheshire Cat floating on a cloud of opium. The question tagged her as one of the uninitiated. Nothing makes kids talk like knowing something adults don't. They fell all over each other to explain.

"Ashes are just in the top. From the shisha. But that's not what you take in. There's vapors."

"They come in all different flavors. Strawberry. Piña colada. It's not illegal, you know?"

"The illegal stuff makes you high, but mostly we just do the vapors."

"I like lemon. It's kind of cool. But yeah, it's still the hookah with the long pipe, the bowl with the water giving off vapors, and the flavored shisha burning on top. That leaves ashes."

"Is it big, this hookah?"

Uncertain of what qualified as big, the sprouting mustache adjusted his hands until they indicated something about a foot high. "And metal," he added with a proud grin. "The real thing. Not some plastic pipe setup."

A rash of new images formed in Libby's mind: a hard metal object. Billy's hand. And a deadly gash on Father Henry's head. Libby didn't want them to get lost in their detailed hookah tutorial. She'd gotten the picture—pleasant or not.

"Do you know if Billy was in school all day Monday?"

There was a halt in their hookah presentation. They looked at each other, checking in with who had seen him first period, who'd eaten lunch with him; the test they'd all endured fourth period.

"Could he have skipped?" Libby asked. "Especially last period. Did anybody see him last period?"

For a moment they all had blank looks on their faces.

"This is important," Libby stressed. "Maybe he snuck out early?"

In the midst of their muttering, trying to find something that would help their friend, a new voice was heard, calm and certain. "No. He didn't skip Monday."

The speaker pulled thick shoulders into his jacket. Bulldog colors—red and white. Definitely football, thought Libby. Everyone swung around to hear his justification.

It did not come quickly.

After much prompting, the words finally spilled out. "Because we helped Allison Talbot carry her stupid ol' science project upstairs last period and we were late to history."

Wolf whistles and teasing started at the mention of Allison's name. "Oooh, Allison. Can I help you carry that?" "I'm soooo strong. You're such a little thing!"

Libby let the good-natured teasing go on briefly, then called them back to the business at hand. "You were both late to class? Any possible way Billy left before it was over? Sneak out, restroom excuse?"

"No." The defensive lineman ignored his peers as he responded to Libby. "We had to stay after to explain it all to Mr. Petosky because the class was in the middle of a quiz when we got there, and he needed to get all his reprimanding lectures in. Billy hustled out of there as soon as he could. He was afraid he was going to be late for work."

"Oh," squealed the ponytailed girl. "I have to get to wo-rk."

The personal lives of the group began to override Billy's dilemma. Libby stepped away, grateful for the information she had acquired.

With more immediate concerns, they chugged, still hooting and howling, out of the Bulldog parking lot in the crowded van.

~ ~ ~

"His alibis mostly check out, although he was a little late for work," said Detective Grass to two uniformed officers. "Maybe did it between school and work? Still a possibility. Okay, remote. Don't need much of a motive for a teenager to steal."

They were in Grass's small, neat office at the police station.

They'd found out that Guillermo—Billy—Garza had been in attendance at school on Monday, all day. Gone to work and left at the regular times. Next place he showed up on the radar was when the store security guard called in.

"Thanks for tracking that down," Grass said. "Anything else I should know?"

A lanky, young rookie checked his notes. "No, sir. Did you get a chance to talk to the folks at the hospital?"

"A visual on the wound had them guessing dirt—either from the steps by accident or whatever someone hit him with on purpose." The detective tossed an empty coffee cup in the trash. "The church higher-ups are tightening the screws a bit. I understand. Nobody looks good losing an old priest like this and then not having somebody to blame."

He stood and reached for his winter jacket. "Gotta run. I just picked up the case of that woman found dead at those new apartments by the stadium."

The officers stepped out of his way. "Anything else you want us to do, sir?"

"Not until the autopsy gives us more on the time of death, on the wound, and probable cause of death."

He paused as they all started for the door. "I'm thinking this is pretty open-and-shut. What we need is evidence to prove if it was an accidental tussle and fall or a malicious hit. I know the lab's already been all over that crime scene, but it was dark and the place had all night to be contaminated and messed up. If you could make one more pass in those bushes and on the church grounds for a rock or something similar. Nice if it came with a little blood on it. Then we could maybe all get some closure, as they say."

~ ~ ~

Libby was torn. Should she try to find the hookah or not? If Billy had used it to hit Father Henry, he would be charged with murder. If she didn't turn it in, the police would likely say Billy pushed the priest, an accident, but one that led to death. He'd still be charged with a serious crime.

Or the police might discover it as she had, and it would confirm what they already believed.

On the other hand, there was the chance Billy didn't have anything to do with Father Henry's death—as his friends, his uncle, and cousins maintained. Testing the hookah might clear him of suspicion and make the police look in a new direction.

Away from Billy.

Chapter Nine

Not only two hours, but most of Tuesday afternoon had disappeared. Libby stood in the Silva living room with Antonio, who was thanking her for things she had not done. He introduced Libby to his wife, who also called on the Mother of God to bless her.

Their home was, like the rectory, graced with aged woodwork and crystal light fixtures installed by the original owners. Colorful paintings spoke of the Silva's heritage; a statue of the Madonna, large and prominent, spoke of their faith.

"It looks like Billy's alibis are pretty good," Libby started, taking the seat on the sofa the anxious couple offered. "He was probably telling the truth about where he was during the day. That's all good."

Antonio's teeth were less than perfect, but the smile they formed was radiant and perfect with hope. "I knew you would help," he said with great satisfaction. "You will get Guillermo free." He patted his wife's knee as they sat across from their guest.

Libby tried to sound more neutral. "There are still many questions the police have to ask. And they're very busy."

Antonio's smiled dropped. "Too busy for my sister's little boy? Too busy for my nephew?"

"I'd like to talk to Paco and Raymond," Libby said. "Are they around?"

"In the shed," said their mother, tossing her head in the direction of the backyard. She rolled her eyes. "Always in the shed."

Antonio stood. "They're working on the science project, Mama. They're good kids. Smart."

Libby followed the short, stocky man, who trusted her so much, through the kitchen where the scent of spices from Mexico lingered. As Antonio reached for his coat from one of the hooks along the wall by the back door, Libby suggested she might have better luck talking with the boys alone. Whatever Libby thought was best was okay by him.

It was getting dark, but Libby could make out the shed in the corner of the yard, past what was a huge garden when winter wasn't claiming it.

To Libby's surprise, Paco and Raymond actually were working on a science project, involving more wires and metal silos than she wanted to know about. Like their friends in the school parking lot, the less she knew, the more they wanted to enlighten her.

The boys were close enough in age to look like twins and duplicates of their father. Their faces looked a little thinner, smoother than the older man's, whose skin was wrinkled from the stress and worry of raising and supporting a family.

The shed was small. Yard tools, cleaned and orderly, lined one wall; while pots and buckets sat on a waist-high shelf. The rest of the shed the boys had obviously made their own. A space heater, a table lamp with no shade, and discarded chairs offered small comfort as the night and cold set in. But a teen hideaway required little except being away from adult eyes, and Paco and Raymond seemed content with their spot.

They knew Libby mostly by sight from church. After covering details about the current science project, Libby brought their attention to the seriousness of the situation.

She began, "Your cousin could be in a lot of trouble."

Earlier, before going into Antonio's house, Libby had sat for a long time in the car going over her questions, as if she was a lawyer preparing for cross-examination, calculating what order to ask things of the boys to elicit one piece of information that might lead to another, and thus get her to where she wanted to be by the end of the visit. The experience in the school parking lot had taught her that interrogation was an art form.

To her surprise, all the pre-calculating had proved unnecessary.

Paco and Raymond turned out to be approachable, even open and helpful. The cold and their agreeableness encouraged her. She went right to the endgame. "I know there's a hookah you and Billy use. Is it here?"

The cousins exchanged glances; both of them blushed.

"Don't know," said Paco.

Libby figured she'd finally hit a teen stone wall. She had to stay firm. Ready to challenge any reticence. "Don't know?"

As Paco stepped over two crates to a third pushed up against the shed wall, he said, amazingly void of reticence, "Depends if Billy has it or not." He lifted a stained towel.

There was the hookah.

Much smaller than the Cheshire Cat's but similar in its octopus tangle of hoses, it was not totally unlike what the fuzzy mustached Bulldog had described.

"It kind of comes and goes," Paco explained. "If Billy wants it, he just comes in and takes it. Then brings it back whenever. I haven't used it for a while."

"Me either," Raymond said, then offered a weak-sounding defense. "I've been … busy."

Before Libby could challenge him on it, Paco smirked as if it were the dumbest excuse possible. "My brother has a girlfriend."

Libby tried not to smile too much at the embarrassed teen, and kept to the business at hand. "One more thing," she said. "Did you work out here on Monday night?"

Paco shook his head. "I had a test to study for. I stayed in the house. It's warmer."

Raymond admitted to being in the shed for a short while after school. "I was waiting for Billy to help with the battery setup on our project, but when he didn't show, I went back to the house, too."

There was no reason to prolong the inevitable.

"We have to take the hookah to the police," she said.

They looked at the floor. They looked at each other. They blew on their hands and lifted their feet in the mounting cold, in their discomfort. "Will it help Billy?"

She meant the words with all her heart. "I hope so."

They consulted each other silently again. Paco voiced what they both feared to put into words. "Do we really have to?"

Libby had seen enough movies to know she could foul things up by how she obtained any evidence. She was more than a little relieved to discover that Paco was eighteen, legally an adult, because no one standing in that cold shed wanted to run this question by the good, but naïve, Antonio. She had both boys sign a sheet of notebook paper saying they were letting her take the hookah. After easing it into a brand-new, unused, plastic garbage bag—careful not to touch it herself or disturb any existing fingerprints—she camouflaged the bag with her thick mittens and a scarf against her coat.

She talked quickly, saying goodnight to Antonio and his wife, saying she would keep them informed. Yes, the boys had been helpful. She adroitly moved through the house and out the front door.

Yes, they were good kids.

"Tell me again who she is and why she's so interested."

Detective Lawrence Davis told Detective Grass what he knew of Libby Kinder. She was a church cantor, a member of St. Hedwig's Parish Council. Friendly. Big on helping the world's needy, like disaster reliefs and collections for local poor families at Christmas. He wasn't surprised that she'd responded to Billy Garza's plight, especially after seeing her in the car with Billy's uncle.

"A bleeding heart, eh?"

It was late in an already long day. Both detectives sat in Grass's office. Davis's blue-plaid shirt, once buttoned down and pressed, was now wrinkled; his sleeves were rolled up on arms stretched behind his head. He was watching a cobweb sway in one corner of the ceiling.

Grass was bent over his desk, his hair mussed from going in and out all day and from ruffling through it repeatedly since Libby Kinder had dropped off a black garbage bag.

A bag loaded with evidence.

With a hookah, for God's sake.

With a whole new line of questions that had to be addressed.

Davis dropped his arms. "I would also say she's pretty smart."

Detective Grass stared at the ten-inch-high hookah and the short hoses shooting off from its base. "Or very lucky."

Davis let it pass.

While the two men often used each other as sounding boards for their various cases, because they had such different styles, one could easily get the other one's fur up. Davis was more likely to let things emerge, allowing for multiple options; Grass liked to have a specific theory in the back of his mind to weigh all his facts up against.

"Let's look at what we do know," Grass said, straightening several disparate piles of papers beginning to stray on his desk. "The facts lean toward—*were* leaning toward—this kid taking advantage of an opportunity that presented itself to him. It is my dumb luck that Father Henry's death was initially labeled an accident. Crime scene sitting out in that sleet. Anybody or anything walking all over it. Clues washing away down the drain. If we knew for certain how long he'd been lying there before he was found, we could eliminate the kid in the murder category. Even a shove would have had to occur earlier than Billy could possibly have been there since all of his alibis are solid. Mostly. That would make him more definitely someone just happening by."

"Didn't the paramedics say the body was already cold?" Davis asked. "Of course, that could have resulted from about a half hour on those steps in this weather."

Grass leaned even farther over his desk and came to eye level with the hookah, his hands held back like a child told to look but not touch a precious object. "Of course, if this baby has blood on it," he said, "we've got a whole new ballgame."

Chapter Ten

When Libby got home, the dog was at the door, the cat at its bowl, both demanding attention. She fed BabyCakes, then laid her old, soft sweater along Dash's back and deftly crisscrossed the woolen arms underneath, back up and around, to tie securely on top at the dog's shoulders. Even little, long-haired pups needed to wear something in this weather. She snapped on Dash's leash and headed back outside.

The timing was perfect. As she walked out her side door, Namita, the renter from upstairs, and her rescue greyhound came out the front door. Nothing seemed more refreshing at the moment to Libby than walking with someone not involved with detectives, hookahs, or deceased priests.

Namita Green. Her name said it all.

Her mother was from India, a biology major who came to study in the U.S.; her redheaded father was the owner of a small hardware store outside of Chicago. Dark complexioned like her mother, bookish and laid back, more of a listener than a talker—until her father's genes kicked in. He'd given Namita height and a sassy sense of humor.

Her flair for wearing edgy, unusual clothes was all her own.

Once out of college, Namita hopscotched jobs and cities across the States, until three years ago, at age twenty-eight, when she landed her job as head of Reference and Technology at the vocational training college.

And moved into the apartment above Libby.

Namita Green was a projects person. Sometimes her interest in something was short in duration, sometimes longer-lasting. The year before, she'd dived into learning how to play the guitar. This year she was knitting up a storm. Libby had been the grateful recipient of trial booties and mittens.

Standing next to the waiflike sweatered Dash, terrier ears and dachshund tail showing he was ready for action, stood Namita's sleek-and-muscular, champagne-colored Paki, in a hand-knit, royal-blue dog blanket that was only a smidgeon too long and artfully tied at the chest and waist.

This evening, Namita had tossed a gold-red-and-brown poncho with a slightly irregular fringe, obviously an advanced undertaking, over her five-foot-eight frame. It must have been wool yarn because it was freezing outside; the contrast between Namita's thin, casual throw and Libby's puffy down coat, scarf, hat, and mittens, all covering every inch of her body, could not have been greater.

Delighted at having human company to walk down the inky, deserted night sidewalks with, Namita quit whatever she was involved with on her cell phone and put it away as Libby caught up with her.

"Am I interrupting you?" Libby asked, as the two dogs sniffed out their familiarity and proceeded in tandem down the block.

"Checking out a Potential."

It was the term Namita used for any man that came onto her dating radar screen. She was currently signed up for an online service and was hoping, as usual, to find a suitable, and permanent, match. Her standards were daunting. She was searching for an intellectually first-class, artistically sensitive, socially liberated, kind, generous, solvent, fun, and animal-loving person.

While Libby made her assessment of people by paying attention, catching a tone or remark, watching reactions, and sometimes going on gut instinct, Namita was more computer-age, and trusted her research skills and technical savvy to piece together a portrait of any given Potential.

Namita could track down personal and professional sites that branched out and networked their way to a profile more thorough than the meager tips any Potential had listed under his name. Conversely, her skills had allowed her to block and thwart any such search aimed at discovering her own vita. Her reasoning was that if someone was clever enough to get through to her information, all the higher marks they would receive in her assessment.

Libby regarded these searches with a mixture of awe, curiosity, and admiration. "Anything interesting popping up?"

"The usual, so far; but I'm only beginning on this one." The wind lifted Namita's short, black hair. "Gee, it's arctic out here. I need to knit myself a hat." She yawned. "Long day."

The yawn was contagious. "Me, too," Libby mumbled into the hand she raised to cover her open mouth.

"How's the grant writing going?"

"Never enough time. Deadlines always show up too fast."

"Hey, I've been meaning to ask. Was that your priest who died?" Libby looked ahead at the dogs. "Yeah."

"That's rough. I'm sorry," said Namita. "Was it an accident or did this kid do it?"

With only two short questions, Libby found herself explaining the whole situation to Namita. As one who often processed things by talking, Libby had discovered Namita's queries and astute observations on their informal walks with the dogs to be helpful.

"Do you think the kid did it?"

"I don't even know the kid," said Libby. "I like his family. What I know of them."

"Did you ever consider not turning in such … damning evidence? I mean, you, it, could really …."

Libby knew the rest of the sentence. She'd weighed all the options and their ramifications before she'd taken the hookah into the police station. The one option she could not escape was that it was the right thing to do, the honest thing to do. In this instance, her conscience would not let her off the hook because she liked or disliked someone.

"After talking to you, though," Libby mused, "I don't think he did it. I know it takes more than looking at something with the naked eye, but even as a possible weapon that fits all the other facts, the hookah, to me, did not look like it had blood on it. Some ashes from the shisha maybe …"

Namita stopped and cooed. "Ooh. Shisha. I'm impressed."

Libby gave a short laugh. "Yes, I've picked up a whole new

vocabulary!" She tugged Dash away from nosing out the smell of another dog's visit to a shrub. "The biggest problem for me is the timing."

Namita reigned in her dog, who was equally obsessed with the bush. "It doesn't take long to whack somebody. If there's no fight."

"The detective said they didn't find any other wounds, so it doesn't sound like there was a struggle. That means the person surprised him from behind."

"Or," conjectured Namita, "the priest knew the person and didn't suspect anything until it was too late. Like knowing the kid from church."

"I just have a feeling Father Henry was dead before Billy could have found him. That's how Maggie, the secretary, described him. The priest. 'Cold. Cold and dead.'"

The two women turned the corner that brought them to the last part of their walk. It also sent them straight into the wind; tonight's biting gusts suddenly whipping Namita's poncho and uneven fringe out behind her. Libby rewound the scarf at her neck. Both of them held tight to leashes as both dogs decided they'd had enough fresh air and pulled in the direction of home.

"Look," Namita called into the wind. "My eyes are watering and the tears are freezing. Right on my cheeks! Incredible."

Libby stopped by the light of the streetlamp.

She stared at her friend, momentarily amazed. "You're right. They are. Freezing right in front of us."

Chapter Eleven

The world stopped when the Host had people to dinner. Meetings were postponed and his secretary deflected non-emergency church business. He certainly felt he worked hard enough as a pastor to deserve a night off—or several days, if preparation warranted that. Besides, it was a gathering of the committee. How he elected to entertain the members and what refreshments he chose to serve were his prerogative.

He had ordered the crown roast of lamb weeks before. After poring over cookbooks and recipe clippings for days, he decided to stuff it with a dried fruit-apples-and-nut dressing. An undertone of garlic added to the rich, meaty aroma that permeated the kitchen. Parsley-buttered fingerling potatoes and creamed spinach rounded out the menu. Oh, and fresh salad greens purchased that morning. Wines were chilled and the special order Charlotte Russe had been picked up from Harper's Bakery just north of the city, along with a dozen of their yeasty dinner rolls.

"It's nothing special," the Host demurred. "The crystal and china were still out from entertaining the Donors not long ago."

The Host denied, especially to himself, that he was approaching middle age. He had always been attractive, and the fact that he was graying handsomely, like a Hollywood movie star, gave him some support in this belief.

He led his guests into the formal dining room at Queen of the Roses rectory:

The Vicar. Tall and naturally slender, he was acceptably dignified and effective, although his head was not particularly turned by his position. Having attended his fair share of dinner meetings with institutional chicken and undercooked broccoli, he did appreciate the occasional home-cooked meals, superbly prepared by the Host.

The Young Priest. Pudgy Father Ramon, newly minted and assigned to a parish two hours away from his mother's own delicious meals, was still awed and mystified by the older priests' habits. Being invited by the Host this evening did, indeed, rotate his head a little.

The Monsignor. A man who had worked and dined with the first and last at tables, he enjoyed the Host's meals in equal measure. The pomp of his title—Monsignor—even attached to his jaunty surname, Flaherty, was always deflated by his informal first name: Jimmy. The name he'd been called as a boy and still answered to at eighty-seven years of age.

Monsignor Jimmy took his seat at the Host's beautifully set table. Fresh flowers were a delight to see in the middle of January, and he leaned over the good china to cup a fragrant star lily to his nose. The slight tremor in his hand from the Parkinson's was nothing he wasn't used to.

The monsignor's outfit was basically unchanged from his daily black garb. He still wore his usual jacket, rumpled by this time of the day, but had removed his white collar. The others, happy to abandon not only the stiff collar, but the black as well, were dressed in bright-colored sweaters, some casual, some cashmere, all depending on their tastes, budgets, or the generosity of a parishioner.

"Pretty fancy for a meeting about a retreat," noted the Vicar, cutting into the tender lamb. "I may have to put you on more committees."

"Your food allowance must be quite generous," said Father Ramon. "All we seem to have is chicken."

"I like chicken," said Monsignor Jimmy. "Pizza, too."

The Host lifted his glass of wine jovially. "I ask. And I receive."

The Vicar laughed heartily. "So that's what 'knock and the door shall be opened' is all about!"

"Potatoes, spinach, a salad," said the Host airily, "nothing out of the ordinary. The crown roast, however," he added with another toast of his wine, "came out of a little pin money. From the Donors."

The four priests ate with gusto and made small talk until the Host rose to refill the wine glasses. "Well, Vicar, any hints on who the Bishop is sending down to St. Hedwig's?"

Ideas erupted around the table.

"It's an inner-city parish. Not everyone is going to want that position. Especially after what happened to Henry."

"It's an old church. With old people."

"*Wise* old people," interjected Monsignor Jimmy, not looking up from his salad.

"No school. That's a bonus."

"It's one of the only parishes in the black financially."

"Frugal Germans."

Father Ramon pushed uncertainly at his spinach. "Then better not send the unfrugal Father from St. Gert's. He'll be ordering new carpet, a new sound system, carillon bells for the steeple, and a trip to Italy for himself. They'll be bankrupt in a year."

The other priests turned to their young, seemingly knowledgeable companion. Realizing what he had just rattled off and how it had been received, Father Ramon bowed slightly as the question hung in the air. "Finance committee. I help with the Diocesan Finance Committee."

"I like Italy," the Host tossed in, reaching for a roll.

"You have enough Donors to allow you to like Italy," remarked the Vicar matter-of-factly. "And, I assume from the quality of the recent new car purchase, you get good personal investment tips from them as well."

"Definitely. Part of the ask-and-receive plan."

"I didn't know Father Henry at all," said Father Ramon, wiping his fingers on the white linen napkin in his lap. "Sounds like he was good with parish money. How old was he?"

"Seventy-two. Only three more years to retirement. Pity."

"I don't think I was ever on any committees with him," said the Host. "Was I?"

"Possibly. He worked in the Diocesan Archives for a period of time. I remember he liked history. Old things. Buildings," the Vicar recalled.

"Architecture," Monsignor Jimmy amended, swirling his wine and taking a hearty drink. "Churches, chapels, convents, basilicas, monasteries. The whole gamut. Knew a lot, appreciated a lot, about their construction, their artifacts and such. I imagine he loved being at St. Hedwig's. Such a beautiful structure. Would be nice to appoint someone who would keep it up."

"A building's one thing," said the Host, reaching to fill the Monsignor's glass. "What is the timbre, the ambience, the vibe of the congregation? Every parish has one. Inner-city can be a pretty eclectic term."

Monsignor Jimmy put his hand across his wine glass and smiled. One was enough for him. "I would say St. Hedwig's is traditional but not overly conservative."

"So, Father Hats-and Chapel-Veils-on all-Women-in-church isn't going to fly?"

Monsignor Jimmy leaned back. "Are you serious?"

"I'm serious that he's serious."

"And must the men remove their hats?" the old priest asked casually, returning to his greens.

The Host scoffed. "Men don't wear hats like that anymore."

"My point exactly."

The Host wielded his knife authoritatively around an innocent potato. "The historical meaning of covering a woman's head ..."

"Is history," said Monsignor Jimmy lightly. "Fashion is one thing. Or is this female submission resurrected for the twenty-first century?"

The Vicar gave an exaggerated cough. "Brothers. Gentlemen," he said. "This is all very distressing business." He laid his fork across the top of his empty plate and put his palms flat out on the table. "You know it could have happened to any one of us."

Monsignor Jimmy put a weathered palm to his heart and closed his eyes. "You are right, Vicar," he said sincerely. "This was a good man. We must pray for Father Henry."

After a brief moment of silence, the Host began clearing dinner plates. "When will the funeral be?"

"Can there be a funeral if the police are still investigating the circumstances?" wondered Father Ramon.

The Vicar let one hand stray to smooth the tablecloth in front of him. "The police said it shouldn't interfere much with the planning. There are, however, some out-of-town relatives to be consulted."

"And the people of St. Hedwig's," Monsignor Jimmy said, his

head nodding slowly. "Their needs should be considered as well." He looked at the Vicar. "The congregation will be in mourning. Given the circumstances, they will be understandably restless. The city, too. So many people, so many stories from the police, so much on the news, and all the disruptions. They will be like lost sheep. I hope the Bishop takes this into account."

The Host sat down. "Our Bishop? Does he even know Felger is gone?"

The Vicar adjusted the remaining polished-silver dessert fork. "I am sure the Bishop is considering many things in this matter, as with any tragic death in a family."

+   +   +

One of the altar boys (Josh) is writing a paper. Very confused. Asked for help. Easy enough for me to write down the hierarchy of the Catholic Church. I'll copy it and he can use what he wants.

Church with a capital C = the Church as a whole. (The Church believes in sin and forgiveness.) Small c church = the building. (I went to church for Mass.)

The Pope is at the top. In charge of the Universal Catholic Church; all people, all ranks are below him. He wears white. The Pope appoints bishops.

Bishops are in charge of a diocese, a geographical location, like a county, that can consist of multiple parishes.

Archbishops are bishops for a consolidated group of dioceses.

Cardinals advise and vote for the Pope. They wear red, especially the big, red saucer hats.

Monsignor is, was—goes in and out of fashion—mainly an honorary title, but they do get to wear a beautiful magenta sash and beret.

Vicar is a temporary position of authority beneath a bishop, like a team captain. Or maybe like the defensive coordinator. (The bishop is always the team captain.)

Priests come from the populace of their own volition. After being ordained, they are assigned to a diocese, where they live, work, and answer to that diocese's bishop. They are called "Father," and for the most part serve as pastors and run parishes. They might also be chaplains at a hospital or for the State Police.

They do not move around willy-nilly within the diocese. It is up to the bishop's discretion as far as where or for how long they stay at a particular parish; usually no longer than ten or twelve years, often less, depending on what's needed.

Priests can become bishops or popes. (Archbishops and cardinals, too). Bishops must be priests. Popes usually are, but it is not a requirement.

People think the priests in a diocese are like a family. That we get together for holidays and confide in each other and go on summer vacations together. Maybe in some dioceses, but not here. Actually, the priests here don't know each other very well. Even in a moderately sized diocese like ours, we're more like relatives you see once, twice a year. True, we see each other at meetings, serve on committees together, and attend communal church events like the ordination of a priest or a priest's funeral.

Occasionally one priest might have a couple other priests over for dinner or to play cards on New Year's Eve, but they're just as likely to spend Christmas with their own parents and siblings or a family in the parish they're friends with. Or they're so tired after saying five Masses, including one at midnight, that a nap is all they can think of.

Otherwise, the association of diocesan priests is like any other where you are related by work not by blood. Classmates might have a special bond, those who follow a certain sport, or have mutual interests like antiques. We do depend on each other to cover for us if we get sick or are lucky enough to have the time or money to go on vacation.

Kind of nice to see a kid interested.

Oh, and diocesan priests take vows of chastity (including celibacy) and obedience (directly to their bishop; ultimately to the Pope). While priests are supposed to live simply, they do not take a vow of poverty. They get a salary, have possessions like cars and jewelry, and manage their own finances.

Gee. Not a lot about serving God in all this.

That is the whole point, isn't it?

Chapter Twelve

Cousin Ruth and Cousin Phyllis sat across from one another in Ruth's breakfast nook. It was usually a cozy spot where the two shared tea and gossip several times a week. They were cousins to each other and also to Father Henry. When Henry's mother, their aunt, died several years earlier, the women left their respective parishes and moved to St. Hedwig's. There, they took over care of the pedestal their grandparents had erected and placed their first male grandchild on. While alive, Henry's mother had followed suit, polishing it for her only child. Now the two cousins tended to it.

Henry, long used to adulation, responded with a mixture of tolerance for being fussed over and gratitude for the perks it granted. The cousins hosted him for holiday dinners, clucked and inquired endlessly about his sleep, fiber intake, and mental disposition, and tried to anticipate his every need.

This morning, Ruth's seventy-year-old, round, pale face was puffier and paler than usual as she sniffed loudly, pulling and shredding the damp tissue in her hands. She was so short, she might have been kneeling on the floor instead of sitting on the bench, her chin barely rising above the table's edge. From the neck down, everything about her went square: broad shoulders extended out from a short neck, a full bosom filled in the middle, and a wide bottom completed the form.

Ruth's short, boxy body contrasted with her cousin's taller, larger, more womanly figure. Inside and out, summer or winter, Phyllis wore a hat, a nondescript pastel cloche, apparently meant to deal with hair issues. It was impossible to tell if she had so little hair that the hat covered a balding head or so much and such unruly stuff that the ever-present hat was needed to keep it under control.

Whereas Ruth wore her heart on her sleeve, Phyllis, when she did encounter emotions, bottled them up or rolled them out and baked them into cookies.

A plate of thick, chewy molasses ones sat between them, next to the pot of tea.

"What are we going to do now?" Ruth inhaled several shallow breaths. She was older than Phyllis by several years, but the few tufts of white hair escaping Phyllis's hat negated the difference.

Phyllis broke a cookie along the cracked fault line running across its sugar-sprinkled, dark-brown top. "The news now says they think some kid might have robbed Henry and hit him. Wish they'd decide something. It's disturbing not to have this settled."

They drank tea. They picked at the yellow floral placemats on the white tabletop. Everything was as neat as a pin.

They ate cookies and stared out the window at the winter light, thin, with no warmth in it.

"Now that it's happened," Phyllis started up again with renewed spirit, "I guess we can go onto the next step." She tossed off the last swallow in her cup. "I suppose we'll have to plan the funeral. Make all the arrangements. Being his nearest family."

Ruth's tea was tepid. "I hadn't thought about that, but you're right. We'll want it to be nice. Even under the circumstances. A grand send-off for Henry. For Father Henry."

"If we'd had our wits about us, we could have been planning these things all along." Phyllis lowered her voice and changed direction. She spoke more pointedly. "It's going to be different now, you know?"

Ruth sniffed again. She lifted a blotchy face to her cousin and closest friend who, in her eyes, looked like she did when they were children—confident and in charge.

Phyllis regarded her tablemate similarly. Even though Ruth was older, she always had a childlike, say-something-to-comfort-me stare.

Ruth wiped her eyes. "Don't you think we should say some prayers for Henry's soul?"

Phyllis patted Ruth's arm. "Some prayers for our own circumstances might be beneficial, too."

~ ~ ~

Sixty-seven-year-old Bird Hawkins was head usher at St. Hedwig's. His florid face was topped with white hair so thick it spiked upward like an egret's, no matter how short he had it cut. He wore a brown sport coat in winter and a robin-egg-blue jacket in summer over his great barrel chest, a chest that gave him a boom of a voice, perfect for assigning seats and reprimanding unruly children.

Bird Hawkins enjoyed his position of authority.

Patrolling the back of church, Bird's objective, in addition to assigning and reprimanding, was the blatant extraction and passing on of information. It could be about illnesses, job changes, births, drinking problems, marital woes, financial successes, or abject failures. A little secret, dirty or not, brightened his day.

Bird Hawkins was, quite bluntly, a news magnet. Besides being tapped into the lives of everyone at St. Hedwig's, Bird's circle of informants widened exponentially outside the church walls as he gleaned the latest from funeral homes, hospitals, political offices, police and fire departments, grocery stores, not to mention the plethora of social media he consulted.

And he always gave as good as he got.

It was not unusual, however, for Bird's retelling to be embellished with less-than-factual aspects. Or be missing some salient points altogether. But news was news, and the people of St. Hedwig's appreciated the direct line, even with the occasional flaw of misinformation.

It was understandable then, that it was from Bird Hawkins that most of the congregation of St. Hedwig's heard about the death of Father Henry Felger. He'd told them the sad news, and they'd taken the grief and horror into themselves.

The next step was dealing with the tragedy.

In such situations, it seems that people come together around the greatest common denominator, however the group sees itself—as a family, as city, as cancer survivors or the like. They seek an outward communal response to tragedy; gathering in solidarity as if the more they lock familiar arms against an unfamiliar enemy, the safer they will be.

And so when St. Hedwig's parishioners began fumbling with the question "What can we do?" it was fitting that they turned to their religious bond. The answer was not unpredictable: we need to pray. And we need to pray together.

Uncharacteristically, Bird Hawkins did not get to the Vicar fast enough. Rather it was the Vicar who, with Monsignor Jimmy's prompting, called Maggie Mueller to offer the Cathedral downtown to the city in general and the parishioners of St. Hedwig's in particular for a prayer service to be held Thursday after the murder.

With that date to look forward to, people's agitation was temporarily put on hold.

For a while, everything about the murder of Father Henry Felger faded into the background. The church building remained closed, scattering St. Hedwig's congregation to other parishes for weekday services. People went to work and took care of their families, secure that they would be coming together as one in the near future.

Few noted the release of Guillermo Garza. The nomadic flock of lost sheep had a direction, a time and place they would be together and could lean on each other in the protective presence of the Divine. That was comfort enough.

To almost everyone.

Chapter Thirteen

They had a dishwasher. That wasn't the point. Doing the dishes together was a sacred part of the day for Daniel Giglia and Paul Thomas Roth. The routine—Paul Thomas washed, Daniel dried and put away—was established when they'd first come together twelve years ago, and was now an anticipated ritual.

Over plates and silverware and pots and pans, they connected after a hard workday to mull over jobs and life—the joys and disappointments—to expose their separate opinions as well as shared points of view or just to reflect on small pleasures of the day.

Thursday night after the priest's death, the topic was the prayer service for Father Henry at the Cathedral.

Paul Thomas rinsed a coffee mug and handed it to Daniel. "Do you want to add the weather as an impediment? How about time to start doing taxes?"

"Hadn't thought about that, but that's a good one." Daniel wadded up the end of the towel and corkscrewed it into the dripping mug. "I'm really tired. Seriously. Besides, hardly anyone in that congregation knows me."

"Don't kid yourself. They all know you. And now that that boy's been released …"

"That might be just a rumor."

"Might be. But some of the parishioners know you were at the church the day Father Henry died. Some of them must realize you could have been the last one to see him alive." Paul Thomas gave his partner a weak smile of encouragement. "Don't you think it's important for you to be seen as …"

"What? Not afraid? Not hiding? Not a …" Daniel left off the word they'd both avoided. He placed the royal-blue mug on the second shelf of the glass-paneled cupboard overhead. He turned its handle in line with the others. "Wish you could be there with me," he said quietly.

"Not appropriate," Paul Thomas replied firmly. But his action was gentle.

There was a place between Daniel's shoulder blades that cradled Paul Thomas's beginning-to-bald head perfectly. The gesture could still send a zap of electricity down to Daniel's fingertips. Tonight it was better than that. Warm reassurance flooded Daniel's whole body and he leaned back against the perfect globe nestled in his back.

"Don't worry," whispered Paul Thomas, soothed himself by the familiar smell of the familiar body. "We'll get through this."

~ ~ ~

Wayne Nichols slouched in his rusty pickup truck parked at the edge of the Cathedral parking lot as he smoked a cigarette. He'd left the motor running. It was cold and he wasn't about to freeze waiting for this prayer service to begin; and he sure as hell wasn't going in early. Eventually he'd make an appearance. Figured he needed to be seen as the grieving maintenance man. Sad for the loss of his boss. Appear concerned. Like when I'm putting out those damn Storm Relief Fund boxes for the poor, he thought to himself. Act like I care.

He picked a fleck of tobacco from his tongue and kept grinding his axe.

Wayne Nichols was a small man. Physically and otherwise. On the short side, he was more muscular than one could readily surmise from the oversized, double sweatshirts he wore and frayed jeans that hung low on his hips.

He had a smallness of character, a limited view of the world that encompassed primarily himself. No one had ever put him on a pedestal.

And he visited that slight every day of his life.

Turning down the radio at a song he didn't like, Wayne let his thoughts ramble. In the tangle of all the negative chatter, a tiny notion wriggled free. Would he now be able to quit his job? Instead of stuck under the thumb of Henry Felger, like I had no options, he thought. Henry probably told himself he was being charitable. A janitor. Shit. If you wanted to be charitable, give me what I deserve.

He sat up. Maybe this was something he should celebrate. He rubbed his hands along the curves of the steering wheel and took a heavy, happy drag on his cigarette. Maybe a new truck?

In the dark, it looked as if all the people streaming into the Cathedral were wearing gray. Gray bumps curved against the wind. Stupid people, thought Wayne. Huddled together to ward off the angry gods. He'd been huddled and herded enough in his life. More than a few times to church. He had gladly thrown off those shackles. A crude, violent laugh erupted from his lips at the irony.

Wayne got out of the truck, flicked his cigarette into the dirt, and shoved balled-up fists into the front pockets of his outer sweatshirt.

And skulked into the prayer service.

Even before passing through the thick doors and into the warm Cathedral, people could hear Bird Hawkins's voice booming above everyone else's. About thirty sympathetic members of the Catholic community milled in the open space at the back; most of them, in contrast to Bird, spoke in hushed tones. Light from amber-colored lamps overhead joined the glow emanating from the racks of candles that sent darting shadows down the aisles and up the walls of the big gothic church, animating the life-sized statues of saints stationed all around.

Libby was in the back, standing with two longtime parish women. "How sad," they were saying. "How awful what happened to Father Henry. … How nice of the Vicar to offer the Cathedral." Did Libby know when the funeral would be?

No, she did not.

Did she know who that man over there was? Their heads bobbled back and forth as they scanned the crowd and pointed out people they could not place.

"That's the man who decorates the church," said Libby, identifying Daniel, who stood alone near the main door, smiling politely at no one in particular.

"He's very good," they agreed. "We love what he does at Christmas with all those poinsettias. And the swags along the pillars. And that one? There?"

Their attention landed on Wayne talking to the Parish Council president.

"Our maintenance man," reported Libby.

Libby spotted many of St. Hedwig's regulars: Jonny Kwan and his wife, the few families with young children, Bird Hawkins, Lawrence Davis and his wife conversing with other lectors, Father Henry's Cousin Phyllis and Cousin Ruth, people from Saturday night Mass, people from Sunday morning Mass; parishioners Libby knew well, and others she only recognized by where they sat out in the church pews in front of her when she sang.

A splash of red Tartan caught her off guard; the two older women knitted their brows with consternation on being told its wearer was a police detective.

"Hello, Miss Libby." Bernie Fruehauf came up from behind, greeting Libby. "A pretty good turnout, don't you think?"

There was general agreement, then more observations about the crowd until the two ladies moved to seats toward the front of the church, where perhaps another hundred people were already on their knees or sitting in quiet prayer.

Libby smiled at the organist. "Glad you're not playing tonight?"

"Probably as glad as you are not to be singing. Any word on a date set for the funeral yet?"

"No, not that I've heard. While I'm thinking of it, do you know what the vigil or wake service looks like? I know it's different for a priest. Is there a prescribed ceremony, or are we left to our own devices?"

Bernie could only remember snatches of other wakes he'd been to. "I know they're laid out in church, not the funeral home. I think there's a program I saved from one in the choir loft files. We can look at that."

A loud laugh erupted in the distance.

"That crazy Bird," said Bernie. As if to temper the outburst, Bernie lowered his own voice. "Hey, did you know Bird says it's definitely not that kid who hit Father Henry? He's even been released. How did that happen?"

"It probably happened because of the soup," said Libby. "Mrs. McGrew's soup. Do you remember it the morning of the Webber funeral?"

He thought for a moment, carefully bringing that day to mind. "Well ... yes. Henry put it in the refrigerator. You were there in the sacristy, weren't you?"

"I was. Father apparently had the soup with him when he left church later because Maggie found the jar by ... his ... body. Frozen. The soup."

"Oh. My."

Libby knew this response. It meant Bernie was hearing the words but either understood a terrible thing had happened or was not understanding something at all.

"The soup would have only been cold from being in the refrigerator when Father Henry left," she clarified. "But it was frozen solid when Maggie found it. That meant it had been outside long enough to freeze. And that meant Father had been outside that long. At least several hours. It's cold enough for tears to freeze on your cheek in seconds these days; so it wasn't a stretch to think a jar of soup, already cold, could do that. The kid, Billy, was at school or work all afternoon. He didn't have time to kill anybody any earlier than five o'clock. Which is when he said he was at the church."

Bernie let all this sink in. "But, he did steal those gift cards, didn't he?"

"Yes. He admitted that right away. And he left the scene of the crime. But he probably didn't kill Father Henry."

"Probably?"

"Maggie ate the soup," Libby said bluntly. "The police only have her word that it was frozen. And there was ... he did have ... a possible weapon."

"That pipe thing? Bird said there was nothing on it. No blood. No hair. No ..."

"Wait," Libby interrupted, no longer the one with the information but the one desperate to get it. "The tests are back? Bird knows this, for sure?"

Bernie nodded.

Sometimes Bird's grapevine drove Libby to distraction. "You know, Bernie, Bird doesn't always get everything right."

As he trailed Libby over to where the head usher was holding court, Bernie kept trying to give Libby the rest of what he'd heard. "Something about the ashes weren't the same. On Father's head and on the pipe."

"Uh-oh. Here comes the music department." Bird Hawkins bowed dramatically.

Libby tugged at Bird's arm as she smiled at the couple he was talking with. "Would you excuse Bird for a minute?"

The couple graciously obliged, and Bird, who merely traded one audience for another, hardly skipped a beat at Libby's question.

"There were ashes on the hookah," Bird answered. "A hookah brought in by, I might add ..." he said, bobbing close to Libby's face, "... our very own Ms. Kinder. But they were not the same kind of ashes. The hookah had hookah ashes. Some kind of sweet incense the kids smoke these days. Which confused the police, because there was something like candy mixed in with all this stuff. Sweet. Like hookah ashes can taste or smell or something. Crazy stuff kids do. But Henry's head had something else. Not dirt, which they also thought it might be. Not hookah ashes."

Bird's eyebrows lifted, his spikes of hair standing up even stiffer. "Church ashes," he pronounced solemnly. "Incense ashes." He straightened up imperiously. "I could have told them from the start. Makes sense. We had a funeral that morning. Incense in the thurible. And guess what? Lo and behold—the thurible is missing! Nowhere to be found. Gone. Disappeared. Police probably over at St. Hedwig's looking for it right now."

Libby scowled. "Who told you that?"

Bird loved having the upper hand. "Sources." He closed his eyes and sniffed. "Somebody used it to bop Father Henry on the head and then ditched it. Pop! Down he goes. Just like that."

Both Libby and Bernie shrank at the crude description.

"And you know what that means?" Bird added, as if the three of them were in on the conspiracy.

Bernie registered a stunned wariness.

Libby worked at processing this barrage of new information.

Bird had them right where he wanted them. "It means, look to those who have access to St. Hedwig's."

He pointed once at Libby, once at Bernie, then to several other people. "Access. As in keys to the church. People who had access might be, and I'm only saying 'might be,' the one or ones who did the bopping."

Bernie paled in horror, which brought out Libby's protective side; not to mention her own defense in the face of someone she found to be a big, loutish gossip at best, someone feeding off a tragedy to frighten people at worst.

"Why would either of us kill Father Henry?" she asked with restraint. "You need to be more careful, Bird, going off the top of your head about things."

Nothing set Bird rolling like a little pushback. It merely made him up his ante. "I heard Father Henry's been talking about firing somebody, and there's more than you two on the payroll. For example ..." He nodded toward Daniel. "Our guy that takes care of the church decorations. He's gay, you know."

Libby did not like where this might be headed.

Bird was undeterred. "He lives with another guy."

"That's their own private business," Libby said lightly, even though she did not feel light at all.

"Not lately. Been showing up at Gay Pride parades. Seen together. Out in public, at least out, as it were." Bird chuckled at his own joke. "And our secretary, for another, sneaking into the Women's Health Clinic. That's a no-no. Bishop wouldn't like ..."

Libby broke in. This time her irritation spilled out. "The Bishop's ignorant. Anyone with half a brain knows Maggie could have been going for ... a ... a mammogram at the Clinic. You don't fire someone for getting a mammogram."

Bird eased off. "Just saying, maybe Father Henry didn't like something going on with somebody. Maybe that somebody just got mad. Shoot, Libby," he tossed in, trying to be more teasing than accusing, "even you have a reputation for an occasional overly strong reaction to something Father did." Bird rocked back on his heels and cocked his head. "I hear there've been some hot discussions at Parish Council now and again."

Libby had to move away. If she kept talking to Bird, she was liable to have an overly strong reaction in the back of the Cathedral at the prayer service, which she did not want to do. If Bird Hawkins didn't have anyone to talk to, she hoped, maybe he'd stop talking. "I think you ... we ... should go to our seats, Bird. And pray. Silently."

The notion must have been in the air because people around them began making their way toward the pews. A hundred and fifty people barely filled a fourth of the cathedral, but no one was counting. Having all been raised to believe that two or more gathered in the Lord's name was sufficient, they were glad for whatever company they had.

Bernie was still with Libby in the back when she snagged Lawrence Davis close to the holy water fountain, a large black-granite pool at the head of the main aisle. He was with his wife, and the four exchanged hugs.

After commenting on the number of people who had made it out for Father Henry's soul on such a cold night, Libby said, "Listen, Lawrence, I know this really isn't the place, but one quick question."

She hadn't planned to unload, but Bird had stoked her, as much with his implications as with the fact that he knew more than she did; even though she was the one who had taken the hookah to the police and told Detective Grass about the frozen soup which put the timing straight and got Billy cleared.

"Yes, Bird is right," Lawrence admitted reluctantly. "Right about Billy. Right about the ashes." He glanced in the direction of the gabby head usher. "We should have put a cork in that source of information sooner. If that's even possible."

He turned back to Libby and spoke more genially. "Did Uncle Antonio call you?"

"No. Why?"

"He wanted to thank you. He's sure you saved his nephew's life. Maybe you did. He'll have his hands full for a while with other charges, but nothing like murder."

"So giving you the hookah did help?"

"Got us thinking a little differently. The autopsy also confirmed the earlier time of death. Definitely scouring for that censer now. Church will remain off limits for the time being."

"Will you be overseeing that?" Bernie asked.

"Not him," said Lawrence's wife with a playful poke at her husband.

Lawrence fended off the razzing. "No. I have to bow out of the investigation. Only briefly, I hope. It's because I was at the Webber funeral that morning and had access to the crime scene. I have to sit this one out for the moment."

Bernie's eyes widened. "You mean, they think you're involved?"

"Better not be," said his wife.

Libby guessed the answer before she asked. "So, who's in charge?"

Lawrence pointed to the man with the red Tartan scarf.

Libby nodded. "Detective Grass."

"Yes, Detective Grass," said Lawrence. "You don't like him?"

Libby shrugged. "He's okay. Doesn't seem to be all that ... thorough."

"He's got his good points. He's working on more than one case right now. And we're getting pressure from the top on this one. People don't like priests being killed."

More lights lit up the main section of the church. "Don't worry," said Lawrence, "I'll be back in the know soon." He took his wife's arm, "Looks like it's going to start." And he escorted her down a side aisle.

Bernie latched onto an old friend and joined the crowd close to the altar. As Libby fell in line, she chafed at watching Bird play usher, pushing everyone just where he wanted them.

A voice came up behind her and blotted out Bird's noisy instructing.

"May I sit with you?" Daniel Giglia stood beside her with a thin but companionable smile.

Libby glanced at Bird and moved farther into a pew making room for Daniel. "Absolutely."

Chapter Fourteen

The following morning, Maggie filled food and water bowls for Dunkirk and Calico Two in the rectory kitchen as a young police officer leaned against the doorway admiring the terrazzo floor.

"Beautiful," he commented. "And they're all hardwood upstairs."

"I'm surprised you can see the floors upstairs. Father Felger was a bit of a packrat."

"Still, beautiful up there. Those huge rooms."

Maggie shrugged. "Upstairs is Father's apartment. His personal space. If he needed help corralling one of the cats to take to the vet or the groomer, he might ask me to come up, but otherwise I didn't have any need to go up there."

The officer tilted his head toward the two felines nosing and clinking food around in their bowls. "What are their names?"

"The tortoise-shell one is Dunkirk. Father was a World War II buff. And World War I, I guess. The other is Calico Two. I think he had Calico One when he was a kid."

"Now, that's what I've got. A kid who wants a cat!" The officer chuckled and folded his arms. They were like two soccer parents chatting while their kids played. "There's a sitting room with a TV in the front, with an easy chair. Is that where he'd have guests or entertain?"

"Not that *I* know of," she said, as if this were the most unlikely scenario possible. "Of course, I go home every evening. He was such a private person. Usually he'd go out or use the living room down here. Upstairs was not used for visitors as far as I know."

"Were you ever in that locked room?"

The officer was no dummy. Neither was Maggie.

They both were aware of her split-second hesitation.

Maggie dropped the scoop into the canister of dry cat food. "No."

"But you knew about it?"

"Yes."

"Know what's in it?"

Maggie shot the officer a quick glance. "Don't you? I assumed you got in there the first time your searched the place."

He smiled. "I wasn't in on the rectory search. They don't tell us everything." Maggie slid the canister into a bottom cupboard near the sink and closed the cupboard door. "As I said, Father was a packrat. Maybe it's stuff from his other parishes. Priests get moved around a lot. Probably drag a lot of cra- stuff with them from one place to another. He also liked going to antique stores and garage sales. I figured it could be junk like that."

"We're mainly looking for that incense burner, so most of the crew is searching over at the church."

"I thought they did that last night."

He smiled again. "As I said, they don't tell us everything."

The parish phone rang for the twentieth time that morning. Maggie gave a short wave in the direction of her office, letting the call go to the answering machine. "Maybe I should have shown up at the prayer service last night. Could have answered all these people's questions at one time."

She looked at the officer still leaning against the door jamb. Still watching her. Still asking questions and noting her answers.

Calico Two sniffed at the officer's shoes. "I'll watch out for the cats," he said, cordial to the end. "You'll get a call when you can go back in your office. Shouldn't take long."

The phone rang again.

Maggie reached for her coat and purse lying on the kitchen counter.

"Take your time."

~ ~ ~

After a short morning outing with Dash, Libby did some sun-salute yoga stretches, started water for tea, set out breakfast for the cat and dog, and assembled the ingredients for muffins. As she softly hummed "Beautiful Dreamer," she mixed up the liquid ingredients, combined that mixture with the dry ones, then gently folded in some walnuts and grated zucchini. After putting the muffins in the oven, she glanced over the grant work she had on her schedule.

And then he had called.

After the phone call, Libby got dressed. Casual. Jeans and a warm sweater—more than the usual sweats under her nightgown that took her through the first half of a day she would spend working at home.

Because of the phone call, she opted to brew a pot of coffee. The muffins were cooling, the coffee hot, when the doorbell rang.

Libby often forgot how frugally cool she kept her house until someone like Detective Grass came and declined to remove his coat. Or scarf. She was so glad she'd put away the Sunday newspaper, usually still scattered over the floor by her haphazard reading style and BabyCakes's habit of reclining on every section at least once.

Dash followed the guest and the muffins into the living room and tried to assume a pathetic look of hunger, sitting as close as possible to his mistress on the couch. BabyCakes was much more discreet and merely lay next to Libby's feet, purring as if this had been his plan from the beginning.

Detective Grass accepted coffee and, on second thought, opted for a muffin from the small platter of them Libby placed on the table between them.

"I understand you have a key to the church," he began. "Why exactly is that? I understand you're just a cantor, a singer. Is that right?"

Libby tried not to hear this as disparaging. The detective would have no idea how far past "just a singer" she was. No one not connected to the inner workings of a church could have a clue how many little things needed to be attended to with an older priest in an older parish with a comparatively small staff and congregation of older parishioners. Everything from washing Communion linens to changing hymn numbers to setting out new bulletins took some pitching in.

"Yes, I am the cantor," said Libby. "I have to get into church to practice sometimes. But I also help set things up for services, and stay afterward to lock up when Father has to be…had to be somewhere."

Detective Grass put his muffin plate aside, wiped his fingers on the napkin Libby had supplied, and lifted a small notebook from his coat pocket. "Did you help set up for the funeral the Monday Father Henry was killed?"

"No. It was nothing special. I had put up the hymn numbers the day before, after I sang for Sunday Mass. Everything else was done when I got there."

"Did you see the censer?"

"When I came in the back door, it was on the table ready for the service."

"What does that mean?"

"A charcoal briquette was sitting in the censer. When it's close to when the funeral is going to start, you light that up. We just use those clicker lighters. It has to get hot, like a coal. When it's time, you sprinkle the incense over the coals, and that's what makes the smoke."

"Did you touch it? Any of it?"

"No."

"How about after the service?"

"No."

"What happens to it then?"

"The ashes get dumped. Outside. And it's put away, I guess. I've never had anything to do with it. Usually Wayne, the maintenance person, takes care of it."

"Did he take care of it last week?"

Libby sipped her coffee and shrugged her shoulders. "Don't know. It was sitting on the table after the funeral, where I assume the server put it. The lady who died had some grandkids who served. Anyway, it wasn't burning anymore. Father said to leave it for Wayne. I think Father also told Daniel—Daniel Giglia, he does the church decorating—not to bother, because Daniel had offered to dump the ashes. I left before anything more was done about it."

"Do you know where it's kept, this censer?"

"Sure. It hangs in the sanctuary on a gold stand. Brass, probably. Gold-plated. It's an old, ornate hook on a pole in a stand that sits off to the side of the main altar. The censer is always just hanging there."

Detective Grass seemed to be able to take notes without looking down. After every response he marked something off on a page in his lap while keeping his eyes on Libby. He acted like she was a coworker and they were on a coffee break trading stories about their weekend. He asked Libby what she had done after the funeral, when she got home to work on her grant, what the grant was about, and if she'd seen or talked with anyone during that time.

She had not.

He took another muffin and asked how she got along with Father Henry. "He obviously trusted you. Any problems between the two of you?"

Libby slowly shook her head. Now that this priest she'd known and worked with for many years was gone, only his positive traits came to her mind. "He wasn't all that demanding. He was efficient. We rarely had meetings to go over anything. Some priests are meeting-crazy. They're either control freaks or they're so lonely they need to schedule a meeting every night. Maybe some parishioners like meetings. Or the parishes are so big they need them. At St. Hedwig's, Bernie and Father and I would simply discuss things like Christmas Eve music while we were sitting in the sacristy before a weekend Mass."

Her coffee mug stopped midair as she went on explaining. "We all always got there early. Plus, Father trusted us to do things. And he liked things relatively simple. Beautiful, but simple. At some parishes everything's big—big procession in, every verse of every hymn, twenty-minute sermons that ramble around to a hundred random points flying off the top of the priest's head or making no point at all, big production for setting the altar or bringing up the collection, big…."

Libby reeled herself in.

"Of course, that's their prerogative," she added.

She took a sip of coffee. "Here, we do things with a little less fanfare. Don't get me wrong. No one likes …" She self-consciously corrected herself, "*liked* pageantry more than Father Henry, but he was judicious. A little went a long way. Maybe because St. Hedwig's, with the big pipe organ and the long, elegant aisle and the three huge altars lit like Christmas trees, is already pageantry personified, he could be more tempered about gilding the lily. He would also tell you the Mass didn't need much embellishing."

The detective reaffirmed the scarf around his neck. "No flaws?"

Libby set her coffee mug on the small table, thinking before she spoke. "I liked Father Henry. Liked working with him and for him. We had a similar cynical sense of humor. But he was not a saint. He could be weak. He didn't like to make decisions. Or rather, he didn't like to tick anybody off; so he'd let things fester that, in my opinion, could have been handled earlier without the fallout that later flared up. Sometimes he was prone to hear the one dissenting voice and try to please it rather than see the bigger picture."

"Was he upset with you about anything?"

"Not that I know of."

"Were you upset with him?"

"Nothing that would warrant killing him." Libby realized too late that not everyone had her blunt approach.

The detective didn't seem fazed. He went on as if asking about the weather. "How about gays? He okay with gays?"

The non sequitur threw Libby. Before she could get her bearings, Detective Grass asked, "There's been some talk that Father Henry was thinking of firing someone. Is it possible he was going to fire Daniel Giglia for being gay? For living openly with another man?"

Libby would later blame her reaction on the coffee. More caffeine than she was used to. She was set to launch, but holding. For the moment.

"Daniel's worked at St. Hedwig's for a couple of years. His being gay never bothered Father Henry before."

The detective pressed on. "Apparently he's been more active in the cause lately."

"I would say that was Daniel's personal business."

"Did Father Henry know about this more public display?"

The term rankled Libby. Why shouldn't Daniel be allowed a 'public display'?

"Maybe Father Henry had other orders," Grass offered. "Orders from higher up to comply with. Your Catholic Church isn't keen on this, is it?"

Not only the Church but society at large had this wrong, thought Libby.

"The Church …" she started, knowing immediately it was a little too loud.

The dog jumped from the couch and the cat's ears shot up.

"The *Catholic* Church …"

And there was lift-off.

"The Catholic Church is out to lunch on this," she said, her voice beginning to rise. "Personally, I think it's going to feel pretty stupid, pretty petty, when its bigoted approach is finally recognized for the backward, un-Christian, un-Gospeled point of view it is."

Again, the detective said nothing.

Gave very little reaction.

Except to take note.

"What about the other people with keys? How about Maggie Mueller? Any reason to fire her?"

Libby tried not to snap back. "You'll have to ask her."

Then it dawned on her where this line of questioning was coming from.

She patted the couch for Dash to return and reassured BabyCakes. She spoke deliberately, but calmly. "I'd be careful what information—and innuendo—you take from Bird Hawkins. He thinks he knows everything, when that might not be the case."

Grass leisurely drank his coffee. "Thanks. I'll bear that in mind." He flipped to a new page of his notebook. "So, as far as you know, no reason to fire Ms. Mueller?"

"No."

"Is your organist always nervous?"

"Yes."

"Did Father Henry smoke?"

"No."

"Any reason to fire Wayne Nichols, the maintenance guy?"

"No."

Libby did not like herself when she got short and disagreeable like this. Detective Grass did not seem to be offended, but she felt she'd been offensive nevertheless.

"Look, Detective," she said more evenly. "We're all pretty ordinary people. Little tics, minor disagreements. Ordinary arguments."

"Murder doesn't usually come from ordinary arguments." He took a last bite of muffin and changed to a less officious tone. "These are really good. Not too sweet. Bet you're careful about that sort of thing."

Libby attempted to be pleasant, too. "I try. Not good for you, you know. All that sugar."

"How about Father Henry? Take everyone out for a hot fudge sundae once in a while?"

Libby laughed out loud. As much as Maggie couldn't picture their priest smoking and drinking, Libby couldn't imagine him scooping up ice cream and chocolate and whipped cream. Pasta and French fries, yes; hot fudge sundaes, not really. "No."

"My wife would love these muffins. Especially with—is it zucchini—in here?"

"Yep. Zucchini."

"Any chance you would give me the recipe? Maybe just jot it down in my notebook?"

Libby was glad for the break. She went into the kitchen and returned with a recipe card, spattered with batter stains. She copied the recipe into the back of the detective's small notebook. He must take shorthand, she thought. The notebook is so small.

After Detective Grass left, BabyCakes yawned and Dash settled back up against Libby's warm thigh. She knew that having animals near was supposed to bring a person's blood pressure down. She hoped this was true.

Chapter Fifteen

Crawling with ants.

It was an apt metaphor describing St. Hedwig's Catholic Church that day, swarmed as it was by dots of dark-uniformed police officers, busy, methodical, searching pew by pew in that holy place for the instrument of an unholy act.

By the time Libby arrived after her interview with Detective Grass, the swarm was near the front altar. For her, the scene was disorienting: the lights blazed for no apparent reason, the jumpy scramble of the police; it was an image that warred with the usual reverential bowing and kneeling. Instead of voices raised in song or communal mumble of prayer, she heard arguing.

Libby paused for a minute to get her bearings as she stood in the back of church. She turned to see that the disagreement was not coming from the bug-like visitors, but instead from Daniel and Wayne facing off not far from her in the opposite corner of the back of church.

In an instant, as soon as they realized her presence, the two men separated. Wayne pushed open the heavy door that led to a vestibule with a restroom and door to stairs leading to the choir loft. Daniel walked briskly into the church and dropped into a pew several rows away.

Libby studied Daniel's profile. He had strong, angular features softened by a slight wave to his black hair. Daniel—kind, funny, artistic. Who spent his days selling flooring and, in his spare time, made St. Hedwig's beautiful; shaping the environment with color and cloth and plants and light to reflect and enhance the liturgical seasons, creating a space to foster the soul. And, at the end of the day, going home to his family, a loving mate. How could this church not be a welcoming place for their souls, too?

Daniel turned. He smiled and waved Libby over.

"What are they still doing here?" she whispered, sitting down next to him and pulling off her hat and mittens. She spoke in hushed, reverent tones out of habit. "Maggie—and Bird Hawkins—told me they finished searching the church last night."

Daniel shook his head. "She told me the same thing." He nodded in Wayne's direction. "Apparently, told him, too. I have plants to water. Him? Just nosing around. The police said we were okay back here." He stared more intently at the ants. "I've been watching, though. Something odd. I think they're moving ..."

Libby surveyed the activity before her. "God help them when they get to all those drawers and cupboards in the sacristy."

Suddenly, Daniel leaned forward. "They *did* finish last night. Look! They're not searching. They're performing!"

Libby twisted to see where Daniel now pointed. Tucked in the corner, hidden by the north confessional, was a TV camera operator, filming the search, which did, on second look, seem to be orchestrated. "You think they're faking it?" she asked.

"I think someone is making sure it looks like all available personnel in the city have been dispatched to recover the likely weapon in the murder of a local pastor. Good news; good politics."

"Amazing," said Libby. "They obviously haven't found it."

"No. Nothing yet." Daniel began to rhythmically slap his gloves lightly against his leg. He stopped long enough to fan them in the direction of the altar. "If you came to do anything up there, I suppose it'll have to wait till the show's over."

"Came to look for a program for a priest's wake. It's a special service. Wanted to see what we're heading into. Bernie thought there was one in the choir files." She turned to look. "So, it's okay to go upstairs?"

Daniel nodded, with no further comment.

"Not at work this morning?" asked Libby.

He slapped his gloves. "Too busy being in hot water. I was on my way over here to do some work when that Detective Grass caught me. He must think the search is over, too. Wants to talk. More. I only talked briefly on the phone with him a few days ago. Said we could meet here. Kill two birds with one stone." With a wry smile he added, "Although I no longer like the term. Think he's planning to talk to Wayne again, too."

"Guess he's making the rounds," said Libby. "I've already had that chat."

Daniel shot her a quick glance. "When?"

"Just a little while ago. Came to my house."

"Don't you rate. How'd it go?"

Libby turned and stared out the church, picturing her interview earlier. She found herself flapping her own gloves at her leg. "It was a little unnerving. But," as she thought back, "he didn't ask scary questions. More like 'What happened that morning? Anything unusual happen after the funeral? Why do I have a key to the church? What did I do that afternoon?' Mostly stuff you read about in novels. Including 'Do you know anyone who would like to see Father Henry dead?'"

"I was at work late in the afternoon. But now they're saying he was killed earlier."

"At least you went somewhere. Were seen by someone," said Libby, her mittens landing noiselessly on her lap again. "I went home. Worked from there. Didn't talk to anybody but the cat. Maybe the dog. I don't remember."

"At least they won't snitch on you."

"What do you mean?"

Daniel hitched his thumb towards the choir loft. "Wayne's telling people he heard Father and me arguing. Said he was in the church basement working, about the time I said I left. I don't believe he was down there. Out having a smoke in his truck more likely."

"Did he say he saw you leave?"

"Oh, no. That would be too convenient."

Daniel stared ahead. "I have even more bonus points than that." He stopped slapping his gloves. "So far, I was the last one to see Father Henry alive."

Libby stopped her mittens as well.

She knew novels didn't give that situation a very positive mark.

At the sound of the heavy main doors behind them opening with a lumbering swish, Daniel and Libby both turned.

Detective Grass took his time, adjusting his eyes to the bright lights illuminating the vast structure before him. He could not miss the grandness, the sheer size and beauty of the church. He had never been to Europe but supposed this kind of architecture was what all the fuss was about. Like many other citizens in town, he had driven past St. Hedwig's more times than he cared to count and had that odd feeling of not noticing some huge thing right before his eyes.

Libby said good-bye to Daniel and walked over to the detective, partially from training to be hospitable, and partially by an unconscious refusal to be intimidated. If that were his plan.

He had just acknowledged her greeting when a member of the colony of ants approached. The detective stepped away and held a brief but quite animated conference that concluded with an abrupt, dismissive wave. The officer went back to the other ants; the detective returned to Libby.

"Your men certainly work long, hard hours," she noted. "I was told the church was clear for us to get back in after being searched late last night."

"It is clear and it was searched." The dismissive wave reappeared, along with a definite tinge of irritation. "This … production was supposed to be out of here by now. We don't have enough officers to …"

Detective Grass cleared his throat and regained his composure. He attempted a smile and quipped, "You people do spend a lot of time in church. If I'd known, I would have skipped going to Bernie Fruehauf's and your place and just met everybody here. Could have taken all your statements at one location. What are you up to?"

Libby explained about looking for the wake program. She informed him that the officers had already checked upstairs and, excusing herself, proceeded in that direction, leaving the detective to interview Daniel.

Wayne had reappeared and was kneeling, tinkering with a light socket, behind a statue of Our Lady of Perpetual Help just outside the door leading to the choir loft foyer. He stood as Libby approached. "I see the interrogator is here," he said, catching her by the arm.

It was a move Wayne used often. Even though the touch was quick and light, it made Libby mildly uncomfortable. She was practiced in the art of pulling away discreetly.

This did not keep him from trying to engage her in small talk.

"Did you get your hair cut? Looks nice today."

"No, but thank you." Libby kept moving, backing into the door behind her while facing Wayne. "Just passing through. I need to get something upstairs."

"Are you in line for the detective?"

"Already talked to him." She flashed a breezy smile. "You're up after Daniel."

Wayne's smooth delivery lost all trace of pleasantness. He glared in Daniel's direction. "I hope that asshole tells the truth. What a phony. Look at him. Falling all over that cop."

Libby looked. Daniel was gesturing. To her, he appeared sincere. Cooperative. He was nodding and writing something in the detective's notebook. Hardly a muffin recipe.

She left Wayne sputtering and slipped up the stairs to the choir loft.

The climb went round and round, up two stories of cut stone steps in a dungeon-like spiral. Although Libby was used to it and comfortable, it was not a climb for the claustrophobic or high-blood pressure lot. The walls were thick and close, with no windows. The pie-shaped steps, barely enough to support a foot at the wide end, tapered to barely an inch at the other.

Once at the top, Libby emerged into the loft. It was all open, but there were small areas on either side of the large central space that housed the three-manual organ console. Behind it, a thousand pipes rose up almost two more stories. Old oak benches, pews moved here after the renovation of the downstairs, lined the back wall, ready for choir members. The far room was used for storage. The closer room that Libby stepped into was like an office with a desk, copying machine, and various cupboards to store music.

She went to a small, old, cranky, metal file cabinet and began to rummage through folders. Drawer after drawer sent a screech echoing out into the church as she yanked each open.

One drawer would not budge. Stuck.

She jumped when Wayne's hand feathered across he shoulder. "Oh!"

Before Wayne could get out his offer to help Libby with the stuck drawer, Detective Grass appeared.

"You make more noise than the whole search party downstairs," he said.

Libby appreciated not only the detective's presence but the lightness of his remark. It took the edge off a situation she hadn't even realized had an edge.

"I'm so sorry," she said, a bit flustered.

"Not a problem," the detective replied. He turned his attention to Wayne. "Mr. Nichols, if you're finished up here, I'm ready to meet with you."

Libby lost interest in her quest for the wake program. "I can do this some other time. Bernie probably knows right where to look."

As she backed away, she could hear Wayne and Detective Grass commenting on how perilously high the choir loft was. The last she heard before she walked out of earshot was the detective asking if anyone had ever gone over the railing and fallen the two stories to the marble floor below.

~   ~   ~

Libby doodled along the edges of the grant proposal for the School of Visual Arts, its small but energetic faculty hoping her skills would help them expand their program. Her attention drifted back and forth from reading their suggestions about computer animation to the ever-darkening circles decorating the side margins, so much that the front page of the proposal was beginning to look like a rare illustrated manuscript.

Libby Kinder was a person who wrote things down. She took notes and made lists, not just to process and organize her thoughts, but sometimes just to get the stuff out of her head. While the laptop was useful for most of her work, a pen or pencil in hand was still her favorite method for pondering things.

She abandoned the doodles on the proposal form and grabbed a clean sheet of paper, and began unloading in ink what was really occupying her mind.

SUSPECTS
Who has keys to St. Hedwig's?
Libby
Maggie

Bernie
Daniel
Wayne

She stared at the list.

She stared at the word **SUSPECTS**. For some reason, putting it down in black and white had a mildly chilling effect. There must be others who have keys and access to the church. The killer can't really be one of us.

*Note: Ask Maggie who else has a key.

Libby thought about each person on the list. How well did she really know them? How long had she known them?

Maggie—at least 10 years
Bernie—forever
Daniel—2-3 years
Wayne—2 years

Everyone had flaws, but like her, each "suspect" seemed to be a basically decent, rational being.

Except Wayne. Granted, he'd been around the least amount of time, but even at that, he didn't seem to fit in with the rest. Not that the staff had to be best friends. She'd worked with other maintenance guys and other decorators who kept to themselves or were busy with their own lives. Wayne, despite his attempts to cozy up to her, was certainly more of a loner, a guy with a chip on his shoulder.

Libby ran a computer search on Wayne Nichols.

2,064 hits. Popular name.

After some narrowing down, she had a local address. Looked like an apartment in a part of town where rent would be cheap, modest at best. Age: 43. No phone number. Nothing else.

She tried additional searches but got nothing of value in return.

Now she was curious. Although she considered herself good at figuring out puzzles and ferreting out information, Libby recognized her shortcomings with technology.

She could be logical and clever and persistent on paper. What she needed was to be all that on the computer. And slightly devious.

She needed Namita Green.

Chapter Sixteen

Banks of computers accommodating students of various ages greeted Libby as she made her way to the main desk in the Reference and Technology Department on the first floor of Caldwell Vocational College. She spotted Namita in a long skirt, laced boots with three-inch heels, and a flamboyant scarf chatting with an older gentleman.

Sighting Libby, Namita lit up. "Hey, hi!"

"Busy?" asked Libby.

"Actually, kind of a slow night."

As Libby explained her quest, they came around to the computer at one end of the central desk where Namita, as if snapped into place by a magnet, began typing in commands. The question, her hands, and the keyboard, were soon all of one piece. "Who are we tracking down?"

Renter and landlady conspired for over an hour, visiting public records and sites Libby couldn't begin to follow. Sometimes Namita leaned in close to the screen or looked up and around the room. At first Libby thought Namita was watching for students who might need assistance. Eventually it became clear to Libby that Namita was pursuing some questionable avenues of information and didn't want to be seen.

At six p.m. the two trackers took a break. They had learned

Wayne Nichols had been in town only a few months before starting his job at St. Hedwig's. He'd never been married. No kids. Member of the National Pipe Fitters Union. No church or social affiliations. Registered for a welding class at the college but dropped it.

"It's obvious he's not from around here," Namita said, sitting back on the tall chair behind the desk. "I don't think I can get much more information without knowing where he's from or where he grew up. So many records are still kept by each state. Did he ever mention anything, drop a clue that might indicate which state to check?"

Libby realized how much she had avoided the friendly chit-chat that would have elicited such information from Wayne, but once he'd begun commenting on how nice she looked in a creepy way or touching her arm …

Touching her arm, for heaven's sake, she thought. Big deal. Yet it bothered her coming from him.

Libby was tired and hungry. It'd been a long day. Namita couldn't take a break for supper; so Libby thanked her cohort, bundled up for the cold, and started to walk out.

The cold.

"I think he's from Minnesota!" Libby practically shouted, rushing back to Namita's desk. "Wayne always complains that we don't know real winters in Indiana. 'You should see Duluth,' he said."

Within minutes, Namita had leaned back triumphantly, unabashed gloating in her voice. "My, my, my," she said. "Here's a nice tidbit. Your maintenance person is a convicted felon. Two years in the slammer." She peered at Libby. "In Duluth."

Libby swallowed. She could barely get her words out. "What for?"

Namita pursed her lips and raised an eyebrow. "Armed robbery."

~ ~ ~

Friday morning, Maggie shut the front door behind Libby, who followed her down the hall to the secretary's office. They each gravitated toward chairs near the portable heater at the side of the big desk. Within minutes, both cats walked in and began vying for a good position near the heat and the attention of their visitor.

"You look refreshed today," remarked Libby. Taking off a

mitten, she gave a good rub to Dunkirk's furry Persian head. "Not you, kitty. The secretary."

Maggie finished writing a note and stuck it on her computer screen. "Me? I finally got some sleep. That and having the police out from under everything."

"Did they find the thurible?"

"Nope. Or anything else important as far as I could gather."

"Wow," Libby said slowly, muttering as she considered the repercussions. "That means no weapon. No fingerprints to process. No evidence pointing to one person. Or eliminating anyone either."

Calico Two yawned so wide her big green eyes disappeared, showing nothing but a gaping mouth and back teeth. One good stretch and she returned to lie inside the lid of a box on the floor.

Maggie stroked Dunkirk, while firmly dislodging the papers he'd taken up residence on. "How was the prayer service?"

"Nice enough. A pretty decent crowd."

"I was planning to go. Then fell asleep. Besides, I felt like I'd already talked to all those people every day for the last week. I couldn't face Bird Hawkins one more time."

Libby knew just how she felt. "First thing out of his mouth was that Antonio's nephew was cleared. How he knew that, I don't know."

"Cleared of everything—or will he be charged for stealing the gift cards?"

"Yes, that. And leaving the scene of a crime."

Maggie shook her head. "Just the kind of stupid thing a kid does that screws up his whole life. It must have been Billy I saw ducking behind the bushes the night Father died." She straightened the papers into two neat piles. "Guess I was too busy foraging for my dinner." She smiled mischievously. "Probably shouldn't have eaten the evidence."

Libby grinned back. "I don't know. Mrs. McGrew's minestrone is hard to pass up." She opened her coat and pulled off her scarf. "Does it seem weird that no one found Father sooner? I mean, now that they think he was dead a while. Long enough to freeze the soup. I always figure you're going back and forth over to church a lot. Or that he's in here pestering you during the day."

"He did do that," Maggie said wryly. "Pester. He wasn't demanding like some bosses, but little stuff. Annoying." She began collating the two stacks of papers, stapling them at the corner and setting them into a third pile. "Like I told Detective Grass, it was too cold and icy to go anywhere. I hardly ever go out for lunch, even when the weather's nice. Plus, I was busy working on the bulletin."

"On Monday? You were ambitious."

Maggie whapped the stapler twice. "There was an insert that had to be run off and stuffed. Nothing else on the calendar, so I decided to get a head start."

She whapped the stapler hard enough to rouse the cat. She stopped to give a reassuring scratch to Dunkirk's ear. "I suppose the omniscient Bird Hawkins knows who killed Father Henry."

"He says it's one of us with a key." Libby slouched into the chair. "Which, unfortunately, makes sense." Suddenly Libby sat up. "Oh, Maggie! Guess what I found out? I have an idea who it might be."

"Oh?" Maggie's eyes narrowed. "Who?"

Libby leaned in conspiratorially, her excitement unrestrained. "Wayne Nichols is a convicted felon!"

"Oh. Yeah." The secretary took it matter-of-factly. "He is."

"You knew?" Libby sank back in her chair, her sleuthing triumph collapsing. And a little surprised that Maggie was not surprised.

"It came up in his background check. Everybody has to go through one to work for the Church. Remember?"

It had been so long ago that Libby had not remembered her own check. "Father Henry knew Wayne was an ex-con? And still hired him?"

"Oh, he definitely knew. We had a conversation about it. If I had known then Wayne would turn out to be so … aggressive. Like I don't see through the phony compliments; that hyper-polite, concerned approach …" She shuddered. "Anyway, Henry was adamant about giving Wayne a chance."

"I suppose that's the right thing to do," Libby said grudgingly. "To give him a chance. But when he turned out to be such a … a … slug of a maintenance man, it would have been an easy thing to fire him. Bird says that's why Father was killed. Because he was going to fire someone."

Slumping deeper into her chair, Libby gazed out the tall windows beside Maggie's cluttered desk, busy with never-ending church matters. The day outside was dull by comparison. No leaves on the trees. No sun. No street traffic. "Bird was full of lots of opinions—and gossip—about who was in line for that. For getting fired," Libby said. "Somebody who then got mad enough to do something about it."

"Like who?" asked Maggie.

"Like Daniel, for one."

"Because he's gay? If anyone had a right to be mad, it's Daniel."

Libby agreed. "Apparently he and Paul Thomas are being more open about living together."

"What?" Maggie gave a sardonic glare. "Are they blatantly going to the grocery store together?"

"I guess they're marching. Speaking out."

"Good Lord." Maggie reclaimed the stapler and went back to whapping. "And how does Bird know? Was he in the parade?"

Libby laughed. "Or maybe the grocery store. How does Bird know anything?"

"I can only guess what he's said about me. I've certainly gotten into it enough times with Father."

Before she thought, Libby blurted out, "He told me about you going to the Women's Health Clinic—insinuating it was for 'family planning.' All full of himself for knowing that. You can't get fired for going there, can you?"

Maggie slammed at the head of the stapler. "Depends."

Libby was always incredulous in these discussions. Always taken aback to learn about or be reminded of some Church rule that she never considered offensive to begin with.

"What do you mean? It's your private business, isn't it?"

Maggie went back to collating. "In this job, you sign a code of ethics. Believe me, if the Church had its nose in the lives of its clergy as much as it does in the lives of its employees and congregations, it might have its eyes opened."

Libby's voice was beginning to squeal. "If you went to the Clinic ..."

Where Libby's voice flew up with outrage, Maggie's dropped and became steely, steady. "I did go. With my daughter. My twenty-year-old, married daughter. Who wanted her mother to go with her in case she got harassed by zealots who don't even know why she was going. And if it was for birth control, it's so that this adult, married woman can go to school so she can get a job so she can afford to take care of a child when it does come. Or maybe it's to regulate her periods enough so she can get pregnant. Or maybe she suffers from migraines. Or maybe ... maybe she's doing it this way because she was raised by a widowed mother who did not have the education or the means to do better for herself than to work for a Church that gives minimum wages and lousy health insurance."

The stapler took the brunt of Maggie's final comments. "So much gossip. Can't even have a private life. Everybody deserves a little happiness." Her jaw set hard. "You know, some things are between you and God."

The phone rang.

Maggie paused. She quickly adjusted and returned to sounding like a secretary, answering the caller's questions graciously.

At the end of the call, Libby said, "Before I forget, do you happen to have a program from any other priest's wakes? Bernie thought there was one in his files in the choir loft, but I didn't find it. OK," she gave in, "I couldn't pry that rusty old file cabinet open to find it."

Maggie dug around in the bookcases behind her. She found a program from Father Kelly's wake and made a copy for Libby.

"Boy, your copier runs like a dream. The one in the choir loft sounds like a cement mixer."

As much as they mocked Father Henry and his scrimping ways, it was an accepted fact that one of the reasons St. Hedwig's stayed afloat financially was by always choosing to fix even the most ancient of machines rather than purchase the latest model. Having lots of experience being economical, Maggie applied those traits to her stewardship of the church's purse strings. Libby, her house thermostat set low to save on heating costs and barrels set out to collect summer rainwater, wasn't far behind.

"Thanks. I'll look at this later." Libby folded it and put it in her coat pocket. "What happens next?"

Maggie fluffed at her hair. The cut was still unfamiliar to her. "I will work," she said with a dramatic sigh, "to hold the parish together as I always do." Then more soberly, "Detective Grass said we'd probably be open for business this weekend, but we'll have substitute priests for Mass until the Bishop appoints someone permanently."

And here was the dreaded dilemma.

Getting a new priest in the Catholic Church was like playing the horses. No one in the parish had any control over the outcome, much less input on the decision. It was not like other religions, where congregations voted on a minister or a board accepted applications and hired according to need and fit.

People in a Catholic parish stood on the sidelines, clutching their tickets with hope and expectation, while the Bishop set the gate. In his defense, he had a limited number in the stable to pick from. But he did have inside information and could hobble any horse in the race. Dumb luck could select the right person for the right spot, the Holy Spirit could prevail, but picking the winner, as in any sport, was an art form. In Libby's experience, not many bishops had the talent.

"Any thoughts on who we'll get?"

"If it's a good match," Maggie said, "we could be all right. If it's bad, we'll close in five years."

She ticked off the points for consideration. "We have no school to bring in young, growing families. We're in the inner city. There has to be something—a good homily, a short service, a kind or vibrant, or just plain nice pastor. Henry hit two out of three—the short service and the good, short homily. Actually, that combination goes a long way to filling the pews. And I *am* kidding. A little. Henry could be … bearable. He didn't ask for a lot out of anyone. Some people are looking for church activities to make them feel like part of a community, to fill their lives or entertain their children in wholesome, religious ways."

"Henry's mode," Libby agreed, "was certainly more get them in for Mass; send them on their way. Beyond that, baptize, marry, and bury 'em. Kind of a streamlined approach."

Maggie picked up the stapler and went back at it. "Most of the people at St. Hedwig's have already done their share of chili suppers, fun fairs, parish picnics, all those sports and programs with their kids. Being in that middle- to upper-age group, they seem happy to come in, pray a little, pay a little, and go on with life."

Libby looked at Calico Two, her furry body filling up the empty box lid lying on the floor like skeins of mohair yarn set aside for one of Namita's knitting projects. "I wonder if that's such a bad thing,"

Libby said, thinking of her own involvement, her own streamlining. "Maybe we shouldn't be so disparaging. Oh, I know a lot of our drop-ins are just that. They're here to check off the Sunday Mass requirement, but so many of the older ones seem like this *is* their life. I mean, I get the idea that coming to Mass is just one part of the whole piece. They've already said morning prayers, a rosary, meal prayers, night prayers, and read Scripture."

Maggie had to agree. "That certainly sounds like my mother."

"I suppose they would be appalled to hear us say we have to offer more than God."

"Are you kidding?" Maggie banged the stapler. "God's a given. Popcorn at the movies is a given. What you have to sit through to get it makes or breaks the evening."

Libby sputtered out a short laugh. "Now that's a spiritually rich analogy! Are you sure you don't have it backward?"

As Maggie straightened up her completed stack of collated and stapled papers, Libby turned to stare out the windows and considered the appeal of St. Hedwig's against that of other parishes. "It does seem that you have to have some tangibles that bring people in."

Maggie brightened. "Oh. I know. The music is good."

"I certainly think so," said Libby.

"No, that counts a lot. And I'm not saying that just because it's you."

"And the church is beautiful," offered Libby.

"If you like big and old. And drafty," countered Maggie, her shoulders slumping. She brightened again. "The organ is spectacular."

"Unless you prefer guitar and piano," conceded Libby. She sighed. Heavily. She was sure most people thought all Catholic churches were basically the same. In their spiritual guidelines, they were. Same rules; rituals roughly the same.

Enter the human element.

If outsiders only knew how each parish was such a world unto itself. The rich filled St. Benedict's, while a tiny group of Vietnamese worshipers met in the basement of an old mission. Sometimes there was lots of interaction and participation at Masses, happily lasting two hours with standing room only in the back like an evangelical mega-church; or the twenty-minute quiet mutterings of a few souls struggling to keep the doors of their neighborhood church open. There could be dancing down the aisles like at San Patricio's or priests with their backs turned, chanting Latin, as if it were the 1500s like at Our Lady of Sorrows.

These differences only concerned a priest's ability to appreciate the variety of ways a parish added its own flair to church ceremonies. Running the business side called up an entirely different skillset. Or lack thereof. A priest could spend with carefree abandon on pet interests—all new shrubs for the parking lot, redecorating the rectory—or carefully watch accounts and prudently make purchases and repairs. The downtown diocesan offices had to approve major expenditures, like a new roof or heating system; otherwise, the pastor reigned supreme.

And priests, being human, came in the same myriad variety. Getting the two elements to meld was no easy task. It wasn't just a matter of matching up temperaments or interests or personalities, because currently there were not enough priests to choose from to fill positions that way.

There also did not seem to be any seminary preparation that cultivated an openness so that priests could be adaptable and responsive shepherds to disparate flocks.

Take a priest, ministering and administering to one of those unique flocks, pull him out, and drop him into the middle of another. Chaos. An immediate and perfect fit of priest to parish, parish to priest was rare. In most cases, adjustment took time on both sides of the pulpit, eventually everyone relying on Providence and settling in for the duration with patient acceptance.

But sometimes, even if only for the stint of one badly fitted priest in an already fragile situation, it could mean the death of a parish.

Both Maggie and Libby recognized this as a real possibility for St. Hedwig's. In unspoken agreement, they both chose not to dwell on it.

"Any date yet for the wake and funeral?" asked Libby.

"First the Vicar was waiting for the police to be finished," said Maggie, uncovering the big desk calendar underneath everything. "Now he's waiting for some out-of-town relatives. The reading of the will has to wait, too. I gather the Vicar is Henry's executor."

Maybe being single, over fifty, and having dealt with her own plans for disseminating possessions and property made Libby more curious. She had never thought along these practical lines for priests. "Do you think he's worth much?"

Maggie picked up a pen and wiggled it back and forth in consideration; to the delight of Dunkirk, who took this action as a cue to play. He lay on his back and wrapped his paws around Maggie's forearm in an attempt to capture the pen. "I can't decide," said Maggie. "Could be a little. Could be a lot. He didn't spend much as far as I could tell. When he first came to St. Hedwig's, he bought odd stuff. Rare books. Relics. He was tracking down spoons with the U.S. Presidents on them. Old cracked teapots. Clocks." She waved her pen dismissively. "That's probably the kind of crap that's upstairs in that locked room."

"Locked room!?" exclaimed Libby, sitting upright and in no way dismissive.

Maggie waved the pen in the direction of Father Henry's apartment overhead. Dunkirk clung to her uplifted arm like an opossum swinging from a tree branch. "There's a small room at the end of the hallway upstairs. Locked. Always been locked as long as he's been here. Other priests used it for linens. Not that I snoop all the time," she said more puckishly than defensively. "Just once in a while."

As Dunkirk came in for a landing, Libby found herself recalibrating her understanding of Maggie Mueller, church secretary. Not only did Maggie have access to records like background checks, she also knew better than anyone else the details of Father Henry's habits and activities.

And she was used to keeping her cards close to the chest. Discretion was undoubtedly an attribute needed in this occupation.

As was, no doubt, equivocation.

"I suppose the stuff could be worth a lot," Maggie said as she disengaged Dunkirk. "Of course, I don't know if he had any taste. Or he could have played the ponies for all I know and made a fortune. Or lost it. That room could be stacked with pure cash—or pure junk."

Libby sniffed. "Priests and their money. Given the Church's parsimony, they probably don't make a great salary, but the perks—people buying them cars, giving them condos in Florida, plane tickets to France to preside over the marriage of their daughters, free meals, free you-name-it.

"On the other hand," Libby persisted, "whatever he had, who do you think gets what's left when a priest dies? Do they just recycle it back into the Church?"

Maggie consulted her mental dossier for Father Henry. "He's an only child. Parents are dead; no siblings. I suppose those cousins could inherit it." Maggie tantalized the cat with her pen again. "Heaven help us if they don't. Phyllis especially. She seems a little overly involved in Henry's life."

"Cousins," Libby nodded. "That makes sense. Maybe they get everything."

"No." Maggie sounded definite. "Not everything."

Libby gave her a puzzled look.

The secretary tapped Dunkirk's haunches. "I get the cats."

Calico Two apparently had been paying attention. At the mention of her fate, she uncurled and jumped up from box lid on the floor, landing squarely on the desktop to be included in the discussion.

"Henry already asked if I would take them," said Maggie.

"That makes sense."

Libby smoothed the tuft of white fur between Calico Two's ears. The cat tilted her head in appreciation. When Libby stopped, Calico Two curled up into Dunkirk's belly, the sound of their purring soon audible everywhere in the office. "I'm glad they're going to a good home. How far away are the out-of-town relatives?" she asked, settling back into her chair.

"Duluth, I believe."

"Duluth? Duluth, Minnesota?!" Libby practically shrieked. "Wayne Nichols is from Duluth. Where it's 'colder than we can imagine in Indiana'."

"That's right!" Maggie exclaimed, all attention. "You don't think he's related to Father, do you?"

"That would explain some things," Libby said slowly, chewing on the thought. "Like, why Father Henry hired an ex-con. And why he kept Wayne on, even if he's not great at the job."

Maggie eagerly followed the new thread. "Maybe he's in Father's will."

Screwing up her face, Libby let the puzzle pieces shift around in her brain. "Do you think anybody would ... kill ... for something they're getting in the will?" She slapped her palm on the desk, causing the cats to jerk, but not be disturbed otherwise. "Sorry," Libby apologized to the felines and continued, still excited but in a lower volume. "Classic motive. Right out of the books!"

"Not for me," Maggie retorted. "I like the cats, but not that much. Don't you think the cousins would know if Wayne's related? Maybe they're related to him, too."

"Good point," said Libby.

"Oh, dear," Maggie said, flumping back in her chair. "They'll all want to be in on the funeral and luncheon planning. At Father Rowley's, the parish handled it. A.k.a., the secretary." She didn't even pause; but from years of training, she smoothly transitioned into making notes. "I hope Mrs. McGrew will be available. She's so easy. Responsible. Wonder if Jonny Kwan would help. Wouldn't blame him if he didn't. How many does one plan for? All those priests …"

"I'm really curious now," said Libby with growing interest. "Maybe I can go see them. The cousins. Get them to blab. Find out about Wayne while asking them about the funeral. Maybe what they want for readings. Or food at the luncheon. Or …"

Chapter Seventeen

*P*eople assume I was doted on as an only child. Not so. Kind of ignored until I was ordained. Mother and Grandmother doted on the collar. Couldn't call me Father enough or have me bless everyone and everything in sight enough, as if I was some saint who could cure leprosy.

A lady Eucharistic Minister here at St. Hedwig's came in to help tidy up Communion dishes once and saw me struggling to lift my vestment over my head. She's convinced I have arthritis. Didn't correct her. Now she comes a little before Mass and stays a little after to help me dress and undress.

She is smooth—makes a little, easy joke—mostly though it's an unassuming gesture. Not hussy-fussy like the Cousins. Especially Phyllis, who makes everything seem like she's doing it more for her own gratification than to be helpful. It's what I imagine a British valet is like, a gentleman's gentleman, or woman as it were, quietly serving. I must say, it's very nice to be tended to this way.

I don't even understand what an atheist believes. Or is that an oxymoron?

Grandpa Leo hated religion. Is that the same thing? Don't think he ever went to church after he was married in one. Not even for my ordination into the priesthood. Other than that, we were such a great pair. All those movies he took me to. Taught me pinochle. Now, there *was a man who doted.*

I think he believed in God. I hope and pray he did. How can you not believe in God? Where do you put that part of your sense of the world—the beauty, the mystery, the way everything works and fits together? Really? Nothing?

I often wonder what priests he knew. Grandpa. Said they only cared about moving up in the ranks, getting titles, bigger parishes, knowing more prestigious people, wearing fancy church outfits. Thought it would make me lazy, being a priest. Too easy to let other people take care of you. And make you feel you deserve it. What a nut. All the while he's spouting that, he's taking care of me and tucking money in my shirt pocket! Even after I went off to join that "seminary cult."

Oh, the money. Keep a ledger, he warned. The old goof. Stay in the black, don't go in the red. Keep track of your own money. Don't trust banks to be on your side.

I'm thinking of you a lot, Grandpa. Now, when my legs won't do what I want. Stupid doctors. You hated them, too. I told them I had the same symptoms. I remember you losing your balance on the back porch steps, even with the railing there. Pretended you were tipsy drunk. Made me laugh. But I saw you at the big bird feeder, rubbing your hands to work out the numbness.

Don't know if they believe MS runs in families or not. You left me so much. You could have skipped this. Just between you and me, I'm not telling anybody about it either. Like you said, a man's got to have some privacy. Some dignity.

Funny what things run in a family.

+ + +

"I thought more people would come to the prayer service last night," said Cousin Phyllis, disappointed as much for herself as for Father Henry. She reached for a square of fresh shortbread, warm, buttery, crumbly, with specks of lemon zest, as she sat at the breakfast nook next to her Cousin Ruth.

The floral placemats matched the tea cozy that was keeping a large teapot in the center of the table hot.

A tea cozy, thought Libby. This is a page from a calendar of the

English countryside. All that's missing is a view of climbing white roses and pink foxgloves in the garden outside the window. Certainly not the mounds of dingy snow piled up out there now.

If it was a formal afternoon tea, Phyllis, the larger of the two, fit the picture best in a pastel cardigan sweater over a plain white blouse. In the shadow of her cloche, she wore the right spot of blush on her cheeks and lips for a woman in her late sixties, and brandished polished nails that showed off several nice but not gaudy rings, all evidence that appearances mattered.

If it had been the gardener's wife's tea, the more boxy Ruth carried the day in her red turtleneck and comfy, plaid flannel shirt.

Libby, concerned mainly with cleanliness and warmth, was wearing all-American corduroys and layered sweaters.

"Perhaps they didn't come because of the weather. It was an awfully cold night," Libby said, sipping tea from the thin china cup, a nice change from the thick mugs in her own cupboards.

Ruth licked an index finger that had dabbed crumbs from her last piece of shortbread. "I still can't believe he's gone."

Libby noted that Ruth was so short she gave the impression of perpetually having her head bowed. Whether today it was from sadness or merely the normal position of her head was difficult to tell.

"Who will ever replace him?" Ruth said.

"You mean who will St. Hedwig's get stuck with?" asked Phyllis, to the point. She turned to their guest, someone possibly in the know on church matters. "Do you know, Libby?"

"Afraid not. Substitutes for a while. Probably until after the funeral at least." Libby set her cup down. "I was wondering if the two of you, as Father Henry's relatives, would like to help with some of the planning. Father might have already picked out his readings, maybe even the music, but the Prayers of the Faithful are a good place to put in some personal petitions by the family."

Ruth brought her head up. "That would be nice."

"Oh, yes." Phyllis jumped at the chance. "We've already been thinking of things. For the luncheon, too."

Libby retrieved a pad of paper and pen from the side pocket of her purse. She made a heading and tried to refrain from doodling right off the bat. "There's usually a generic request to pray for the Pope and Church leaders at the start. I can take care of that one, if you'd like." She wrote an abbreviated note next to the numeral one. "You might pray for deceased family members. Father Henry's parents. A relative he was especially close to ..."

The cousins needed no prompting to come up with the name in unison. "Grandpa Leo."

"He liked all the grandchildren," Phyllis recalled with obvious delight. "Had a big yard. About twenty bird feeders."

"Played cards—pinochle, gin rummy—out on the porch with us in the summer," chimed in Ruth. "Grandma Felger was kind of stern, but not Grandpa. He adored Henry."

Phyllis reared up in her seat. "Aw, Grandma adored him, too. Are you kidding? First male grandchild? Then off to be a priest? She couldn't have been prouder." She removed the tea cozy and poured a round of tea. "Grandpa Leo wasn't so thrilled about that. But it was Henry's decision, and Henry could do no wrong."

With Ruth's encouragement, Libby helped herself to another piece of shortbread. Tea alone is not nearly as satisfying on a cold afternoon as tea and a treat. Homemade, at that. "Sounds as if there were more than just you two and Henry. I understand there are some relatives coming in from Minnesota."

"Weingartners. More cousins. There were three of them," said Phyllis.

"Are they all coming?" wondered Ruth.

Phyllis was sure they were. Remember, she reminded Ruth, she'd asked them to stay with her, but they were going to a hotel. No in-laws. Just the three cousins.

Libby drew in a breath. "Kind of odd. Wayne Nichols, the maintenance man, is from Minnesota." She looked away self-consciously and added a splash of milk to her tea. And waited.

Not for long.

"Not odd at all," Phyllis said matter-of-factly. "He's another cousin. Once removed. He's our cousin Germaine's child. She was the youngest. Died first, though. Cancer. Wayne was her only child. Black sheep. Moved here not more than two years ago."

Without being asked, Phyllis nudged the sugar bowl in Ruth's direction. Libby recognized an unspoken sisterly kinship, having four sisters of her own. These two were cousins, but circumstances and compatibility made them more than that just cousins. They often attended church functions together, husbands in tow.

"We tried to be nice," Phyllis explained. "Invite him for dinner.

For holidays." She set her cup down with a forceful clank. "Gave up."

Ruth stirred a spoonful of sugar into her tea. "Henry was being more than generous to give him a job. He's not very dependable. Wayne, that is. Surprised he's lasted this long without getting fired."

Excited doodling was beginning to take hold. Libby tried to stay focused and remember all the questions she wanted to ask; now that she'd found her way into the subject. "Do you think he'll want to be involved with anything?"

Phyllis let out a sarcastic snort. "The will maybe. If there's any money floating around for him to bump into, he'll be there. Like a magnet to a refrigerator door."

A row of loops cascaded with a life of their own down the margin of Libby's pad. She kept her eyes on the pen making them. "I don't suppose there's much to divide. Father being a priest and all."

"Unless he saved all the money from our grandfather," said Phyllis. "I didn't. Frank and I put it in our house. By the time Grandpa Leo died, his own kids, our parents, were all grown and doing well enough. He skipped over them and left everything to the next generation. Each grandchild, the six living cousins—Ruth; me; Henry; and the three coming in from Duluth, a boy and two girls—we all got something. But it was not an equal split. The girls got less, probably old-fashioned thinking that we'd get married and be taken care of. Which was sort of how it worked out."

"But unfair," Libby commented, half to herself.

Either Ruth was in sync with that other time, or she had adjusted long ago. Nothing in her manner hinted that she was upset with the distribution. "Henry got the lion's share, that's for sure. Even Edward, the only other male cousin, didn't receive as much as Henry. Like I said, Henry was the favorite. The first born male. And a priest."

Phyllis defended the split as well. "He worked for God. All those years. Being moved at the Bishop's whim. No spouse; no children. The most he ever did have was a nice car. Never went more than two years without a new one."

"Maybe there is a lot left to divide." Ruth pondered this, adding another spoonful of sugar to her tea and staring wistfully out the kitchen nook window.

Phyllis was on her own path. "I'd like a new car."

A different thought crossed Ruth's mind. "Maybe he gave it to the poor. His money, I mean."

Phyllis looked askance at her. "I hope—." She checked herself. "Maybe so. God bless him. It was his money."

Whether this last was a sincere comment or for Libby's sake was debatable from Libby's point of view. "So," Libby said. "I gather Wayne won't want to do anything at the funeral?"

"I doubt it," said Phyllis, reaching for one more piece of shortbread. "An atheist the last time I spoke to him about such things. Hates religion. Sees no need for it."

Ruth folded her napkin and lined it up with the vine winding across her placemat. "One man a priest; the other one an atheist. Funny what things run in a family."

Chapter Eighteen

The Fruehauf house had a museum-like quality. Furnishings were from Bernie's childhood, old and sturdy. Sentimental paintings of angels and Popes hung on the walls, while statues of saints mixed comfortably with lamps and travel artifacts on end tables. A large Blessed Virgin Mary, her benevolent arms outstretched, welcomed visitors from atop the small organ in the corner of the living room. Thick dark drapes covered all the windows, keeping the sun's damaging rays from fading the furniture. But the furniture had not paid attention and gone on fading anyway.

A neatness prevailed in the home; mostly from lack of use, as Bernie was a do-er, an out-and-about busy guy. He played the organ whenever asked—if the event met his criterion for being low-stress—substituted for other organists on vacation or ill; made countless sick calls to parish shut-ins; dined modestly but often with friends from choir days gone by; and in any spare time, attended free concerts, which in a city of so many church organs, small ensembles, and community bands, were plentiful.

The little money Bernie received from his small church pension was spent on travel. (Social security paid the bills.) Had he sat long enough to read anything as contemplative as poetry, he might have identified with Tennyson's "Ulysses," weighing in on "how dull it is to pause."

It was late Friday afternoon when Libby arrived at Bernie's to go over music for Father Henry's wake, Bernie greeted her in his browns—slacks, shirt, and sweater vest—a mix of solids, plaids, and patterns coordinated only by having the one color in common.

Libby folded her coat and laid it next to her on the stiff couch as she commiserated with Bernie about the recent events surrounding Father Henry's demise, including the distressing experience of having the police rummage through their personal belongings and personal habits. Both had had their houses searched for the thurible.

"I understand why people feel violated," said Libby.

Bernie drummed his fingers on the arm of his brown recliner, practically blending in. He closed his eyes and sighed. "It'll be such a relief when all of this is over."

"Good thing your dad wasn't here."

"I don't know," said Bernie. "Might have been a distraction for him."

Libby looked across the room. "I remember the last time I saw your dad. Hospice had set up the bed right here in the living room."

Bernie regarded the room, which he rarely did. Nightly news or an occasional music program on PBS were about the only times he sat down. "Wish we could have kept mom home, too." He smiled briefly. "Not at the same time, of course. But for her sake."

"And yours, no doubt. It is a drain to visit somebody you care for like that. Every day. For so long."

"Oh, you get used to it. Just part of your day. You know me. I'm always out anyway. Got to know lots of other people at the nursing home. I'd play the organ and they'd all sing. Old hymns. Show tunes. They were always grateful for the visit. Mom was a little cantankerous when I'd leave. Even more after the stroke."

Libby had heard tales of Mrs. Fruehauf berating Bernie when he'd say he couldn't take her home. Alice Fruehauf may have been a good wife and mother early on, but she had not become an agreeable old woman.

"So, what have you got here?" she asked, looking at the music books on the doily-topped table in front of them.

"I got all this from the Vicar this morning," Bernie said, sitting forward. "Looks like Fr. Henry had some of his funeral already planned. Mostly songs he *didn't* want. No "Amazing Grace." No "On Eagles' Wings." A few favorites he wanted worked in. The rest he left to us."

Originally, long before they had become friends, this approach had bothered Libby. Bernie was St. Hedwig's Music Director; it was his responsibility, not hers, to select music. He had begun by telling her to pick what she liked, which did appeal to Libby. This gradually turned into his saying she was so much better at putting a service together than he, which she fell for. Over time, their roles had, for the most part, been reversed, and then so blurred by the growing friendship that it was no longer an issue. The royal *we*, however, always meant Libby.

As she pulled her own planning sheet out of her bag, Libby told Bernie about being at Father's cousins' earlier and learning that Wayne was a relative; not only of theirs, but of Father Henry's. She figured it was news that was soon to come out anyway. Unless Bird Hawkins already knew.

"If he did," said Bernie, "I think he would have told me."

Bernie again drummed his fingers. "Do you suppose that's why Father Henry kept Wayne? Because he was family?"

"Wouldn't make me keep him. He does a lousy job."

Libby's bluntness often made Bernie laugh, but it also tended to make him come back with a more charitable response to balance it, albeit couched in Bernie's own style of veiled criticism. "Maybe he's the best of a bad lot out there. He's not my favorite person either," he said. "Guess it was for Henry to say." Bernie's eyes went soft with sympathetic allowance. "Just between the two of us, priests aren't always so good at this sort of thing. Hiring people, I mean. I heard that over at St. Stephen's, the custodian forgot to adjust the heat and the water pipes froze. I guess Wayne could do worse."

Libby listened to Bernie return her comments about Wayne with a slightly kinder response. It compelled her to hold off saying anything about Wayne's ex-con status. If by some rare chance, Bird Hawkins did not have that piece of information, she decided she wasn't going to be the one to spread it around.

Bernie noted the program on Libby's lap. "Oh. Did you find the thing for the wake? I'm sorry, but I couldn't get that cabinet drawer open. I thought we could call the Vicar or the Chancery and get the information ..."

As the organist prattled on, Libby's mind took a detour. Bernie had known Father Henry for a long time. They had traveled together, which is certainly an up-close-and-personal situation. Eight hours on a plane—that alone can reveal a lot about a person. "Bernie? Do you know if Father Henry had a lot of money? I don't mean that he spent, but that he might have squirreled away?"

Bernie gave it some thought. He and the priest had talked about money many times. Neither spent it frivolously. Bernie's biggest concern was that his savings last for his own needs more than worrying about what to do if there was anything left over.

"You mean, like under the mattress or in a will?"

"Yes. Like that he might leave to someone. Money."

"Oh. My." The implication began dawning on the organist. "Do you think Wayne was going to inherit money?" His eyes grew large and bright. "That would give him a reason to … you know … kill Father Henry."

"It's a motive that makes sense."

Bernie's fingers drummed along more rapidly; his interest piqued. "Wayne sure doesn't look like somebody who has a lot of money. I mean, he looks like he could use some. Maybe he has a lot of debt or something."

Libby, too, picked away at this line of reasoning. "Although Father was willing to keep paying him a salary when he was worthless in the job. Why didn't Wayne just ask for money?"

"Maybe he did," Bernie said slowly, fingers at a standstill as he carefully considered the possibility. "And maybe Henry said no."

"And maybe they were just standing on the steps …" Libby pictured the scene. "Those icy steps. They argued. Wayne had the thurible, which could easily have been gotten rid of."

Bernie joined in, imagining the situation. "He … Wayne … just got so mad. So mad at Henry."

"In the books it happens just like that. In an instant. Or," she went on conjecturing, "Wayne could have been planning it for a long time. He'd already asked for the money and been turned down. And suddenly, the opportunity just presented itself."

They sat in silence.

Bernie spoke first. "Should we … should we tell the police?"

Libby found she had inched forward to the edge of her seat. She sat back and let out a healthy sigh. "I don't know. I'm not that impressed with them. Lawrence Davis says they're short-staffed and dealing with several cases at the same time. And apparently there's a push from the top because Father Henry's death is a higher profile; so more pressure to find the murderer fast. Maybe they are taking some shortcuts, skimming over some of the options on their way to finding anybody who fits in where they need them to fit. Besides, we don't even know if Father Henry had any money to leave to anybody much less whether that anybody was Wayne Nichols."

"I guess his cousins, Phyllis and Ruth, could be in the will, too," Bernie admitted grudgingly. The scene with Wayne had been shaping up so smoothly, he was reluctant to let it go. Reluctant to give up the possibility that it could all be over soon—the police invading their lives, the disruption at church, the emotional confusion at the sudden loss of his longtime friend.

"And there are three other cousins coming in from Minnesota, who might also be getting a share," Libby added. "That's why nobody's set a date for the wake or the funeral."

"Oh. My."

Libby returned to the music papers and looked over Father Henry's list. She laughed. "He obviously avoided all the standards. Looks pretty simple, although a very different lineup than we're used to."

She placed Father's suggestions in the appropriate slots on the outline, ran by Bernie her ideas about what might round out the funeral music with other hymns she knew would have pleased the priest.

Bernie put up no opposition to her choices.

"Only thing left for us is planning the wake," she said, rifling through the program Maggie had found for her. "The cousins are more interested in planning the luncheon. But I think we can follow this program from Father Kelly's wake that Maggie gave me practically as is."

Bernie was amenable. Or perhaps worn out. "Whatever you think."

They made a few simple changes to the wake for Father Henry and considered their assignment completed. As Libby reached for her coat, Bernie reached for his as well.

"A new rattle in my car," he said by way of explanation. "Want to get it checked out. I don't like to wait until it's something big and expensive."

"Do you need a ride?"

"No, thanks. If it has to be there long, my neighbor is usually around to pick me up. And I know he drives you crazy, but believe it or not, Bird would always come get me."

Chapter Nineteen

A jaunty piece by Handel, with a plucky mandolin part, popped in and out of Libby's humming as she set out the infamous red Storm Relief Fund boxes in the back of St. Hedwig's. She had found a new box to replace the one that had fallen down the steps with Father Henry.

The relief project had been going on for several months and the boxes were showing their wear, making this fresh replacement stand out as a blatant reminder of the sad event connected with it.

By the time five o'clock Saturday Mass finished, it would be pitch dark outside, but for now, an hour before the start, the church was quiet, except for the blowers sending warmth into the building, and softly lit, as dusk let go of a winter evening.

There was no light Libby did not think her church was beautiful in, and this late-afternoon glow took her momentarily out of time and place. Even the few ushers readying collection baskets and bulletins did not disturb the mood. Thankfully, Bird Hawkins's tour of duty this week was on Sunday.

Lavina Woodson regularly arrived early to claim one of the back pews for her elderly father and his walker. Lavina was an active parishioner, at different times having served on and been head of various committees and councils, like her parents before her, who were some of the first African Americans to join St. Hedwig's. Lavina had no spouse or children, and when her mother died, she had taken her remaining parent into her own home to care for him.

Once her father was settled into his pew, Lavina moved in Libby's direction. "How you doing?" Lavina's voice was low, melodious and friendly. She and Libby had not only worked on many projects together, but had what Libby considered the same rational, practical approach to most church problems.

"I'm good," replied Libby. "You?"

"Like everyone else, I suppose. Getting used to Father's death. Nice to get back into the church. Have they set a date for the funeral yet?"

"No. Waiting for relatives."

"Well, you be sure to call, girl, if you need anything. I can lector or help with the luncheon. Maggie knows to call, too."

In any season, Lavina wore eminently sensible dark slacks but topped them with silky blouses in rich-jewel tones, always on display because she had the habit of shedding her coat as soon as she arrived, even on cold afternoons. She was not tall but had a full figure and face highlighted by eyes that were gentle yet always attentive.

"Hey, I'm sorry I had to tell the police about that Parish Council meeting where things got a little heated between you and Father."

Libby hadn't recalled it when Bird Hawkins had been blathering on about her temper in the back of the Cathedral, but now she knew immediately what meeting Lavina was referring to. The one where Father Henry and some people on the Council had wanted to order cassocks and surplices for the boy servers. But not for the girls. The girls were to wear those apron-like …

"Oh, yeah," said Libby. "It all comes back to me. You're right, Lavina. I was heated."

"For what it's worth, I did tell the police I was angry, too."

Libby envied Lavina's version of angry. Where Libby's nature gave it a physical, heart-thumping, voice-raising reaction, Lavina let others spew out their frustrations and merely watched until they were out of gas. Then, if warranted, she would add her opinion.

"I wouldn't have thought of it," Lavina said, "except the detective kept digging, asking for any big disagreements at meetings. Bird Hawkins was standing right there with a bunch of us at the prayer service and, you know Bird. Everything is big to Bird. If it's any consolation, you weren't the only subject. They seemed keen on

Daniel Giglia, too, as someone with a possible conflict with Father."

"Excuse me, ladies." Lawrence Davis said, as he pulled off leather gloves and unbuttoned his topcoat. "Are you on to read this evening, Lavina, or am I?"

"I'm pretty sure it's me," said Lavina. "I hope you didn't make the trip in vain."

He winced. "That means I'm on tomorrow morning." He shrugged it off easily. "It's all right. My family wanted to come tonight anyway. Thanks. Sorry to interrupt."

"No, it's okay. I have to get over to my dad." Lavina moved in the direction of her father, but looked to Libby. "Call if you need me."

Lawrence tucked his striped tie into the suit jacket under his topcoat. "Guess I'll have to get cleaned up two days in a row."

"Yes," teased Libby, "you'll have to stretch that one set of old rags." To Libby's knowledge, the man had never worn a casual piece of clothing in his life. "Any news from headquarters? Or is your presence on the case still verboten?"

"I'm staying up on things."

"Are they still investigating everyone?"

"Kind of."

Libby was never accused of beating around the bush. "Why is everybody so sure it's Daniel?" She followed Lawrence as he stopped to pick up a church bulletin at one of the usher's stations. "Do you think it's Daniel?"

Lawrence put up a hand, smiling at her insistence. "Libby, Libby. I can't tell you anything. I shouldn't even be talking to you about it." He spied his wife and daughter taking a pew toward the middle of the still empty church and walked toward them.

Libby followed him like a puppy expecting a treat. "Could you possibly just happen to nod at some basic yes-or-no, noninvasive questions?" Hoping to spark his interest, she added, "I might know some things, too, you know."

Lawrence could see Libby was going to be dogged about this. She was certainly in touch with lots of the undercurrents that ran through St. Hedwig's. And she was not unobservant. Even possibly helpful, like uncovering the business about the frozen jar of soup before the autopsy confirmed the time of death. He stopped beside a rack of flickering vigil lights and gave her his full attention. "Okay. Try me."

Libby wasted no time.

"Have you found the murder weapon yet?

"No."

"Do you know that Wayne Nichols is an ex-con?"

"Yes."

"Do you know he's a relative of Father Henry's and may inherit money. Or something?"

Lawrence tried to stifle his surprise, but Libby caught it.

Emboldened, she plowed on. "Are they hot on Daniel's trail just because he was the last one to see Father Henry alive? I know that's a big deal in mystery novels. The last one to see the victim alive."

Lawrence raised his hand again. "It's a big deal in real life, Libby. His alibi for the rest of the afternoon isn't solid either."

"Does Wayne have an alibi?"

"Yes."

They were like two people raising each other in a poker game.

"And you believe him?"

"So far."

Lawrence pulled up. "You really dislike him, don't you?"

Libby fumbled. "He's … creepy. I don't trust him. You were there in the sacristy when Father said he had to fire someone. Could have been Wayne."

"Could have been Daniel."

"You've been listening to Bird Hawkins."

"He has a point. Church policy and gays. A militant advocate in opposition to that. Makes sense."

"Not to me it doesn't."

"That's because you disagree with the policy."

"That's true."

"Look, Libby," said Lawrence. He rolled up the bulletin and tapped her lightly on the shoulder. "You have to see things the way they are, not how you want to slant them because of how you feel."

"The facts."

"The facts. Daniel emptied the thurible—the murder weapon, or so we think. And now it's missing, along with any possible fingerprints. Daniel was the last one to see Father Henry alive and Daniel has a lousy alibi."

Libby sulked. "How's yours?"

"Better than yours." The retort was meant to be funny, but beneath Lawrence's grin, Libby heard the slight edge to his voice and understood the fact it was pointing out.

More people began to drift into church, their winter boots and wet rubber soled shoes squeaking along the marble floor.

At the head of the side aisle, a serious moment passed between Libby and Detective Lawrence Davis. Again he warned her. "Be careful, Libby. Please. Let the police handle this."

On every other Saturday at this same time, Bernie would have been sitting in the same chair at the sacristy table. Every two weeks, like clockwork, Father Henry would hear Bernie's confession. Otherwise, Bernie waited for him to return from opening the doors and setting out bulletins, seemingly disgruntled about everything, about being old and achy, the weather, some new guideline from the Bishop on bowing— head bow only; waist bow; deep, full-body bow. Libby would go nuts.

Bernie would listen, agree, tease, and add his own complaints about not sleeping well and having heartburn; waiting until Libby came in to pick up her end of the exchange.

This evening, Bernie sat alone and looked, for the tenth time, at his list of hymns for the service. He fanned the pages of the liturgy book and let his eyes roam the room, pausing at the cupboards, the hanging vestments, the sound system lights blinking.

How things had changed over the forty years he'd been at St. Hedwig's. The old sacristy had no bathroom and only priests were allowed in the area. Certainly no female cantors in to joke around. Only the nuns, ironing altar cloths in the next room and laying out vestments for the Good Father.

Four thirty. No confession today. Who would Bernie go to now? He supposed it didn't really matter. Sin was sin; forgiveness was forgiveness. But, as with so much that is human, a little familiarity with a confessor at a vulnerable moment could be reassuring.

"Sorry I'm late. Yakking in the back." Libby breezed in through the door from the sanctuary. "Is the altar all set up?"

"Oh. My. Forgot all about it." Bernie stood. "So used to Henry having most things ready."

Libby patted him on the shoulder and smiled. "Sit down. You can direct me from your place of honor. I assume our sub isn't here yet?"

"No," he replied, accepting the order and dropping back in his chair.

"Maggie says he's one of the young ones."

Reaching for gold goblets on the shelf over the sink, then wine from the small refrigerator in the corner, Libby moved about the sacristy, deftly pulling things together for Mass.

"Maybe it's that one from St. Joan of Arc," suggested Bernie. "Remember how he bounced around? All that talk about joy? Like that missionary last year. Remember how loud he talked? Walking up and down the aisle for his sermon. Just between the two of us, he sounded a little phony, a little showy. Not that priests can't be happy. I always think humility is important. For a priest." Guilt from speaking so negatively about the clergy always brought an apologetic reversal from Bernie. "I'm sure the priest from St. Joan's will be just fine."

Libby was less apologetic, more for calling things as she saw them. "He was so new," Libby said. "Hard to read a person through all that untested delight. Hard to tell in someone so young how they will turn out."

Passing through to midlife had given Libby some experience with being tested, with forks in the road. As a person, she'd encountered questions and made choices about life in general; as a Catholic, after a long run down the straight-and-narrow path, she had, especially recently, faced challenges in her spiritual life. Beyond the original package of talents, shortcomings, and inclinations, she knew experience shaped a person's life immeasurably. Surely the influences that yielded a declared religious life had to be profound.

Over the years, Libby had seen her share of priests. Being in the sacristy, listening, observing them up close, seeing them as mortals, not just stand-ins for God on their best public behavior.

Her observations inclined her to believe that if faith and grace were on his side, a young priest flourished and grew in wisdom as a Good Shepherd to his flocks. Dynamic ones ran schools or food pantries; quiet ones walked around the neighborhood saying a rosary and made untold visits to the homebound. Both types officiated at the marriages of children they'd baptized; and happily went on to baptize their children's children.

On the other hand, if the twig was bent early toward an appreciation and thirst for the things of this world, he gradually sought out the best food, wine, cars, and beautiful things—artwork, antiques, jewelry—and cultivated persons who could bestow such gifts.

Because the gifts included matching donations to a church's roof fund, all parties involved felt magnanimous and believed it only proper they make use of their capacity for appreciating the good things God put on this earth. The priests who thrived on this, often, not always, but often, became bishops and higher; those who did not have the opportunity or flair to make the connections became bitter.

Libby turned at the sound of the back door opening, then closing gently, then footsteps padding down the carpeted passageway from the bride-side sacristy. She exchanged looks of anticipation with Bernie.

The man appeared to be neither the joyful fledgling shepherd nor one bounding down the path toward excess physical comforts. He entered the room, head bowed and pious, self-deprecating, looking more like a scrubbed altar boy ready to assist at Mass than one old enough to celebrate it.

"I'm Father Alex," he said, bending low in his worn parka.

Libby had seen this version as well. If their piety was true and genuine and wholesome, they kept their message simple, their lives extraordinarily ordinary. And they inspired more people than they ever knew.

Or.

Or their piety became a badge, an outward sign of their own significance as a man of God and a standard by which they judged others. They insinuated guilt with every word that came out of their mouths. As they flaunted their own shortcomings, they felt justified calling out everyone else's and granted redemption for all clinging tightly to a compulsive fervor for rules and rituals and their version of God's will.

After subdued introductions, Libby locked the back door then returned to fill the ciborium with unconsecrated hosts while Bernie went to put the small purificators for wiping out the used chalices on the altar.

Father Robert stepped in close and spoke intimately. "I'd rather those were properly placed somewhere to the side."

Bernie found himself bowing—full body—before following the priest's instructions.

"Yes, Father."

Chapter Twenty

Paul Thomas opened the door, welcoming Libby, not hiding his surprise. Or pleasure. That her appearance was unplanned did not seem to make any difference. He busied himself escorting her in, replacing the rolled towel at the bottom of the front door to keep out the draft in an old house. He straightened the rug for her to step on, as if he'd spent the last few hours preparing for her arrival. With an embarrassed, absolutely charming smile, he apologized for being in stockinged feet.

"I am so sorry just to drop in like this," said Libby, stomping off the snow that had fallen during Mass and covered sidewalks all over town. At Paul Thomas's insistence, she slipped off her boots and stepped into the warm living room. Both of them now in stockinged feet.

"I wondered if Daniel was home by any chance? I … uh … I talked to Lawrence Davis at Mass."

"He works till six thirty," said Paul Thomas. "No plans. Should be here soon, with Papa O'Reilly's baked spaghetti. You're welcomed to stay."

Libby feigned disappointment. "No baba ghanoush?"

Paul Thomas held her coat while she stuffed scarf and mittens into the sleeve like a third grader. "Sorry," he said. "Middle Eastern on Fridays. Saturday night it's Italian. Come on in. Would you like some wine? A beer? Or something hot?"

Daniel's spouse had roots less cosmopolitan than Daniel's Sicilian heritage. A sandy-haired Midwesterner, with a splash of freckles cultivated in a childhood on a soybean farm north of the city, Paul Thomas had a face more open, his features softer, than Daniel's chiseled dark-Mediterranean ones, in tune with the good-natured manner of an occupational therapist.

As she was steered into the spacious front room, a crackling fire sent its own invitation, and Libby realized she was cold and tired and hungry.

January was holding on tightly to winter. Father Henry's death and the investigation heckled her working hours. She didn't know which took more energy—obsessively churning clues and murder motives in her mind or the effort needed to pry herself loose from that to concentrate on grant proposals.

"Wine would be wonderful," she said, rubbing her hands together. As they stepped farther into the cozy room, Libby exclaimed, "You've changed everything around!" The couch was pushed closer to the fire, making a more intimate space at the far end. A new poppy-colored piece of modern art brightened the taupe wall to the left. "When did you get the piano?"

Offering her a crocheted afghan with one hand, Paul Thomas quickly retrieved his shoes with the other and set them aside, out of his company's sight. "It's been in the basement for years. When we moved the couch, it left the perfect spot."

"Do you play?"

"I can't even get one hand of chopsticks down." He fluttered his ten digits out before him. "Fat fingers. Daniel, he's like an octopus. Hands fly all over the keys."

Libby laughed. "I didn't even know he played."

"Classical. Rock. Honky-tonk. I don't know exactly what he's playing lately. Heavy stuff. Somber." He shook his head as if to shake the heaviness off. "Come on. Let's get the wine."

In the kitchen, immaculate by any standards, Paul Thomas took three glasses from the cabinet. "Pinot Grigio okay? Nothing fancy. Although Aldi's has some really good wine at great prices." He made space on the countertop by pushing aside two large pineapples.
"On sale this week," he said, patting the spiky fruit tops. "Nothing more refreshing than tropical fruit in the middle of winter. Do you like

pineapple?"

Libby was used to Paul Thomas's chattiness. To her, it was homey, put a person at ease. She could see how he'd be good at distracting a client from the torture of therapy with his engaging conversation.

Back in the living room, encouraged to do so, Libby curled her feet up under her and wrapped the afghan over the rest of her. She saluted Paul Thomas, who had dropped into the overstuffed chair across from her, and they settled in by the fire.

After a few words about the weather and the wine, the discussion turned to the unspoken topic. "How are you guys holding up?"

Paul Thomas weighed his response.

Then the floodgates opened.

"Frankly, I'm scared to death. The police have asked Daniel a million questions, over and over. What time did you last see Father Felger? When did you get to work? You say nobody saw you between church and work? Nobody? Don't you two text each other? That's a long time, etc., etc. Are you sure you and Father weren't on the outs?"

He set his wine on a monogrammed coaster on the table next to him and folded his arms. His voice was low but impassioned. "He should have been on the outs. Daniel *was* out. Whether he wanted to be or not. That nosey jerk usher. We don't care if people know we're a couple. Even if it's none of their business. But your Church and your congregation seem hell bent on making sure that if you're 'that way,' we will, quote, 'love you as you are, as long as you're not who you are with another human being.' Frankly, I don't understand why Daniel stays connected to such a patronizing, hypocritical, judgmental, bigoted religion. I don't get it."

Libby said nothing. She had no rebuttal. There were days she wasn't sure she could stand up in front of the congregation, welcoming everyone to St. Hedwig's, singing about being "one in the Lord," when knowing the reality of not only the Church's stance, but the belief of the people sitting in the pews. Some of them. Okay, most of them.

It smacked of the same injustice she felt for her gender. The Church demanded marital relationships must have a man and a woman, but somehow that didn't translate into men and women being equally in demand in other circumstances.

Interpretation was everything. She was getting tired trying to apply the Be Nice Principle to its fullest when men at the top were interpreting their own definition of kindness and love and demanding that that be everyone's definition.

Was she being a coward by staying?

"Why does Daniel stay?" Libby asked.

While it was a practical question in light of recent events, it was also a question Libby asked herself. More often than she'd admit.

"I mean at St. Hedwig's." She made a slight detour, not sure she wanted a firm spiritual reason that would put her own reasoning to shame. "I'm assuming the House and Home Outlet is a decent job?"

"House and Home pays the bills. Many of the bills, that is. Money from taking care of the church is definitely part of what keeps us afloat."

Paul Thomas took up his wine, rolling it gently to reflect the firelight. "It's also important for Daniel. Gives his artistic side a place to breathe."

Libby understood this completely. If a person loved to sing, letting loose in a room like St. Hedwig's was unspeakably gratifying—the wood and space reverberating sound like the body of a giant cello, the organ coming up under you as if a fifty-piece orchestra sat upstairs. Add five hundred jubilant voices on Christmas Eve belting out "Joy to the World" with you and there was nothing that compared to it.

"Not much artistry in selling flooring," said Paul Thomas, "even though he defends it that way sometimes. But to spend hours arranging flowers, moving angels, candles and ferns, and all that swooping fabric into a beautiful space—that feeds a part of Daniel that no geometric design in bathroom tile can. God knows why."

He tipped his glass toward Libby. "And I mean that literally. Daniel loves that church. Big C Church and little c, St. Hedwig's church." He smiled. "I call it Hedwiggy's. All that ornate, carved woodwork; the grand gothic structure." Paul Thomas stared into his wine and spoke with a sense of wonder. "And a God he firmly believes loves him and wants him there. I don't get it."

He looked across the room and stopped Libby before she could speak. "No. I don't expect you to explain. It's a part of Daniel, and that's all that's necessary for me to accept it. Daniel or not, organized religion has always left me cold." He shifted in his seat and let out a huge sigh. "I ... I'm sorry. Like it's your fault."

"It is my Church. It is me ...." Libby stumbled. "I can't understand it any better than you. Do I stay because it's what I was brought up with? What I'm used to? Am I fooling myself that I stay because I think I can help change things? Sometimes I think I'm like Daniel. I stay because I sing. It gives a part of me artistic nourishment." The fire snapped and sputtered. "Or is that just self-serving vanity?"

They paused and listened to the back door open, followed by the familiar stamping of snow-covered feet.

"Sounds like carryout has been carried in."

"What a treat," declared Libby, luxuriating in the idea of an impromptu meal showing up before her. As much as she loved to cook, once in a while it was heaven to fall into this situation: no deciding on a menu, no shopping for ingredients, no chopping or boiling or baking. No cleanup. Just voila! O'Reilly's baked spaghetti!

Daniel appeared in the living room doorway, having come in noiselessly, as if on Sandburg's little cat feet. Well, stockinged feet.

"Thought I heard talking." A wide grin broke out between Daniel's wintry red cheeks. "Although, as Paul Thomas heads toward senility, talking to an empty room is to be expected."

"I've had a lot of practice lat ..." Paul Thomas cut himself off.

Libby watched an exchange of looks between the two men. She saw a split-second decision being made by Paul Thomas: whether to give a snappy retort or to be nice. Nice won out.

Daniel turned to Libby and switched gears. "Proverbially speaking, what brings you out on a night like this?"

The question was congenial and fitting enough, but Libby thought she caught a hint of wariness.

"I talked to Lawrence Davis this afternoon at Mass. I didn't know if you knew him. From St. Hedwig's. Lectors. He's a detective, too. So he's interested in what's going on, but not the one in charge."

"That would be Detective Grass."

Libby nodded. "Not that I'm any expert, but I'm not crazy about how Grass is working on this ... situation. I thought if I ...we ... those of us in the line of fire ... put our heads together, maybe we could make better progress."

Daniel unzipped his leather jacket. "Considering I'm the main suspect, I'm not sure I want to make any more progress."

"I don't know," said Libby. "Wayne turns out to be a relative of

Father Henry's. He could be in Father's will. Maybe there's a motive lurking there."

Paul Thomas sank back into his chair. "I guess just being a jerk isn't enough to qualify him." Halfway through crossing his legs, he sat up. "Although, I certainly like having more than one motive option."

Libby swirled the wine in her glass, then looked directly at Daniel. "I'm not off the hook yet either."

Daniel held up the large white carryout sack. "Will you stay for baked spaghetti?"

"I already told you, told everybody, that I was probably the last person to see Father Henry alive. Except the person who killed him."

Daniel pushed his plate with a half-eaten meal aside to make room for his legs, which he stretched out and brought to rest on the large round ottoman in front of him. "Yes, I dumped the ashes because that idiot Wayne never came in to do it. I wasn't going to leave everything smoldering there on the table. Dumped the ashes. Thurible back on the hook in the sanctuary where it belongs. Father and I talked briefly. And no, I did not argue with him."

The baked spaghetti was delicious. A blanket of cheese was no exaggeration. But it soon lost its appeal for Libby, too. "Why do you think Wayne said you did?"

"Because he's a lying jerk. And not particularly fond of me. I'm sure by my doing things he should be doing, I make him look bad. This was an opportunity to return the favor."

"So. No conversation with Father about firing you?"

"No."

"Didn't he ask you that morning if you'd be around later? Sounded like he had something he wanted to talk to you about."

"He asked how hard it would be to put up purple swags along the pillars for Lent. It's not hard. A little pricey. But it's such a quick switch to red for Good Friday and then Easter Vigil white a day later."

"So. Nothing about firing you?"

"None."

"Was that a possibility? Firing you?"

Daniel hesitated, briefly glancing at Paul Thomas. "When you're openly gay, living with another man, out for the world to see—pun intended—it's always a possibility. But you know Henry. Keeps his head firmly in the sand. Not always a bad place these days for a Catholic priest who doesn't really want to deal with social issues. As long as he could pretend I'm just a guy who comes in to decorate his church, he was fine. In that respect, he is, I suppose, better than some. But if someone raised the question, forced him to face what's right there in front of him … I don't know if he's too nice or too weak or too much in lockstep with the Church to react differently. I don't really blame him."

Paul Thomas waved a bread stick and smiled sweetly. "Whereas I do."

Daniel laughed. Paul Thomas could be ingratiatingly equivocal in any number of situations, but when it was between the two of them, when it mattered, there was only the unvarnished speaking of his mind. Daniel found his bluntness endearing.

"This is what Father Henry, et al, has been taught," Daniel went on, without raising his voice, without the rancor lacing his partner's statement. "Taught, trained, indoctrinated with for all his life. It's the Church, the Pope, and bishops he's vowed to follow. It's just that they miss the mark of Christ's message. Instead of seeing human beings made in the image of God; oh, yes, us, too; instead of finding a way to embrace us, they choose to shove us to the edge, just outside the main. We love *you*, but not how you live. You can participate, but leave your heart at the door. I'm not asking that gays be tolerated, that they make room for us. No. They need to acknowledge that we've already been given a place by God. We already belong."

Libby listened. Daniel seemed so calm. Seemed as if this was something he had settled for himself long ago. Yet she wondered if there wasn't some rage, righteous as she considered it to be, simmering under it all. Could there have been a moment when all the years, all the struggles against the opposition, added to an immediate threat to financial security, that erupted unbidden?

"How was Father when you left him?" she asked.

Daniel sighed. He closed his eyes and gave what repetition had hardened into a formulated response. "I was finishing up, had my coat on to leave, when Father came in. I presumed from the funeral luncheon because he said he ate too much. He remembered the Storm Relief boxes. Said he always worried about leaving them out. Too much of a temptation in that neighborhood. Had forgotten to empty them on Sunday after the weekend. I said I'd help collect them. He said just dump all the cards into one box and he'd take them over for Maggie to count."

"Do you remember how many cards there were?"

Daniel looked to the ceiling for the answer. "Four boxes. Easily five, maybe eight cards in each. Could have been twenty to thirty cards."

Libby compared this to her own calculations as she tapped her fork against her bottom teeth. "That's what I thought. The kid who was arrested had fewer than ten cards he was caught cashing in. They never found any more. Guess he could have hid them really well."

"Or given them to someone else," suggested Paul Thomas. "A girlfriend maybe?"

Libby couldn't remember any of the kids in the high school parking lot emerging as such or indicating one existed.

Daniel picked up where he left off. "Father and I talked. He asked about the swags. Then about the people getting the relief funds. The storm. What it must be like, in practically a split second, to lose all your belongings, your home, even just losing power for days on end. Like when everything went out on us those couple of hideously hot days last summer."

"Was the conversation loud enough to sound like an argument?"

"Hardly. I asked if he wanted any help locking up. He said to go on. He had to get some soup, I think, from the refrigerator, and he said he might stay and pray while it was quiet. It was around one o'clock because I figured I had time to get some lunch or stop at the craft store before I had to be at work at three. We both genuflected at the altar.

He went left to the priest's sacristy; I went right to the bride-side, put on my coat, and went out the door. Locked it behind me. Saw no one."

"Were the steps slippery?"

"Of course they were slippery."

Being accused of killing a priest didn't raise Daniel's ire, but the incompetence of the maintenance man certainly did. "It was sleeting and cold and everything was iced over, and Wayne hadn't put any salt out. He's such a …"

Daniel didn't finish the sentence. Perhaps too many options.

Libby pressed on. "Then you went to work. Or the craft store? Didn't anyone see you?"

"No, no one saw me in a way they could vouch for me. Didn't buy anything. Didn't ask for assistance. Just slipped in and slipped out."

"For two hours?"

"I did stop at home for a sandwich first. No. No one saw me here either. Paul Thomas was at work."

Libby tried to picture Daniel going through these actions. "Did you leave any evidence of lunch? A used coffee cup? A knife in the sink that Paul Thomas could have seen?"

"I don't leave knives in the sink."

Paul Thomas shrugged apologetically. "He doesn't."

Libby had to laugh as she considered her own habit of letting rinsed dishes collect throughout the day until a comprehensive loading of the dishwasher and pots-and-pans scrub occurred. She couldn't go to bed without the kitchen being clean, but during the day, the accumulation of miscellaneous bowls and plates didn't bother her.

The humor was lost on Daniel, who was finally hitting an exasperation point. As if to put an end to the question once and for all, he rattled off the summary of his day. "I went to church. Worked there as usual. Saw Father. Helped him and left. Had lunch. Roamed the craft store. Went to work. Worked. Went home. Maggie Mueller called that night and told me Father Henry was dead. No one, no one between church and work can vouch for me."

Libby saw no humor either. Her situation corresponded all too closely. "And my animals won't vouch for me," she said plainly, turning to her wine.

The trio fell silent. Fire, friends, good food—all meant to make a winter weekend evening comforting—had failed.

Paul Thomas rose and gathered up dishes. "Another glass of wine, anyone?"

Daniel shook his head, more a gesture of distraction than refusal.

Libby also declined. "I have to drive. Besides, my brain is already muddled with trying to figure out how things might have happened. Trying to see how the police are figuring it. At least that way we can know what we're up against, what we have to disprove."

She pulled her legs up more snuggly under her and tucked the afghan up at her neck, letting it drape around her shoulders. She spoke out loud, although more to herself. "If they're thinking of me, they must think I was still at church when Father Henry came back from the luncheon, we got into an argument about women's issues, I got mad and killed him, then went home to work on my grants."

She watched Daniel's stockinged feet tap at each other on the footstool by his chair, his elbow on the arm of the chair, his hand balled up against his cheek. She said, "The police must think you argued with Father about being fired because you're openly gay, got mad, bashed him on the head, stole most of the gift cards, killed ... er, spent two hours looking at silk plants, then showed up at work. Presumably on time."

Daniel yanked his feet off the ottoman and sat bolt upright. The fire in his black eyes was not a reflection of the flames next to him, but of some inner burning. "Libby?" he practically shouted. "Do you really think I could do this? Do you think even if I was angry enough to hit someone? That hard. How repressed do you think I am that I could leave him on those icy steps and just go on to work? Just chat the afternoon away about kitchen dimensions and laminates?"

The room went dead as if a vault door had slammed shut and pushed all the oxygen out.

Still, the question hung in the air.

Libby had already asked herself if she could ever have been angry enough to hit, to harm, to kill. In the darkest corner of her mind, she admitted it was possible. Not premeditated. Not starting out after someone purposely.

But she knew anger.

What she hadn't thought about was this second point of Daniel's.

Could she, having done such a violent, horrific thing, something so contrary to her natural inclinations, could she then just go about her day as if nothing had happened?

+ + +

Had to move all the shadow boxes of World War I medals so the new Liberty Bonds poster could fit on that south study wall. A little faded but still in good condition. Should not have started rearranging things so late at night. Exhausted today, but what a find. Will have to go back. That shop had some interesting clocks and candleholders. Can't be more than an hour, hour-and-a-half, from here. Lots of beautiful old church linens, too.

Funeral on Wednesday. Wonder if I can get Fr. Halberstadt to take it for me. Thank goodness he's still driving, probably not very well at ninety, but he gets around. Always says he doesn't mind subbing.

The Bishop, via the Vicar, keeps pestering all of us to get our wills and any final business in order. I suppose he's got to worry, since three-fourths of his priestly population is old enough to drop dead on the spot. The MS seems to be only a nuisance at this point—"stable" and not flaring up at the moment. Tired a lot. Eyes not so good sometimes. Not enough to do me in.

Pretty set on who gets what. Two biggest concerns already on paper. Need to get that other info to the Vicar. Thank goodness I'll be dead and won't have to listen to how anyone feels about my decisions. Granted, not everyone will be happy.

I can trust the Vicar and Maggie to sort things out. If L. is still around, she'll plan an OK funeral. Sometimes I think she has the right idea—just put me on the compost pile. At least she and B. know the songs I'm sick of. If "Amazing Grace" is anywhere on the list, I shall rise up out of my closed casket and scream. Frankly, I'd like a little soft rock-and-roll mixed in and then go out to "The Battle Hymn of the Republic."

+ + +

The knife slid easily down the firm red flesh.

No. That didn't sound right. Why did everything lately have a gruesome connotation? wondered Libby as she quartered the organic ruby Bosc pear she had splurged on from the Health Food Shop. She was nestled on her plump couch between Dash, already walked and inside for the night, and BabyCakes, snoring like a hibernating bear cub.

Her own fire crackled in front of the three of them. Sated, for the most part, with wine and Papa O'Reilly's spaghetti, she was topping off the unexpected meal at Daniel and Paul Thomas's with her pear. Sweet and succulent and as good as any pineapple.

Too much talk about murder and killing.

She stared at the fire, the only light in the room. The only light in the world—if the living room windows squaring off the black night outside were any indicators.

With only a very few substitute cantors available for vacations and emergencies, Libby sang for most of St. Hedwig's services. She would sing again in the morning at the nine o'clock Sunday Mass. For the moment, everything at church was stable, holding together for the time being. The pews were modestly filled for both weekend services, but as she and Maggie had concluded, with no school attracting the next generation and the stigma of being an inner-city parish, a good portion of the congregation were transients, people looking for a place to worship with no strings attached. And Father Henry had given it to them.

Libby sliced the last half of pear and watched the fire throw animated shadows around the room. How happy she was to have relinquished the frantic plan-making of youthful Saturday nights. These days, a movie and popcorn at the home of a neighbor, a good book, and the amateur sketching of her animals when they would pose for her were satisfying options.

When Namita had first discovered her landlady was more than the person who collected rent and made sure the kitchen drain worked, she began inviting Libby to book clubs, knitting nights, foreign language classes, and medieval re-enactment weekends.

"You're too young to sit at home," she complained. But the longer Namita observed and connected with Libby, the less she pestered her and, in fact, finally admitted that Libby seemed not anti-social, introverted, or dull, but self-contained, selective, and anything but dull. Namita saw her own candle often crazily blazing at both ends. More than once, she envied the rich simplicity of Libby's life.

Into Libby's fireside reverie, the phone rang. The name and number that came up made Libby abruptly stop the final wedge of her dessert from reaching her mouth.

"Good evening, Vicar," she said, careful not to upset cat nor dog. Neither of them stirred, even when she reached for her calendar, squinting at it in the firelight.

It was a short call.

"Yes, I can be there," she said. "Yes, I am a little surprised. Thank you. Yes. Good night."

Libby's fingers gently rubbed the scruff of BabyCakes's neck, massaging soft rolls of flesh and fur until the hibernating bear purred steadily.

Libby leaned down and whispered into the black velvet ear. "Don't tell Dash. I'm in Father Henry's will."

Chapter Twenty-One

For Libby, Sunday night dinner always meant family dinner. After their parents' deaths, Libby's older sister, Jane, had taken over hosting the event.

Jane, four years Libby's senior and the oldest of the five Kinder children, had assumed the caretaker position in the family. She rushed about, her still dark, thick hair usually pulled back simply from a face comfortable without makeup. She wasn't particularly tall and fussed perpetually about losing a few pounds, but her focus was always and abundantly directed selflessly at the needs of others.

Jane's Sunday night dinners were open to all, including stray siblings, in-laws, grandparents if mobile, an occasional neighbor, and primarily Jane's husband, Joe, and their own progeny—four grown married children, their spouses, and eleven grandchildren under the age of seven.

This was the same assortment of people Libby enjoyed while growing up. The house was different, but it was the same table, with laughter and conversation and great food.

As silly as Libby's four siblings could act when they were together, in childhood they were held in check by their mother's insistence on civility and basic manners. Nothing too rigid, but staying seated for the duration of the meal; passing bowls and platters in one direction, preferably clockwise; and no snorting milk or otherwise playing with their food.

In contrast, at Jane's, a kind of Montessori daycare atmosphere prevailed. Jane and Joe had encouraged their children, and now their children's children, to build, color, jump, draw, paste, and explore on any surface in any room of the house. They were like a family out of Dickens, tumbling all over and into each other with raucous amusement and delight.

On this particular Sunday, there was a pot-and-pan drum corps banging accompaniment to a Suzuki-esque piano concert in the family room; chairs and blanket tents in the living room; and everyone sporting multiple Band-Aids in solidarity with one of the babies who had acquired a small, yet genuine, gash on his head.

For a few hours on Sunday afternoons, Libby loved being immersed in the cooing, oohing, and ahhing; teasing and being teased by three-year-olds.

For a few hours.

The bonus for the day was a meal of equal indulgence. On this night, the fare included roasted chicken, two kinds of rice casseroles, broccoli with cheese sauce, corn pudding, dinner rolls, and Aunt Lib's fresh-fruit medley. For picky eaters, there was always macaroni and cheese out of a box. Picnic-style serving replaced the business of passing food in any given direction, snorting milk was taken for granted, and playing with food considered an investigative endeavor.

By Jane's decree, no one was allowed to help with the dishes after dinner. Instead, people drifted toward the TV to watch sports or sat and chatted around the table. On this particular evening, child-rearing dilemmas and job dramas paled in comparison to Aunt Libby's present circumstances.

"In his *will*?!"

"What do you think he left you?" asked Libby's niece Caroline, as she slid discs of sliced banana across the highchair tray to her youngest.

"I haven't a clue," confessed Libby, as she mindlessly brushed a small unicorn's unruly pink ponytail, per instructions from the child leaning across her thigh.

"Money?" another niece conjectured.

"Maybe a big, hoggy ring," said Caroline. "Don't priests wear rings with all those jewels and precious stones?"

Caroline's husband unwrapped a popsicle and handed it off to the boy squirming on his lap. "No. That's bishops and popes with the jewels."

"Maybe Father Felger had a thing for you."

"Oh, come on."

"Purely platonic. Or unrequited." Caroline paused in the banana slicing and rhapsodized on the whole affair. "Romantic, I think. The struggle between God and Aunt Lib."

Aunt Lib and the husband rolled their eyes.

Jane wiped cheese sauce off a picture book. "Don't tell me you aren't curious, Lib."

Libby had to admit she was.

"When do you find out?"

"The reading of the will is tomorrow. Monday morning."

Another in-law roamed in from the kitchen, nursing a mug of coffee. "Did they ever figure out how he died?"

Libby explained about Father Henry being hit on the head on the back steps of the church. Probably with the thurible. The censer.

The coffee was too hot to drink. The in-law blew on it and asked, "What's somebody doing on the back steps in the middle of winter with that thurible thing?"

"It was used for a funeral that morning."

"Are they sure he didn't just fall and hit his head?"

Caroline considered a banana slice intently. "They should be able to tell those wounds apart. The laceration from a sharp metal edge ..."

"Okay, Nurse Caroline," they all teased.

"Hey, don't make fun of Nurse Caroline," her sister said in defense. "She was right about Rufus's ears. The vet finally gave him some drops to help."

"See," said Caroline, happily vindicated.

"Honestly," her sister went on. "Pets and vets and groomers and kids and doctors."

Libby handed cream to the in-law. "You're right. They did assume Father Henry fell to start with."

"Didn't they think some kid did it?"

"Our neighbor's dad goes to St. Hedwig's," the husband interrupted, "and he said the ushers were talking about you, Lib. And that guy who decorates. And maybe the church secretary. Said any one of you could have done it."

For a split second, no one spoke. In the silence they exchanged quick glances.

Then came an explosion of questions.

"Are you a suspect, Aunt Lib?"

"Is it because you're in the will?"

"Were you *involved* with Father Henry?"

"Why would they suspect you?"

Libby had gotten relatively used to talking to church people about the murder. Had had more than one exchange with two different detectives, her renter, in addition to endlessly running over things in one-sided conversations with her pets. But the sudden interrogation by family, in a place that was usually an oasis from the concerns of her daily life, took Libby aback. Carefully she set the unicorn with the pink, neatly coiffed ponytail aside.

"I have a key," she said succinctly. "We, all the people you mentioned, have access to the church. And the probable weapon."

Jane sent a plate of fudge brownies around. "Why would you kill Father Henry?"

"Why would anyone kill him?" Caroline said airily as she added bits of brownie to her child's tray. "He says a good, short Mass. He doesn't rag on about money. Our priest, that's all he talks about."

A new line of theories.

"Maybe he abused somebody."

"Yes. Blackmail!"

"Maybe somebody from his past. His family. Knew something secret about him."

"Held a grudge."

"A grudge?" Caroline shot a sideways glance at her mother and added in a teasing, sing-songy way. "Who would *ever* hold a grudge?"

This was an old chestnut in the family. Which Caroline never hesitated to drag out. "Like still being angry about someone fifty years ago throwing away that plastic bracelet from fourth grader Vinnie Pedewski."

"Petroski," Jane corrected and trotted out her long-standing defense. "The bracelet was important to me."

There was a practiced chorus of daughters. "Mom. Let. It. Go."

Jane shrugged. Everyone laughed good-naturedly. The men at the table reverted to crime.

"Father Henry could have stolen parish funds."

"Or played the ponies at the track."

"We don't have a track."

"Online, dummy. You can gamble your life away online."

A fight among the little kids that had been brewing in the family room spilled into the dining room and distracted most of the adults. Aunt Lib was handed a baby for safekeeping while Jane passed the brownies for another round.

Caroline lowered her voice and leaned toward Libby. "I heard Father Henry was all fuzzed about the church secretary because she went to the Women's Clinic for birth control."

"I thought her husband was dead," said Jane.

"Maybe she's fooling around."

"Maybe," said Libby, not lowering her voice, "maybe she was taking her married daughter there for contraceptives."

"Why is that a problem?" asked Caroline's sister.

"Duh. The *Catholic* Church. Birth control. No-no."

"I still don't get that." Caroline wiped water that had dribbled down her child's front. "It's one thing not to have any kids—although I think that's a person's own business. Seriously, three is looking like my limit. My daycare lady won't use the pill because the Church says not to. She won't even use it to regulate her periods so the *natural method* will work. They have eight kids. In a three-bedroom house. What's the point? We don't need ten kids to work the farm anymore. And, it used to be that it took ten pregnancies to give you two or three healthy children. Either way, it all seems very personal. Between you and God."

Jane poured herself a cup of coffee. "That's fine with me. As long as it is between you and God."

"What do you mean?"

"I mean, I hope we raised you to know that you don't stand alone in making such decisions. In a vacuum. That you consider more than your own, self-interested point of view. That God and morality play a part."

The rebuke was not new.

"I don't blindly disregard God and cater only to my needs, but I don't blindly disregard my needs and mindlessly follow a Church law," responded Caroline.

Jane was content to leave her concerns at that. She'd had her say.

It was infinitely more comfortable and interesting to dig around in someone else's life. "So," she said, "would Father Henry have to fire the secretary if she got caught?"

Libby had wondered the same. Father Henry was funny about controversial topics. Unpredictable. As Daniel had noted, he didn't like to rock the boat. Would he have fired the person who ran his parish and made his life easier? In which direction would he be willing to turn his blind eye?

"I don't know," was all she could answer.

At a certain moment on Sunday nights, there seemed to be an internal signal that enough was enough. Enough food, enough conversation, enough squabbling. As if choreographed, a cry went out from parents to their offspring to pick up the toys, get down off the piano, find your shoes, stop whining.

"Goodbye, Aunt Lib," Caroline shifted her youngest on her hip at the front door. "Hope you hit the jackpot tomorrow!" She pulled a fuzzy knit cap over his ears and called back, "I hope it's a ring!"

Chapter Twenty-Two

Sitting inside his car, Detective Mark Grass peered over a steaming cup of coffee at the rectory for St. Hedwig's, noting how its brick structure and slate roof matched the huge church across the street. The rectory was also huge, with five bedrooms at least, he guessed.

The house looked like something from an old movie, a place a wise and benevolent pastor lived and instructed young men on the joys and trials of being a parish priest. A plump, amiable housekeeper kept his Roman collars clean and his table laden with wholesome home-cooked meals; and when the dishes were done, she retired to her private quarters and sipped a small brandy while she prayed or crocheted doilies.

Detective Grass could entertain such an idyllic scenario because he had, in fact, very little experience with priests, housekeepers, churches, or religion. He was not without morals; he adhered to firm boundaries for right and wrong—because they seemed logical and natural, a prescription for the common good; not because a God ordained them. His job was to sort out the guilty from the innocent in this life; he did not need a judge to take care of that in the next.

Grass had a wife and three sons, who, by all accounts, were on their way to becoming good men and productive citizens. Detective Grass did not overly credit himself with being a successful parent nor did he blame others for being less so. Luck and circumstance, he thought, had as much to do with how kids turned out as anything. As a police officer, he'd seen kids raised by druggies, who raped thirteen-year-old girls and bullied gays. Children born with that luck into those circumstances usually ended up as dropouts or gang members. They often landed on his watch, and were often on their way to lives in and out of prison.

He sipped at the scalding coffee, which was barely cooling, even as it made steam condense on the car window. At fifty, he was glad he had risen to detective status, using his brain more than his body to chase down the bad guys. He couldn't complain. This Father Felger investigation was a treat compared to his other murder cases.

Although it wasn't exactly a white-collar crime, the suspects were all pretty normal. And hardly contentious. Average. Granted, one had stepped out of the normal range and murdered the Good Father, but the pool of possibilities was somewhat defined and limited—only a small, identifiable, locatable, handful of people had keys and alarm codes to get into the church and at the murder weapon.

All right. The almost-for-certain murder weapon.

At this point, the most elusive element was motive. He hoped the gathering that would take place shortly would help with that.

Detective Grass already knew what was in Father Felger's will. He wasn't here at the reading of it to get that information. He was here to see how those named in the will would take the information. Maybe they already knew and would pretend they didn't. There had been addenda. Changes. Maybe that would make a difference.

Maybe it already had.

The reading of Father Henry Felger's Last Will and Testament was at ten Monday morning. At 9:15, Detective Grass was let into St. Hedwig's rectory by Maggie Mueller. He was again struck by the ten-foot ceilings, the polished marble floor of the hallway that ran from the front to the back of the house and from which other rooms, all outlined with the original, wide, dark woodwork, shot off to the left and right.

The detective stepped into the parlor, passed through a wide opening where pocket doors had been pushed into their slots, and entered the formal dining room. At one end of a large, shiny mahogany table, under the glittering prisms of a chandelier, sat Mr.

Kenneth Becker, lawyer.

In a subdued voice, he was going over paperwork with the Vicar. Both men looked serious and business-like; the lawyer in his dark suit; the Vicar, formal and official in all black except for the crisp, white, clerical collar. Black-rimmed reading glasses added a scholarly look to the Vicar's otherwise plain, but perfectly groomed, face.

The chair at the head of the table was already occupied. Dunkirk and Calico Two, side by side, paws overlapping with easy confidence as if they were ready for the Board Meeting, alternately watched the proceedings with curious interest and dozed in complete boredom.

Maggie offered the detective coffee, which he accepted; more to have a prop in his hand than to drink it, having had his fill from his observation post earlier.

The secretary disappeared through a swinging door into the kitchen and left him to tour the religious paraphernalia in the room. Statues of saints. Clocks cradled in the arms of angels. Jesus at every age—babe in the manger, boy lost in the temple, preacher of the multitudes, savior on the cross—depicted in various art forms.

Detective Grass viewed these things with a non-believer's eye, seeing each piece as one might see displays in a museum. In turn, some were charming, even beautiful; some sentimental; some quite maudlin bordering on the macabre. He supposed any religion, because it chronicled such a long span of historical events, as well as mystical phenomena, might present a collection no less fantastic.

Having been acknowledged by the lawyer and Vicar, the detective turned to meet up with Maggie in the kitchen, which, to his surprise, was thoroughly modernized with contemporary appliances. Even the cabinets and countertops were of the latest style and materials.

The doorbell rang.

Maggie handed the detective his coffee. "Cream and sugar on the counter," she said before leaving to answer the front door.

She's more attractive than she gives herself credit for, thought Grass, catching a splash of color at her neck, a bright green that was subtle but noticeable. Widowed young. Church secretary. Pay can't be much. A daughter to raise alone. Nose to the grindstone. Working for an old priest. Cranky, maybe. Demanding. All things considered, frustrating enough to murder?

Voices filled the rectory vestibule as the two cousins the detective had met, Phyllis and Ruth, spilled into the parlor with their three out-of-town ones he had not.

In the commotion, the cats dived for cover.

Only one cousin shared any resemblance to the in-town relatives. She was short and round and a little puffy around the eyes like Ruth. The other two seemed related only to their other sibling—thin but sturdy.

Until Wayne arrived and joined the group. He steered toward the edges of the room, and for a brief moment, when he tried to smile and look interested, a certain shape of the nose connected him with his relatives. It was the persistent downturned expression, the pessimistic slump of the shoulders, as if he were permanently huddled to protect the lit tip of a cigarette, that set him apart.

A few minutes later, Libby arrived. Shortly thereafter, Bernie. They hung back, shedding coats and scarves. After letting everyone in, Maggie reached around to lock the front door. She was obviously surprised to see her colleagues. "The Vicar said to set places for ten. I had no idea that included you guys."

"Shocked me," admitted Libby. "Vicar only called Saturday night."

"Me, too," said Bernie.

"I think everything fell into place once the out-of-town cousins got situated." Maggie rattled off the slate for the days ahead. "Wednesday the wake; Thursday the funeral. Of course, this morning," she added dramatically, "the reading of the will."

Bernie sniffled with the move from the outside into the warm hallway. "Henry used to kid me about putting me in his will. I always said I'd return the favor. I thought it was just a joke."

Maggie set the bolt. "Can I get you a Kleenex, Bernie?"

"No, no. Just a little drip from the cold." He pulled out his own tissue and wiped his nose. "Better than being a little drip, I guess." He gave a short, giddy laugh; then seeing the lawyer and the Vicar, he quickly became serious. "Oh. My."

Maggie started back toward the other guests.

Libby caught her by the arm and whispered, "Vicar said there was an addendum?"

"Oh, I don't know," Maggie whispered back. "Did he say what you were getting?"

"No."

Bernie leaned in. "Me, neither." He shot a furtive glance . "Those must be Father's other relatives."

"I see Wayne's here," said Libby. "All cleaned up for the big day. I hardly recognized him without his sweatshirts."

Maggie moved into the group and announced that there was hot coffee and water for tea in the kitchen; then offered to take people's coats to the study, which Libby pitched in to help with.

Libby hadn't known what to wear to the reading of a will. It wasn't covered in any fashion manuals. She'd finally decided on gray slacks and a short, gray-and-white flecked boucle jacket. Warm, comfortable, but a little professional.

Although for the most part, Monday was a regular workday for Maggie, she felt that, in lieu of Father Henry's being unavailable, she was the de facto hostess and had scoured her limited wardrobe for something appropriate. A plain, black pencil skirt always worked. She topped it with an emerald-green turtleneck, which drew attention up and toward her new haircut. A bulky black cardigan was a concession to the cold. It looked warm but was a bit shapeless and a little frayed at the cuffs. She rolled them up and artfully displayed a bit of the green top underneath and several pretty bracelets she'd borrowed from her daughter's jewelry drawer.

Libby laid the cousins' coats in the study over the backs of several chairs. Hers and Bernie's were in their own pile. "Are you here as welcoming committee, heiress, or in some other official capacity?"

Maggie adjusted the last coat, which was threatening to slide off the full chair. "Making coffee and cutting up some pastries. Otherwise, I'm here same as you are." As they rejoined the group, Maggie smiled mischievously. "Only, I know what I'm getting."

Libby watched the cousins with interest. Either time, distance, or temperament kept their connection from looking anything more than mildly cordial. Libby's family would have been falling all over one another, each one talking louder than the next, stories and memories tumbling out like the waterfall of a burst dam.

Both Libby and Maggie had hospitality bones. Libby asked the Minnesotans about their flights; Maggie about their accommodations.

Edward, a tall stern man of eighty, with thin hands and thin lips, gave terse responses. His sisters, in their late seventies, seemed grateful for the concern and replayed engaging stories of their layover in Chicago and the pleasant surprise of the size of their hotel rooms.

Edward wore a neat suit and tie; his sisters, simple dark slacks, unpretentious blouses, and sweaters highlighted by a few heirloom pins and earrings. Helen, the shorter one, had the same shy way as Ruth; Catherine was tall like her brother, but more robust physically. She had strawberry-blonde hair that matched her gregarious personality, though not all that natural for her age. Libby sensed the women were more given to humor than their pinched brother.

Ruth, Phyllis, and Wayne were also dressed up, but nothing flamboyant. They did their best to appear friendly. But Phyllis especially, in a new navy-blue cloche, gave the impression that, really, her nose was out of joint. Libby wondered if their hallowed spot in Father Henry's hierarchy was being threatened.

Wayne had plastered a not very believable smile on his face, which only caused Libby to ask herself why the ever-petulant maintenance man would set himself to the unnatural task of trying to appear warm and cordial.

At the moment, the only tie that bound them was the thread that led to Father Henry Felger. And his will.

How thick or thin that thread was, would soon be determined.

As Libby mingled, she concluded that Father Henry was a conglomerate of the gene pool. He could be dour like the terse Edward and occasionally self-absorbed like Wayne, seemingly happier to be left alone. And he could also be very funny. Dry and witty. And surprisingly, just plain silly. While Libby often found him at prayer, reading his breviary before Mass in the sacristy, more than once she had arrived to hear the seventy-year-old priest drumming out a baseline with his fingers and singing a low but credible version of "Light My Fire."

The lawyer suggested everyone get something to drink, help themselves to the sweet rolls on the table, and then take a seat, where each place had been set with two pens and a packet of papers in folders stamped in gold with the law firm's logo; put down such a precise distance from the edge of the table and from each other that they might have been laid out with a ruler.

The nine beneficiaries fit comfortably: Edward, Helen, Catherine, and Maggie took one side; Bernie, Libby, Phyllis, and Ruth sat opposite them. Wayne replaced the cats at one end, while the lawyer directed the proceedings from the head of the table.

Detective Grass and the Vicar found chairs against the wall

beneath the high leaded glass windows. Not much light came through from the darkening day outside, leaving the chandelier to glow alone, its splintered light reflected in the high sheen of the dark-wood table. The room looked as if dinner at an English estate was about to be served. Had a murder not already taken place, thought Libby, surely this was a great setting for one.

Right out of the books.

The lawyer flexed his arms forward as if he was getting ready to carve a roast for the main meal. Instead he took up the first page of the Last Will and Testament of Reverend Henry Leo Felger. "From the start, let me caution you," he began in a clear, firm voice. "There are several sections to this will. You are advised to refrain from comment or discussion until the entirety of Father Felger's wishes be made known."

All sociability drained from the room.

Being cautioned, being advised, inflicted a formality on everyone and brought Libby to an attentive state. This was the will of a murdered man; someone in the room was likely his murderer.

As the lawyer inched his way through the document, people wrote in margins, underlined or circled portions, turned pages in one unified flip, as if the English dinner guests were now engaged in the evening's entertainment, a play of sorts, and they were following the script of the drama they'd all been cast in, watching intently, carefully, as they learned of their character's fate.

After several pages of legal jargon, the lawyer cleared his throat. "To each of my living cousins …"

Six simple words charged the atmosphere.

Moments before, the beneficiaries had been struggling to stay alert through verbiage about jurisdictions and executive duties. Being named riveted their attention; they ceased all outward movement to mask racing hearts and shallow breaths.

"To Edward, Helen, Catherine, Phyllis, Ruth, and Wayne, I bequeath $5,000. For any and all who had to incur any expense in order to travel to this reading, those expenses shall be reimbursed." The lawyer did not wait for a reaction, but read on.

"Addendum One. As agreed, Maggie Mueller shall assume all care and responsibility for my cats, Dunkirk and Calico Two. They come with their bedding, litter boxes, collars, and toys. In addition, food, veterinary care, and grooming needs shall be compensated for."

The out-of-town cousins looked to confirm who Maggie was, this person who was not a blood relative inheriting something of Henry's, even if they were just pets.

Maggie nodded, acknowledging her presence.

"To Libby Kinder, for all her help to me and to the parish, I bequeath the antique angel clock on the dining room sideboard."

Unconsciously, everyone turned to the location described and stared at the small, delicate, porcelain clock as if it had just miraculously materialized. Then, simultaneously, they swung back around to stare at Libby; as if she, like the clock, had also just appeared.

They barely had time to raise an eyebrow or ask a question before the lawyer methodically droned on.

Detective Grass picked lint from his pant leg. He knew all this. No surprises so far.

"To Bernie Fruehauf, longtime friend to me and the Church, I bequeath whatever vehicle is currently in my possession. This includes the remains of the booklet for a year of unlimited carwashes."

Libby felt Bernie tense next to her at the mention of his name. At the mention of the car, his eyes widened slightly, but, as with the others, he refrained from any overt reaction. Had he wanted to jump or smile for joy, the atmosphere in the room held him in check.

The lawyer stopped talking.

The pages of the will he had laid aside, having been dutifully read and decreed, were collected and flipped right side up. He straightened the pile at each corner and inserted the will into its original home in his folder. He then adjusted the unit with the synchronized movement of his thumbs, nudging it until it was parallel to the edge of the table.

Silence.

No movement.

No more pages to read.

Wayne looked up and down the table. He looked at the lawyer. He rifled through his copy of the will. "Is that it?" he blurted out.

Cousin Phyllis found her voice. "Yeah. Is that it?"

Wayne consulted the scratchings in his margins. "That's only about $30,000. There has to be more."

The cousins turned to one another.

"He's a priest. He couldn't have spent all of the money," declared Helen.

"He didn't have a lavish lifestyle," said Phyllis. "He certainly never gave lavish gifts. A poinsettia at Christmas, a basket of fruit at Easter."

Ruth thought hard. "He didn't travel much anymore. Or wear expensive clothes."

In the end, after a babble of conjecture and innuendo and irritation spilled out onto the table, as if everyone had tasted the dessert and deemed it unappetizing, the overriding question that came out of every cousin's mouth in some form or another was: "What happened to all that money from Grandpa Leo?"

After several minutes of lively conjecture, the Vicar stood and stepped into the fray. With his commanding clerical presence, the fuss died out and the lawyer deferred to the priest.

The Vicar tipped his head and spoke over his dark reading glasses. "There is," he said with a slight cough, "a second addendum."

Phyllis sat back, triumphantly crossing her arms over her bosom. "See. I knew that wasn't all there is." Vindicated, she took a sweet roll.

The Vicar, having performed his function of quieting the mob, turned matters back to the lawyer. The lawyer cupped one hand inside the other and brought them to rest on top of his closed, gold-lettered folder. "That *is* all there is." He looked around the table and spoke gently, as if he were a doctor delivering a terrible prognosis. "For you."

The cousins' brows knit in consternation.

"But ... there is ... more," he said slowly. "Sort of."

Wayne reared back in his chair. "What the hell does that mean?" He gave a swift wave of his hand at Maggie. "She can have those stupid cats."

Mumbles of agreement from around the table.

He flapped at Bernie. "And Bernard, here, he can have the car. It's nice, but it's not worth what Henry inherited from Grandpa."

Louder muttering.

"Un-l-es-s ..." He dragged the last out to about five syllables.

As if it dawned on everyone at the same time, an unseen string slowly pulled all their heads. Toward Libby.

Wayne chewed on and then spit out every word. "Unless that damn clock is worth millions."

Suddenly Libby felt trapped.

Detective Grass imperceptibly shifted in his seat. He quit picking the lint off his pants.

"Just a moment." The Vicar's voice again rose above the clatter, as he glided smoothly over to the lawyer at the head of the table. He gathered himself up, as he must have done a million times in church prior to launching into a homily. It was enough to temporarily distract the chorus of objections. The Vicar removed his reading glasses and, as he folded them carefully, meticulously, the rumblings subsided and made way for his pronouncement.

"Father Henry had two addenda to his will," he said. "Kind of. What you have before you is the will itself, covering monetary gifts to beneficiaries who are related by blood. Namely, Edward, Helen, and Catherine. Phyllis, Ruth, and Wayne. The addendum, the first addendum actually, includes bequests to Maggie—the cats. Libby— the clock. Bernie—the car. There is, however, a second addendum."

The Vicar looked to the lawyer, who handed him a new pile of documents from a hard black briefcase on the floor near his feet. As the Vicar passed a set of the new papers to each person at the table, he explained, "This second addendum, such as it is, pertains to the remainder of Father Henry's estate."

Justified and pleased that their clamoring had produced the desired effect, the cousins nodded and congratulated each other. "Yes, finally," they said. "The remainder of Father Henry's estate. Now, that's what we came for."

The Vicar took a step back. Once again unfolding his glasses, he stared at his own set of papers, but yielded to the lawyer, who read from the official copy before him:

"The remainder of my estate, is to be used to build a chapel in my name, on Lot 67, 400 East, County Line Road, its boundary adjacent to the Franciscan Retreat House …"

"Where's that?" asked Wayne, his impatience barely disguised.

Maggie put her hand over her mouth. "That's the Shinnick property." Under her breath she added, "They did like him."

For the first time, the terse Edward was animated. "A chapel?! He had enough money left to build a chapel?!"

The lawyer and Vicar exchanged looks.

"We're not sure," said the lawyer.

The table erupted. "What do you mean?!" said the cousins.

Even Libby, Bernie, and Maggie could not hide their dismay.

The lawyer waited for an opening.

"The addendum is legal," he said. Surely he'd faced other uprisings at the reading of other wills. He proceeded calmly, in a voice lower than those around the table, causing them to quiet down in order to hear him. "The request that the remainder of Father Felger's estate go somewhere of his choosing, outside the family circle, is totally legitimate. However ..."

The lawyer's calm took on a note of discomfort.

Or was it trepidation?

"However, after reviewing all his known accounts, with the help of the Vicar ..." Each word came out distinctly. "That. We. Could. Find. Totaled a little over $50,000. That just covers the beneficiary bequests and leaves what scarcely covers funeral expenses and legal fees."

"You mean, it doesn't leave enough to build a chapel," observed Libby.

"In his name," quipped Maggie.

The lawyer looked at the Vicar. The Vicar looked at the beneficiaries. The beneficiaries looked at each other. At their papers. At the ceiling.

All searched for some kind of understanding.

"As most of you know," began the Vicar, "Father Henry was a little ... different. ... One might even say, eccentric, about money."

"I'll say," sputtered Wayne. "He left more money to the church secretary to take care of his damn cats than to his own family."

"That part's okay by me," declared Phyllis with a harrumph. "I don't need those shedding machines in my house."

Ruth ran her finger up and down the edge of the latest set of papers. "I like those cats."

The Vicar continued his explanation. "Henry also did not have much trust in financial or legal institutions. He seemed to have a kind of ... diversity program, a combination of ways to handle his wishes."

Edward cut to the chase. "So, where'd he put all this money?"

Detective Grass watched from the sidelines. He knew the squabbling could be instructive.

The Vicar cleared his throat. "Believe me. I asked him many times. He always told me that the information about where the money was ... was in ... his diary."

Cousin Catherine suddenly found this mysteriously fun. "His

diary?"

Not so, Cousin Phyllis. She was like a bloodhound onto a scent. "A diary? What kind of diary? How much are we talking about? How much does it cost to build a chapel?"

The lawyer placed his hands flat on the second addendum as if to keep it from rising up with a life of its own. "Probably several million dollars."

Blood relative or not, Libby couldn't contain herself. "He put several million dollars in a diary?!"

Bernie screwed up his face. "Henry kept a diary?"

The Vicar raised his voice to correct this notion before all hell broke loose. His diction was precise. "Henry put the information. About where to find the money. In the diary. At least, that's what I understand."

A mantra kept repeating around the table. "Several … million … dollars."

Ruth could be reasonable. "Okay," she said. "At least we know there's more." She turned to the Vicar. "What does the diary say about where the money is?"

After another exchange of looks with the lawyer, the Vicar, some strain beginning to show, simply said, "We don't know. We don't know where it is."

Bernie exhaled audibly. "Oh. My."

Maggie stifled a laugh. She thought she'd witnessed every possible Father Felger quirk.

Libby tapped her pen, clarifying each point. "You don't know where Father Henry's diary is. That has the information about where the money is. To build a chapel."

"In. His. Name." Maggie completed the overview.

"Henry kept saying he'd get the details to me," said the Vicar, now sounding plaintive and not a little defensive. "I only asked him once or twice where the diary was, and he just shrugged it off. Neither of us thought he'd be…that we'd need it this soon. This way."

"Maybe you don't need the diary," ventured Wayne. "Where else could the money be, supposing it's not in the normal bank accounts? In a lock box?"

"Under his mattress? In a sock drawer?"

"Perhaps it's not cash at all." Edward scratched at his chin. "Perhaps it's been invested. Stock certificates? Annuities? Property?

Some art treasures like…."

"Like that clock?" Wayne suggested.

Libby sucked in a sharp breath. She'd admired the clock, certainly. The delicate, white, porcelain angels, with a soft blush of color on their cheeks, their lips. But she'd never said she wanted it or hinted that it would be nice to have. Or …

Detective Grass held up his hand to curb this angle of discussion. "Just a minute," he said.

Everyone turned abruptly, startled, having completely forgotten he was even in the room.

"We've already checked the clock," he reported. "It's nice, but it's not worth any million dollars. From what I'm gathering about Father Henry, the money, so to speak, could be in just about any form. In just about any place."

All the nervous energy at the table sent Phyllis to the plate of sweet rolls. As she eyed the selection of Danish, she noted the flow blue plate under them. "Maybe Edward has something. Henry did go antiquing a lot. Not so much lately, but he used to go all the time."

She turned to Ruth. "Who was that guy with the big, gaudy amethyst ring? He and Henry used to drive to Illinois to some church antique auction or store."

"Sam Cartwright," said Maggie succinctly. "He's dead now."

Phyllis pointed at Maggie in confirmation. "Yes, that's the name. Maybe that's where Henry's money is. Maybe Henry bought priceless works of art."

Wayne jumped in. "Could be right here and we'd never know it. The beneficiaries need to be told. I'll contest!"

The lawyer felt the wind change. He had to stem the tide before the nine inheritors fantasized more than was ever going to be realized. He tried to be reassuring within his given parameters, while not completely sidestepping the truth. "Some of these items have been located."

But mutiny was afoot. Libby, Bernie, and Maggie watched with interest, but were not maniacally involved like the relatives.

Edward drew himself up and demanded. "Where are they? How do we know you received the proper amount for them? That some of that money doesn't rightfully belong to us?"

The lawyer glanced at the detective, then the Vicar, with no visible response from either. "I understand your concern, sir," claimed the lawyer, his somber composure unchanged. He was, undoubtedly, used to this particular challenge and went on unintimidated. "You have my word on it."

"Bah! Don't trust lawyers," barked Edward.

The Vicar's voice topped that. "You have *my* word on it. We have the antiques."

A priest's reassurance was the last thing in the world that would placate Wayne Nichols. "Excuse me, Vicar, but I'm not sure I believe you either. It is, after all, in the Church's best interest to get as much as it can out of this, wouldn't you say?"

The debate was going in the relatives' favor. Self-interest, masquerading as getting what they rightfully deserved, outweighed regard for both the law and the Church.

Edward pressed further, his terseness lost in the shuffle. "I know a little about art and antiques. My sister Catherine here reads about that stuff all the time."

Catherine gave a confident nod at her brother's acknowledgement. Then she agreed with the others. "Maybe we ought to have a look at these treasures."

If a vote was going to be taken, the ayes would definitely win. Even the nonrelatives had joined forces, being sucked in by curiosity, if nothing else.

The lawyer looked to the Vicar. The Vicar looked at the detective that fly on the wall, who folded his arms and gave the smallest shrug of his shoulders.

The Vicar closed his eyes; took a long, slow, meditative breath; and let it out with equal length and deliberation.

When his eyes opened again, he turned, and simply said, "Follow me."

The Pied Piper would have envied such an immediate and complete response.

Bringing up the rear, it was Maggie who hissed in Libby's ear. "The locked room!"

Chapter Twenty-Three

T hree and four abreast they followed the Vicar up the wide rectory staircase; around the landing; and down a long, ominous, unlit hallway with rooms shooting off to the left and right; similar to the setup of rooms on the first floor.

Whether the group of inheritors was awed by a trip into the sacred, forbidden territory of a priest or simply spellbound about finding hidden treasures was hard to say. Whatever the case, no one said a word.

They trooped past Father Henry's private living quarters, a front bedroom, a sitting room, a study, a guest bedroom, bathroom, and several closets. To a small door at the end of the hall.

The Vicar removed a key from his pocket and, without comment, opened the door. He flipped a light switch and stood aside, allowing the mute search party to enter.

The room was like an attic, with bare beams above and exposed wood lath on the walls. A naked lightbulb dangled overhead and sent large, dense shadows bobbing across the space. Which there was not much of. Hardly a large room to begin with, its size was diminished, not only by all the people, but also by the number of objects haphazardly housed there.

Huge, four-foot tall gold candlesticks flanked a crucifix so life-sized and realistic it made the first to come upon it gasp. Against one wall leaned several stained glass windows of different heights depicting well-known apostles and saints. Two ornate monstrances, used to house the consecrated Communion hosts during adoration time, with spikes of gold radiating from their center glass cases, were wedged in by an overflowing box of altar linens near the back.

Attached to each item, in Father Henry's handwriting, were notes that began with the same designation: Chapel. Chapel candlesticks. Chapel linens. Chapel windows. Etc.

The Vicar gave the group ample time to touch, lift, turn, compare, and otherwise examine the items; which they did with utmost thoroughness and in almost complete, stunned silence.

Maggie gave things a cursory glance. She was disappointed to find a bunch of church paraphernalia in the locked room, when for years she had visions of fantastical plunder or some forbidden debauched hobby of her boss.

Bernie saw the items as coming from and going to a place of worship and afforded them their due respect. Many were pieces he fondly remembered from days gone by.

Libby, figuring that none of it was in any way hers to inherit, and not being overly impressed by anything, concluded these were nothing more than things Father Henry had collected to furnish the chapel. In his name, as Maggie had pointed out. Thus Libby stood back to let the more vested persons have their fill of examining. She let her observations shift to the cousins themselves and the idea of how quickly the thought of potential wealth had brought out the mercenary in them all.

Did it also bring out enough greed and jealousy to kill for? Almost everyone in the room was in the running for having committed murder.

With that thought, Libby caught sight of Detective Grass, standing in the shadows, eyeing, not the crazy array of religious objects, but the people looking at them.

Eventually the lot of them wore out, and the Vicar made his case. "As you can see, there are some lovely, even expensive, church artifacts that Father Henry collected. I can assure you, as can Mr.

Becker, our lawyer, that their values have been assessed by more than one—independent—appraiser. While these objects are indeed valuable historically, their total worth does not exceed $10,000. Nowhere near the several million that Henry alluded to. Let me suggest that we all go back downstairs, get some fresh coffee, and see if we can come up with some clues about where to find this diary."

Detective Grass led the beneficiaries downstairs to the kitchen, where they mindlessly fixed hot cups of tea and coffee. It didn't seem to matter. They spoke quietly now, having seen what they had clamored to see and found it wanting.

The detective was getting frustrated. He hadn't known what to expect, but he'd expected more. A tipped hand. One person reacting more than another. Was the killer that clever or had he missed something? Had his attention lapsed during plain, petty, ordinary family bickering?

Under prisms of light from the chandelier, Grass waited until everyone was settled at the dining room table. Then he stood and started his own line of inquiry.

"Apparently no one knows about this money," began the detective, using the official voice he used to woo information from someone not inclined to give it. "What about the chapel? Other than you, Vicar, did Father Henry ever discuss plans for a chapel with anyone?"

They shrugged shoulders and shook heads. No one had any idea of Father's intentions in this matter. In fact, all of them were still dazed and incredulous about the whole diary, chapel to be built in his name, and room full of church artifacts.

The detective reached for his chair from against the wall and pulled it up next to the lawyer. He laced his fingers and set them on the table in front of him. "The people in this room were in Father Henry's closest circle. You're related. Some of you saw him often. Worked with him practically every day. Did you ever see him writing in a journal? In a diary? And that includes you, Vicar."

More head shaking. Including the Vicar's.

"Ever see anything that looked like a notebook or a tablet lying around? Or that he had with him?"

General pondering.

Negative.

"Could it have been on his computer or some other technical gizmo?"

While the cousins from Minnesota considered this a possibility and began enumerating the newest gadgets they were using or that could be used for storing one's personal thoughts, Maggie laughed.

"You obviously didn't know the man. Paper and pencil at best."

Wayne lifted his chin and let an edge of sarcasm have its way. "I assume you've looked through all his things ..."

If the remark was meant to annoy, Detective Grass did not bite. Nor did Maggie.

Instead, the detective dropped his wooing technique and rattled off a summary of the police search. "We went through his apartment upstairs and searched the study, the offices, and all of the other rooms. Twice. Same as the church. First when we were looking for the murder weapon. Then after we learned about the diary. We will search a third time if necessary. We merely thought if someone here ..." He made eye contact with each person as he slowly took a visual sweep around the table. "... if someone here might have information that could be helpful."

Everyone stayed frozen in his or her seat as Grass made another sweep, his eyes wide, inquisitive, expectant.

The detective always hoped for productive results when questioning suspects, but he was not disappointed if it did not happen. This was merely one step in a series of many to get the information he thought they might have—even if they did not realize they had it or would not admit to it at the moment. They might not be ready to give up some detail, or they might not want to share it in front of someone else who was present.

He reached into his shirt pocket and passed a business card to each person at the table. "Please, call me if something occurs to you. Even the smallest, oddest detail could be a clue." He folded his hands again in front of him. "I will say this. I am getting a clear picture that Father Henry had his own particular way of doing things."

With that, Catherine burst out laughing. It was such a hearty, infectious laugh that it set her sister, Helen, followed by Ruth, involuntarily giggling along.

"I'm so sorry, Detective. I know this is serious." Catherine's copper-blonde hair bobbed to the contrary. "It's just that this is all so Grandpa Leo. Nothing I've heard today surprises me at all. Come on," she said, throwing her hands out gaily to the whole table. "The detective's right. We know, knew, Henry better than anyone." She looked specifically at her cousins and siblings. "Grandpa and Henry were two peas in a pod. They hated banks. Didn't trust lawyers." She regarded Mr. Becker to her left. "You must have passed some test for

Henry to let you in on as much as he did." She pushed the sleeves of her sweater up comfortably, as if she were going to pull weeds in the garden on a summer afternoon. "And don't fret, Vicar. We got used to these Felger men and their ways long ago." She gave a chummy nudge to her brother.

It was hard to resist Catherine's teasing. No part of her seemed mean-spirited. Everyone at the table relaxed, hardly realizing how wrought they had become until Catherine's laughter broke the tension.

Libby was happy to find her original impression of Catherine's sense of humor justified. She was equally happy to have someone in the crowd given to being friendly and unaffected.

Edward couldn't totally acquiesce to his sister's playful poke, but his defense was less formal, less biting, than it might have been without it. "We Felger men are a practical lot," he said with no shame or embarrassment. "We're careful about money. We always know where it's coming from and where it's going."

"A little stingy. A little frugal. A little obsessive-compulsive," persisted Catherine. She patted her brother's arm. "Then, once in a while, they're so crazy generous it makes your head spin." She went on more soberly, explaining to those around the table not privy to the family history. "Once Grandpa Leo gave most of the proceeds from selling the farm and land to Henry, Father Henry, it was out of our hands."

Phyllis tried to keep the bitterness out of her voice as she responded to Catherine's comments. It came off as a little loud instead of curious. "Weren't you at all upset when so much went to Henry? After all, he was going to be a priest. What'd he need the money for?"

"But we all got some," Catherine retorted. "All of us grandchildren. Henry just got more. I wasn't surprised. No one should have been. Like I said, two peas in a pod. Grandpa and Henry. I honestly think Henry was more like a son than a grandson. Besides, it was Grandpa's money. Same as this is Henry's. I've got no claim on it."

Wayne slumped in his chair at the end of the table. "Easy for you to say."

Phyllis squared her shoulders. "Would have made my life easier then. Could help now."

Ruth smiled benignly. "Maybe we've got everything we need, Phyllis. God has provided generously by comparison to others. Maybe we should just be thankful."

Pushing her chair back, Catherine stood and brushed a few crumbs of Danish from her lap. "I got a nice trip paid for and five thousand dollars I didn't have yesterday. We could do worse than have the money go for a chapel. I figure by now Grandpa has met God and found Him not so despicable."

No one of authority, not lawyer nor Vicar nor detective, rose to detain her. Catherine shook each person's hand. As she politely addressed Detective Grass, she said, "I'm sorry I can't help you with the diary business. If Henry stays true to Grandpa Leo's lead, it could be anywhere. And I mean anywhere. Somewhere truly odd and hidden. Or simply right under our noses."

She took one of the detective's cards. Everyone followed suit, in at least an outward show of cooperation; and since there was little else to deal with, they all stood and began disassembling.

Libby and Maggie crossed into the study, where Dunkirk and Calico Two had found refuge away from the uproar in the dining room, curled into and cushioned by the out-of-town cousins' coats.

"They're probably all allergic to cats," Maggie said, gently shooing the animals aside. She brushed off the coat on top of the pile and gathered up the others, tossing them over her arm.

Libby swooped up the scarves and gloves that had broken away from their moorings. "What did you think of the locked room?"

"It all made sense once we heard about the chapel," said Maggie.

"Yeah," said Libby, her amazement rekindled. "What about that? And what about the diary? Kind of crazy. Kind of ..."

"Typical." Maggie finished Libby's sentence as she lugged the coats into the hallway. "Typical Henry. Typical priest. Off on their own cloud. Never thinking about how things are going to affect anyone else. 'Course, you get that pretty little clock. It's certainly one of the nicer things he picked up. Less overtly religious. Angels are bearable. And Bernie, here, you hit the jackpot."

Bernie rounded the corner, nearly crashing into the two women and their load of coats. "Oops! What? Oh. The car. I still can't believe it."

Maggie playfully bumped the organist with her bundle of coats. "Practically brand-new."

"I … I don't deserve it," stammered Bernie.

"And you don't deserve a hand-delivered coat either," Libby joked, flicking her head back toward the study. "We figured you were used to fending for yourself."

Not far behind Bernie, Phyllis was cornering the Vicar. Libby watched her block the priest's way and heard her speak to him in a soothing, restrained way. "Now, Vicar. Just when did Father Henry come up with this chapel idea?"

Not far behind Phyllis, Wayne was keeping an ear to his cousin's conversation with the priest.

"He started planning it several years ago." The Vicar was obviously pleased. "It was truly generous of him."

Phyllis agreed sweetly. "Yes. Truly. That was probably before Ruth and I moved into the parish. Before we welcomed Henry into our homes. Before we all really connected as family. Henry always teased us on the holidays that we would receive our reward for our kindness. Not that we ever expected anything," she demurred. "I was thinking, perhaps he set aside more than was necessary for the chapel, for inflation and such. Perhaps once the building is completed, what might be left over could be divided, equally, of course, among the cousins. That's something you, as the executor of the will, would surely see as the fair way to handle the excess. We were all commenting on how a modest chapel would surely be most in keeping with Henry's humble way of life."

Before the Vicar could respond, Phyllis said with a sincere pat on his arm, "But let's not talk about material things at the moment. Better that we all pray to know God's will."

She turned and floated away, waving to catch her out-of-town relatives' attention.

As Detective Grass sidestepped the Vicar and approached the small group in the hallway, Bernie turned around and walked into the study for his coat.

The detective stood next to Libby. "Your favorite suspect didn't get much of a motive boost today, did he?" Before Libby could react, he added, "Actually, you and Fruehauf came out on top. Unless Ms. Mueller's cats are some rare breed worth a fortune that we missed."

"As far as Ms. Mueller is aware," said Maggie, "the cats were both rescue babies. If you'll excuse me, I need to get these coats to their owners."

The detective stepped toward Maggie. "I'm sorry. May I help you with those?"

"I've got them, thank you. In fact, Libby, if you give me those scarves and things, I'll deliver those at the same time." She collected everything from Libby and was gone before the other two could object.

Detective Grass wasted no time and continued as if Libby and he were in the middle of a friendly chat. "Did you know you were getting the clock?"

"No. Not a clue."

"What do you know about it?"

"Nothing about its worth. I did admire it. Father Henry pointed it out when we had a dinner meeting in the dining room once. I have a small mantel above my fireplace where it will look nice."

"It's worth about $1,500."

"Are you serious?"

"We had it appraised. Wanted to see how much everyone was inheriting."

Even with his chatty, companionable tone, Libby bristled. It felt like an intrusion. As if a gift for her had been opened by someone else first. An arrogant someone like Detective Grass.

"Any reason Father Henry singled you out for such a gift?"

Libby looked squarely at Detective Grass, to see if she was misreading a man whose job it was to ask questions or if his implication was serious. "I admired the clock one time. I did a lot for Father Henry."

That didn't sound right.

She tried again. "There were a lot of little things, like editing his fundraiser letter or coming in early to help set up for Mass. We were …" Libby stopped. This was not going in the direction she wanted.

"Sounds very chummy," the detective said.

No, he wasn't gloating at her discomfort or goading her to say something she didn't want to. It was all of her own doing.

And that drove her nuts.

"We worked together." She repeated the words, emphasizing *worked*.

"And in all that working together, did you and Father Henry somehow ever *not* get along?"

Libby became more wary. "What are you aiming at?"

"Let's say, at a Parish Council meeting maybe? Heard you could get pretty steamed. Something about girl altar boys, girl servers, I guess. What they should wear?"

"What they should wear should be the same as the boys."

"Kind of a women's rights thing? Sort of a feminist take on it?"

Libby wasn't sure which was pushing her buttons more—being reminded of the stupid opposing Council members at the time or the fact that people were still blabbing about it, focusing more on her reaction than the underlying injustice she was responding to.

"Depends on who you heard it from," she said.

The detective remained passive, as if this was the least important conversation he'd had all day. "It happened at a parish meeting. Kind of public knowledge. I understand you got pretty angry."

The less a person seemed to get Libby's point of view on what she considered a meaningful subject, the more she felt she had to make it clear. She hadn't backed down at the Parish Council meeting; she wouldn't back down now. "Yeah. I was angry."

"Must be important to you."

"It is important to me. Very important." Her voice had gone up several notes before she knew it. The defense flew out of her mouth as quickly and sharply as if the meeting had just gotten underway. "Father Henry saw nothing, *nothing*, wrong with dressing those boy servers in cassocks and surplices like little priests. Not the girls. No, the girls had to wear some garb with a slash of material down the front that looked like an apron. He thought it looked like a cross, but a woman knows an apron when she sees it. Servitude. Anything to keep women in line."

"They don't make generic, unisex robes?"

"Of course they do. But not for St. Hedwig's. Tried to placate me by saying we're lucky girls are on the altar at all." Libby glanced at the detective. He had a quizzical look on his face. "You're not Catholic, are you?" Libby asked.

"No. Is that a prerequisite for all this?"

"You don't understand. There's a part of the Church going backward, running to the past so fast. Those bishops. Those male bishops. They could rescind the 'privilege' of girl servers any day they want. Some of them already say it's up to the pastor. And some pastors say no."

She had to meditate more. Where was the peace of deep breathing when she needed it?

Bernie reentered the hallway just as Libby was proclaiming her last point. He slid an avuncular arm around her shoulder. "Sounds like Ms. Libby is firing up."

Many people irked Libby, but Bernie Fruehauf had always escaped the quick annoyance she jumped to with so many others. Maybe because he never patronized her. Okay, a little manipulative sometimes to get her to help with church music chores, which she did enjoy doing, but he had a knack for naively stating the obvious when she was so perilously engrossed in an argument. In some ways, he was good for her, like an uncle, a brother, helping her not to take things so seriously—if he could catch her in time.

Libby took one of those deep breaths and tried to regain her composure. This was just what Grass wanted—to see how angry he could get her. The fury almost re-ignited as she realized how she'd fallen into his trap.

Another deep breath. Thanks goodness she'd been able to keep Father from knowing about her singing at Deb Draper's upcoming ordination. A conversation about a woman priest? Grass would love digging into that. A sure-fire explosion.

More breathing. Libby was happily able to latch onto Bernie's presence for a diversion.

Meanwhile, Detective Grass smiled inwardly. He had gotten what he wanted from Libby Kinder as far as how easily she could be provoked and how strong her feelings were, especially about certain issues. He was only too happy to steer his attention to Bernie.

Grass gave a congratulatory nod to the organist. "Nice new car, eh, Mr. Fruehauf? Was it a surprise, like Ms. Kinder's clock, or expected like Ms. Mueller's cats?"

Bernie worked to unravel the question. "How do you mean?"

"Did you and Father Henry ever talk about him leaving you his car?"

Normally on guard with the detective, Bernie was relieved to have a straightforward answer to what seemed like a simple question. "We talked about how bad mine was. Oh, I guess sometimes he'd say he'd leave me his, and I'd say I'd leave him mine. Like we joked about putting each other in our wills. But it was just something we joked about. He always got these fancy new cars, and I'd drive mine till they fell apart."

Libby watched helplessly as her friend walked into the same trap she had just left. On one level, she understood the detective was doing his job. On the other, she hated the constant insinuation that she or the people she cared about were criminals. Always with dark, ulterior motives.

"Bernie's one of the frugal Germans," she said lightly. "Always been more practical than indulgent."

Bernie regarded all this as a point of pride. "Eighteen years in the one I'm driving now." He gave a thoughtful pause. "I always figured the next car I got would be my last. Considering my age. I guess people do drive into their eighties and nineties."

The detective went on pleasantly. "Nice not to have to worry about money for a new one."

"Oh, yes. With my small pension. A big save." Bernie dropped his voice. "It was awfully nice of Henry to do this. You know, he didn't have to leave me anything. I didn't expect anything."

"I understand you were pretty good friends. Knew each other a long time. Worked together. Even traveled together."

"Once in a while."

"Ever get mad at each other? A friendly spat about something?"

"Bernie never has a …"

The look Detective Grass shot Libby clamped her mouth shut before she finished her sentence. He might as well have been a nun from her grade school days. For all her perceived outspokenness, Libby's be-a-good-girl bones could still be tapped. Besides, she thought, she had to start accepting the fact that the detective approached everyone with the same suspicious mind.

"Not really," Bernie said sincerely.

"All those years? Never?"

Bernie had been taught by the good nuns as well. He hesitated, but eventually conceded. "Oh. I suppose. Nothing ever very big really."

Voices rose in the parlor and came into the hallway as the lawyer, surrounded by the Vicar and Father Henry's family, made their way to the front door. The conversation in the hallway was no longer private.

The detective lowered his voice. Even while keeping a pleasantness in his tone, he did not avoid sounding firm as he spoke to the organist standing next to him. "Sometimes people can get pretty upset about not very big things."

He then turned squarely to the cantor. "Or things that are really important to them."

That was Father Henry's will.

Libby and Bernie heard Maggie lock the door behind them as they paused outside on the big, brick, rectory porch.

"It's not that cold," observed Libby, "but it sure is damp. Feels like it could snow any minute. Didn't they say it wouldn't begin till tonight?"

Bernie adjusted his wool cap, fussed with his wool scarf, and started down the steps.

"Bernie?"

"Huh?" he asked absentmindedly.

She followed him down the cement steps and saw that his thoughts were somewhere else. "It doesn't matter. I was just talking about the snow."

Bernie squinted at the gray clouds puffing in on top of an even darker, puffier layer. "Yes. It's clouding up." Wriggling his fingers into thick gloves he added, "I'm sorry, Libby. Talking to that detective kind of upset me."

Libby scanned the sky herself. "Me, too," she admitted and tucked her scarf up close to her ears.

They continued down the rectory steps together.

"Kind of takes the edge off your new car, doesn't it?" Libby's attempt to humor Bernie was short-lived when she saw that his eyes were beginning to water.

"You know I don't care about that car," he said with little emotion and walked on.

As Libby opened her car door, she watched Bernie cross the street, past the detective's car to his old car a few yards down. He looked small and bent. All those years leaning over an organ had given him a permanent stoop. Today it was more pronounced in a way only sadness and grief could weigh a person down.

Libby understood. Given how everything had come about, the porcelain clock with hovering angels meant very little to her.

Chapter Twenty-Four

Nothing until a meeting at four." Namita tromped down the indoor apartment foyer steps with Paki, where Libby stood with Dash, leashed and ready to go.

A few large, fluffy flakes of snow greeted them outside: Namita, in an oversized army surplus jacket; Libby, re-bundled for the walk, changed out of the good clothes she'd worn to the reading of Father Henry's will.

Namita inhaled deeply. "Aren't they beautiful?" Snowflakes dotted her black hair before they melted into it like butter sinking into a piece of hot toast. "Want to walk through the park?"

Dash and Paki, both familiar with *walk* and *park*, set their noses in the air and their sights in that direction, revved for a nice, long trek. They were wonderfully accustomed to each other; Dash's quick, short, dachshund-terrier steps marking double-time to Paki's long-legged stride.

The snowflakes landed on the sidewalks, cleared of what had fallen Saturday night and ready to take on the new layer that was predicted to fall.

The foursome took their typical route down Apple Street. Except for the tree-lined sidewalks that unified block after block, the neighborhood boasted the variety of architecture that was the norm when it was settled in the mid-1900s. Most houses were two-story homes with an occasional bungalow interjected. There were brick houses with large porches and wood houses with shutters and modest, canopied stoops. Usually Libby delighted in the variety and liked to take note of how different weather affected their looks.

Not today.

Libby had not meant to, but because Namita was such a good listener, Libby had soon disclosed most of the events from the morning, including the cousins' inheritance and her clock, the locked room, and the chapel to be built in Father Henry's memory.

And Detective Grass's conversation.

"How could I have been so easily lulled into thinking I was off the hook?" a disheartened Libby asked. "Exactly like in the books. The way police flush you out. Make you say things to trip you up somehow. What was I thinking?" she said with exasperation. "This is a murder investigation. A real murder. And we're all, including me, suspects. For murder."

Namita knew things were serious, that Libby was rightfully concerned. But there was no need to add to the fear beginning to take root in Libby.

Instead, Namita's reaction was droll, her voice several octaves lower. "You sound a little unnerved."

Libby sailed on. "Every time this Detective Grass talks to me, he makes me feel like I'm the main person he's considering."

"How endearing."

"Maybe that's why Lawrence Davis—he's a detective from the parish—wouldn't tell me much. If I'm really that high on the list, I've got to figure this out," said Libby with conviction. "At least how to get myself out of the running."

"Well. It seems to me," Namita said, stretching her gloved hand out to catch the free-falling flakes, "you either need to knock down your own qualifications … and/or build up someone else's."

How reasonable, thought Libby. How logical. How hopeful.

"Hmmm. Yes. You're right," agreed Libby. She frowned. "Wonder how you do that."

"Is it too early to get everybody in a room and let Hercule Poirot eliminate you one-by-one?"

"Afraid so."

"Is it a large contingent we're considering?"

"Not really," Libby explained. "Mostly we made the cut if we had a key to the church. And the alarm code."

Namita tugged at Paki, who was burying his nose to locate a scent hidden in a pile of dirty, old snow. Besides listening, this renter had come with a researcher's knack for asking questions and pressing for more than perfunctory answers, irreverently as they may be worded. "I thought the holy guy was killed outside. Why is having a key to the church such a deal breaker?"

"They think the murder weapon was from the church. Only somebody with a key could have gotten a hold of it."

"The keys can't be duplicated?"

"No. You need authorization. So that would be me; Maggie, the church secretary; Bernie, the organist; Daniel who decorates; and Wayne, the custodian.

"Hmmm. No Colonel Mustard. Is Wayne our ex-con?"

"The very one."

"And that's all who have a key to that big church?"

Libby brushed away some snowflakes sticking on her eyelashes. "Big church; small congregation. Actually big, old, inner-city church. Maggie said a few other people do have keys, but they seem unlikely candidates."

"Don't be dismissive," Namita cautioned. "Those are just the sort who pop out of the shadows with some twisted motive."

"Ted. Doyal, head of Buildings and Grounds. In Arizona for the month."

"Okay. Dismissed."

"Lavina Woodson. Parish Council President. Can't imagine a motive. Retired bookkeeper. No husband, no kids, takes care of her elderly father. Runs the big chili supper in the fall. A good, practical person. Keeps the parish on the right track."

"She has a key? And the code?"

"A key, but not the code."

"Could be a pickled herring."

"Red."

"Pickled red herring."

Libby took a long sideways look at Namita, who didn't flinch. The upstairs renter finally cracked the smallest edge of a smile. "Trying to add a little levity to your plight."

Reaching to slap her knee for the joke, Libby nearly slipped. The snow was no longer melting but was covering the sidewalk and hiding the occasional patch of ice. That and the dog tugging her forward, made her footing precarious. "I guess I could check to see if Lavina has an alibi. Or not."

She recovered her balance, but proceeded more gingerly. "Guess we should be careful. Snow's coming down harder."

The park appeared just ahead—six city blocks tucked into an otherwise residential area. It was a fortunate aspect of this established neighborhood that the city planners had set aside such a fine plot of nature for the nearby residents to enjoy. Libby never ceased feeling lucky and grateful to live within walking distance.

Libby and Namita and the dogs came to a halt as the street dead-ended into the park entrance. The snow gave a soft gauzy look to the bare trees standing guard around the small pond. Clumps of fir trees outlined a soccer field and playground, both uninhabited on this wintry afternoon.

Namita checked with her walking companion. "Still game?"

She was. "I love this place in the summer," Libby replied, "when it's full of kids playing and picnickers and joggers. But it's so peaceful and pretty in the winter. Besides, we can't disappoint the dogs."

The dogs got their way and the entourage crossed into the park, heading west on the paved path around the soccer field.

Namita resumed the investigation. "Anybody else outside the little key club who could get access?"

"Not officially with a key. Wayne supposedly leaves the back door of church open sometimes. Says he's always downstairs in his workshop or out in the church when he's waiting for a delivery. Not sure he's reliable on that score. Maybe he left it open accidentally. Or on purpose."

"Does that mean you're expanding your suspect list to include the surrounding neighborhood at large, the whole central part of town, or just the city in general?"

Libby paused to give this some serious thought, even though Namita's exaggeration was meant to be only half so. "This doesn't seem to be that random," said Libby. Was that just a feeling or did the circumstances she'd been reflecting on bring her to that conclusion? "On the other hand, we were all—police included—willing to blame Billy, Antonio's nephew, for a random, spur-of-the-moment crime."

Namita held Paki from racing after a squirrel. The dachshund strain in Dash barked in support of the endeavor.

"I was thinking more of the cousins," continued Libby, firmly holding Dash until the squirrel scrambled up the trunk of a willow tree into a hole and out of the snow.

"As in cousins collectively?"

"Two really. The ones here, in town. They belong to the parish. Although not for that long. They're kind of a Mutt-and-Jeff, tall-and-short team. Okay, maybe just one of them. Cousin Ruth seems genuinely upset. Like she cared about Father Henry. Used to bring him cookies and cake and things. But Cousin Phyllis ... she's a big girl. Could have easily done the hitting on the head part. They were both in the will. Thought they were going to inherit money that Father Henry had gotten from their grandfather."

"And they have a key?"

"No. But ex-con Wayne is their cousin, too. They could all use his." Libby frowned again. "They don't really seem to like each other, though, Wayne and the ladies. Or even act connected. I didn't know they were related until practically the reading of the will this morning."

The quartet turned to come around by the playground, lonesome swings filling with snow, swinging on their own as the wind made its presence known. Namita lifted her royal-blue scarf, which matched Paki's, from around her neck and pulled it up to cover her snow-dusted hair. "Means. Motive. Opportunity," she proclaimed.

Libby leaned against the wind, blinking into the snow. "Everybody had opportunity—access to keys and code. Either directly—me, Maggie, Bernie, Daniel, Wayne, and Lavina—or indirectly, the in-town cousins. I suppose, even though it is remote, the out-of-town cousins too, through Wayne. Or in cahoots with Wayne."

"Cahoots," repeated Namita with glee. "What a terrific word."

Libby gave a short officious bow. "Very technical."

"Proceed."

"Therefore, they all had access to the means. To the thurible."

Namita grimaced. "That's the name of the means?"

"Yes. A censer. For the incense. A thurible. Sorry, more technical terms."

Namita stopped, turned, and this time looked directly at Libby. "The fact that you know the proper name for the murder weapon would alone be enough for me to arrest you."

Libby's swiped at her wet cheeks. "Oh, great."

The dogs had slowed, pushing against the wind, their coats beading up with snow as it fell faster and heavier.

"It is beautiful out here, but I'm getting cold," said Namita. "And all this police work is making me hungry. Want to detour around to the Muffin House? I have money."

Libby flipped her own scarf, blown loose, back tight around her neck. "Hot tea? Lovely. What about the dogs?"

"As long as they're leashed I think they'll be all right."

Namita reeled in Paki and shifted directions. "Let's go be in cahoots!"

~ ~ ~

Maggie loaded the last cups and saucers into the rectory dishwasher. As she pressed enough buttons to make it hum, she felt a familiar head butting at her ankles. With a well-practiced swoosh, she lifted Calico Two, cradling the cat like an infant in her arms. The cat's lemon-yellow eyes gazed lovingly back at her.

"Oh, Callie" cooed Maggie. "He had a diary. Just what do you think he wrote about me in that?"

Calico Two heard the footsteps first and jumped down to hide behind the trash bin at the end of the kitchen counter. Maggie turned to see the red Tartan scarf in the doorway.

"I'm leaving. Everyone else is gone."

Detective Grass stepped aside to let Dunkirk nonchalantly amble into the kitchen and saunter over to his water bowl.

"Will you be taking the cats home, now that they're officially yours?"

Maggie wiped her hands on a dish towel and folded it neatly. "I'll probably leave them here a little longer, now that things are settling down. With no place in the rectory off limits to me, I can track them anywhere. Besides, they're comfortable here. Still getting my two animals prepared for their arrival anyway."

"I've been told they are actually expensive cats, as far as cats go. Valuable."

"By definition. By breed," said Maggie. "Not by circumstance. Father Henry rescued both of them from the shelter. I'm not sure dubious lineage like that gives them much value. But expensive? To me, they are. Long-haired Persians that need lots of trips to the groomer unless you brush them every day. Both of these have delicate stomachs and dry skin. Lots of trips to the vet."

The detective took the coat tossed over his arm and began to put it on. "And what about your job here at the rectory?"

Maggie hung the small towel to dry on the door under the kitchen sink. "The Vicar definitely wants me to keep running things until a new priest is appointed. After that, it all depends. If the new pastor is happy that everything is already set up and running smoothly, that somebody's in place he can work with and who knows all the books, contacts, routines, essential people and such, I stay. Sometimes there's a clash. Priests can be territorial, particularly about how things are handled, or they can come with their own secretaries. Then, I'm out."

"Does that happen very often?"

Maggie shrugged her shoulders.

"So you're in a decently secure position."

Maggie couldn't tell if it was a statement or question.

Calico Two ventured out from behind the bin, but stuck close to Maggie's legs. Dunkirk had plopped next to the water bowl, content to monitor the situation from a low vantage point.

Detective Grass regarded the cats. He did not have pets. Maybe his kids had a guinea pig, once. Didn't have them in his own childhood. It was not a connection he missed or, frankly, one he understood. He could see people cared almost inordinately about whatever animal they had in their lives. But it didn't register to him as anything other than an added chore, expense, and responsibility. The whole attraction mystified him.

"Do animals really miss people? Do you think they know Father Henry's gone?"

Maggie eyed Detective Grass, standing in the doorway, keeping his distance. "You don't have pets, do you?" she asked.

The question was rhetorical. She did not wait for an answer but leaned down to run her hand gently along Calico Two's side.

"They're curled together, sound asleep on his pillow upstairs, whenever I get here."

Chapter Twenty-Five

Once the women were unbundled and seated, they rubbed their hands together, partly to warm them and partly in hungry anticipation as they decided on and ordered the Tea-for-Two special.

Within minutes, a miniature cobalt-blue pot of steaming jasmine tea for Libby and a daisy-covered pot of Earl Grey for Namita arrived; along with four right-out-of-the-oven muffins of choice placed on a small doily.

Dash and Paki, patiently awaited crumbs from their spot on the floor near their mistresses' feet. With only a few afternoon customers, the ladies had practically first choice of tables, and had chosen one near a window, which kept the falling snow in view but without the blustery wind.

The Muffin House was a cheery shop: a renovated, brick firehouse flanked by a candy store and small library on a well-traveled street that cut through Libby's neighborhood, a neighborhood that otherwise saw sparse and only local traffic.

Inside, the Muffin House was white—white walls, white tablecloths, white-painted chairs. Besides the pleasant, clean feeling this gave, white was the perfect backdrop for the colorful mixed and matched teacups, pots, and vases that brightened up each of the eight tiny tables. Tea brewing and muffins perpetually baking sent an intoxicating aroma above companionable chatter and invited all to linger in the cozy atmosphere.

Namita inhaled the ambience and let out a satisfied sigh. "Let's talk motive."

Libby unfolded a white paper napkin, smoothed out its creases, and began to write with a pen borrowed from their young waitress. She put down each person's name on her list of suspects. Her letters were neat, her mind clear. She was ready to tackle this part of the puzzle.

Namita reached for sugar. "You first."

Libby looked up. "Me?"

Namita was unfazed. "Have to be thorough. No one gets a free pass. Might as well rule you out right away." She stopped stirring abruptly. "Unless there is something you want to … talk … about?"

"No," Libby said immediately. "Happy to be ruled out first." Libby selected an almond-date muffin and laid out her most recent cause for concern. "I got an antique clock. In the will," she stated.

"Fancy? Expensive? Something to die for?"

"More than I'd ever pay for a clock. Not, however, anything I'd kill for."

Namita stirred her tea daintily. "From what you've always said, it sounded like everything was more than okay between you and Father Henry. Would that be a fair assessment? No friction?"

Reaching for a small white ramekin filled with delicate butter curls, Libby said, "There were, I suppose, things I irritated Father Henry about. Things he irritated me about. I'd say it was a draw."

"Is that how it works? You tick him off, he ticks you off, and that cancels out everything? Presto. No motive?"

Libby hesitated, caught between flippant humor and serious defense. "Not … quite."

Namita went on airily. "What was the subject of these ticking-off matches?"

"Once in a while he'd go xenophobic on me, but generally he was ethnically open-minded. Gave homilies about welcoming immigrants into the neighborhood—but he did have a burr up his butt about Muslims. Thinks they're all rabid militants. I'm sure he's never met one." Libby quickly took a bite of muffin before the butter she'd slathered on could slip away. "He was also," she said, pausing to swallow, "staunchly opposed to people of other faiths, now that I think of it. He was cordial, never rude to their faces, but underneath I think he felt that old Catholic superiority. Us versus Them. And God forbid, literally, if you were Catholic and left the fold. The ultimate betrayal in his eyes." The tea was very hot, so Libby carefully sipped across the top. "Mainly, we got into it over women's rights."

Namita, too, sipped her tea carefully. "Talk about Us versus Them."

"I could understand some of his opposition to other faiths. Not agree with it, but understand it. It seemed like a God thing, understandable. Henry's area of expertise."

Before Libby could go on, Namita broke in. Setting her cup down she said, "I might not be any help here, Libby. I was brought up with a Hindu mother and a father who started out Methodist, but who didn't keep up with it. Certainly didn't pass many teachings onto me. Personally, I feel strongly about our spiritual nature, about having an appreciation for our existence."

Libby stared out the window. The snow had such an easy drift to it, steadily falling without hindrance, without a plan or destination. Namita's words fell with equal lightness, as if they were not connected to such a heavy subject.

"Again, personally, I think God, or the Creator, is bigger, more dimensional, than most traditional Catholics, as far as I can tell, give the concept credit for." She dropped a few crumbs of muffin for each dog. "Did you and your priest clash about mostly contemporary issues or down-to-the-core tenets?"

"We never discussed the basics. I knew how he felt. At least, I was pretty sure. Since it was the same as I was taught and grew up with, it was something I could leave alone. Nothing I felt I had a leg to stand on for arguing against or wanted to change his mind on. Not the same as how I felt about people's rights."

Libby leaned forward on her elbows and wrapped her fingers around her tea cup, as if embracing something warm and tangible would help. "To be honest, I'm a little muddled on my own exact belief in this area. I seem to be constantly revising my concept of God, Creator, Being, Power, Energy. I don't have a strict or clear position, but I'm not so positive that Father Henry's thinking was, is, all wrong either. Not sure. But women," she said, her eyes narrowing over the fragrant brew, "our rights, our place in the scheme of things. We're in the same clan, for heaven's sake."

"Women's rights. That's a bit broad. Anything specific that got you roaring?"

Libby launched into the brouhaha over servers' outfits. It wasn't the only example, but it had been so recently brought up and hashed over, it's what she immediately jumped to—the boys looking like little priests to encourage their aspirations in that direction; the girls looking like servants. She also had to admit that this was particular to St. Hedwig's. Not every parish had this rule. Some places were better, some worse, in her eyes.

She always started out sounding reasonable. She drank tea to slow herself down, but Namita being a neophyte about the Catholic Church's centuries-long repression of women skyrocketed Libby's dissertation on the matter through the roof in no time.

"Maybe you need to be a Unitarian," Namita said calmly. "Something less rigid. We don't have servers. Everybody is a server. We feel like we're all in this together."

Libby took a breath, let her shoulders, which had reached ear level, relax. "Sounds like our Franciscans."

"The ones in the sandals? The brown robes with the hoods?"

"Not all of them do robes and sandals, but you're in the right ballpark. Their role model, St. Francis, was more of the 'no servants' type."

"Are they still Catholic?"

Libby smiled at the thought of the can of worms she was on the verge of opening to explain religious orders in the Catholic Church and decided it was better to save the long version for another time. "Yes, we come in a variety of flavors. Underlying doctrines the same; slightly different takes on application and spiritual priorities." She had to laugh. "The Franciscans are actually a lot about being a servant. In service to others. They would probably put the boys in those apron outfits, too."

Namita shared more poppy seed muffin with Paki and Dash, who happily snatched the morsels out of her hand. When no more was forthcoming, they reluctantly settled back into nap positions and fell into soft-snoring sleep.

Wiping her fingers and pouring more tea, Namita said, "Let's get back to a motive for you. So. Were you angry enough about the server outfits to bean your priest on the head? Seriously."

"Seriously? No. Besides, that meeting was several months ago."

"And people are still talking about it?"

Libby hung her head. "I was rather vocal."

"I guess," said Namita. "Nothing more recent?"

Libby considered the last months. No topics they had wrestled with came to mind.

Except.

Except there in the background lurked one *potential* for contention: Deb Draper's—a woman's—impending ordination. To become a priest. That Libby was singing at. Undoubtedly, Father Henry would rather she not, but as far as she knew, he didn't even know about it. Not having had any conversation about this allowed Libby to feel justified at keeping the subject right there where it was— in the background. "Nothing" she said, " that we've actually disagreed on. Had any confrontation on."

Namita studied her landlady and tea partner. Libby over-circled the loops of the L in her name on the napkin.

Libby looked up when she realized Namita was waiting. "No," said Libby bluntly. "We weren't ticking each other off at the moment."

"Okay, then," Namita said resolutely. "I say you're good. For now." She lifted her cup, grinned devilishly, and asked, "Who's next?"

Libby passed over her name with the mutilated first letter and went to the next suspect. "Maggie. Church secretary. She was seen taking her daughter to the Women's Health Clinic. The evil ones would have her getting an abortion, but it was for birth control pills."

"For her or her daughter?"

"She's widowed. Not that that rules her out."

"Isn't her daughter married?"

"And a student. And poor. And, in my opinion, too immature to have a child at this point. Wants children later. The Church …"

"Don't tell me," interrupted Namita. "If the Church won't let girls wear male server outfits, they're not going to let them have control of the care and maintenance of their own bodies. Not to mention be responsible for planning their own families. I've heard about this in the news. Didn't know how far it had gone."

"The Church, Father Henry, I presume, would say it was immoral to prevent any pregnancy. That they were being selfish, thwarting God's plan. Only looking out for themselves, their own needs."

"As opposed to looking out for the child's, who's going to be brought into a world of possible poverty and raised by adolescent love alone? Are you thinking Maggie and Father Henry argued about that?"

"Maggie's an employee of the Church. There's a code of ethics she works under. She might have been the one Father Henry was going to fire. Which is something he said he was going to do the morning he was killed. Maggie's been at St. Hedwig's fifteen years. She has limited education and experience. Not that she isn't really good at what she does, but in this economy, where's she going to get another job? A new pastor could possibly mean job security. At least, it would buy her time. Keep this clinic trip off her resume."

Namita wrinkled her nose. "Seems a little thin for murder. Are you sure that's why she went to the clinic? And if it is, the daughter broke the rules, not the mother."

"I'm not sure how the code works. Just being a Church employee and being seen at such a clinic, to some, would be scandalous. Or seen as encouraging the forbidden behavior."

Namita was not won over.

Libby reworked her theory. "Let's push it to a heated argument about the scandal, the ethics violation, and being fired. All three."

"A crime of passion."

Libby sat back. She let this motive sink in.

"That would be Daniel, too. The guy who takes care of decorating the church. Also possibly in line to be fired. Gay. Living with another man for, I'd say, at least ten years. Recently they've been more open though. Marching for gay rights. According to his partner, it sounded like they really counted on Daniel's job at St. Hedwig's to help keep them afloat financially."

Daniel. A new suspect to consider.

Namita paused to evaluate the circumstance and motives Libby described. She swirled the last swallow of tea. "Hey," she said, setting down her cup. "Maybe the murder was *indirect* passion." She looked out the window, envisioning all the satellite human connections one has, as if Daniel was one of her Potentials and she was set on unraveling his current entanglements. "Maybe someone, like a partner, killed Father Henry for someone else. They were angry, but angry about the treatment of someone they cared about. Maybe the motive was more personal."

"Hmmm." Libby began a row of perfect squares down the left side of her napkin. "Hadn't thought about that." The last square reached the bottom and Libby let her pen hover above the perfectly drawn boxes. "Maggie and I were definitely protective of Daniel. Both of us are outraged at the Church's position on the whole gay thing. If I thought Father Henry was going to fire Daniel, I'd be mad. I'm angry about Maggie's predicament, too."

"Whoa," Namita edged in before Libby's voice could start its ascent. "I did not mean for that to point the finger back at you."

"No. No, not good," Libby agreed quickly. "Curb that thinking. Dismiss it."

"I was only thinking who else would be affected if anyone on your list was fired. A spouse, let's say. A partner."

Libby couldn't fathom Paul Thomas doing anything so brutal. Then again, if he believed his life with Daniel, their happy family unit was in jeopardy …

"What about a daughter? What about Maggie's daughter?" Libby suggested. "I don't know her that well. She doesn't seem like the type, but I'm out of my element on that score. Nobody on this paper seems like the type."

The waitress brought fresh hot water and new bags for their teapots.

"It's just a thought," said Namita, removing the old tea bag to a saucer and dunking the new one into her pot. "It would mean they had to steal the key, that day, at just the right time."

"And somehow get the access code to turn off the alarm. A lot to do spur-of-the-moment."

"They would have had to feel the threat of Daniel or Maggie being fired and then acted. I agree. A lot to do at the last minute."

Libby consulted her napkin of suspects. "Okay. I'd say unlikely, but I'll let that simmer for the time being." She checked off three names: Libby, Daniel, Maggie. "Bernie's next."

"Which one is Bernie?"

"The organist. He got Father Henry's car in the will."

"Somebody would kill for a car?"

"Normally I'd put Bernie low on the list."

Namita grinned as she poured the fresh, hot tea. "He gets extra points for that. It's always the character you least suspect."

Libby split open another muffin, still warm enough to melt the generous smear of butter she spread on it. "Well, this character is practically living at poverty level. As a diocesan employee, his pension is probably enough for groceries, the basics. He told me recently he couldn't afford to move into the apartment complex he'd always hoped to when it came time to sell his parents' modest house."

"Does he have a car?"

"About twenty years old. Needs brakes. Eats oil and gas."

"That would be a no. Did he understand he was in Father Henry's will? That he was getting the car?"

"He said not. He said they joked about it. About leaving each other their cars. Maybe he did know. If I were being thorough, I'd have to figure Bernie is seventy-six years old, on a fixed income supplemented by social security and playing funerals all over town for extra money. Don't know how long he'll be able to get around like that or even have the mental and physical agility to play the organ."

Libby caught a large drip of butter on her chin. "If anything, it would have been a crime of desperation. The other piece would be that, on the surface, the gift cards might have been tempting. Except all of us with keys could have stolen them outright any weekend. And Bernie, more than anyone, would have had to override the longstanding relationship, friendship, he had with Father Henry. They go way back. Traveled together. Have very little friction personally."

Both women checked on the snow falling more heavily outside and patted their respective charges slumbering at their sides.

They were down to the last on the list.

Wayne.

Namita had already heard about Wayne. His being related to Father Henry. And the cousins. Who Namita thought fell a little too neatly into the murder-mystery suspect category.

"I could be happy with neat," said Libby. "I'm afraid my opinion of Wayne puts him on equal footing in that same regard." Libby described how Wayne, even if she discounted the ex-con factor, was truly an unpleasant, self-centered guy. Creepy even. That's what Maggie always called him. He was not, as far as Libby could tell, made of money. A juicy inheritance would have been welcomed.

Namita countered by saying he'd be killing the hand that fed him, employed him, when getting a job with his criminal record wouldn't have been all that easy. "However, maybe Wayne considered the situation oppressive. Stuck under Father Henry's thumb," she conjectured. "Just went off because of demands he thought were beneath him. Or sick of taking orders, especially from a patronizing family member."

Libby agreed. "A healthy inheritance would have made all that unnecessary. I didn't get the impression Wayne met Father's employment with any sense of gratitude. And I still think he, and the cousins, really believed they were getting a good slice of money. They seemed visibly shocked at the reading of the will. Wayne is probably over at St. Hedwig's right now, ripping up the pews for that diary."

"Diary?"

The young waitress asked if the two ladies wanted anything else, which they declined. The break forced them to look at the time.

"You'll have to fill me in on that tantalizing piece later," said Namita. "I need to get the dog home before I head out to my meeting."

Before donning all her winter garb, Namita examined one last time the napkin notes Libby had taken. "Well, that did not get you very far. Each one of your suspects had access to the priest and the weapon. The motives of anger over Church issues or job security and financial gain seem a bit thin, but equally so for everybody." She extricated her long, blue scarf and took a second to admire her handiwork before tossing it with a flourish about her neck. "I have to say, Libby, as an outsider, I have two observations. First, if being with Father Henry in the Church was so oppressive for any one of you, why not just leave? Why bother getting so worked up that you kill the guy? Don't forget, he did often look the other way. Besides, if your Church is like all other human institutions, wouldn't you run the risk of getting a pastor who was even more restrictive?"

Libby hated having to agree with that.

"Second," Namita said, "if the treatment of women, gays, Muslims, employees, etc., was as uncharitable as they appear; and the other grievances on the list so untenable, then—and understand this comes from a pacifist—maybe, just maybe, Father Henry and his ilk ought to be done away with."

~ ~ ~

Swish-swish. Swish-swish.

The wipers on Detective Grass's car made quick work of the snow landing thick and wet on the windshield. He hardly noticed.

Having recently left the reading of the will, he was preoccupied with Father Felger's case and found himself revisiting his earlier expectation that it would be simple to discover the perpetrator. Here was a small, limited group of suspects, none of them in the sophisticated-criminal category and a high enough profile victim to light a fire under the lab for quick results on the evidence.

Simple.

And yet, the very plainness of everything itself seemed confounding.

The people involved lived lives that were ordinary to the point of being boring. Motives were flimsy. Their killer arguments mostly amounted to hotheaded bickering. And, who could get murderously upset about being fired from a job that paid such a paltry salary?

Maybe things would liven up when they located the priest's missing diary.

Until then, Detective Grass eased his car down the slick streets while turning his thoughts to an uncomplicated, overtly violent gang shooting on the near west side.

Chapter Twenty-Six

Libby's brain had become so saturated with data about Father Henry's murder it was a relief to immerse herself in the current grant project she had spread out on her work table at home. For the remainder of the day, after hashing things out with Namita at the Muffin House, she had focused on cutting and pasting as she hammered out an appropriate assessment tool for the Visual Arts Department.

Late the following morning, she hummed and re-hummed the opening notes to Tchaikovsky's *Piano Concerto No. 1* long after it had played through and faded out on the classical music radio station. Preparations for a second cup of pomegranate tea were underway. She had calls in to several community business partners she wanted to connect with to be local underwriters, and she was waiting for them to get back to her.

The mug of tea was too hot to hold, much less drink. Cautiously, Libby took the handle in one hand and let the tips of two fingers on the other guide its decent to a coaster on the edge of the table overrun with the grant work in progress.

Outside the multi-paned solarium windows, a red male cardinal balanced on the branch of a bush. Only two inches of snow had fallen overnight, but it was enough to freshen the remnants of the previous layer.

It was the typical weather cycle for January in the Midwest: weeks of cold, maybe a heavy snowfall, then rain; rain turning to sleet turning to snow, leaving a pretty, pristine scene that over days eventually gave way to sooty, grimy stuff and a view much less attractive. Snow on the ground either melted away on a sunny afternoon or waited to be covered by another clean blanket, which is what was out the window this morning.

It was all good and distracting. For a while. But the longer Libby stared at the inert landscape, the more her brain was activated. And not about Visual Arts.

She chewed at her dry cuticles like an addict.

Finally she got up, dug around the shelves and drawers, and finally located an old spiral notebook with lots of good pages left. She collected all the stray scraps of paper and napkins on which she had ruminated about *The Death of Father Henry Felger* (title at top of page).

First page, bold heading: **Means** (Key and code allows access to probable means, i.e., thurible)

List of suspects with keys: Libby, Maggie, Daniel, Bernie, Wayne, Five cousins, Lavina W., Ted N. (Bldgs. & Grnds.)

Second page heading: **Motive**
She retrieved her napkin from the Muffin House.

List of possible reasons:

Being fired (M., D., W.)

Angry (L., M., D., W.)

Inheritance (W., Cousins, L., B.)

Third page heading: **Opportunity/Alibi/Movements on day of Murder**

Libby twiddled her pen, slapping its end on the open notebook.

Start with what you know, she thought. Me. And wrote her name. *Libby*.

How tedious. She knew where she had been, what she had done. She also knew of no one who could corroborate any of it.

She stared at her name. *Libby*. Top of the list.

Get yourself off the hook by putting someone else on it. Not by fabricating something but by discovering a timeline of movements, like she had done for Antonio's nephew Billy that boxed someone in as having the opportunity to hit Father Henry on the head.

Or not.

She inched ahead.

Maggie. Easy.

Up. Arrives for work at 9 a.m. Sees or talks to no one. Five p.m. discovers dead body.

Too easy. Too bare.

But it was all Libby had. Except a slew of tiny question marks sprinkled down the side of the page.

She tried to quit. But like all addicts, once she started, once she let the smallest bit of interest in, the addiction took hold.

It was not long before Libby was diving into all the "key" people, noting what they had actually told her or someone else had told her they had said about their actions that day. She marked circumstances that needed verification. Was anyone lying? Even fudging a little about where they were or what time they got there? How much could be corroborated by an independent source?

She tried to imagine each person going through his or her ordinary day, and then, in one extraordinary moment, committing the most egregious act one human being can inflict on another.

Libby closed her notebook and sighed. Her tea was cold.

It was extremely disconcerting how easy it was getting to be to think someone so close to her could do such a horrible thing.

+ + +

Reference to World War I and the mustard gas worked really well. Several positive comments. Josh asked how homilies are put together—how do I pick one idea out of all the themes in the readings? How do I find an opening story? Where did I learn so much history? How do you say something important but keep it short enough not to bore people?

Genuine interest???

I hate asking for money. Even for a good cause like the Storm Relief. Grateful Libby K. is willing to make the pitch. Well-written pitch at that. Happy for no big fuss to get the fundraiser underway.

Not like Cousin Phyllis, Virgin and Martyr—well, martyr anyway—after Mass in the sacristy. All fuss. Starting to notice my eye problems. Hesitations. Told her everybody moves slower when they get old. Won't be happy till I get a checkup. Didn't tell her I've already been more than checked up. I don't eat right, don't come to her house for a good dinner, etc., etc. She means well. I would rather warm up soup and watch TV with Dunkirk and Calico Two.

Bird Hawkins in after Mass to say a lady lost some expensive ring. Took it off near the Tenth Station. Thought it rolled somewhere. Who takes their jewelry off in the middle of Mass? World War I obviously not riveting to all. I went out and it looked like a scavenger hunt for ushers—on the floor, under the pews, behind the pillars. Futile. Libby says maybe someone picked it up and just took it. In church? A thief among us? May their hand wither, I said. Started laughing. L. had to turn away. Left her to lock up. Last I looked, church still crawling with people searching for the lost treasure.

+ + +

A kneeler dropped with a loud thud, its echo ricocheting around the big empty church.

The sound no longer jarred the police officers combing the pews of St. Hedwig's. They merely continued to run their hands along and under the long wooden planks padded for worship, lift and examine the floor beneath, then methodically move to the next, through thirty-odd rows, down the center and both side aisles.

"We didn't see any diary, journal, notebook, or whatever when we were in here or in the priest's house the first and second time looking for that incense burner thing," one of the officers muttered to himself. "Can't see how all of a sudden we'll hit on it this time."

Up front in the sanctuary, by the St. Joseph side altar, another officer tilted the large, wooden board for hymn numbers forward as far as he could.

Again.

His partner sent a beam of her flashlight to search behind it, the wedge between it and the church wall too small for any hand to reach.

Nothing.

Again.

"I'm beginning to feel like I'm back in grade school, with those grumpy old nuns dragging you to daily Mass," she said, clicking off the flashlight.

"I'm Baptist," he said, "but I told my wife, after this detail, I don't need to go to church for a month of Sundays." They eased the numbers board back into place.

They had found nothing.

Again.

Pausing, the two officers considered the warm oak wood everywhere; the colors from the stained glass windows dappled on the walls, on the choir loft above, over the back section of pews.

"Are all Catholic churches this beautiful?" he asked.

"No," she said in an odd staccato, as if she knew more than she was telling. "They are not."

~ ~ ~

Tuesday. Libby flexed her fingers inside the mittens that gripped the steering wheel. She was lulled by the rhythmic click-clack, click-clack of a late-morning freight train lumbering by that had temporarily halted her mission to verify alibis.

Mittens are definitely warmer than gloves, she reflected. Namita had made the ones she was wearing from bits of leftover, 100% wool yarn. They did not match except for the wild array of colors and lack of pattern, as if a box of broken crayons had been melted down and put to good use. But the stitch was tight and three extra inches at the base tucked far up into her coat sleeves to keep cold wind out. They were the warmest mittens she'd ever owned.

Mittens.

Instead of her usual systematic reasoning, progressing step by step, Libby kept catching herself for long minutes staring down at the organized chaos of her mittens.

A blast of train whistle startled her and called her back to the moment. She patted the spiral notebook on the passenger seat. She had a lot to do.

Libby tried again to pull into focus information and clues that might point to one person definitively. No matter how she sliced up the hours of the day Father Henry was killed, each one of the key holders, herself included, had a chunk of unsupervised time.

Enough time to commit a murder.

Libby knew that Detective Grass and the police were ahead of her on these details, but she was spurred on by believing she was closer than they were to the people and the situation, and that she might possibly hear or see or know something they would miss.

Something that would drop her name lower on the list of suspects.

And move someone else's higher. To the top, if possible.

It was going to be a zig-zaggy day around town. Libby sat in the parking lot of her first stop, snow piled in great mounds at the edges, but otherwise the black asphalt completely cleared for the few cars parked there. She opened the notebook beside her, scanned the headings, and tried to lock in her mind the questions earmarked on pertinent pages before closing it back up. Admittedly, she was a little anxious. Or nervous? Or just excited to be doing something concrete, something more than shoving information around on the pages of her notebook and doodling it into undecipherable blobs?

Don't be so anxious, she coached herself. How hard can this be?

A muted sucking of warm air was the only sound to greet Libby at the door of Fleck and Fleck's Funeral Home. Inside, several hallways leading to viewing rooms presented themselves. She started in one direction, moving tentatively in the eerie silence as if she was intruding, uninvited.

No one.

She turned around and whoa!

Within inches stood Don Fleck.

Libby gasped.

Don grinned. "It's the carpet. Thick. Thick carpet, thick pad. Muffles sound so you can't hear anything." He winked. "Or anyone."

Libby exhaled and let her heart rate slow down. She knew Don Fleck; had sung at enough funerals presided over by his company not to be surprised at his appearance. She had, in fact, hoped he would be the one on duty.

"I don't usually sneak up on people," Don said. "Can't help it sometimes. With this carpet. Besides, when I saw it was you …"

Libby recovered quickly. "More funeral home humor, eh?"

Don Fleck was his usual immaculately dressed, personable self.

"Come on in. What can I do for you?"

A sure and comforting gesture guided her to chairs at the back of Viewing Room B, empty and nearby. Opening her coat and sitting, Libby began, "I just wanted to ask you a few questions. About the day Father Henry was … that he died."

Don Fleck unbuttoned his navy suit coat and smoothed a dark silk tie. "Very creepy that was. Which is saying something for me. In my line of work. Very sad, too." Libby saw the initial lightness in Don Fleck's manner evaporate. It seemed sincere. Then again, he was a man who spent his days adjusting the tone of his response to accommodate any situation, any emotion he might encounter. "I liked Father Felger," he said. "Dry sense of humor. Always on time, which in my line of work is a plus." He bent over to pick up a dead plant leaf on the floor missed by housekeeping. "When I talked to the police, they were trying to figure out who was the last person to see him alive. I drove Father back from the cemetery, after the Webber funeral that morning. Well, you were at the service. 'Spose it could have been me, except I dropped him off at the church hall with the family. A few hours later he was dead."

"Did anything weird or unusual happen at the cemetery?"

Don Fleck winked as his humor returned. "Playing a little detective, are we?"

Libby responded in kind. "Not quitting my day job yet, but I was just curious. You're right. I was there to sing, and the police asked me about that morning, too. I didn't go to the cemetery."

"Can't blame you for that. Terrible icy rain. We were under a tent, but that damp cold goes right through you. Days like that I wish I had a regular office job inside."

"Did Father seem … upset? Edgy? Or distracted?" Libby asked. "Different in any way?"

The funeral director stroked the errant leaf. "No. Although that was unusual. Everybody else was edgy and distracted. We had that guy in shackles. Well, under close watch. The son. The convict. Didn't seem to faze Father Henry. Guess he's seen it all."

"And Bernie. He was there?"

"Fruehauf? Yep. He's probably seen it all, too. Mainly everyone kept polite distance from that Webber kid, but I wouldn't say anything else unusual."

Libby digested this. "Hmm." Be open. Be thorough.

"You weren't here at the funeral home for the Kwan showing later, were you?" she asked.

He shook his head. "Left at four. I had gotten back around noon, maybe one o'clock, from the Webber business. Kind of a dull afternoon at that point. Few phone calls. Heard lots of people came that night, though. Especially given the bad weather. But the family requested one long viewing session. Four to nine."

His voice softened. How often he must attend this area of people's lives, Libby thought. Don Fleck had undoubtedly, and literally, seen it all. "Always sad when a young person dies," he said. "Sounded like he'd been sick a while."

Libby picked at her crazy-colored mittens. She had known the Kwan child the way one knows children in a church, watching them week after week grow from squirming toddlers to gawky teens. Unless there was a reason to single them out and relate to them, they became a fixture, an expected and unremarkable place holder, third pillar back on the south aisle plopped unceremoniously next to their parents. On the other hand, these parents were active, involved parishioners and longtime friends. The loss of their youngest, their baby child had, she agreed, been sad.

Libby mentally reviewed her list of questions. "Any chance Father Felger came in early? I know once in a while he'd sneak into a funeral home, sign the guest register, and duck out. Kind of there without being there. Sometimes Bernie would bring him."

Don Fleck shook his head. "I came back here right after the Webber funeral and was on call till four. Did not see him."

Until this firm response from the funeral home director, Libby hadn't realized how much she wished Father Henry had relented and made even the slightest showing of compassion by slipping in for the few seconds it took to put his name on a piece of paper.

In reality she knew better.

"Not a lot of wiggle room with Father Henry when someone leaves the faith," she said. "There was a family once, a good family, whose son married a non-Catholic and joined his bride's church. Father wouldn't even let this brother do a reading in the service at his sister's wedding at St. Hedwig's."

There was nothing more Don Fleck could think to offer. "I would have seen him. Them. If Bernie had brought Father."

"Bernie was here later," said Libby. "I saw him when I came to the visitation around four forty-five p.m. He had another funeral to play for at six. At St. Bede's."

"Can't say. Not one of ours."

"You can't have everything," teased Libby.

"Believe me, I've got all the work I want. Sometimes more than I want."

"I'm sorry," said Libby, reminded that she was not sitting in someone's living room, much as the furnishings and décor and carpeting attempted to resemble it. "I should let you go."

"No. No," he objected. "I didn't mean that."

"It's okay." Libby's eyes drifted to the framed pastoral paintings of horses on the walls of Viewing Room B. She sighed and smiled briefly at the funeral home director. "I can't think of anything more to ask you."

Don Fleck automatically countered Libby's disheartened tone with sympathy and reassurance. "Like I said, the last time I saw Father Felger was after the drive back from the cemetery. Dropped him off at the Parish Hall for the family luncheon. Bernie Fruehauf must have been in a car close behind us because they went in together. Sorry. That's all I've got."

He walked her to the door, which he opened with a smooth graciousness.

"Thanks for your time, Don."

Stepping aside to let her out, he said, "I don't feel like I helped much. What exactly were you looking for?"

"I'm not sure." Libby felt the cold rush up at her. She pulled on her mittens of the unruly colors. "Too early to tell."

Chapter Twenty-Seven

The automatic glass doors at House and Home Outlet parted, and with some trepidation, Libby realized that as apprehensive as she'd been about talking to Don Fleck at the funeral home or even to Antonio's boys earlier, it was a whole lot easier to play detective when the person being questioned was somewhat familiar.

Not so easy with a total stranger.

"What was your name again?" A bald, middle-aged man with shoulders wide and strong like cross beams in a log cabin hoisted a box of lightbulbs onto an overhead shelf in Aisle 1.

Libby repeated her name, adopting a pleasant customer's tilt of her head. "I missed an appointment with Daniel in flooring last week. I thought the appointment was on Tuesday, not Monday. My husband said to go in and apologize. I'm still not sure that … well, was Daniel Giglia even here last Monday? My appointment would have been at three o'clock. Do you know if he was here then?"

She kept smiling, while inside she was rolling her eyes and thinking how lame she sounded. Her excuse felt ridiculous now that it was spoken out loud. She was sure the sturdily built General Manager eyed her with suspicion, but he remained agreeable.

"Tell your husband it's okay. Just go back and make another appointment."

Libby stuck by his side down an aisle of lamps and porch light fixtures. "I really liked Daniel. And I will. Make another appointment. My husband always says to be sure the supervisor knows it wasn't the worker's fault if you screw up." She rambled on as if she'd run into an old friend at the grocery store. "But just for my own satisfaction, I wanted to see if Daniel was here waiting around for me. Last Monday."

The General Manager abruptly stopped at ceiling fans. "Who are you?"

The confrontation rattled Libby, but she was too far into the charade to back down. "Like I said. I ... I had an appointment with Daniel in flooring a week ago. Monday. That didn't ... that I missed." Libby was sure the idea of strangulation was slowly but surely making its way to the front of the General Manager's mind.

Instead, he thrust both hands into the bold-yellow company half apron at his waist. "Look. All this sounds a bit fishy, if you'll pardon me. That Monday was ... kind of an unusual day, and the ..."

He hesitated, then gave way to surly. "Let's just say other people have been asking some of the same questions. Yes, Daniel was here. Yes, he was on time. Yes, he stayed the whole shift, three to nine. If you had an appointment with him on that day, you missed it. Daniel's a good employee. Now," he said, his stance firm, his eyes unwavering, "if you really want an appointment for flooring, go back and let Jewel take care of you. Aisle 4."

Pride and saving face propelled Libby down Aisle 4. She would not let the General Manager believe she was anyone but who she said she was. She certainly didn't have to talk to Jewel. Jewel wasn't even in her notes.

Jewel. Probably a pasty, old grandmother earning Bingo money, thought Libby as she passed kitchen-cabinet hardware. At paint chips she reprimanded herself for stereotyping the woman before she saw her.

It didn't matter. No one was in flooring.

Libby flipped mindlessly through wood laminate samples. No need to run into the General Manager before the time it took to set a fake appointment.

She pondered how uncomfortable the pretending—okay, lying— had made her. Kind of. Actually, as she reviewed the encounter, she thought herself pretty nimble at it. Perhaps the discomfort was because the bald manager had been more guarded than Don Fleck.

Perhaps because she hadn't been such a great success.

But wait.

True, she hadn't become best buddies with Mr. Manager, but she had gotten information. Daniel had told the truth about the time he went to work the afternoon Father Henry died. It didn't help with where he was the hours before that, but she was content taking one step at a time.

She wondered if Daniel could have snuck out once he was at the store. Kind of close timing if Mrs. McGrew's soup in the jar needed time to freeze. And why go back if he was at church to start with?

"May I help you?" A young, very tall, very thin, very non-pasty, African-American girl sporting a bold-yellow half apron offered a cheerful alternative to her boss. "My name is Jewel."

No more stereotyping.

Emboldened by this eager, let-me-help-you employee, on top of her revised view of the success of her previous interview, Libby, rather easily, fell into her customer persona and improvised. Lied.

"I don't know," Libby started slowly, with a studied hesitancy. She flipped more laminate samples. "I just spoke to the manager about …" She stopped flipping samples and confided in Jewel. "Is he always so …? I mean, he seemed a little … put off."

Jewel laughed generously. "He's not bad. Depends on what kind of day he's having. He gets lots of whacko customers, you know, complaints. Dumb questions. That sorta thing."

Libby understood better than she let on. "I've been here, in flooring, when Daniel's working. He seems pretty nice."

"Oh, Daniel's awesome." There was nothing hesitant or self-conscious about Jewel's admiration. "He trained me. Always taking time to explain stuff. And there's a lot of stuff to learn about flooring and handling customers."

While Jewel demonstrated her acquired knowledge of tiles and grouts, Libby did her best to pry out some useful nuggets about Daniel and those precious hours she was concerned with.

"I hear Daniel had some rough days last week. Somebody he knew got killed."

Jewel was not the leery general manager type. She barely paused. "Yeah. His priest or pastor, I guess." She cringed. "Cree-py. Somebody Daniel actually knew."

"Were you here the day it happened?"

"It was Monday, wasn't it? I'm always here on Mondays." Jewel tidied a rack of small carpet squares. "But Daniel didn't know about it then. So he wasn't upset about that."

Libby tried not to look too interested.

"You know, Daniel's an ex-Marine?"

No, she didn't, Libby admitted to herself although not to Jewel. The solid muscle tone now made perfect sense. A mental door opened to the idea that there might be other things, relevant things, that she did not know about Daniel Giglia. That she had not needed to know before.

"He's an upfront kind of guy," Jewel went on with her considered assessment. "If he's disturbed about something, you know it. Doesn't let a lot slide by. Brings it up. Gets steamed. Gets over it."

"Was he steamed that day? Mad that Monday? Before he knew about the priest?"

Jewel folded her thin, dark arms, letting one long, expressive finger bend up against her lips as she recalled the day. "Not mad. But not totally his usual self. He was like … distracted. Like there was something buggin' him. Daniel's not a moody kind of guy. Not at work anyway."

"I wouldn't think so," said Libby.

Jewel cocked her head and narrowed her eyes slightly. "You a friend of Daniel's?"

Libby was liking Jewel. Not just her candor, but her attempt to stay clear-eyed in her observations, to give everyone a fair shake. Libby had no trouble coming clean. "Yes, I am."

"Then you know he's gay?"

"I do."

"Buff, handsome man like that. A little short, but in good shape. We talked about it sometimes. Both of us having social challenges, as they say. I don't care. Daniel's a good guy."

Libby gave an exaggerated scan of the flooring department. "I'm kind of out of the mood to look at anything more today. But thanks. I really appreciated all your time."

Jewel flashed her customer-pleasing smile and waved her fingers elegantly. "You're totally welcome."

As Libby turned to leave, Jewel lightly touched Libby's arm. Her face clouded as she added seriously, "I'll tell you one thing. Daniel's fair. If he was steamed about something, he probably had a right to be."

She stepped away from Libby. "And that's exactly what I told the police."

St. Bede's was an ultraconservative parish on the east side of town. While St. Hedwig's was far from progressive, limping its way into the twenty-first century, St. Bede's, from Libby's point of view, was firmly rooted, and happy to remain, somewhere in the 1500s. Weekly they offered an old-style Latin Mass, in addition to weddings and funerals celebrated in that tradition if requested.

The Latin Mass was the service of Libby's childhood and, as such, had a certain nostalgic charm. Like many students, she had taken Latin in high school, so the language rolled off her tongue more effortlessly than for most. Some Catholics felt the Church should never have translated the Mass into English or made any of the other changes implemented in the 1960s.

As much as Libby could appreciate the tradition, the Latin Mass, to her, was a leftover sign of a male-dominated, hierarchical, devotion-driven Church concerned more with keeping people in their place by guilt and fear than by kindness and love. Of course, the nature and extent of that love, in the Biblical and religious sense, could be, and would be, hotly debated in many families, rectories, convents, political venues, and in each individual's heart.

Given her current association with St. Hedwig's and definitely by comparison to the House and Home Outlet, Libby approached the church offices of St. Bede's on firmer ground.

Fred Snyder, sixty, was the music and liturgy director. His heritage was German on both sides, but from the flush of his red cheeks and quick laughter, he appeared to be more from the beer drinking and singing lot than the dark, stoic line.

"Oh, excellent!" Fred popped up from his desk in greeting. "It's Laura? Louise? No. Libby. Right?"

Libby took his hand and smiled with the effusive shake. "Very good."

"How grand to have someone break the monotony of this interminable afternoon." He offered her a chair in the tiny office after clearing the seat of stray sheets of hymns and church bulletins. Returning to his desk, he tapped at several open music books. "Trying to get a jump on Lent. Be here before you know it. Although a bit dreary planning all those somber hymns. Beautiful, but somber. Are you still singing at St. Hedwig's?"

"Yes. Still there."

With dramatic sympathy, Fred bent over his desk, his bushy gray eyebrows collapsing along with rows of wrinkles lining his forehead. "Terrible about your Father Felger. Terrible."

"Yes, awful." Libby's knees brushed the side of Fred's gray metal desk.

St. Bede's was a small, old, neighborhood parish, abandoned for many years, stripped of vestments and ordinary church trappings. New interest in old structures and old ways was slowly resurrecting it. The office it afforded its part-time music minister was closet-sized at best.

"Really a shock," she said, careful not to bump a stack of choir music crisscrossed into piles for soprano, alto, tenor, and bass next to her on the floor. "Very sad. Especially for those of us who worked with him."

"Any idea who will replace him?"

"Not yet."

"Up to the Bishop as usual." Fred tipped his head back and chuckled. "Wouldn't want that job. Nobody's ever happy. Each parish is so different. 'Course, not as if the congregation has any say-so. Even under normal circumstances, they get used to their chummy, grandfatherly pastor or lively young one—for what? Eight or ten years if they're lucky? Then poof! Time to rotate, and you end up with a crabby recluse going through a midlife crisis. Even if you get a priest you love, it means somebody else lost a priest they loved." He tilted his head in consideration and chuckled again. "I suppose you could also be rejoicing, if you were dumping the midlife crisis guy."

Fred's sympathy returned. "Probably worse dealing with your situation at St. Hedwig's. Losing someone with so little warning, under such drastic circumstances. No. Would not want the Bishop's job."

Relaxing into his ancient tweed sweater with the rolled collar, Fred rested his elbows on the arms of his chair and laced his fingers together. "So. What brings you to darken my door this chilly afternoon?"

Libby was better prepared with her story this time.

"I was out this way and stopped because Bernie Fruehauf thought he forgot all his Latin Mass music when he played that funeral a week ago last Monday."

Fred tapped his thumbs together and raised his eyebrows. "Didn't forget it. Because he didn't remember it."

This was not exactly where Libby thought her opener would go. Fred glanced up at the clock on the wall behind him and, as if some factory work whistle had blown to signal the end of the shift, busied himself closing up music books while he talked.

"Bernie was his usual frazzled self. Weather was bad; driving worse. Forgot half the funeral stuff he was supposed to bring. Forgot his music. Not that that's a problem. Bernie Fruehauf knows almost everything by heart. Especially the old Latin. Played it for years before all the bastardized English stuff took over."

Libby grit her teeth and let the comment slide as Fred rattled on. "Said he'd come from another funeral."

"Yes. That morning, at St. Hedwig's."

"No. I think this was just the funeral home."

"Oh, right. Jonny Kwan's son."

"Seemed to be someone Bernie cared about. Seemed quite upset about it."

Libby had not unbuttoned her coat. The room was warm enough, but her host, though hospitable, did not hesitate to indicate that his workday was coming to an end. She kept her explanation to a minimum.

"The Kwans have been longtime parishioners at St. Hedwig's. I know Bernie would go visit the whole family. Kind of went through the son's illness with them all." Libby feigned interest in separating the strands of fringe at the end of her scarf. "Not surprised he was upset. And the roads were pretty icy. Did he get here on time? That frazzles him, too. To be late for anything."

Fred turned to a wall calendar bearing a picture of Jesus preaching to the multitudes and tracked down the appropriate date. "Funeral was at six o'clock. Bernie was here, oh, about half an hour ahead."

"Guess he wouldn't have stuck around long then, if he forgot his music." Libby pressed forward. "He sometimes stays if there's a meal or reception with food after the service."

Fred tightened his lips and shook his head, all forehead wrinkles on duty. "It was already unusual to have a funeral so late in the day. It was small. I think only the immediate family was going out to dinner. Bernie stayed and talked to a few people, but mostly everybody headed out rather quickly after the service. Weather wasn't conducive to hanging around. I saw him out the side door of the sacristy and watched him cross the parking lot to his car. Wanted to make sure he didn't fall."

After stuffing several pens into an already stuffed holder, Fred's desk was cleared for the night. "They were in; they were out. I waved good-bye to Bernie, locked the doors, and was warming up soup at home by seven thirty."

Chapter Twenty-Eight

Vitelli's West End Plumbers and Wayne Nichol's alibi were on the opposite side of town from St. Bede's. Late in the afternoon and down to her last interview for the day, Libby cranked up the car heater and sang "You Are My Sunshine," both at full blast.

As much as she loved making lists, Libby loved crossing off things even more. Regardless of what she'd gleaned from the day's conversations, the mere fact that so many assignations in her notebook could now be counted as done designated the day a success.

If she left St. Bede's and drove through downtown's business district instead of around it, she could go by St. Hedwig's and clock how long it took to get from there to the plumber's.

To anyone who would listen, Wayne claimed he was on time for a one o'clock appointment the day Father Henry died. Daniel said he left the church around the same time and Father was still alive. Libby bet Daniel was none too pleased at the possibility of being Wayne's alibi on that crucial end of the afternoon.

Seventeen minutes. With no ice on the streets.

The timing was tight. Wayne could have killed Father after Daniel left and still made it to the plumber's. Or if he was only at the plumber's a short time, he could have come back to the church and killed Father later, after Daniel was gone, and still left time for Mrs. McGrew's soup to freeze.

Vitelli's West End Plumbers had been around for three

generations. Originally a residence for an old, prestigious family, the house had been converted to a shop over fifty years ago. The business held firm as the houses around it were razed and grocery stores and pizza parlors took their places. A thick row of arbor vitae shrubs hid those establishments of contemporary life; if Libby did not look in either direction as she walked up the stairs and across the beautiful, expansive porch, she could almost feel as if a full century had not occurred.

Frankie Vitelli, Jr., looked like a child to Libby. He was probably in his early thirties, but black hair, buzzed short, and skin like a baby gave him the face of a preteen. Body type—wrestler maybe. The grandson of the founder and no doubt brought up in the family business, Frankie, Jr., confidently manned the counter, which was backed by a large bay window. In its glory days, this room would have entertained guests for high tea instead of customers searching for plungers.

"Hi. Can I help you?"

Libby responded in kind to Frankie, Jr.'s, infectious smile. "I hope so. I'm Libby Kinder, from over at St. Hedwig's Catholic Church."

"That's Wayne Nichols's territory," he said, stretching his muscular arms forward on the counter and leaning casually, is if he were at a bar and had just ordered a friendly beer.

"Yes, it is," said Libby, impressed at the young man's good business sense. Already he was pulling client's names and situations from his brain's file. It bode well for getting some dependable feedback on her queries.

He was true to his offer to be helpful. "I hope that doesn't mean the toilet in the Parish Hall broke again. I told Wayne those old porcelain fixtures can be a nightmare. Granddad says to always warn people they could last another hundred years or maybe only another month."

"I think it's doing all right."

"Good to hear. Was there something else?"

"Two things." Her plan was to be direct.

As a landlady, an economically prudent landlady, she had determined early on that she could be as capable as anyone of doing minor home repairs. "I need a new flap for my own toilet. One with a rod, not the chain. Like the church, mine is also archaic."

She figured it was an inexpensive purchase, something she could stockpile for later use, and an item she knew enough about to keep a credible conversation going.

"That's easy." Frankie, Jr., came around the counter into the room and led Libby down hardwood floors that disappeared under free-standing shelves packed with plumbing accessories. In the conversion of home to showroom, someone had loved the fireplace enough to allow it to remain and be functional. Nothing seemed more welcoming than the gas fire burning, albeit incongruously, just beyond an assortment of the latest showerheads. At the end of an aisle of flush levers and ballcocks, Frankie, Jr., located the package with the appropriate flap for Libby.

It was all very painless. While she examined the product, Frankie, Jr., ventured, unbidden, into the very subject she'd hoped to address.

"For an inner-city church, you guys must be doing okay. Busy even. The day I was over there to help Wayne, I had to park around the corner. Squeeze in between a hearse and repair truck, funeral people and ladies bringing casseroles to the Parish Hall."

"Yeah, it's nice to see all that activity." Libby turned the package over in her hand and compared it to one hanging from another row on the shelf. "You must have gotten there early."

"About nine. Streets so slick even my big truck was sliding around."

"Scary," said Libby. "If you were there at nine, that was before … other things happened."

Frankie, Jr., switched to the same serious tone everyone defaulted to when they hit the topic of death. "That's the day the priest got killed, isn't it?"

Libby nodded. "Later anyway. Guess you were gone by then."

"Wayne and I worked in the Parish Hall restroom all morning. Tight old fittings. Rusty threads. Pain in the rear. We decided it was better to bring the pipes and stuff back here to work on." He gave a boyish smirk. "Not great PR having grimy workmen traipsing in and out of the restroom during your funeral dinner."

"That's for sure." Libby handed over the selected package. "I think this'll work."

Frankie, Jr., took it and Libby's credit card and rang her up. He started to hand her the receipt, then stopped. "Oh, wait. You said there were two things."

Libby smiled. For several reasons.

Frankie, Jr., had made this stop incredibly easy, answering questions before they were asked and then generously responding to further inquiries. In addition, he was a fun combination of a man with years of experience running a business and scrubbed kid playing store in his grandfather's shop. He was young, but his attention to a customer's needs predicted a successful career in his inherited field.

And he was just plain nice. He had again, beat her to her own point.

Libby took the receipt. "There's nothing else I need to buy, but since I was already coming, the church secretary asked me to double-check that you got paid enough for that job last week at St. Hedwig's."

"Boy, we don't get asked that very often."

So much for being smooth, thought Libby. "No, I don't suppose you do. I … she just wanted to make sure Wayne hadn't talked your leg off."

"He's not as bad as some. I'm pretty good at keeping an eye on the clock. Family training, you know. Blabbing is fine as long as we keep working."

"Wayne's a funny guy," Libby offered. "Sometimes all jokes and teasing; sometimes head down, all business."

"He was pretty normal, given the old toilet and trying to get it fixed before the funeral people came in. Once we decided to bring it back to the shop, he was like everybody that day—mostly bent out of shape about the weather. Kept on about people driving crazy. Sliding in his way."

"Wayne said he was here most of the afternoon. Secretary was waiting on him for another problem she had going; so, you know, just kind of squaring up times."

"Let's see," the plumber said, pulling up a file on the computer screen. "You probably want specific numbers. I know we worked in the morning till about eleven. I came back here to cover lunch breaks. Because the funeral meal was going on, Wayne said he had other stuff to do till we met up after lunch."

Frankie, Jr., continued scrolling, continued talking. "He's got a sweet little setup over there in the church basement."

"I suppose." Libby carried on her end of the banter. "It's a big church. Lots of little things go wrong."

Libby hadn't been down there since Wayne had come to St.

Hedwig's almost two years ago. She and the former maintenance man had gotten along well, especially since he had been a willing resource for some of her landlady repair questions.

"Fancier than most church workshops I've seen. All those power tools. New stuff." Frankie, Jr., ran his finger down the screen, carrying on a running commentary as he scrolled through the records. "Monday … labor … hours. We agreed to meet at one o'clock, after lunch, and that's when that part of the billing began. He was here just over two hours monkeying with the whole thing, finding parts. We did some soldering. I remember him talking about going home from here and putting the toilet together the next day at church. By three thirty he was bummed about heading into school buses and more icy driving. I didn't blame him."

Frankie, Jr., was pleased with how everything in front of him added up properly. "Two hours we worked; two hours you got charged." He squared his shoulders confidently. "I'd say we're all good."

That did it.

Collecting information for the day was complete.

Processing could wait.

Libby saw that it was after four. She would be hitting the tail end of the same school bus traffic that had bummed Wayne more than a week ago. With great relief, Libby reached out to shake Frankie, Jr.'s, hand. "Thank you so much. You've been awfully nice to take the time."

An older gentleman came through the front door.

"Not a problem," said Frankie, Jr., alert to his new customer, yet never neglecting the current one. "Happy to help. Sorry it took so long. After the police were here asking about all this, I should have been quicker."

Why the news that the police had been to Vitelli's West End Plumber's suddenly deflated Libby was unclear. Maybe it was from sheer exhaustion. It had been a long day of pretending and ferreting and trying to be clever. Maybe because all the work she'd done that day only amounted to rehashed pickings the police had already gleaned.

She sat in her car on Washington Boulevard. Behind a school bus. As children spilled out, the bus's sidearm STOP sign flashed at Libby, forbidding her to advance.

~ ~ ~

He should have ordered decaf. It was too far into the day for a cup of regular coffee to do anything but set him over the edge. Detective Grass looked out the window of a midtown java shop and watched cars lining up for the drive-thru.

One by one, they streamed by.

One by one, his suspects passed in and out of his mind.

A church secretary. A church decorator. A maintenance man. A singer. An organist. Possibly some cousins.

The facts of each of their days lay before him. The work schedules; the appointment; the hours at home, alone, working, eating lunch, and napping; at the rectory stuffing bulletins.

Somewhere roughly between twelve thirty p.m. and two thirty p.m. on a cold Monday in January, one of them had killed Father Henry Felger.

At this point in a murder investigation, Grass always hoped for one person to emerge as the probable guilty party. He preferred to be tracking down corroborating evidence instead of, as in this case, feeling as if he was starting from scratch every morning.

The prosecutor was unhappy with the case's lack of progress.

The Bishop was also unhappy.

And he was unhappy. He had information. Times and places; movements verified. Something wasn't right.

Something was missing.

Chapter Twenty-Nine

When an artist draws a bird in the sky, most people focus on the bird. Yet the shape of the space around the bird—the sky, the light—can be just as interesting, just as important, as the bird. In art, it's called "negative space."

Libby stood in her kitchen and stared at the carrot sitting on a white dinner plate and let her eyes move back and forth between the carrot and the plate—the shape of the orange, the shape of the white. Negative space.

She had entered the afternoon's findings in her notebook under each suspect's **ALIBI** heading on his or her particular page. Her page, the *Libby* page, glared back at her as blank as the white dinner plate.

"Be thorough." She heard Namita's directive flitting around at the back of her mind.

What she wanted was to be thoroughly done for the day.

What she wanted was to close her murder notebook, ladle out a big bowl of the sausage-lentil soup bubbling on the stove, slice up some lemon-thyme tea bread, and sit by a warm fire.

But the notebook page, where nothing but *home, working alone* was written, haunted her. Was there something in the negative space, something going on around her that she had missed?

Dr. Amanda Whelan was a widow, a respected former

neurosurgeon and semi-invalid. At eighty-four, she was happy to watch documentaries and history programs on TV; along with all the comings and goings of people on Apple Street outside her front window—which was kitty-corner from Libby's solarium.

Dr. Whelan liked Libby and her occasional container of homemade soup or casserole. She didn't know it, but sausage-lentil soup was already set aside for her.

"Dash is fine," Libby reassured her neighbor as they spoke on the phone. "Yes, we're being very careful in the cold. No ice out there today." She wrapped up two slices of tea bread and set them alongside the soup. "Speaking of that, do you, by any chance, remember a week ago Monday, if you saw me walking Dash? In the afternoon. Usual time after lunch?"

"Oh, honey." The voice on the phone was stronger than the frail body attached to it. "I don't know Mondays from Fridays anymore."

Libby knew it was a longshot when she called. "It was really icy that day. Sleet. Ice. School delays in the morning."

"Winter is all icy days to me," said the doctor. "Now, you ask me about a day the sun was out shining, and I'll probably have that circled on my calendar!" She laughed. A good hearty laugh.

The laughter slowed to a chuckle with a little wheeze at the end. Then her voice changed. "I think I should tell you, Libby. The police came by and asked me the same thing a while ago."

Libby stopped her second bite of carrot. "Really?"

"It has to do with that priest getting murdered, doesn't it? That's your parish."

"You don't miss a trick, do you, Dr. Whelan?" Libby tried to keep the fluster out of her voice. "I was at church that morning, for a funeral; and then came home to work. Alone. Their checking everyone's alibi." She didn't want to worry the older woman. She was almost upbeat.

"Libby?" Dr. Whelan dropped any trace of cheeriness. Nowhere near upbeat. She could easily have been back in the operating room, clinical, serious. "I'm sorry. I did not see you, Libby. And while I may not know, exactly, what day of the week it is, I do know to be careful talking to the police. Truthful. Be truthful. But careful. If I may offer the advice of a nice, old-lady neighbor with a modicum of worldly experience, I suggest you do the same."

Bits of carrot caught in Libby's throat as she stammered, "I … uh … okay. Thanks, Dr. Whelan. I appreciate the advice. I really do."

Libby swallowed. Several times.

The police had talked to Dr. Whelan. Her close neighbor and friend. About her. They were tracking her movements.

Why should that surprise me? Libby thought.

But it wasn't surprise. Surprise had moved to the bottom of the list these days. No, it wasn't surprise.

It was fear.

+   +   +

… and, of course, there's joy in saying Mass. Admittedly, it's not always spiritually uplifting. You try, but things creep in—distractions, familiarity, an unpleasant phone call you have to make, upcoming meetings, not sleeping the night before. You're tired and just want to get it over with.

We are all Peter sinking in the stormy sea.

I guess a high point would be a vocation. Someone in your little sphere who chooses to enter the religious life, someone you might have influenced, even in the smallest way, to give their life to God.

Josh B. has a girlfriend. Seems pretty serious. Suppose I'm disappointed—all those questions when we were working in the garden. He seemed to show real interest. Would have made a good priest.

Well, and a convert. Oh, yes, there's definitely joy in that. I can baptize a hundred bawling babies—I'm sure they delight their parents and God as new little souls entering the Church. But an adult, struggling—and you, just the right person at the right time and God telling you what to say that touches them in the right way. An adult making a conscious decision to convert can bring you to tears. Yes. That's a great joy.

Dear Father Henry,

All my life I have searched for a spiritual home. Today, you and the people of this parish have become that for me.

When I first met you, that afternoon BJ showed me around before the Christmas concert, you were sitting quietly in the sacristy praying. You didn't seem to care that we broke in on this sacred time, but instead welcomed me, even though I turned out to be one of those "non-Catholics."

Through our talks—which were always funny, interesting, and challenging—my instruction, your wonderful homilies and personal example, you have lighted for me a path to the God and Community I so longed for. No other relationship has meant more to me on this journey of Faith.

Thank you for all you have done and all you are.
Blessings and peace,
Andrew C.

+ + +

Early Wednesday afternoon, Maggie scooped up the petals from a cream-colored mum that were scattered across the shiny marble floor in the back of church. It looked as if a flower girl had come in first and made way for the casket. It was a tender thought in the quiet left by the funeral home people.

Maggie refused to give in to it.

Their stomping in and about with huge bouquets, floral sprays, and planters had distracted her in the beginning, along with straightening prayer cards (a picture of Jesus as the Good Shepherd, Psalm 23 printed on the back with Father Henry's birth and death dates), squaring donation envelopes for those inclined to give to the Church Preservation Fund, and setting open the Guest Book next to the envelopes on a small wooden podium.

A Guest Book.

For who? Maggie wondered. He was an only child and his parents were dead. Who would want the keepsake? He was childless in life, doted on in every way, and died an orphan in the end.

Regionally, the custom was for Catholic priests to be laid out for viewing in the church, not a funeral home. Earlier that morning, the Vicar had received the body of Father Henry Felger at the front door of St. Hedwig's. It was an unremarkable event. A few prayers.

Only Libby and Maggie were there to let them in, to see them wheel the casket down the center aisle, the same route he'd taken for all the Masses celebrated, bringing it to rest before the marble steps that led up to the main altar.

The Vicar would not return for the visitation. He would miss the viewing by family and friends and a short ceremony to end the evening wake. The funeral Mass itself would be the following morning.

A sunless day made the stained glass windows dull, and the empty church seem a lonely place. Libby came in from the side door entrance to join Maggie in the dim foyer. "It's cold out there," she said with a shiver.

"It's cold in here," was Maggie's retort. "I suppose we should hit the thermostat override so it warms up by the time people come."

"I left the front doors locked. It's only one o'clock. Wake doesn't start till four. We can open the doors at three."

There didn't seem to be anything else to do in the back.

Libby and Maggie walked slowly down the main aisle toward the front.

Toward the casket.

Maggie wadded together the mum petals in the palm of her hand. "Are you staying till then?"

"Don't know. I have someone taking care of the dog in case I can't get home in between. I need to go over stuff with Bernie. Want to make sure everything is ready for tonight and tomorrow."

A few feet from the casket they instinctively stopped.

The lid remained closed as per strict instruction by the deceased.

"So. There he is," Maggie said with little fanfare.

+ + +

It's Holy Week, for God's sake! What the hell am I supposed to do? Of course, I remember the guy. Haven't seen him in church for twenty years and all of a sudden he's dying and wants a priest. Maggie lays it on by telling me the family said he's only got two days to live. I have an eye doctor's appointment and confessions and things to set out for Holy Thursday's Mass!

I told Maggie to tell them she couldn't get a hold of me.

They'll call someone else.

+ + +

"Yes," repeated Libby, "there he is."

The two women stood near the casket; absorbed; their attention seized as if a piece of good family china had been dropped and broken, all the memories connected with it coming unsolicited to their minds and stunning them. Memories of Father Henry, some shared, some personal and private, showed up in the instant without invitation.

Libby countered the emotions stirring up inside her. "I was wishing he was Irish, and we could all just laugh and drink and tell good stories at the wake."

"I can arrange the drinking part," Maggie said dryly.

Libby nudged the cynical secretary. "Come on, Maggie. You have some good stories. I have some good stories."

Maggie's sarcasm prevailed. "I have some stories. Not all good. More irreverent than might be permitted."

Libby let out a long, loud sigh. "Pretty unreal, isn't it?"

Maggie stared at the casket. "I wish it was all over."

That was not a wholly unwelcomed idea, and they both tried to let the relief waiting in the not-so-distant future carry them.

"Libby?" Maggie said softly.

"Yeah."

"Wanna look in the casket?"

It was both ludicrous and hilarious. Libby choked on a stifled laugh. "What do you think he's wearing?" she whispered.

Maggie clapped her hand over her mouth and honked through her nose. "Whatever it is," she said, "I'm sure it's that red violet color for the monsignor title he always barked about not getting."

"I hope they got his hair right."

The loud whrrr of a vacuum cleaner halted their speculations.

Reality broke in with a jolt, calling them back to their sober agenda, and like moths to a flame, they were drawn away from the casket, on through the shadowy sanctuary into the priest-side sacristy.

Lights. Sound. Action.

The room was ablaze—overhead lights, countertop lights, lights in the display cabinets. At the nearest end of the great oak table, Bernie was absorbed with a spread of music sheets and notes on the order of impending services. At the far end, a crisp, white, altar cloth gathered in intentional folds as Daniel ironed it smooth, foot after foot, up from its wrinkled heap at his feet across the ironing board and onto the table.

The vacuum roar ebbed and flowed with Wayne's in-and-out, push-and-pull of the machine. He whipped its electrical cord behind him undeterred by any chair, person, or table leg.

It was warmer in the sacristy than the rest of the church and, by contrast, bursting with human activity. To the outside observer, the scene might have looked like busy elves preparing for a big event, a harmonious lot working in unified anticipation.

Not for long.

Wayne cursed when his vacuum cord caught on Bernie's chair. Bernie stood to free the cord and sent his music flying. Libby came around the table to catch the sheets, colliding with Wayne, who overcorrected and backed into Maggie.

"What the hell are you doing?" Wayne shouted at her over the vacuum roar.

"You ran into me!" she yelled back.

Daniel stepped out of the way, raising a hot hissing iron over his head into the air. The vacuum began to eat one of Bernie's notes until Libby rescued it.

She waved the sheet at Wayne. "Turn that off! Please!"

Abruptly, the roar ceased. Dead away.

The bickering did not.

Wayne brought his face in close to Libby's, his voice silky with sarcasm. "I'm just making things nice for all our visitors. Just doing my job."

"That's a first," muttered Daniel.

Wayne swung around. "Don't want to hear that pretty boy had to do all the domestic work." He shoved the vacuum toward the ironing board.

Daniel didn't move. "Don't. Step. On the altar cloth."

Bernie stood, taking the papers from Libby. "I can go to the other room."

"You're good right there, Bernie," Maggie said resolutely.

A dozen smart-mouth remarks jumped to Libby's mind. For once, she fought the urge. There was no time to get into a big argument, and the one blowing up certainly was not worth the energy. "The room looks fine, Wayne. All those priests traipsing in and out, no one will notice."

"The Bishop will," Wayne snarled with mock affection. He squirreled around and yanked the vacuum cord plug from the socket behind Daniel, who remained aloof.

"As if you'd recognize him."

"As if I cared."

Libby reached for an escaped sheet of music, then sat next to Bernie. "Are we all set?" she asked, trying to effect normalcy.

The tension did not dissipate, but the yammering quit.

Maggie tidied the countertop, putting away pens, stacking old bulletins, chucking someone's lost rosary in a drawer.

Wayne wound up the cord for the vacuum, then shoved it noisily to the other sacristy.

Daniel ironed.

Bernie sat and worked to reorder his music. "I think I have everything for tonight," he began tentatively. "The priests sometimes sing the "Regina Coeli" a cappella. Do you think that would be all right? To let them do that?"

"Works for me," said Libby.

"Anything you want to practice for tomorrow?"

Wayne reappeared. Without a word, he laid the cream-colored pall that would drape the casket in front of them on the table. Next to it he placed the aspergillum, for the holy water. A small crucifix. A thurible.

Daniel looked up from his pressed altar cloth. "What's that?"

Bernie went silent.

Libby stared.

"What's it look like?"

The heater clanked; Daniel's iron pulsed steam.

For a second, no one moved. A bomb had been laid in front of them.

And it was ticking.

Maggie turned to see her colleagues gone cold. "Oh, for heaven's sake," she said, pushing in the chairs Wayne had pulled out to sweep under. "It's not *that* thurible. It's one we borrowed from the Cathedral."

No one really believed her. They looked at each other out of the corner of their eyes and glared at the censer until firmly convinced.

If there was ticking, for the moment, it had stopped.

Maggie spoke like a preschool teacher talking to a four-year-old. "That wasn't funny, Wayne. You know we don't need any of these things until tomorrow."

"Like I said. Just doing my job." Wayne lifted two edges of the pall and made a great show of lining them up exactly. "Making sure this was folded right."

Bernie tucked the music into his worn satchel, his head and his voice low, not to rock any boat, but not to let Wayne get by. "It should be perfect," he said. "St. Bede's is very careful when they borrow things."

Daniel resumed pressing. Libby turned to Maggie. "Is there anything else we have to do for tonight?

On her fingers, Maggie checked off wake and funeral preparations. "Somebody from the Cathedral will deliver the matching vestments for all the priests to wear. I got servers for tomorrow. One for tonight if we need one."

Bernie stood. "I might as well fill the ciboriums with hosts."

He went to the cupboards; Maggie offered to help.

Wayne pretended to adjust the pall, all showy, away from Daniel's altar cloth. Libby checked the wine. A civil tone descended on the sacristy, while an underlying tension remained.

Daniel set the iron on the side counter to cool. "Libby, would you help me carry this altar cloth out?"

There was much fussing and giving of directions from everyone on the best way to transport the unruly, six-foot wide, twenty-foot long piece of starched white linen. Daniel, used to Paul Thomas's steady hand, instructed an unsure Libby as she backed into the sanctuary, Daniel following with his end of the cloth.

They were coming in line with the casket.

"Maggie. Flip on some lights," Libby called, moving toward the altar, her footing uncertain in the dim light.

The side bank of lights snapped on.

As Daniel swung around to the front of the altar he felt a tug. "What?" he asked testily, halting mid-step with the delicate cargo.

"Daniel?" Libby had stalled at the edge of the altar.

He could barely hear her.

Exasperated, Daniel adjusted to keep the cloth between them

straight and off the floor. "What? I just spent hours ironing this …"

"Look."

They inched over, the crisp cloth going slack between them. Light bounced off the brassy-gold filigree.

Hanging from the hooked stand was St. Hedwig's missing thurible.

Daniel swallowed. "Doesn't look like we needed to borrow one."

Chapter Thirty

Detective Grass didn't do much second-guessing in his job. He based decisions on facts and trusted himself and his department to assemble those with a high level of competence. He was not like some investigators who had uncanny instincts or a knack for understanding the human condition.

Facts usually got him where he needed to go. Once in a while, he was lucky.

Being in the right place at the right time to catch a clue or to stumble on someone in the situation—a nosy neighbor, a friend, a boss who unknowingly dropped an incriminating hint, could all help the cause. In the end, though, his method was primarily to keep after the facts until things fell it into place. It was a method that was better than some, not necessarily as good as others.

Grass had originally toyed with the idea of collecting all the keys to St. Hedwig's Church as soon as Father Henry's death was labeled a homicide. Instead he decided to permit everyone to keep their keys, allowing them to continue their routines, to go on as if nothing had happened to be wary of and perhaps, in that familiarity, reveal something incriminating. Damaging.

This had been his decision—based on the fact that the church had been searched three times, with as many officers for as many hours as his budget would allow—and nothing was found.

No murder weapon.

No incriminating diary.

In and out his suspects had gone, singing and playing for services, keeping the snow cleared; the heat going, and the plants inside from shriveling up. Now, one of them, in those comings and goings, had brought back the original thurible.

The likely murder weapon.

Short of dunking the object in acid, which most amateur murderers would probably not do—and he was convinced this was the work of an amateur—some evidence was bound to be on it. Even if tests did not tie someone specifically to the thurible, they could, at least, tie the weapon firmly to the crime. That, by extension, would reaffirm for Detective Grass that these holders of the keys to St. Hedwig's Church were the rightful pool of suspects; that they did, in fact, hold the key to the murder.

Arriving at the sacristy after receiving Maggie's phone call, Detective Grass realized that, for the first time, all the major suspects in Father Henry's murder were in the same room at the same time. The priest's wake had brought them together for those preparations. The return of the censer found them conveniently assembled for unplanned, unrehearsed questioning.

The detective considered this a fortunate opportunity.

In many ways, St. Hedwig's was an unremarkable, old, inner-city church; but as the detective had witnessed more than once, even in his own department, every kingdom, no matter how small or unremarkable, exhibited all manner of relationships. Here he would get to see who supported who, see if there were allegiances or rivalries for attention or power.

Although Grass sat on one side of the long, oak table, not claiming any head position, there was no doubt he was in charge. He stared down at his small, open notebook, lying on the table in front of him, considering.

Libby. Bernie. Wayne. Maggie. Daniel.

Libby watched him, wishing she had her own notebook. So much easier to keep things straight when they were trapped on a list under a neat heading. She listened carefully.

No one had seen the thurible since the day of the murder.

What a surprise.

And today?

No one had seen it hanging where it belonged until Libby and Daniel ran into it bringing out the freshly pressed altar cloth.

It was Wednesday. According to Bernie and Libby, the thurible wasn't there for Saturday night or Sunday morning Masses over the weekend. Substitute priest. Regular ushers, servers, lectors. No one else.

Except everyone who attended the services.

On Monday afternoon, after the reading of the will, Maggie and Wayne said they were in church moving kneelers and chairs around on the altar for the added number of priests coming to the wake and funeral. The police were also there, searching for Father's diary.

Daniel heard Bernie practicing on Tuesday. Before he left, Bernie helped Daniel tidy plants and replace candles.

No one noticed anything out of the ordinary.

It seemed that just as everyone had gotten used to the thurible always hanging in its place, they'd just as quickly gotten used to it not being there.

Today, the funeral home had brought the body at noon. Maggie had let them in. The Vicar was here and gone within the hour. Each suspect at the table had walked in and out of church whenever they'd wanted.

Because they all had a key.

"In and out of church," the detective summed up. "In and out of the sanctuary. And nobody noticed a missing murder weapon reappearing out of the blue?"

No one spoke unless spoken to directly.

They looked at their hands; they folded and unfolded their arms.

Grass rotated his pen in his fingers like a small baton, staring past it at the shorthand in his notebook. "What I'm hearing is that when you were in church, you either came with one of the others, worked with one of the others, or, at the least, saw one of the others. Convenient."

He looked up and down the table, eyeing them separately, then as a group.

"Are you sure you're not all in this together?"

They couldn't quite catch the tone of his voice. Was he being funny? Or truly serious?

"Yeah," Wayne piped up, while his entire body seemed slouched into his sweatshirts. "That would be us. Real chums. We planned it at our regular Tuesday poker night."

Bernie's mouth dropped open.

Daniel turned and glared at Wayne.

The women rolled their eyes.

Whatever the individual reactions, the table as a whole seemed uncomfortable with Wayne's attempt at humor. They regarded each other with less-than-chummy stares.

Seizing on their discomfort, the detective pressed the point. "You are, after all, the only ones with keys."

"Except Lavina Woodson and our man from Buildings and Grounds," Maggie reminded him.

"Noted. But that's it for having access to the church. I understand that without authorization you can't get a duplicate key made."

"Correct," Maggie confirmed.

"And you, Maggie, are the authorizer. Right?"

She took a moment to answer. "Yes."

She pulled up in her chair, then said evenly, "Sometimes Wayne leaves the back door unlocked."

Wayne yanked his hands from his sweatshirt pockets and grabbed the edge of the table. "I do not!"

The secretary stayed composed. "It was open right before Christmas when I came over. And once a few weeks ago."

The maintenance man sat back, justification rolling off his lips. "I leave it open for the florist. Or a delivery. But I'm always in the church or in the basement and I can hear them. I'm expecting them. Not just leaving the door open willy-nilly."

"And did you leave it open, willy-nilly, recently?" asked Grass.

"No." It was succinct. It was defiant.

"So, again," the detective said, "any one of you, any combination of you—or all of you together—could have come in here any time of the day or night and just hung that censer back on its hook."

He paused.

He clasped his hands and laid them across his notes before addressing his suspects. "Why do you think anybody would do this?"

Whether the assembled group was puzzled by the question or puzzled for an answer was unclear.

The detective coaxed them. "Is there anything special about this thurible?"

"Like an heirloom?" ventured Libby.

"I don't think it's a relic," said Maggie.

"It is part of St. Hedwig's history," offered Bernie. "Maybe somebody didn't want it lost."

Libby turned to Maggie. "Is it worth much?"

Maggie shrugged. "They're often solid brass with a gold coating. Antique. Nice, but with so many churches closing down or going modern, you can probably get one cheap."

"Great," Wayne tossed in, "a murderer who gives a shit about saving money."

Grass smiled invitingly at Wayne. "Got anything better?"

Wayne slouched back in his chair, but took the challenge. "Sure. Our chummy group here went out after the poker game; had a few too many beers; and decided to, let's say, wipe down the thurible; sneak into the church at oh, say, midnight; and just dangle the murder weapon out for all to see. Thought we could help by giving you some evidence against us."

Buried in Wayne's outrageous scenario was the solid, but unwelcomed, reasoning that a murderer would have to be daft to return the thurible.

Daniel chose a different tack. "Are they sure this is the murder weapon?"

"That's what the lab's going to tell us," said Grass.

Maggie was doubtful. "Don't you think whoever did this would have wiped ... things ... stuff ... off it?"

"You mean, like Father Henry's blood and fingerprints?" Wayne was enjoying himself.

Libby grimaced. "How gruesome."

Bernie blanched. "Oh. My."

"There are things the lab can detect even when an object has been wiped off or cleaned in some way," said Detective Grass.

He closed his notebook. He took a last look around the table.

Wayne smirked and picked at his fingernail. "You gotta say, Detective, kind of clever hiding that thing out in plain sight. Kind of throws things off."

Inwardly Grass agreed, but he would never give Wayne Nichols the satisfaction of admitting it openly. He made a final sweep of the faces around the table, looking for the typical expressions of those under police scrutiny: Confusion? Defiance? Nervousness? Contempt? Faked nonchalance?

What he saw made him re-consider Wayne's suggestion of a Tuesday night poker game.

Detective Grass was finished. The thurible was on its way to the lab. He'd seen and heard what he wanted. What he could get.

As people rose from the table, the detective, gathering up his notes, asked in general, "Who will come to the wake?"

Maggie stood and pushed in her chair. "Members of the congregation. People from Father's previous parishes. Priests from nearby parishes. Although many of them will wait until the funeral tomorrow. A few relatives."

"Will you all stay for it?"

Everyone simultaneously checked the clock above the door to the sanctuary.

"It's already three thirty," said Libby. "I might as well stay."

"Me, too," said Bernie. "I can finish setting out things for tomorrow."

Maggie rubbed her hands together then hugged her shoulders. She was cold. "If you're staying, I'll go. I have food to pick up for the funeral luncheon. Thank God Mrs. McGrew is helping, but I need to get with her this afternoon."

Daniel decided to stay for a little while, too. "To give my regards to the family. There won't be anyone else I know to pay my respects to. I'll be back before the funeral in the morning, but if you'll help me put that altar cloth out, Libby, I can be done for tonight."

Wayne stood in front of Daniel and held out his hand. Daniel regarded the gesture warily.

"Thought you wanted to pay your respects to the family," said Wayne. "That would be me, don't you know?"

Daniel registered some dismay, but mostly he looked leery. He caught Bernie's eye. "Is he telling the truth?"

"Yes," said Bernie.

"This time," said Maggie, reaching for her coat.

"A cousin," Bernie added.

Daniel did not soften his disdain. "Not sure I could tell by how close you seemed to Father Henry."

Wayne retracted his outstretched hand. "Close enough to get a little something in his will."

Detective Grass left. He left his suspects bickering and planning. And yet, seemingly, getting on as usual in the sacristy.

As he pulled out of St. Hedwig's parking lot, it crossed his mind that, in one sense, they worked well together. Each had a job, they got things done, picked up the slack when necessary, knew their places. Either Father Henry had trained them well or he was lucky.

Or.

Or did Father Henry threaten this little cohesive unit in some way? Would firing one or more of them upset the delicate balance?

Because it did appear that, collectively, they did run the place.

His thoughts returned to little kingdoms and he wondered anew, Why had this king been murdered?

Maggie slipped out of the back door of church and hurried past Wayne, who was lighting up a cigarette. She had too much to do to waste time with his stupid comments.

Wayne exhaled, smoke and wintry breath mixing in a stream of cold air. He was too engrossed thinking about all of his witty retorts during the detective's visit to care about needling her.

He was also thinking about what else he had to do to get the most out of the present situation. Plans for the next phase of his life bubbled like a pot of stew on a low burner, simmering just below the boiling point.

Bernie didn't like dealing with Detective Grass. He was glad they had all been together for this interrogation. He took some comfort in being surrounded by people he knew. He took strength from them as well. When they didn't crumble with the detective's questions, he could follow their lead. He'd spent his life being embarrassed at his nervousness in these kinds of situations.

Of course, a murder investigation wasn't a normal situation.

He looked at the sacristy clock again. He figured he'd go upstairs and wait in the quiet of the choir loft where he felt safe. At home. He could say a rosary. Pray.

That's what he could do. Pray.

Libby and Daniel smoothed out the last wrinkles on the ironed cloth, finally in place on the altar. It was a beautiful piece with five inches of hand-tatted lace along the front.

If asked, Daniel would say he loved these beautiful things, loved taking care of them, loved being in a place where they were still used. St. Hedwig's was filled with beautiful things.

Libby, too, appreciated them, but also someone like Daniel, who cared; who took the time to dust off or clean or press or repair whatever was necessary—what too many Catholic churches tossed or sold or let sit in a box somewhere.

And that, that is where Libby stood so often: loving the things of the past in her Church, but longing for it to embrace the realities of today; to have a future, not just a past. The irony of having these thoughts as she stood next to Daniel, a man who wanted to belong fully, spouse and all, to that same Church, did not escape her. Nor did the idea that being rejected, fired, might cause a great deal of anger and hurt.

Possibly violence.

As had been the case recently, it did not make her feel good that her brain could jump so easily to such thoughts.

For the moment, Daniel and Libby paused and faced the high main altar; so ornately carved, with gilt-edged nooks for statues of angels and saints, rising a hundred feet above them. It was hard to keep one's eyes from traveling upward, heavenward, as the architect had intended, inspiring awe in the presence of God.

Eventually, Libby's and Daniel's eyes came back to earth, and they found themselves staring at the thurible stand. Empty. The thurible. It was like Lazarus. It had been dead and buried, only to be resurrected. And like Lazarus inevitably had to be, was gone again.

"What do you think?" Libby asked quietly.

Daniel shrugged his shoulders and looked for an answer somewhere in the still sanctuary. "Maybe the angels brought it back. One more time. For Father Henry's funeral."

"You know," Libby said, "he hated funerals."

Daniel nodded. "Despised them."

Chapter Thirty-One

One is born into a family; one is ordained into the Church. Attendance at the wake was modest. Persons related by blood were outnumbered by priests and parishioners from near and far, in both time and distance. Father Henry had bounced around a diocese of some seventy parishes, and along the way, made friends and generated his own particular clan based on his particular attractions.

The cousins greeted and accepted condolences at the back of church, leaving Father Henry at peace by the altar in his closed, never opened, casket. Cousin Wayne grew bored with his place in the family and retired to his less public spot in the basement maintenance workshop after an hour.

Bird Hawkins was heard occasionally blasting out historical tidbits about the intricate latticework of the confessional, the design of the narthex, the heritage of families who donated German-made stained glass windows, now almost black with the night coming down behind them. Although it was another cold January evening in the Midwest, Catholics are rarely deterred by the weather for services; so those who wanted to come, came.

"Who's that you were just talking to?" Libby sidled up to Maggie, who had been periodically straightening the prayer cards by the Guest Book for the last two hours. "She's standing behind Cousin Ruth now."

"To the left? That's Father's secretary from St. Christopher's."

Libby squinted in the low light. "What about the guy in the furry parka?"

"Classmate. Grade school, I think."

"Really? Kind of fascinating who comes to a funeral. Even more interesting who comes to a priest's."

Odd and curious and moving, thought Libby. So far, there had been old classmates, the waitress from Father's morning breakfasts, the cats' groomer, people he'd married, priests he'd served with on committees, and people he went to high school football games with. Libby continued to watch the mourners, bundled up, mostly shuffling in, wet shoes squeaking on the marble floor as they walked to the casket, dropping into a pew for a brief prayer, then squeaking back out with little fanfare. They knew Father Henry; he was their sole purpose for coming.

Libby reflected on the disparate group of people. Who are we really close to? she wondered. Who do we confide in? If a person is single, like I am, or Father Henry was, who gets your true self? Are pieces of us parceled out to different people—the classmate? The secretary? The waitress?—so that no one person knows us totally? Where do we go with the extra pieces? Our pets? Our garden? Our diary?

While some wakes can be boisterous, jolly with reunions and reminiscence, Father Henry's was a subdued occasion. St. Hedwig's was warm, comfortable for a change. Whether according to Father's typical frugal wishes or the dictates of the Office of the Dead for the Burial of a Priest, lighting was soft, lots of candles flickering noiselessly. The church felt intimate, with light only reaching human height level before fading into an arch of darkness overhead.

Two Knights of Columbus, the ancient order of guards, silently flanked the casket. They wore black tuxedo-like suits; white shirts crossed in front by the Order's red sash; and knee-length black capes, folded back at the shoulder, displayed brilliant red-satin linings. They wore white-plumed hats; swords, long and sharp, were drawn to attention before them.

By six thirty, Libby took refuge in a pew a little off to one side near the front of the church. It was the first she'd had time to herself all day. She looked around, saw Maggie slip out the main door as one or two last-minute visitors slipped in. Not really very many people, she thought. Maybe murder kept them away—or coming into the inner city at night.

More likely, those in front of her were not thinking about murder at all; instead thinking about sadness, loss, and remembering the gift of the man they had come to pay respects to.

Libby consciously fought not to go there.

Eventually, it would all catch up with her. She knew that. For now, she had to keep her wits in check. At the funeral the next day she would sing, and singing would completely engage her, along with making sure that everything surrounding the service went well.

Hostess bones.

Her mind flitted about like the candles' shadows, jumping quickly from place to place unpredictably.

She thought about Father Henry's will.

She thought about updating her own.

Who would get her money, if any was left? Who would take her pets? Who would take that clock?

She thought about heaven.

If there was one.

Ever since a trip to Rome, Libby had wondered if a thousand years hence the world would look back at her time in history and consider what she had considered as she confronted the ancient ruins: that their beliefs, religion, and the machinations of their God could be just so much superstition and ignorance.

In her heart, Libby knew that much of why she stayed at St. Hedwig's was because she sang. Because her family still peppered the pews. Because the rest of the pews were filled with good people who had become family by association. And because there was beauty and comfort and inspiration in so many of the trappings: the music, the pageantry, the candlelight, and the seasonal celebrations.

Trappings. Yes, they could be traps. Obsessive concern with how to light a candle, when to bow, how deep, how often. Who could be allowed on the altar.

Was her faith merely a product of cultural conditioning? And, if yes, was that so bad? Her quandary dipped into more than questions about the Church's stance on social issues. And once doubt had hit her, she had read, prayed, talked, meditated, and searched.

By her own account, she was a mess.

The spinning around of all these notions in her mind frustrated

Libby to no end. She didn't object to working on a puzzle; in fact, enjoyed it, but the effort had to be directed toward a resolution.

She understood better the love Elizabeth Barrett Browning "seemed to lose with my lost saints," and Libby longed for her own "childhood's faith." She had been told by greater minds than hers that this whole trying to figure things out was useless. That faith was a mystery.

It drove her nuts.

There had been no rush to help from the priestly ranks; only Monsignor Jimmy was kind enough to offer to lead the evening prayers at Father Henry's wake. It was not a great imposition—a brief service following the visitation, more like a few night prayers at the end of a day; still, a priest needed to step forward to do it. And Monsignor Jimmy did. Tomorrow, thought Libby, the funeral, as Catholics viewed it, would be about light, resurrection, glory, and the passing into the triumph of eternal life. But tonight, at the vigil wake, the mood was reverently dark.

Libby caught sight of the Monsignor coming in and walking past her pew. She joined him and escorted him to the sacristy. Arriving in plain clerical black—no monsignor purple to set him apart—Monsignor Jimmy donned a simple white alb tied at the waist and a generic white stole around his neck.

Libby stood at the doorway to the priest-side sacristy and waited for the time to start. She could feel the Monsignor standing behind her, his presence warm and solid.

"Always puts one in mind to question his—or her—own beliefs about the hereafter, doesn't it?" he said quietly.

Libby smiled at how close to the mark his comment was. "Even you?" she asked.

"Oh, definitely me," he said. "But then, if you don't ask, you don't get answers."

Her smile was rueful this time. "Lucky you. You get answers."

From the sacristy doorway, slightly hidden by the wide pulpit, they could look out and see the casket. Two four-foot brass candlesticks stood at one end of it while the two Knights of Columbus, motionless like toy soldiers, stood at the other.

"How's that search going?"

Libby twisted her head in amazement. Could he tell by so little interaction what her soul's confused state was?

Keeping his gaze out toward the pews, the old priest smiled, the soft folds of skin around his mouth quite used to the expression.

Libby turned away. "Not so well." After a moment she added, "It always gets so … complicated."

"Ah," he said.

Libby wasn't sure what she expected. She'd only been around Monsignor Jimmy on a couple occasions. His wit was quick, but also seemed insightful. And like tonight, offering to do the wake for Father Henry, with the big funeral tomorrow to attend as well, seemed to come from an unassuming spirit of generosity. His "ah" was refreshingly candid.

"Easy for you to say," she said in a like manner.

"It is," he said. "I gave up complicated long ago. Too old to fuss with it now."

Libby gave a bit of a glib sniff. "You're a big help."

Upstairs the organ switched on, sucking in a great "woof" of air in anticipation of the service. As Bernie and the organ began a thoughtful, plaintive prelude, the Monsignor added, "I will say, you can never go wrong starting with kindness. And if you can lean a little toward goodness and mercy, you'll be okay."

At eight forty-seven p.m., the last visitor left Father Henry's wake. Bernie joined Libby snuffing out candles on either side of the altar. "What time are you coming tomorrow?" he asked.

"About nine." Libby looked around the sanctuary, taking stock as she shifted focus from wake to funeral. "Numbers are up. Everything laid out for Mass. You and I are all set, right?"

"I hope so."

Instead of becoming more relaxed with time and experience, Bernie seemed to have gone in the opposite direction. Any deviation from routine shook him. After so many years together, Libby was used to soothing her music partner. "You'll be fine, Bernie. It's all stuff we've done a million times."

"I'm glad you're singing. I know it's just another funeral Mass. Sorry I'm so nervous. Guess I'm always nervous when the Bishop comes."

"The Bishop doesn't bother me. I just hope I don't get … that I can … I don't usually fall apart singing for the funeral of someone I know. Until the commendation near the end. Or maybe I will on one of the songs I know Henry liked." Libby's shoulders rose with a deep breath and fell with an audible sigh. "Okay," she said quickly, "not going there. I'm too tired."

Bernie flipped off all the church lights from the panel in the priest-side sacristy while Libby waited. Picking up their music bags lying on the oak table, they crossed through the passage behind the main altar, accompanied only by a few creaks of their footsteps on the carpeted passageway.

"Oh!" Libby gasped. She balked in surprise as Bernie and she came upon Wayne rearranging chairs in the bride-side sacristy. "I didn't know you were still here." Once she caught her breath, she was able to get her bearings. "Want some help?"

Wayne gave a noncommittal shrug. "Soon as I'm finished stacking these extra chairs, I'm done."

Libby and Bernie donned their coats, lifting them from the row of hooks along the wall, pulling out scarves and caps and mittens.

"Want us to wait?" Libby didn't ask out of politeness or friendliness. The offer arose from being alert to the normal dangers of life in any city across the country. Closing up a church, inner-city or not, no matter how people felt about each other, there were precautions everyone took. In view of the events that had them all there that night in the first place, a murder occurring fewer than ten feet away just outside, Libby's proposal carried more implication than usual.

Wayne was curt. "I'll be fine."

Switching open the large, brass, deadbolt on the back door, Libby asked again. "Sure?"

The quick glare Wayne aimed in Libby's direction and the loud grunt as he adjusted two chairs beginning to slide made the answer clear. "You two, go. I'll check the front doors and set the alarm. Be out of here in a few minutes."

Libby went first, out into the cold and dark. The thin light from the overhead safety lamp sent shadows twitching on the brick walls that rose up waist high on each side of the steps. She held the outer glass storm door for Bernie, who was right behind her. "Do you have your key?" she asked.

Bernie pulled the main door shut behind him and locked it. "I've got it."

He paused to let Libby, still holding the outer storm door open, take a step down. Her everyday brain registered Bernie locking up as usual, but for a split second, her new investigative brain saw the action overlaid with suspicion.

"Gosh, it's freezing out here," Bernie said, bringing her back to the moment. He scrunched down into his coat and slapped on his cap.

Libby shivered. "I am really tired."

"Me, too." Bernie hustled past her down the remaining few steps over to his car parked in the nearby lot, calling back that he would see her in the morning.

Usually Libby would have followed on Bernie's heels, but she could not get something out of her head. She stood for a moment, reminded of all the times this sequence had repeated itself with Bernie or someone else. Sometimes it was she locking the main door and Father Henry holding the storm door. She could easily picture the priest on the step. Someone else locking up above him. She imagined Father Henry pivoting, carrying the red Storm Relief box. She saw Mrs. McGrew's jar of soup, heard bits of a friendly conversation. Was it someone he knew? Trusted? A friend?

But they were not friendly. Were they angry? Could it possibly have been an accident? The icy footing, an unplanned whirl around? Were they seizing an opportunity or finalizing a plan? This someone lifted the thurible. Father turned. To say good-bye? To say "you're fired"?

Libby looked up. Bernie was gone. Wayne's truck and her car remained.

And one other.

She recognized the car. Detective Grass. In the parking lot. Watching.

Watching me, thought Libby. Always watching.

Suddenly, Libby felt herself being pushed forward. She grabbed for the railing, but her 100% wool, crazy-patterned mittens couldn't get a grip and her hand slid like a child's down a polished banister, her music bag swinging as she tried to get her other hand around to stop the fall.

She felt her knees buckle and her body lurch forward down the steps, ricocheting against the elusive railing. One foot took hold, but her head kept spinning onward. Dizzy. Her breath came out in locomotive puffs. Even with his face in shadow, she saw it was Wayne above her. Rushing at her. Grabbing.

She twisted away from Wayne, away from the railing, trying to get both feet under her, frantic to make a run for it. At the bottom of the steps, two rough hands pinned her arms to her sides and stopped her. Dead in her tracks. The voice was harsh, demanding. "Libby!"

Her lungs hurt from gasping in the frigid air. She tried to wrestle free, but she was completely surrounded, held tight.

"Libby! Are you okay?"

Her body kept up the struggle while her mind began to clear, to hear the concern from the one calling her name.

"Libby! You're all right," he repeated.

In a shadowy light, Libby caught a glimpse of red Tartan plaid.

"I ... I ... what?" Her words came out in a sputter.

Once she recognized Detective Grass, once she was sure he was there to help, not to harm, she quit fighting.

He, in turn, relaxed the iron hold he had on her arms.

Wayne edged up next to her. Libby shrank from his hand coming to rest on her shoulder.

"I didn't know you were still out here," he said. "I must have backed into you. Or maybe the outer door bumped you when I was locking ..." He turned to the detective. "What the hell are you doing here?"

Grass released Libby once he saw that she was steady. "Just making sure everything gets closed up for the night. Safely."

Wayne took a step away from Libby and stared squarely at the other man. "You don't need to give me that look. If you were spying on us, which is how it looks to me, you'd know I didn't push her."

Grass raised his eyebrows, an unspoken question to Libby.

It had happened so quickly. She tried to replay the event. "I felt ... I was just standing there. I was ... knocked off balance."

Libby expected Wayne to get defensive. He did not. He sounded sure of himself.

Her suspicious brain was now fully engaged. She couldn't decide if Wayne's explanation made so much sense because it was true or because it was rehearsed. Or that it was the kind of excuse he was used to making up on the spot.

"I didn't even know she was here," Wayne said, still not sounding defensive. He looked at Libby. "You and Fruehauf left ten minutes ago. How the hell was I supposed to know you were standing here?"

It made sense. Although Libby knew that if a person wanted to see the church steps, there were windows that gave a partial view from the sacristy hallway. Detective Grass probably—no, given the lighting, only possibly—could have seen an overt attempt by Wayne to shove her down the steps.

She had seen the detective, knew he was in his car; Wayne had probably not. And Wayne was right about how you back into the one outer door while locking the inner door. That, too, made sense.

The logic did not necessarily comfort her.

"I'm cold," Libby said. "I want to go home."

"That makes two of us." The surly tone returned in full force as Wayne zipped up his sweatshirt and lifted the hood over his head. He jutted his chin out at the detective. "Sorry to spoil your stakeout."

Detective Grass looked Wayne up and down. Then he looked at Libby. "Do you want me to follow you home?"

"No. I'm fine. I … I'll call Namita, my renter upstairs, and tell her to watch for me. I'm fine. Really."

The detective stood aside and waited until Libby and Wayne got into their vehicles, car and truck, respectively.

Once behind the wheel, Libby took off her mittens briefly and blew warm breath on her stiff fingers because her hand was shaking too much to put the key in the ignition. A dozen emotions churned through her body, from her stomach to her head and down to her frozen fingers. Once the shaking calmed, she slid the key into the ignition; the engine wobbled and turned over. The most welcome sound was that of the automatic locks engaging, keeping her safely in—and everyone else out.

In the cab of his truck, Wayne lit a cigarette and inhaled deeply before shifting into gear. He glanced over the cold steering wheel at the detective watching from the bottom of the back steps of the church. Wayne exhaled a long trail of smoke and cold and profanity. "Fu-u-ck."

In the novels, Libby would have come home and walked Dash with Namita and Paki. Over tea, she would have elaborated on how unnerving it had been to stand on the church steps and imagine Father Henry's murder. How she'd caught sight of Detective Grass watching her and how creepy that had been, feeling that he was just waiting for her to do something that would give her away as the guilty party. She'd have rubbed at the wrench in her forearm, reliving the missed grasp of the railing, the pressure on her back that had propelled her forward. Was it the unintentional swing of the door—or the all-too intentional shove of Wayne's backside? Just enough of a scare to warn her, to frighten her.

Away from the danger, fears quelled, the storybook mystery would have unfolded in front of the fire; the conversation would have been delicious and reassuring.

In reality, it was nearly ten o'clock when Libby reached her back door. Namita was out with friends, leaving the apartment upstairs dark. Only one lamp downstairs, on a timer, registered the most meager of receptions. Dash eagerly met his mistress. While still dressed for the cold, Libby took him out for his nightly-duty run.

On one hand, she refused to be intimidated by the episode at church. On the other, she refused to be stupid. She tucked her cell phone in her coat pocket, snapped a security whistle on an elastic cord over her wrist, and made a quick trip around the block, alert to every movement, while tugging mercilessly at Dash to hurry up.

The nighttime temperature in the house had already begun to drop as the thermostat had been programmed for it to do. Libby pulled on a pair of thick, knee-high ski socks to warm what wasn't already covered by her long flannel nightgown and crawled into bed on the side BabyCakes had left for her.

She should have listened to the novelist.

Without the tea, the conversation, the decompressing, everyone fell down the steps all night long in Libby's dreams. Father Henry tumbled again and again. Bernie fell. She fell. Maggie fell with Mrs. McGrew's jar of soup. Sometimes Wayne was at the top step; sometimes Detective Grass. They fell down church steps, Libby's home steps, and neighborhood sidewalks that morphed into steps. No matter where Libby put her dreaming foot, the firmament gave way until her waking legs jumped and jerked her back into the real night.

After tossing and turning for hours, she laid there, her muscles contracted tight against the imagined fallings. She knew her only hope for circulation and sleep was to uncurl. To relax.

At the end of the bed, Dash was oblivious and content. BabyCakes butted up against Libby, taking advantage of the body heat she threw off. The cat adjusted as Libby forced herself to unbend arms and legs, to loosen her tight fist of fingers. With little fuss, BabyCakes re-curled himself into Libby's new position.

After long minutes of counting backwards from a hundred, then staring at one point of light on the bedroom door until her eyelids went stiff, Libby gave up her regular methods of lulling herself back to sleep.

Finally, she let one hand steal forth into the cold night from under the covers to locate BabyCakes's side, to feel the comforting, rhythmical rise and fall of his soft warm belly.

The Meditation Masters said to focus on the breath.

They did not specify whose.

Chapter Thirty-Two

On Thursday, no one thought about murder. Final preparations for the funeral of Father Henry Felger blocked out everything else.

Bernie added a sweater vest under his sports coat. Neither heat nor air conditioning adequately reached the choir loft, so he prepared to be chilly. Playing at so many funerals, he did not dress up for most of them. But today, Bernie wore his best outfit: a navy jacket, sweater vest, dress slacks, and a white shirt.

Standing before the bathroom mirror, he combed through his wispy, gray hair and approved the tie he had chosen, the one with the navy and blue diamonds. It occurred to him that this was the same outfit he'd worn for his father's funeral. And his mother's. His hands began to shake at the thought.

He needed something to eat. He wasn't in the mood for his regular oatmeal. Instead he fixed a piece of toast and sat at the kitchen table where mother, father, and son had eaten together for most of his life. Prayers before the meal. Prayers after the meal.

It was still early.

Par for the course, he hadn't slept well. Bernie stared past the toast at the painted wood tabletop, while his thoughts jumped around like water testing a hot skillet. His family had recited the rosary together at this table, led by his mother; her voice, in prayer at least, reassuring and sweet. At the same table, his father had shined his shoes every Saturday night for church the next day. He'd lived to be ninety-seven. That would be twenty more years for me, thought Bernie.

He returned to the present and thought about the Bishop saying the funeral Mass. Thank goodness Libby was singing. He wondered how many priests would show up. There would be ones he liked and admired and didn't get to see very often. There would be a few who made him uncomfortable with their lack of … What to call it? Priestliness? All that pretending to be reverent when they were often arrogant. Or mean.

It wasn't right.

He caught himself; reprimanded himself. It wasn't, after all, his job to judge those priests. Men of God.

A slew of thoughts veered toward Father Henry: The last time Bernie had seen him; the pilgrimage to the Holy Land they had gone on …

Bernie squelched every one as soon as they entered his mind. Not today, he cautioned himself. Not before the funeral. Eat your toast. Wear your scarf. Play the organ. Pray.

Finally, Bernie headed off to church.

Maggie poked at her hair. She'd never had it cut this short before. Did it really make her look younger, more stylish, like Julia said? Tipping and turning her head in the rectory mirror, Maggie considered there might be some truth to her daughter's flattery. The blues and yellows in her new shawl added a nice pop of color, too. Of course, she would leave it in her office for the funeral, the dark-print dress beneath more suited for the day ahead.

It would be a busy day, a heavy day. But the image in the mirror hinted at a certain lightness, bubbliness, just below the surface. There was too much to do yet to acknowledge it and too many potential missteps to give it free rein, but it was delightful to admit its existence.

Maggie let Mrs. McGrew, Jonny Kwan, and Lavina Woodson and her crew into the Parish Hall. Side dishes, salads, and desserts would begin arriving shortly, while the caterers would deliver the entrees closer to noon.

Maggie checked the arrangement of tables set for eighty. Not all visiting priests would stay for the luncheon, and the number of people in the congregation who would come was hard to gauge. There was always more than enough coffee and desserts to satisfy any number who might show up.

One more time, Maggie surveyed the room with approval.

Then Maggie headed over to church.

Libby lined up her music on the kitchen table. Again. She walked herself through the sequence of the service—each hymn, each response, each solo section, each added piece for funerals—stopping occasionally to practice a tricky musical passage.

She buttoned up the jacket to a wool suit, black with an almost indiscernible gray windowpane check. She'd added a white turtleneck because she was still cold from the night before. The herbal tea had helped, but the small bowl of oatmeal, even with specially added almonds and dried apricots, had been eaten more for sustenance than pleasure.

Namita had already left for work, which allowed Libby to warm up her voice vigorously and loudly for a good chunk of time instead of only getting to go full-throated after she was in her car. Namita appreciated Libby's singing, but not so much to wake up to a full blast of "Holy God, We Praise Thy Name."

Most people thought singers just showed up and sang. Some did. Libby was not one of them. Even before age started requiring more preparation, Libby's own standards for being in good form called for it.

For an eleven o'clock funeral, an important funeral, with a big congregation she would be responsible to lead; with challenging songs, songs she did not sing often or songs that went unusually high, it was best for Libby to be up several hours ahead, not singing the whole time, but getting the instruments, the voice and body, ready. She would eat early enough to have the food digested, drink enough fluids to hydrate everything, get the morning gunk out of her throat, and flex her mouth all around for clearer articulation. And then …

Time to go.

Libby packed the books and separate song sheets, along with the outline of the service in her music bag; cough drops and tissues went into a side pocket. She gave Dash an extra treat, BabyCakes an extra hug, and reminded them to be there when she got home, when she would need their support and company.

Then Libby headed for church.

Daniel got up earlier too, so he could have the breakfast and companionship he needed to carry him through the day. Before heading downstairs, Daniel pressed his blue cotton shirt until it could have stood on its own; changed ties twice.

Paul Thomas had gotten up even earlier, to make sure things were ready and available for his partner.

Daniel sat across from Paul Thomas, who loved him and knew him so well. The thought of losing it all made Daniel's stomach lurch. He sipped the strong, rich coffee; freshly ground, freshly brewed; and hoped it would settle his nerves. He poked at the beautiful omelet and tried, for his partner's sake, to eat. In time, Paul Thomas gently tugged the fork from Daniel's fingers, set it beside the plate, and lightly brushed the top of Daniel's hand.

Then Daniel put on his coat and headed for church.

Wayne had a hard time finding a tie, not to mention one that matched his only good plaid shirt. It wouldn't matter much anyway, he reckoned, zipping his dark sweatshirt over it all. He knew he would be inside and out, helping with parking and on call for problems at the Parish Hall. Hopefully, there would be no plumbing issues.

He had opened the church and turned up the heat, and thanked a generic deity that it was not snowy or icy. He finished his cigarette and tossed the butt into the flower bed that edged St. Hedwig's small parking lot in the back. Last summer, he'd planted it with red and white petunias. Today, he couldn't care less.

Several cars, probably priests', had arrived since he'd been in the basement. He spotted a familiar one located in only a slightly different spot than from the night before. Did that man never go home?

Wayne popped a breath mint into his mouth. He grinned broadly and waved at Detective Grass, who returned the salute.

Then Wayne headed back into church.

+ + +

No. Never wanted to be a saint. God forbid. Too much work. I suppose some priests look in that direction, when they're young, full of inspiration, wanting to be good, perfect. I can see more of them wanting to be Pope. Like a kid wanting to be President. It's probably good that somebody wants to take all that on. Hard enough running a parish, much less the Universal Church.

Saints sure come in all shapes and sizes. Built hospitals, founded monasteries, some just washed dishes. I imagine some were fun to be around. Harder to be with if they were confronting hypocrisy, challenging you to really live the Gospel. Probably half of them you didn't notice until they were dead.

Glad I can leave some money, the chapel, otherwise my legacy is pretty thin. As if priests need a legacy. You do what you can do. I don't think there are any saints in this diocese. There are some really good men. Ordinary—no more, no less. Mother Teresa had it right—God doesn't call us to be successful, only to be faithful.

I know faithful confessors, prayerful priests, good examples, good guides to holiness.

God help us, I also know the pompous, the self-righteous. The lazy and indulgent.

May God have mercy on us all.

+ + +

There was a set of traveling diocesan vestments that showed up for special occasions where more than several priests gathered for a liturgy. Such as the funeral of a priest.

The garments were large circles of cloth folded in half with a cutout at the center to slip over the wearer's head. One size fit all as the material draped from the shoulders over whatever slender frame or full girth it had to cover.

In centuries past, vestments were works of art—appliques, embroidery sewn with threads of gold. The ones delivered to St. Hedwig's the morning of Father Henry's funeral were contemporary, utilitarian—plain, cream-colored, with a panel of faux gold material across the shoulders and down the front and back.

Ten fifteen. Forty-five minutes before the eleven o'clock funeral.

Many of the vestments still waited on hangers, while some had already been put on by the nine or ten priests milling about in the bride-side sacristy chatting informally in groups, as they leaned against the counters, sat at the round Formica table, or used the restroom in the corner under the high shelf packed with Christmas decorations.

The Host, a priest known for his love of lavish dinner parties, stood in front of a full-length mirror attached to the restroom door. His movie star good looks were enhanced by a golden tan obtained in warmer climes. He examined his reflection and set about carefully combing hair that had been mussed while pulling on his vestment.

Next to the Host, a middle-aged colleague held his arms out and studied the fall of his garb. "Is my panel straight?" he asked no one in particular. He twisted his torso for a view of the back. "Does it hang evenly on the bottom?"

The Host continued repairing his part. "Do you want a ruler?"

"Do you have one?"

The Host took leave of his reflection and sat with the group at the table.

Giving up adjusting his hemline, the colleague craned his neck over the Host's shoulder, eyeing the tabletop and asking in a reverent hush, "Is that … *the* thurible?"

"You mean the murder weapon?" the Host replied with dramatic detachment.

There were grimaces all around.

"That's what it is," insisted the Host.

"Not this one," another priest said sensibly. "This one's from the Cathedral. I'm sure the … the other one … is with the police."

Mention of the police and murder drew the attention of everyone in the small room. It was not a topic anyone wanted to pursue, but it could not be ignored, sitting as they were in the place it had happened, getting ready to bury the man it had happened to.

"Very sad," said Monsignor Jimmy.

"Very creepy," said a standing colleague. "Killed on the steps coming out of church."

The Host sat back casually. "Could happen to any one of us. You piss— irritate some nutcase parishioner."

A young Nigerian priest helping out in the diocese bowed slightly. He spoke softly, gently. "We must pray for his …"

"Murderer."

The standing colleague rolled his eyes at the Host. "Do you have to be so blunt?"

"I was going to say *soul*," the soft-spoken one finished.

A large, old, bespectacled priest by the counter folded his arms. "Better have your lamps trimmed and ready for the Lord's coming, brothers."

"Indeed. We know not the day nor the hour," added another. "We must all be prepared for our God."

The Host smoothed his hair. "Or some nutcase."

Libby had intended to get to church and spend a little quiet time by Father Henry's casket before things got too crazy. But crazy they got; more quickly than planned.

Early-bird priests had already invaded both sacristies. Wayne was plunking down hymnals, mumbling his usual complaint about the pews not having built-in book racks. Bird Hawkins met up with Libby. Wayne had told Bird to tell her that the cousins were asking if the programs had arrived. A priest bumbling through the church inquired loudly where the restrooms were.

Libby led Bird to the programs in the priest-side sacristy, then led the old bumbler around to the restroom on the other side, where he would have to wait his turn.

"There's our singer," said the large, bespectacled priest, leaning back against the counter. "Oooh, that angelic voice," he said with a swoon.

Several priests turned and smiled in greeting. Libby was always pleased but embarrassed by such recognition. A good number of those present knew her from singing at weddings or funerals in their own parishes, in addition to ones they might have concelebrated at St. Hedwig's for a former member of their congregation or a relative.

"Thank you," Libby said graciously. "And thank you for coming today. I'm sure Father Henry appreciates it. On behalf of the parish, I've been asked to invite you all to the church hall across the street for lunch after the prayers at the cemetery following the funeral. I know some of you have to get back to your own business of the day, or have some distance to drive. Please, go to the head of the food line." She cracked a smile. "As with all high-end eating establishments, carryout is available."

The back door opened and another clump of priests shuffled in.

Between unbuttoning heavy black coats or unzipping jackets of their favorite teams, they acknowledged their fellow clergy. Close on their heels came Bernie, through the door, his capped head down, music satchel snug under his arm.

If several priests knew Libby, they all knew Bernie Fruehauf. It was as if invitations had been sent out, and they were all waiting for the guest of honor.

"Ber-nard, Ber-nard," two of them chanted.

A robust chortle was followed by a chorus of "How's old Flew Off? Flew Off the handle?"

Monsignor Jimmy roared out, "Now, we can start!"

After fifty years of playing everywhere in the diocese, at practically every parish, Bernie, in turn, knew each of them by name and returned their welcome, just as friendly, but in his self-deprecating way.

"Good morning, Father Ramon. Monsignor Jimmy. Father Walter. I see your old Ford made the trip."

"Missed you at St. Margaret's fish fry," someone called from across the room.

A paunchy, Friar Tuck-looking priest put his hand on Bernie's shoulder. "Nice job at St. Bede's the other week. Thanks again for playing that funeral Mass."

While always polite, Bernie's familiarity allowed for wide latitude in his teasing. "You know I'd do anything for you, Father. You're such a sweet person."

Hoots and howls from the others.

"Well, now, that's debatable. But the family was grateful. It was so late in the afternoon," Friar Tuck went on. "She and her husband were both converts of mine, and I knew he really wanted a Latin Mass."

The pudgy priest turned to include Libby. "And you. You should come sing for us sometime."

"Happy to," replied Libby. "Not the Latin Mass, of course. No cantors in the Mass of those days."

"You'd be the wrong gender anyway," said the Host, crossing to the restroom door and going in as the bumbling priest came out.

"Yes. Definitely no women," several said, nodding their heads, some with a serious look, some making a face.

The old priest leaning against the counter huffed a steaming breath on one lens and polished his glasses on his vestment. "Did you hear about the woman supposedly being ordained at the Episcopal church downtown?"

"Not unusual for the Episcopalians," came the retort.

"No," said the leaning one. "She's supposedly Catholic. League or Federation of Roman Catholic priests or some such thing. They've got a renegade bishop coming in from Cincinnati to ordain her."

Reactions were mixed—shock, disapproval, mockery, approval.

Not to mention Libby's heightened interest.

"Wonder if she'd come sub for me," a plucky, young priest considered as he traded his winter coat for a vestment. "I'd like to go to Florida after Easter."

A bent, old priest next to him was horrified.

"Easy for you to be horrified," the younger one said. "Your age group is going to die off and leave about five of us male priests to run all seventy-two parishes in the diocese."

The old priest blinked and lowered his head even further. "I shall pray for you, my son."

"Wouldn't hurt you to pray for your daughters, too." The young one took out a tissue and blew his nose. "Golly, it's cold this morning. Are you playing for that ordination, Fruehauf?"

There was good-natured snickering.

Friar Tuck removed his hand from Bernie's shoulder. "I think you'd be excommunicated if you did."

Libby caught her mouth from dropping open. She dragged out her skepticism. "Noooo …"

"Fired probably," the young one asserted. "Excommunicated? Depends on the powers that be."

Bernie looked mildly aghast. "Oh. My."

Libby swallowed. "Yes. Oh. My."

"Guess I won't put that on my schedule," said the organist with firm resolution.

The restroom door opened. The Host, his tan in sharp contrast with the pale priest next in line, re-entered the conversation. "Hail, Bernie. I see you're still wearing that ratty, old cap. How is the captain of the marry-and-bury 'em team? Libby Kinder. How's your family?"

Libby wasn't as starstruck as most. To her, the Host was a little too slick, interested in dropping names and picking up gossip wherever he landed. She didn't think of it as being catty, merely talking to him on his own level when she said in return, "How was Fort Myers?"

The Host tilted his head and corrected her as if she should have known better. "Naples, dear. Better beaches."

The standing colleague had taken a chair. "Don't you worry about skin cancer?"

"No, I don't. I focus on the vitamins."

"I focus on the cost," the colleague said, pulling the gold panel of his vestment into line as he sat. "Or are you at some Patron's condo?"

"Bingo! You ought to go sometime," the Host expounded. "You, too, Bernie. Put a little color in those cheeks. Do you good to get away. Travel. See the world. And you, Jimmy. Would help with that Parkinson's."

Several priests turned with solicitous inquiries about the monsignor's condition. He merely laughed heartily and declared the human body a fascination to him every day.

"Still," the Host continued, "You deserve it. We all deserve it."

Friar Tuck said, "I hear Father Henry left millions to the Church. Wants a chapel built in his name."

A hint of whininess crept into the colleague's voice. "Now there's a patron. He could have given us all a nice trip. A little getaway. It didn't have to be to Europe or China. I'd settle for … Arizona."

Friar Tuck touched Libby's forearm. "Is it true Henry's diary is floating around somewhere? That they can't find the money till they find the diary?"

"That's my understanding," said Libby.

Several priests inched closer to the conversation. A wide-eyed one said what they were all thinking. "What else do you think is in that diary?"

Conjectures went round the table, running the gamut from serious to frivolous.

"Trysts? Gambling records?"

"Probably just his doctor appointments."

"Maybe he wrote poetry. His homilies were always quite literary and historical."

"He'd love to hear that," one scoffed. "It's probably loaded with his great theological babblings."

"Do people really keep diaries?" wondered the young, soft-spoken priest.

Monsignor Jimmy scratched at his ear. "I keep a diary. Not so unusual. Although I do hope no one ever reads mine. I'd like to keep my theological babblings to myself."

"Quit calling it a diary." The colleague rose from his seat. "It's a journal. They can be very therapeutic. An outlet for …"

All talk stopped.

Everyone's attention diverted to the Master of Ceremonies gliding in from the other sacristy. For any ceremony involving the Bishop, there was an assistant—a Master of Ceremonies. It could be a priest, a seminarian, a deacon, or a layman that the Bishop relied on to guide him through elaborate and complex rituals, making sure all necessary accessories, personnel, music, and assistants were on hand and onboard. A little like managing a Broadway roadshow.

Libby liked this MC. His good humor smoothed over the sharp edges often on display in a collection of clergy; perhaps, in part, because as a married lay person, he was not one of them. She judged him to be fit and forty. Short, sandy-colored hair and a nose pointier than was attractive, granted him a note of seriousness and underscored his position of being in charge.

Whether they liked him or not, everyone in the room, including Libby, respected him because he alone knew how and in what order everything was supposed to happen. He alone could make them look good or like they hadn't a clue.

"Greetings, everyone." The MC strode into the room, his long, black cassock swirling at his feet, his white surplice starched and neatly pressed. "Always sorry to see you under these circumstances. My condolences, especially to you who were close to Father Henry."

He glanced in Bernie's direction. "Bernard. You and Libby holding the parish together?"

They smiled at the acknowledgment, but kept to the periphery. Priests at the table parted to let the MC in close to light the charcoal in the thurible.

Bernie checked the clock above the sanctuary door. "Oh. My. It's getting late. I'd better go upstairs."

The Host gave an irreverent snort. "The Bishop's not here yet, is he?"

The MC looked at the clock. "Too early. Relax, Bernie."

10:40 a.m. It was too early for the Bishop, but it was not early. And *relax* was not in Bernie Fruehauf's vocabulary. He excused himself and proceeded upstairs to the organ. Libby followed him into the sanctuary where she, also a stickler for being totally prepared and on time, looked over her things at the cantor's podium. Out in the church, many people had already arrived. The casket remained closed, front and center.

Libby viewed the sanctuary, the altar, the extra chairs, the special place of honor for the Bishop. All set.

From the far-side sacristy, the pale, old priest she had encountered earlier looking for a restroom hobbled in Libby's direction. "I've broken my glasses, dear," he said in a loud, reedy whisper. "Do you have some tape I might use to repair them?"

He smiled a smile Libby recognized. It was meant to produce enough guilt to get whatever he asked for. Her uncle had it. A fourth-grade nun had it.

"Some black electrical tape would be preferable," he added.

Libby tried to locate Wayne. The clock was ticking; the old priest, demanding. She grabbed her keys. This was just the kind of crazy, last-minute, unnerving kind of thing she often ran into. No time to bother with a coat. Libby picked her way through the cloud of clergy, out the back door, and down the steps in her high heels, then around and down a flight of stairs into the workshop in the church basement.

The plumber was right, observed Libby. There were lots of new tools. Expensive tools. No time to look at them now. No tape on the wallboard or workbench. She opened a drawer and saw several kinds of tape.

And a pile of store gift cards.

Bernie's prelude music overhead kept her on task. She grabbed the black electrical tape and trekked back upstairs where she delivered it to the old priest. She was in a flurry; he, cool as a cucumber.

The MC caught her and asked if there were programs for the priests. Bird had taken them all to the back, she told him. The MC looked at his watch and adjusted easily, telling her he would send the priests to the back. They can get their own programs and begin lining up for the funeral, he suggested. Libby took a breath and smiled at the MC.

"Relax," the MC repeated. "Remember, nothing happens until you and I say go. And no, the Bishop is not here yet. I suggest you go suck a cough drop. It could be another couple of minutes. Or so."

10:58 a.m. No Bishop. From her cantor's seat, Libby watched the

MC standing calmly at the sacristy door. The casket had been rolled to the back of church, where it was lost in the crowd of mourners filing in, thirty priests in uniform vestments, and more than a dozen Knights of Columbus, their plumed hats rising above like drum majors before the parade got underway.

Bernie's playing could hardly be heard above the chatter. Libby lifted her head to see someone upstairs touring the church, pointing things out to a child leaning over the organ-loft railing. All Libby could think of was the child falling and killing itself.

She was now at full-tilt nervous energy.

11:03 a.m. Father Henry, the most punctual man Libby had ever known, would be appalled. But he no longer had a say.

11:10 a.m. The Bishop, a plump, ruddy-faced man, strolled down the side aisle of St. Hedwig's, nodding at people and shaking hands as if he were running for mayor. Or President.

It was the smell of incense that calmed Libby. It took her, not to a murder, not even to the immediate concerns of the dead, but to the familiar motions of the funeral Mass, which she knew by heart. She settled into that familiarity.

Finally, it was time.

The MC swung the smoking, borrowed, gold thurible as he led the Bishop, dressed in cream-and-gold embellished vestments, wearing a mitre and carrying a shepherd's crook, to the rear of church, head of the parade.

Once in place, the MC nodded at Libby. She stood up at her podium and the music stopped.

In that hush, she watched as the casket was pushed into the center aisle, pallbearers surrounding it and family gathering behind. Don Fleck lay the white pall over it; then the Bishop sprinkled holy water on it, adorned it with a small crucifix, and briefly prayed over it.

In those few moments of ceremony, Bernie took stock of his seventy-six-year-old hands poised above three manuals of ivory organ keys. Not a hint of arthritis. At how many more funerals would they play? he wondered.

The MC turned his eyes again toward Libby and nodded. At her command, everyone stood. Marshaling all her nervous energy, Libby directed the congregation to join the organ in the robust, triumphant, gathering hymn.

Into a filled-to-capacity St. Hedwig's, ablaze with lights and candles, came the procession: a cross bearer, two servers, the MC swinging spicy-scented incense from the thurible, the Bishop, the casket, cousins; and thirty priests, their rich male voices singing out, bold and bright.

As he walked beneath the drawn swords of the Knights of Columbus lining the center aisle, Wayne felt exhilaration he hadn't expected; a sense that there were possibly more perks to the situation than he'd anticipated. He deserved this kind of respect, a kind of compensation, even if it was at the expense of his cousin Henry. The swords looked valuable. He'd have to check them out on eBay.

St. Hedwig's looked splendid. Daniel was happy with the white calla lilies and baby's-breath he'd chosen for the main altar. Elegant. He felt that art and material beauty were not only expressions of the Divine spark in humans, but a means to draw humans closer to the Spiritual. Father Henry's casket moved slowly, majestically, down the aisle. Father Henry. Was he closer to the Divine? pondered Daniel. Did he now understand things that had failed to make themselves known to him on earth?

First one, then another priest Daniel knew to be gay passed Daniel's pew. One was a rich baritone, the other practically tone deaf. Both made Daniel smile.

Reaching the front, Father Henry's family was steered left while the clergy veered right, filling several rows not far ahead of Maggie. She picked out the five or six priests she'd worked for or had had extended interactions with. In turn, they were dumber than Father Henry, more arrogant, maybe more thoughtful, more caring. She'd tried to be nice, to see them as human beings, but mostly they had ticked her off. All water under the bridge now, she thought. All water under the bridge.

The service proceeded. Was the Bishop worth the wait? Not particularly. Libby gave his homily a C-. The delivery was strong, jovial, articulate; the content, vapid and generic. Anecdotes about the newly departed member of his flock made her think he had never met the man. Maybe not so surprising given all the conferences the weekly diocesan paper reported he attended. All over the country. Yes, the Bishop was a man on the move.

Mostly on task throughout the Mass, Libby did not fall prey to emotion until near the end when the thurible, re-stoked, sent its sweet smoke gently streaming forth. The MC rounded up the Bishop, the servers, and concelebrating priests on the altar. The congregation bobbed to its feet unevenly; collectively representing the Church Militant on earth, then stood poised for the final commendation of Father Henry Felger, hopefully now a member of the Church Triumphant in heaven.

During the pause, as the main participants moved into their places to process out, Libby suddenly sensed relief was near, felt the stress of preparing, hosting, and performing the last few days, felt the awful and ugly specter of death and murder recede and melt into the tender words of "In Paradisum."

She faced the casket. Feelings of sadness and guilt and mercy stole into her solo. The first words she sang were shaky, but soon the priests joined softly. Feeling their support and Bernie's sure hands on the organ, Libby let the music lead her:

May the angels guide you and bring you into Paradise, and may all the martyrs come forth to welcome you home. ... May the angels sing to welcome you. And like Lazarus, forgotten and poor, you shall have everlasting rest.

If the final commendation at the funeral Mass sent Father Henry Felger's soul into the welcoming arms of the angels, the commendation at the cemetery sent his body into the earth, to the dust unto which he was returned. Only the cousins and a few others braved the cold to gather on the hard ground at the outside gravesite. The prayers there were unpretentious and brief, hurried along by the bone-chilling temperature.

Then, just as Robert Frost had predicted, "they, since they / were not the ones dead, turned to their affairs.

Chapter Thirty-Three

Detective Grass had been to funeral luncheons before, on duty and off. Never one for a murdered priest.

Inside St. Hedwig's Parish Hall, he tried to appear casual, but continued pressure from the county prosecutor to find Father Henry Felger's killer was starting to make him fidgety. He'd been handed what he thought was an open-and-shut case: neighbor's teenage nephew caught in an impromptu robbery turned deadly. That solution quashed, the circle of suspects had widened to antagonized neighbors who hated cats, relatives counting on an inheritance, and most pointedly, five employees who had keys to the church and access to the now confirmed murder weapon. Alibis were lousy; motives slight.

As usual, something was missing.

At this juncture, the fact-based detective longed for just a touch of intuition. He could put data together and draw conclusions, but he wasn't necessarily great at collecting all the pieces—catching an offhand remark, deciphering an action correctly. Sometimes hints slipped by him, only later for him to realize their importance. Sometimes he spent more time incorrectly jamming little pieces in rather than holding off and waiting to see how they might accurately fit—or not—in the big picture.

Loitering about Father's Henry's mourners, he planned to ask a lot of questions and hope something would fall in his lap.

Soon.

Wayne watched Libby watch Grass talking to someone by the coat rack. Several long tables for the priests ran along the front of the hall near the food. Elsewhere people visited respectfully, then fell into clusters of family or friends at the smaller, round tables; all set with white cloths and small vases of fresh flowers, compliments of the Social Committee.

"Who's our little detective chatting up over there?" The custodian stood closer to Libby than she liked. When he exhaled, his cigarette breath grazed her ear, which reminded her of college bars at midnight and deadbeat dates.

In the light of day, however, labeling him a murderer still seemed a stretch. Even adding up his unattractive qualities, Libby found it difficult to stand next to someone she knew and worked with and see him in that horrific way.

Even after the episode the night before on the back steps of the church.

Even with one official and one unofficial detective in the room.

"That's Lawrence Davis," said Libby, moving a step sideways to put a more tolerable distance between her and Wayne's nicotine aura. "He's a parishioner. And a detective."

"Great. Now we've got both of them breathing down our necks."

Much of Libby felt the same way. Go away, she wanted to shout. Get on with it. Go figure this out and arrest somebody, but leave me and the people I know alone.

"Listen," said Wayne, his voice unusually relaxed. "I'm sorry about your fall last night. I hope you're okay."

Libby could never get a firm read on this guy. She kept a wary eye out, even as he continued to sound sincere.

"You want something to eat?"

She did not.

"Come on. Let me take you to lunch," he said playfully. "If you sit with me and the family, boring as my cousins might be, you can be the first in line. After all the priests, of course. The line's going to be long."

She didn't care.

Across the room, the two detectives parted. Lawrence aimed for his wife at a table; Detective Grass headed straight toward Wayne and Libby.

Libby abruptly turned toward the buffet. "I hope they have

something hot."

They did. Homemade soup. Perfect.

A seventy-eight-year-old woman, tiny as a pixie, bubbly as a child, ladled the soup from a large pot into a plastic bowl. Libby had never seen Mrs. McGrew in anything but casual slacks and a tailored shirt, topped with a tightly permed halo of white hair. Today was no different, except she'd added a white chef's apron from the church kitchen. Her perennial fashion accent was a pair of blue rhinestone earrings and matching necklace that made her eyes sparkle as if they were part of the set.

With practiced care, Mrs. McGrew placed the bowl on Libby's tray. "Your singing was beautiful this morning," she said. "As usual. I just love that song at the end about the angels welcoming you into Paradise."

Libby reached for a crusty baguette. "Thanks. I love it, too. A little tough to sing today."

Mrs. McGrew's eyes softened, along with her voice. "I'm sure it was."

The serving line stalled ahead at a relish tray, keeping Libby by the soup and its server. "I see you have extra crew here today."

"Jonny and Bird rounded up reinforcements. Wasn't sure Jonny wanted to do another funeral, so quick after his boy's, but he said it was better to stay busy. And busy, that's Bird's middle name."

Mrs. McGrew tittered as she ladled out a bowl of soup for Wayne. "And you, Mr. Maintenance. Bet you're glad we aren't dealing with that old toilet again."

"Yes, I am," said Wayne, trying not to spill the full bowl handed to him.

Libby couldn't help it. Mentally she flipped open her notebook to Heading: Alibis. Wayne. Plumber. Timing. "Heard that plumber was here for hours," she started out. "Before the Webber funeral luncheon."

"All morning, far as I could tell." Mrs. McGrew looked to Wayne for confirmation. "You were already working at it when I got here at nine. Didn't leave till we shooed you out with the family coming at noon. Luckily we have more than one toilet. Thank goodness that's over and all fixed. Especially for today."

The food line started to move. "Soup is enough for me," Libby said over her shoulder to Wayne. She turned toward a table where

Father Henry's cousins were seated on the opposite side of the room.

Libby saw that Detective Grass had steered in the direction of the table set up for coffee and desserts, either in earnest or by default when Wayne and she were no longer in his path. He was stirring a steaming Styrofoam cup, his lips testing the steam, when Maggie walked out of the kitchen. As she laid out plates of cake and pie, he offered her a mint or some lozenge then appeared to engage her in light conversation. Light, thought Libby, but undoubtedly probing.

Wayne dragged over a chair from a nearby table and squeezed in next to the one Libby stood by. Cousin Phyllis stopped a forkful of rice casserole halfway to her mouth and scooted over to make room.

"Is that all you're eating?" the stocky, quiet Ruth asked, looking up from her full assortment of casserole samplings and side dishes. "No wonder you're so thin."

Libby laughed good-naturedly. "Don't worry. I'm just getting started." She quit staring at Maggie and Grass and sat down, letting herself be absorbed by the cousins. "I was so cold. Just wanted some soup to take the chill off."

"I hear you." Out-of-town cousin Catherine stabbed a green olive. "That cemetery was freezin' butt cold."

Laughter and agreement circled the table.

Although the group was the same, the atmosphere was noticeably chummier than their meeting in the rectory. "Are you staying long?" asked Libby.

"No," replied Catherine, cornering another olive. "Don't need to hang around for our big inheritance. We've signed papers and the lawyer will mail checks to us. You folks let us know if or when you find that diary."

Wayne snorted. "The one that confirms that all Henry's money goes for a stinking chapel? Not sure I care if they find that. Not sure if the police on this case are up to finding it."

He hitched a thumb toward Detective Grass, who had moved and was taking a seat next to Daniel at the far end of the priests' table. Libby noted the congenial look on the detective's face, the casual demeanor, and figured the same breezy, similarly probing conversation was taking place as when he'd been talking with Maggie.

Libby could be breezy and casual, too. She could find things out. Get answers and get on with it.

She broke off a crust of bread and buttered it. "Must have been a terrible shock to hear about Father Henry," she said, looking to engage the male cousin to her left. "When did you people in Minnesota find out?"

Edward spread mustard on his sandwich. He had proven to be taciturn, not unfriendly. "Phyllis called me. I called my sisters. Yes, it was a shock. Don't talk much to Henry, but a sudden death like that. Takes the wind out of your sails."

"The Vicar called me," Phyllis piped up. "I called Ruth."

Ruth gave a forlorn look at her rice casserole. "We were both …"

"… shocked," Phyllis finished for her. "We were both shocked."

Libby tried to sound casually conversational, not obviously fishing. "I know you were close. Had you talked to Father Henry recently? Sometime during that day perhaps?"

Phyllis checked with Ruth. "Not me. That was bridge day. I worked like a dog all morning making cabbage rolls so I could get them there and warmed up by ten forty-five a.m. We eat at eleven, play bridge until four. Gosh, I had terrible cards that day. Came home, fixed dinner for the two of us," she said, elbowing the beefy husband at her side. "We were watching TV when the Vicar called about eight o'clock."

Ruth sadly poked at her casserole, separating the rice from chicken as if they had been mistakenly put in the same dish. "I'm sorry I didn't get to talk to Henry either. Tom and I volunteer at the soup kitchen on Mondays and Wednesdays, seven a.m. to two thirty p.m. We were both pretty tired after that. I think we probably just came home and took a nap. There was no reason to call Henry." She turned to Phyllis. "What time did you say you called?"

"Right after the Vicar called, around eight."

People talked; people ate. St. Hedwig's Parish Hall relaxed and as with many well-fed funeral gatherings, eased into the banter and table hopping of people who didn't see each other often and so took advantage of the unplanned chance to connect.

Wayne never did anything more than remain socially pleasant, which was not necessarily reassuring to Libby, who continued to regard him with suspicion. She kept an eye on Detective Grass as he left Daniel and was snared by a Knight of Columbus, now minus his scarlet-lined cape and white-plumed hat, obviously happy to see the detective.

Eventually Libby excused herself from the cousins and made her way to get a cup of tea, by the table where Maggie continued to monitor desserts. "Bake sales and potlucks," mused Libby. "I'm such a sucker for people's homemade desserts. More interesting than any restaurant. Aren't you tempted?"

"I sampled practically everything in the kitchen," said Maggie. "The triple-berry pie wins hands down. Sorry, won. None left."

"I'm going to pass for the moment anyway. Tea will suffice." As she filled a cup with hot water, Libby gazed out over the hall. "Nice reception. A lot more priests stayed than I thought would." She dipped a tea bag into her cup. "Do you suppose many people here are aware there's a detective, two really, nosing around among them?"

Maggie made a cup of tea and busied herself rearranging the dessert assortment, pushing plates forward to fill in the empty spaces on the table. "Lawrence Davis blends in because he's a parishioner," she said, "but Detective Grass sticks out like a sore thumb. Maybe I'm just overly sensitive since he's so unsubtle about asking questions."

"I saw him over here," said Libby. "More where-were-you and what-were-you-doing kind of thing?"

"Those questions I can handle. I know where I was and when I did what. What I don't like are the questions about other people. Makes you feel like you're ratting on your friends. And at the man's funeral, for God's sake.

"Look at him, scavenging through the food line," she continued. "Pumping Mrs. McGrew. Now bothering Jonny Kwan. He makes it look like a friendly chat, but trust me, he's drilling for oil. What can I say about Wayne that's printable? Creepy. Slimy. Especially when he tries to be nice. Like he's always on the make. Then he wanted to know if I thought Bernie was that poor. As in so poor that inheriting a new car would be enough to make him kill Father Henry. I didn't think so, but how should I know?" Maggie laughed at the thought. "Lord knows, Bernie can be passive-aggressive when it suits his needs. Minimal as those are."

Libby swirled the tea bag in her Styrofoam cup but didn't interrupt.

Maggie obliged by going on. "Lots of questions about Daniel. Honestly, I wonder if he's ever met a gay man. Stereotype blather about him being the *decorator* at the church. His *relationship* with Paul Thomas. Maggie punctuated *decorator* and *relationship* so hard it made Libby wince.

"That's the kind of stuff he's asking?"

"Didn't leave you out of the mix," said Maggie. "Wanted to know what other *interests* you have. *Outside* of church. Any serious relationships. Did you and Father Henry have anything going on."

Libby's cup halted before it even reached her chin. "He wanted to know what?!"

"Oh, he asked a lot about you. Asked about how you and Father Henry *really* got along. How much did he *really* depend on you." Maggie folded her arms, careful not to spill her drink. "I told him Henry was like every other priest I ever worked for—an opportunist. If somebody was willing to help, he was happy to sit back and let them do the work."

Libby sent a scornful glance in the direction of Detective Grass, who was shooting the breeze with the Knight. "I don't blame you," Libby commiserated, "being asked for the dirt on other people's private lives."

"Oh, that doesn't bother me." Maggie's laugh was full-throated. "I don't want other people giving the dirt on mine!"

As Maggie retreated into the kitchen, Libby backed away from the pie and stood against the wall, sipping her tea and watching Detective Grass, now crossing to new pawns. Yes, thought Libby, it's what they say in the movies. It was like watching a giant chess game. He moved around the hall sideways, on the diagonal, up and over, cornering, capturing, eliminating people like pieces on a game board. To others, it must have looked like random encounters. But he's the official investigator, reasoned Libby. There must be some plan.

That's what Libby needed. A plan.

She decided to follow up each move of the detective's with her own countermove. If he got information, she would get the same. She wouldn't pry. She wouldn't make anybody rat on anyone else. If she could help it.

Bird Hawkins let out a loud chortle. Whatever information he was passing on to Grass, as they stood munching potato chips from a large bowl, must have been amusing. Even Bernie, at Bird's elbow, was laughing and looking more relaxed than Libby had seen him for the last week, probably like her, relieved at getting the wake and funeral behind him. Maybe he was wooed by the roll of candy mints the detective was offering.

Libby's black high heels clacked over the linoleum in the

opposite direction. Daniel had separated from the priest he'd lunched with and was pulling his coat from the back of his chair when she reached him.

"Surprised to see you still here," she said.

Daniel lifted his dark eyebrows as he slid a burgundy-plaid scarf over his head. "I hadn't expected to see an old friend. We used to jog together before he was transferred up north. Nice guy. Struggling like the rest of us with the Church on a lot of issues."

"That's heartening," said Libby. She tipped her head toward Grass. "I see the Head of the Inquisition is making the rounds."

"Yes. We had our little chat."

"Maggie said he asked her more about other people this time around."

"Same with me."

Daniel frowned and echoed Maggie's complaint. "What do I know about Wayne? Other than that he's an incompetent asshole. Correction. He's a very competent asshole; he's an incompetent custodian. Surly and unpleasant. What do I know about Maggie? Conscientious and easy to work with. Always has my paycheck on time. Bernie? Old-school reverent. Nice. When he's not playing for Mass somewhere, he's out visiting the sick."

"Boy," said Libby, "he's covering all the bases."

"Oh, rest assured, he did not skip you. But by then, I was bored giving personal evaluations. I lied. Said you were intelligent. Said your extracurricular activities include European mountain climbing and collecting African death masks."

Before Libby could object to the outlandish comments, Daniel amended his last bit with a sly smile. "I don't know if he believed me about the mountain climbing or African masks. And I let that part about intelligence slide."

"At least most of what you said seems true. Did you really call Wayne an incompetent asshole?"

"No."

Daniel's shoulders sagged, fatigue crept into his voice. "I need to quit letting him get under my skin. Maybe he had a rotten childhood." Daniel rubbed at his forehead. "I tried to remain factual. I don't enjoy tearing someone down. What difference does it make after all? What he wanted to know was could or would any of us kill Father Henry. Much as I would have liked to hand him the incompetent Wayne on a silver platter, I couldn't even do that with any conviction." He slipped his arms into his jacket. "So, did you get any unusual questions?"

"Haven't gotten any questions yet. Escaped him altogether so far."

"Be ready. He's digging."

"Anything you want me to say about your ironing skills? Or avoid about your decorating competence? He always seems pretty hot on your trail."

Daniel wrapped the scarf around his neck and zipped his black-leather jacket up next to it. "I can't fathom why." The sarcasm was front and center. "I'm gay and overtly opposed to the Church's stance on gays, which means I could be in danger of losing my job. I have a key to the church building. Wayne says he heard me arguing with Father Henry right before he apparently was killed. And I was the last to see him alive. For starters."

"Okay. Okay," Libby conceded reluctantly, "his interest in you sounds reasonable."

"I'm not sure every direction this detective is going in is entirely reasonable. For one thing, he seems hot on your trail, too. And not in a good way."

Libby took a minute to digest this. Her temptation was to be flip, but before she could get her retort out, Daniel put a firm hand on her arm. "Look, Libby, you've always seemed very open and honest. Not given to being hypocritical. Be careful. Don't give away more of yourself than you want. And don't worry about anyone else."

Libby wondered if Daniel was related to Dr. Whelan. He was delivering the same message, the same warning. His words were disturbing, but his concern and friendship, touching.

"Again," she said quietly, "I'm surprised you came."

He shoved both hands into his pockets until the search brought up his keys. His answer was also quiet, but unmistakably determined. "I came to the funeral Mass for Father Henry. I came to the luncheon because I won't be intimidated."

Libby sat at the spot at the table left vacant by Daniel and his priest friend. It was far enough away from the next diners conversing among themselves to give her the privacy to nurse the half cup of tea she carried with her and to collect her thoughts.

Lots of questions the detective was asking. About her.

She stared at the now dark tea and white Styrofoam cup.

She stared at the white cup surrounding the tea.

Libby longed for her notebook. At least a pen and a napkin. Across the table, several bundles of silverware lay, rolled neatly, unused. Libby undid two rolls and separated out five utensils; named them, respectively, Wayne, Daniel, Bernie, Maggie, and Libby. She lined them up in various ways, puzzling over their namesake's actions, words, and relationships. She knew from other puzzles that just one clue could get her on the right path.

She swirled the cold dark tea. In the white cup.

Stop looking at the tea, she told herself. Look at the cup.

Up to this point, she'd been looking at all the suspects' movements around Father Henry. What about Father Henry's movements?

She placed her cup on the table and rearranged the knives, forks, and spoons to radiate out from there. What were Father Henry's words? His actions? That had affected any of these people?

Be thorough.

Father did the Webber funeral the morning he died. Anything unusual? The felon. Detective Davis. The soup. Firing someone. Was that just frustration or a real threat?

Went to the cemetery. The felon. The cold.

The Webber luncheon. Did something happen at the luncheon? A conversation? An unwelcomed guest? Unplanned guest?

Back to church. The sacristy. The Storm Relief box. The argument. The thurible. The hit. The fall.

"Playing with your food again?"

Bird Hawkins boomed into Libby's reverie. With a jolt, she looked up to see him standing in his brown winter jacket beside Bernie, the two of them gawking over her shoulder at the implements on the table in seeming disarray.

"Just thinking," Libby said.

Bernie, appearing like one of those tiny birds that flit about huge rhinoceroses, hovered next to Bird, his coat on, cap under his arm. "Be sure you stop thinking long enough to get some dessert," he said, holding out a napkin-covered paper plate as if he'd won first prize. "Brownies. For tonight. I've already had two pieces of pie."

"I'll be heading to the kitchen for my own plate later," Bird boasted. "The longer you wait, the more leftovers they're happy to send you home with."

Libby tapped unconsciously at her knives and forks. "I see you were having a nice talk with Detective Grass," she said. "More investigating or just a chat?"

"A little of both, I guess," said Bernie, a wave of seriousness drawing his face downward.

"Don't be fooled, Bernard," Bird broke in. "They're always gathering information. Or verifying. Like the lab, confirming that the thurible had Father Henry's blood on it and ..."

"He tell you that?" Libby snapped.

"That, I already knew." Bird rocked back on his heels, expounding magnanimously. "And ... ashes."

Bernie's eyes widened. He never failed to be in awe of Bird's font of inside information. "Is that why he asked about where Wayne dumps the coals?"

"And about him smoking. You know—ashes."

Taking a moment for this to sink in, Bernie turned to Libby. "He asked about getting along with Wayne again. And Daniel. What I knew of them outside of church, which isn't much."

Bird rocked forward on his toes, bobbing his head with exaggerated emphasis. "He asked about you, Libby. Your friends. I told him you didn't have any." He let out a great buffoonish laugh.

"Oh, you did not," said Bernie.

Libby stacked the spoons on top of each other, making small clinks, and smiled. "I was thinking about the Webber funeral. Were you at that one, Bird?"

"I was. In the back. Did you know Stanley Webber was there? From prison?"

"Yes. Did you go to the cemetery?"

Bird nodded. "And the luncheon. They invited everybody who was at the cemetery. It was a miserable, cold day. And I was hungry."

"Did anything unusual happen at the luncheon?" she pressed. "Anybody unusual show up? Talk to Father Henry?"

The two men gave it some thought before they answered.

"I see where you're going here, Libby. Not too many people came, since it was so icy," Bird recalled. "Way too much food. Went home with a lot."

Libby re-stacked the spoons, trying to figure out what else to ask.

"Who did Father eat with?"

Bernie looked to Bird for confirmation, then shrugged. "Nobody special. Phil Bloom. Donald Klein."

"He sometimes sits with them while their wives are serving the food," Bird added. "He doesn't ever stay long. Kinda just puts in an appearance."

"Excuse me." Cousin Catherine ducked her head into the conversation, her siblings bunched up behind her. "Before we leave, we wanted to thank you again for singing, Libby; and you, Bernie, for playing. The Mass for Henry was lovely."

There was an exchange of pleasantries and good-byes, after which all three out-of-town cousins wound their way to the Parish Hall door, stopping occasionally to thank priests and parishioners. The cousins' departure tripped an unseen signal for the first wave of people to leave. Bernie fell in with a pair of priests, leaving Bird to begin clearing some of the deserted tables.

Slouched against the wall, waiting for the clogged exit to clear, was Wayne.

It was too convenient for Libby to pass up. In the midst of the last-minute farewells, Libby crossed over to the custodian and didn't waste any time with preliminaries. "You said you heard Daniel and Father Henry arguing on the day of the murder."

If he was caught off guard, Wayne didn't register it. "Yeah. So what?" His pleasantries were obviously short-lived.

"What were they arguing about?"

He kept his eyes on the movement at the door. "Couldn't tell. I heard their voices and then they got louder. Then they quit."

"Yelling? Screaming? Gruff? Possibly joking?"

"Like I said, couldn't tell what they were saying. They were loud enough for me to hear. And they were not joking. Not happy."

A gap presented itself in the group at the doorway. "Gotta go," he said, already pulling out a pack of cigarettes.

Libby turned back into the Parish Hall.

Right into Detective Grass.

Chapter Thirty-Four

His winter coat and red Tartan scarf lapped over his arm, Detective Grass stood not more than three feet from Libby.

"Guess I'm next," she said with a resigned smile. "Do you mind if we sit down for this?"

Contrary to what Libby expected, the detective was disarmingly nice. He brought her a fresh cup of hot tea to a table out of the way of those still lingering over lunch.

"Hard to get past Maggie without another piece of pie!" he said genially as he sat down with his own cup of coffee. "I will admit, there are some good-looking desserts."

He took his time. No rush.

Libby relaxed.

A little.

"Maggie's good-looking, isn't she?" he observed in a casual tone. "Attractive, really. You don't notice it so much when she's running things over at the rectory. How long has she been a widow?"

Libby glanced at the secretary; her new haircut and good figure evident under the prosaic funeral clothes. "Fourteen, fifteen years, I suppose. Her daughter's about nineteen or twenty at this point."

"You and Daniel Giglia are pretty good friends, aren't you?"

Relaxed switched to wary. The digging had begun. "What makes you say that?" she said, remaining noncommittal, as if she were talking about the weather.

Grass caught the switch and deflected it with a smile. "He got a little defensive where you were concerned. Not that I didn't enjoy finding out about your European mountain climbing and African art collecting."

It was funny and Libby relaxed again. But to laugh felt like a concession. And a snappy retort would get her nowhere. She had to remember that she wanted information out of him as much as he wanted it from her. She toyed with an earring and said nothing.

He sipped at his coffee, his attention momentarily drawn to Bird's loud laugh at the table of priests. Grass set his coffee down, removed a small roll of candies from his jacket, took one, and then offered them to her. "Care for a Lifesaver?"

"No, thanks."

"Not into candy?"

"Rots your teeth."

He folded the paper flat over the top of the roll and returned it to his pocket.

"What's the connection," she asked, "to the case?"

"What do you mean?" He, too, could have been discussing the weather.

"I mean, I've watched you offer a Lifesaver to almost everyone in this room. It's a nice gesture, but seems a little … forced."

"Not so subtle, eh?" He shrugged, only mildly concerned that she'd noticed. "There was something sweet, candy-like, on Father Henry's collar near the wound. And possibly minute traces of the same substance on the thurible. Just running a little test on the crowd here today." The detective looked out over the dwindling number of friends and parishioners. "A pretty nice turnout for the pastor, wouldn't you say?"

Relaxed was wearing on Libby. "Look," she said, "what do you really want to know?"

Grass eyed her carefully. She wasn't stupid and he granted her that. He decided to be direct.

"Who killed Father Henry?"

Too direct. Libby choked on her tea.

"Sorry," he said, handing her a napkin. "My take was that you were the sort who'd appreciate the straightforward approach."

Libby blotted the spilled tea on her hand. How this man could be so respectful of her intelligence and so arrogant about his own drove her crazy. She, on the other hand, frustrated him with her studied reluctance bordering on defiance. He did not retract the question.

On the face of it, selecting one name out of the five suspects seemed an easy way to go. But it was not a simple multiple-choice question.

Knowing or not knowing who killed Father Henry did not begin to cover the possible responses available to Libby Kinder. There was the educated guess, the shielding of a friend, the diverting of attention, the hiding of her own guilt.

And she could lie.

Lying was always an option.

Libby simply said, "I don't have an answer for you, Detective."

"No insight that might help?"

"What helps you, hurts one of us."

He sat back. He did not have enough evidence to put her in check. Confrontation did not outwardly intimidate her; she would move out of its direct path, but it would not be a surrender, only a retreat to regroup and come back at him from another angle.

He chose a different move.

Beyond disarmingly nice, he spoke gently. "You know, Father Henry's death could have been an accident. The one who's hurting might be the one who needs to come out of the woods on their own, easily, freely. Before we track them down."

He refrained from adding "and we will," but Libby heard it all the same.

He stood. If this was what she needed to hear, he wanted her to have all the time he could give her to take it in.

"Good afternoon," he said. And he left.

The emotional weight of the day, from the funeral, from conversations in which she tried to ferret out information, to trying to give away as little as she could to Detective Grass, left Libby worn out and pensive as she sat at the table.

While her mind went about sorting things, her hands began picking up used napkins and Styrofoam cups. It was not out of the ordinary for Libby to stay to clean up, and as more people left the luncheon, the task merely presented itself. It was a familiar and comforting activity, collecting trays and stray dishes, tossing trash. Other regulars were pitching in, and it gave her a boost to see Lawrence Davis, the sleeves of his stylish shirt rolled to the elbows, his front protected by the bib of a well-worn church apron, mucking about with big messy buffet pans.

In the kitchen, his wife washed pots, while Mrs. McGrew consolidated cheese platters.

"Soup was great," shouted Libby, handing off a pile of trays to a woman who was slapping them into the dishwasher, as the noise of cleaning up after a large affair bounced around the room.

The pixie in blue-rhinestone jewelry waved off the compliment. "Only kind I make for parish events anymore. Everybody always seems to like it. I can make it in my sleep." She flashed an impish grin. "Which I have been known to do!"

Libby nibbled at a piece of parsley she picked off a platter of leftover cheese. "It's the same soup you made for the Webber funeral, isn't it?"

"It is."

"Same soup you gave Father, I guess."

Mrs. McGrew said nothing, but continued sorting the cheese. She wiped her hands on a kitchen cloth.

"I felt really bad," she said finally. "I started to make Father Henry a plate of food to take home from the luncheon that day. He loved rice casseroles," she remembered happily. "I throw in veggies, too. I don't think he fixes them for himself. Men. Of course, not Bird Hawkins. Bird eats anything that isn't nailed down. And Bernie. Bachelors, you know. Shoot, I gave Bernie a whole pie that day. He cuts them into pieces and freezes them for later. Not Father. He didn't take desserts very often. Didn't even want the rice casserole that day. Said soup was enough."

The tiny woman brought out plastic baggies, and she and Libby bagged like cheese cubes together.

"Why did you feel bad?" asked Libby. "You said you felt bad."

"I … I did … I do feel bad. About the soup. I took the soup to him. It was in a jar. I put it in jars so he doesn't, didn't, have to wash something out and return it. I have plenty to pass along. I took it over before the Webber funeral and gave it to Father. He puts it in that little refrigerator in the sacristy. 'Just enough room for church wine and soup,' he always said."

Her smile came with great effort.

Libby wanted to hug the small, generous woman. How many times she'd watched Father Henry beam with delight at the thought of a delicious, no-fuss-dinner-in-a-jar waiting for him to take home.

"Father always appreciated your care packages," she said.

"And I love, loved, giving them. But see, that's why I feel so bad. Because that's why I think he went back to church. To get the soup. My soup. He said he was going to get his prayers in, too. He was a holy man, you know? But if he hadn't gone back, maybe …" Mrs. McGrew's voice faltered. She quickly put a tissue from her apron pocket to her mouth to stop the emotion, to stop the grief.

A chirpy helper delivered a tray with the last of cold vegetables. Mrs. McGrew sniffed a little as she handed Libby another clump of baggies, and they set about sorting out and saving what was salvageable from the tray.

"That's the other thing," the older woman said, clearing her throat. "When Maggie didn't come back to the Hall for the key. I didn't blame her, with the weather like it was. I just dropped it off. Put it in the rectory mailbox on the front porch. It was so icy and slippery that afternoon…" Her voice trembled again. "Oh, the thought of Father Henry just lying there."

She paused, fanning at her face as if that would keep the image from forming. "But I didn't see anything. I told the police I wish I had. Maybe I … But I was double-parked, it was sleeting; so my head was down, and I just dashed in between some van and Maggie's car. That cute little red one she drives. Sometimes I get so tired of driving that big ol' beast of mine. Of course, it does hold all the food I always seem to be carting around."

Libby bagged carrots while Mrs. McGrew zipped shut a bag of broccoli flowerets. "What time did you leave?" Libby asked gently.

Mrs. McGrew closed her eyes briefly, calculating. "Probably around four. It was already dark. So cold. And slippery. I just wanted to get home. But Father … he was lying there. Terrible. Just terrible." She looked at Libby, the pain evident in her watery eyes. "Who do you think would do such a terrible thing?"

It was the same question Detective Grass had put to her. Suddenly Libby felt as if everyone thought she had an answer—or that she ought to.

Or, maybe they thought something more serious.

More dirty dishes, half empty platters of food, and crusty casserole pans were carried into the kitchen. Mrs. McGrew sniffed hard and snapped into action. "Here, I'll take those. Put those pans by the sink."

The aproned Lawrence Davis appeared in the doorway. "Salt and pepper shakers? Stay on the table?"

"No," said Mrs. McGrew, bustling to a pantry shelf. "Here are the boxes they go in; then back on that shelf."

"I can help do that," offered Libby. "Cheese and veggies are all taken care of."

Libby and Lawrence fell into easy teamwork, collecting the glass shakers and storing them neatly in the divided box, table by table, clearing the last remnants of the funeral luncheon. Only a few people remained in small groups.

"Off the record," ventured Libby, "parishioner to parishioner, is Detective Grass any good?"

Lawrence toasted her with a container of salt. "I see you've been working on your subtlety. Why do you ask?"

Libby smarted at her clumsiness, but was undeterred. "I don't know. He just seems so … random. Like everything is a fishing expedition instead of being well-thought-out. A methodical strategy."

"All investigators have their own style," said Lawrence. "Like singers. That shouldn't come as any surprise."

Libby reached for a shaker that had fallen on the floor. "It might also be because I feel like I'm at the top of his list. Random or not. Like I'm the one he's gunning for. Like every question to everybody else is always about me."

Lawrence gave Libby a glance just short of rolling his eyes. "Am I hearing a little paranoia mixed in there?"

"Sure seemed like it today," she went on defensively. "Maggie, Bernie, Daniel. He asked all of them about my habits, my friends, my *relationship* with Father Henry."

"You are a suspect, Libby."

"No more than the others. I have a key to the church, my motive is not stronger than anyone else's. And we all had time to commit the murder. Only that rotten Wayne has any semblance of an alibi." Her voice was rising. "Give me one thing that makes me more suspect than the rest of them."

Lawrence knew the split second he gave himself away.

Libby called him on it. "You know something, don't you?" She moved closer to him.

He edged away, taking the box to another table.

She followed.

"Come on. Off the record," she pleaded quietly, but earnestly. "Parishioner to parishioner."

"It's not always something big, Libby. Sometimes it's just a small thing."

"Like what?" She tried to keep the volume down, but her voice had already hit soprano. "What kind of small thing? Something I said? Something I did?"

"Maybe if you were more helpful to Detective Grass, he'd get off your back."

She was trailing Lawrence now, unabashedly pestering. "If you told me something that made sense, I'd have reason to be more helpful, to pass on any insights, any clue or tip I ran across. C'mon, Lawrence, what do you know? This is a murder. How am I different? Huh? How?"

He turned and bent into her face. "You're left-handed, Libby. The killer was possibly, but not certainly, left-handed."

He stood back up. Then he closed his eyes, as if doing so might obliterate the last two sentences. "Aw, shit."

Chapter Thirty-Five

Of course, the recipe.
Love those zucchini muffins. My wife would appreciate the recipe if you would just write it out for me.

With. Your. Left hand!

Then Daniel's interview in the back of church. Writing out those directions or diagrams or whatever.

Blatant. Right out of the movies.

And it had worked. Some way or another, Grass had gotten each of his key suspects to demonstrate their handedness. Libby already knew Bernie and Maggie were right-handed. She could visualize Daniel using his right hand that day; and she surmised Wayne was also right-handed—making her the only left-handed person in the group.

Leaving her the one likely to be, literally, in the best position to swing the thurible down onto Father Henry's head at just that angle. Forensics said so.

~ ~ ~

Fear would have been a logical reaction, and it would eventually show up; but for Libby, anything that threw her off-base usually landed first on annoyance and jumped from there quickly to anger.

She admitted the detective's conclusion was reasonable. She was, after all left-handed. But it felt as if she had been tricked, that Grass had gotten her to focus on one hand flying up in the air so the other could pull a coin out of her ear.

She felt stupid. Duped.

The feeling propelled her down the block so fast that Dash gave up stopping at trees to relieve himself. He knew to hurry along when his mistress set off at this pace.

Libby didn't wave at the mail carrier, didn't wait for the car taking its own good time till she could cross into the park, and didn't hear Namita calling to her until her renter gave a mitten-muffled tap on her shoulder.

"When did … the race … start?"

Namita's words came out in a sputter between pants. "And what's the prize because … you are surely in … first place."

Libby stopped her sprint, and they each caught their breath. Dash took advantage of the pause and addressed the nearest bush. Namita let Paki's leash out for her dog to join Dash. "Kind of late for your afternoon walk, isn't it?"

"My priest's funeral and the luncheon were today."

"Oh," Namita said, immediately sympathetic. "Are you walking off emotions? Need to be alone?"

"No. No, no. No." Each syllable slowed Libby's heart rate a little more than the one before. "No, it's probably better for me to have some company. If you're game."

Intermittently, the sun poked through strips of pale clouds. It was cold, but as was often the case, the warmest temperatures came late in the afternoon.

The two women and their dogs fell into a steady pace as they entered the park; brisk enough to keep circulation going but moderate enough to be able to carry on a conversation.

Namita asked lots of questions about the Catholic funeral service, especially one for a priest. Not only were her experiences different, they were limited. Whereas Libby had racked up singing at hundreds of funerals, Namita had been to two.

Libby started out by being generically informative, but gradually the specifics of the day, the ever-present specter of Detective Grass with his prying and incessant questions, sent her voice pitching up and her steps quickening. It also sent her headlong into disclosing her trips to the plumber and funeral home and House and Home Outlet's flooring department.

Alibis tumbled out for inspection. Her scary slip on the church steps, cousins, singing, Wayne, Mrs. McGrew, questions, questions, and more questions until she turned sharply to Namita and blurted out, "Don't you get it? I'm left-handed! The murderer is left-handed. Everybody else is right-handed. Don't you see? They think it's me!"

And then came the fear.

Tears stung as they dropped onto Libby's cold cheeks. She swatted at them as if they had not come from her but were some unrelated annoyance, a bug or a gnat.

The park path bore the brunt of Libby's turbulence. Beyond a light rub across Libby's back, Namita let the walk absorb Libby's pounding emotions, a sponge for her fury and frustration. And panic.

But as the group rounded the pond, Namita noted that her landlady's breathing had become regular; her head lifted as she faced forward instead of glaring at the ground.

"Are you okay?" Namita asked.

Libby shrugged her shoulders and said nothing.

As if she were testing the ice on the pond for its thickness, Namita took a risk and said, "Tell me if you don't want to talk about this, but how did you find this out? Was the detective so stupid he told you?"

"One of our parishioners is a detective, too. Not officially on the case, but in the know, and he told me." Libby pictured the aproned Lawrence Davis with the box of salt and pepper shakers. Dodging her questions. "Rather, I kind of pried it out of him."

"Won't he get in trouble for that? Seems like a big clue to toss out to anybody who asks."

Libby told Namita how Lawrence had regretted he'd let the information out as soon as he said it. "In the end, he said he hoped it might actually induce me to be more open. Probably thought it would make me dig deeper or think harder to clear myself." She took a frayed Kleenex to her nose. "Maybe not such a bad ploy."

Her eyes went back to the path at her feet. "I'd like to think Lawrence doesn't think I'm guilty. Even with such a … damning piece of evidence."

Landlady and renter, little dog and big dog, came around the last leg of the park path that would lead them back into the neighborhood and home.

"I have one last question," said Namita, both animals pulling, eager to go in the direction that meant warmth and comfort. "If you are such a strong contender, if all this is so incriminating, why haven't they arrested you?"

Chapter Thirty-Six

Confessions at St. Hedwig's were scheduled for the general congregation on Fridays at three p.m. In light of recent events, the plan was to keep the parish routine as close to normal as possible until a new pastor was assigned. Thus, Friday, the day after Father Henry's funeral, Father Richard Lanski, eighty-four, substitute for the current duty, arrived at two forty-five with a benign smile hovering above his stooped shoulders and shrunken frame.

Libby did not know Father Lanski. Only that he had a reputation for being endearing and mildly daft.

On the murder front, Libby had not been arrested.

Yet.

Instead of feeling reassured, she actually found this nerve-racking.

Unable to concentrate on grant writing, she volunteered to open the church for Father Lanski's one-hour shift for the souls of St. Hedwig's to unburden themselves of their sins, figuring she could occupy herself making out a list of hymns for yet another funeral on Monday.

The deceased was an old bachelor, a former teacher, she thought. In life, he was the man who sat on the north side, middle aisle, third pillar down on Sunday mornings; who nodded politely if she happened down that way during his pre-Mass rosary.

In death, he was the man who requested that she sing "Ave

Maria" at his funeral.

Libby tended to be surprised by these wishes, not for the request of the song but so specifically for her to sing it. Weekend after weekend, year after year, she looked out over St. Hedwig's congregation and knew people more by where they sat than by name or any other qualifier.

But they knew her.

For good or bad, she was often the voice of the music that accompanied their spiritual lives. And for some, when their final Mass in their church home was celebrated, they wanted her "Ave Maria."

Libby considered this an intimate bidding, as if at some time being in each other's presence, a random act of kindness had occurred, unbeknownst to her, connecting them in this personal way. She could not avoid the pride that came with the request. In her heart, Libby knew it wasn't just her. She was the instrument for the music, that transcendent art; and yes, from their standpoint, also a means to the God they aimed to be in contact with.

It was not her fault the bachelor had died. True, she had changed the hymn numbers for the weekend; and no, that did not interfere with Monday's service. What it did do was make her miss Father Henry's teasing her about putting them up prematurely, claiming this surely invited Death into the parish.

But Father Henry was gone.

And no one was waiting in the empty church either.

Father Lanski gave a dismissive wave at Libby's attempt to show him the ropes of St. Hedwig's hundred-year-old confessional tucked in a slight jut of the building near the front side door of the church under the twelfth station depicting Jesus being nailed to the cross.

As a child, Libby thought the confessional was like a charming, wood-carved dollhouse; a tiny room in the middle for the priest, just enough space for a cushioned bench for him to sit on; doors on opposite sides, like a front and back door, for penitents to enter their own area, partitioned off from the priest. The doors came to gabled points on either side of a flat roof that lay over the priest's miniature home. With all its gingerbread woodwork and curtained windows it looked like a playhouse to Libby's young eyes.

That was before she received the burden of guilt that accompanied reaching the Age of Reason and having to tell, out loud, inside that tiny cubicle, what sins she had committed. The dollhouse image was never the same.

The setup did not interest Father Lanski. He paid little attention to Libby's instructions about the light switch, the spring on the door, etc.

I'm practically as old as this church, thought Father Lanski as he shuffled toward the confessional. They sure don't make them like this anymore.

His nostalgic musings were abbreviated once inside. The priest's bench remained in the center, but to his left, the partition had been removed and the kneeler replaced with a chair, allowing the penitent the option of a face-to-face confession. To his right was the original divider wall with a small sliding panel and curtain, which provided separation and anonymity.

Father Lanski settled in. He hadn't listened to that parish lady tell him where the light switch was. He could have read. Maybe this place was so old they hadn't put electricity in the confessional. He sat in the dark and wondered about those days so long ago.

No one came.

At first it was peaceful. What a big old church, he thought. Quaint. Empty.

He took his ever-present companion of black beads from his pocket and began to say a rosary.

Maybe he dozed for a few minutes.

Something woke him. Startled him.

A door? The wind? It was an old church.

An inner-city church. Where anyone could walk in off the street.

Where a priest had been murdered.

"Get a grip," he admonished himself.

Footsteps. Did he hear footsteps?

He clenched the beads in the dark and prayed faster. Between Hail Marys he tried to reassure himself it was someone coming to confession. Just someone coming to confession.

The dollhouse door creaked open. There was movement behind the wall to his right.

What if it's ...?

The panic in Father Lanski's stomach crawled up into his throat. In the blackness, he clawed for the sliding panel. Was he desperate to face the terror or hoping the sight of a friendly human would give him relief?

A sinner? A vagrant? A lost soul? A …

Just get it open!

The old panels always slid from side to side. Did he remember that right? No handles. He pushed it to the left. To the right. Stuck. Push again. Nothing. Who's in there?! Why aren't they speaking?

Snap!

A small catch let loose the panel.

Snap!

The panel under his sweating palm shot upward and caught on a tiny latch as someone, something slapped down his arm. He recoiled in the cramped dark space and let out a frantic yelp. "Who's in here? Get away! Please. Get away!"

"Father?" came a deep voice through the curtain, now exposed in the wall, but in the pitch black, revealing nothing.

Still agitated, still waving wildly at his lap to fend off the unseen object, Father Lanski grabbed it, trapped it. He and the would-be penitent clambered out of their respective sides of the confessional at the same time.

They both looked down at Father Lanski's hands.

The penitent recognized it immediately.

"Oh, Father," he said. "We'll have to call the police."

The penitent knew immediately, because the penitent knew almost everything.

Hearing the commotion, Libby rushed from the sacristy toward the two men newly ejected from the confessional.

Bird Hawkins hollered out to her, "Found the diary!"

+ + +

… and sometimes nobody comes in for the whole hour. It's quiet. I pray. I take a nap.

If they come, I listen.

After so many years, they all sound the same. Repeat offenders. It's not rehab. Or therapy. I just listen.

Don't remember why I started writing. All this quiet time in the confessional, I suppose. A diary, for heaven's sake. Like some teenage girl. They all had them when I was a kid. Pink plastic, with little gold keys for the lock. When I sit in here, in the quiet, hidden, anonymous, like the people on the other side of the curtain, so nice to write and say what I really mean. Feels a little like someone is listening.

Josh B. left the Church.

He's not only marrying a non-Catholic, he's leaving the Faith! I know he'll be sorry. You can't just throw your soul away like that. Suppose I should pray for him. God knows I tried to foster the seeds of a vocation. I really thought he had the makings of a good priest.

I truly dislike this Bishop. He's a pompous, patronizing, bloodsucking, spirit squashing ... Money. That's all he cares about. Raising it, courting those who have it. Being seen. Making the papers. Moving up the ladder. Do we need money? Of course. Does he raise the teachers' salaries? Does he help keep the poor schools open? Does he do anything for his priests except issue decrees? Add to our well-being? Recognize our efforts? If I weren't wearing a collar, he wouldn't recognize me on the street. He moves us around like ...

Waste of ink.

So nice to unload without trying to sound pleasant, having to watch every word. Wears me out. Even talking to other priests it's mostly innuendo, mostly euphemistic, veiled shoptalk.

Maybe it's because I don't have a family. Cousins don't count. Maggie M. has her daughter. Daniel has—let's not go there. Bernie and Libby are single. Libby has siblings she's close to. Bernie has some friends, longtime friends. Maybe it's just me. Maybe it's all that seminary training—don't make any Particular Friends, don't associate unduly with women. Remember, you're moving from parish to parish. Leave those relationships behind. Always make a clean break.

Either way, I don't need a lot of company. Prefer not to have it these days. Too exhausting. The cats are company enough.

Some people would say I have God. He listens.

I don't know. I suppose.

I hope.

+ + +

I know there's more to listening than just hearing the words." Detective Grass thrummed the steering wheel as he waited for a garbage truck to clear his lane. "But sometimes you have to be lucky enough to be in on the right conversation."

"She's not dumb, either," said Detective Davis as he adjusted the passenger side heat vents, which as yet were sending out more noise than warmth. "I hope it turns out that letting her know about being left-handed helps more than it hurts." He looked over at his colleague. "I am sorry I went out on that limb after we'd only talked briefly about telling her."

"We'll see. Could work in our favor. Besides, I got a free Saturday morning out of you, didn't I?"

"Pure guilt. You're lucky I'm Catholic."

Grass turned onto a main artery a few blocks away from the central police department and headed downtown—a well-developed core for a city of two hundred thousand. "Originally I'd hoped you could be my in-the-loop guy. After all, St. Hedwig's is your parish."

"Unfortunately, right now, they see me mostly as a detective. Can't get inside as well as I'd hoped either."

"Under other circumstances, Libby Kinder could have been really helpful. Like you say, she's not dumb. She's clever. Pays attention. *Listens*," he added with emphasis. "She doesn't tip her hand readily. But it's not going to happen right now. Right now she's on a very different list."

"Not to mention she bugs the hell out of you."

Grass drummed the wheel harder than before. "Let's just say she makes me bristle a little. Occasionally." The vents were beginning to give out heat; he spoke louder to be heard over the sound of the blowers. "I'll admit, it is frustrating. Occasionally."

He accelerated forcefully from a stop sign. "She talks to the same people, probably asks the same damn questions. And gets the same answers. But I just know, like at that luncheon, she heard, yes, heard, something important."

"Give yourself a little credit, Grass. If something important was said, it'll fall into place." Davis looked ahead out the windshield. "But let's try not to be too confrontational. Not put her off."

Cutting through the business district was smooth sailing. The weather was clear. Snow piles glistened in the sun, streets were plowed, and traffic was minimal on the weekend morning.

Once on the other side of commercial buildings and the city's art complex, the car turned right onto one of the bridges that crossed a small river separating business district from residential area. Along

River Avenue, grand old houses, now mostly converted to apartments, signaled the shift to family neighborhoods.

"I've always liked the way this street curves around by the park." Switching the blower to low, Grass spoke in a more moderate voice. "Tell me again, Davis. Your church, your Catholic Church, would some of the issues in this case really be cause for firing someone? I mean, was Father Henry that kind of guy or didn't he have a choice? Pope rules and all that?"

Davis gave several thoughtful pats to his knees, formulating his response. "There are rules and then there are interpretations of the rules. Not to mention the enforcement of rules. Like any organization. You know that. In the Church, there are some priests who will go after you on these issues, hardliners who get in your face about your life, your moral decisions, your contributions, your standing in the eyes of God—as they see it. There are others who are actually as militant about social justice as any layperson."

Davis worked to give a fair picture. "I don't know how Father Henry personally felt about gay marriage or Maggie Mueller's trip to the Women's Health Clinic, but he did take a vow to uphold the Church's teachings and that, I think, he took very seriously. He was not a man who liked to rock the boat. Did not like confrontation or making big decisions. All of these transgressions might have been not so much tolerated or condoned as overlooked—which could be seen either as an act of charity on his part or as a man burying his head in the sand."

The pond in the park, ice-covered, cold and hard, came into view.

"However," Davis added, "if any of these things became public, Father Henry would have little choice but to address them."

"Big sins, eh?"

Davis swiped his fogged-up window and nodded. "Mortal."

Chapter Thirty-Seven

Libby was halfway through her second cup of jasmine green tea and the Saturday morning cryptoquote. BabyCakes slouched over the top half of the newspaper; his long, black tail swishing like a windshield wiper on a drizzly day, now and then, now and then, over a critical portion of the puzzle, prompting Libby to sing low and slow in rhythm with the cat's tail, *"Are you sleeping, are you sleeping ..."*

The doorbell startled them both.

The practiced response plan went into effect: BabyCakes kicked the newspaper out behind him for traction to fly off the table, through the nearest doorway, and shot under the bed; Dash, alert, barked and barked and barked.

Libby went to the door.

Outwardly, she tried to appear casual. After all, they hadn't said anything like "find someone to take care of your animals while we arrest you." Inwardly, she was barking alarm and following the cat under the bed.

Pushing aside her boots and a small basket of scarves and mittens and dog leashes by the back entrance she had directed them to, Libby let in Detectives Grass and Davis and the cold air that came with them.

"I have hot water for tea, gentlemen. Or I could make coffee," she said.

At Libby's insistence, Dash stopped barking duty but sniffed every inch of the invaders from the knees on down until Libby called him off that detail as well. "I'm surprised to see you so early. Figured you'd be up all night glued to the diary." She said this in a light, breezy voice, smiling.

Grass couldn't get a good grasp on how much was teasing and how much was making a dig. He tried to match her tone. "What? No muffins?"

"No," she said, still smiling. "So, I guess you won't need any recipes either. You know, you could have just asked which hand I write with."

"I don't always find that a reliable approach for a mur—."

"We won't be here long, Libby," Davis jumped in. "No thanks on the coffee and tea."

Libby led them to the living room. Dash kept up surveillance, coming to rest at Libby's feet when she sat in a wingback chair next to the fireplace. BabyCakes, having crept out from under the bed, kept watch from afar.

The two men unbuttoned their coats and settled on the couch. Grass unceremoniously laid Father Henry's diary on the coffee table before them—a simple, thin, five-by-seven-inch black notebook, worn at the edges.

"Did you know Father Henry kept a diary?" asked Grass.

"Hadn't a clue," answered Libby. "Never saw it before yesterday."

The detective handed it to her.

She arched an eye. "Fingerprints?"

"Processed. Easy enough. Father Henry's and Father Lanski's."

Libby accepted the diary. She studied the front then flipped it over and around as if it were a magical tome. "Small, isn't it?"

"Small enough to shove between the partition wall and the sliding panel in the confessional box. My officers searched the church, more than once, and that panel didn't budge. They figured it was old and didn't work. Or was painted shut. Apparently it lifts up instead of side to side."

"Which I tried to tell Father Lanski," Libby interjected.

"You knew?" Grass shot a glance at Davis, as if to confirm his earlier evaluations.

"Of course. I just assumed your officers poked around enough to discover that and hadn't found anything. And Father Lanski acted like he knew everything. Where exactly was it?"

Davis demonstrated with his hands. "There was just enough room in the dividing wall to wedge the diary once the panel was down. You had to know what you were doing to pop it out of there."

"Unless it came out while you were fighting off an attacker," a bemused Libby said, recalling the frantic old priest. "Poor guy. I did try to tell him where the button for the light was in there."

She held the diary out to Detective Grass. "Sorry. I don't think I can help you much with this."

"Hold onto it a second," said Grass. "I have some papers that were in the diary that I'd like you to look at."

As he passed several plastic bags in Libby's direction, BabyCakes, his curiosity aroused, jumped straight up in the air, landing without a sound on Libby's chair back. He tucked one paw under his chest and let the other dangle over the wing like a fish line dropped in the lake on a lazy, summer afternoon.

BabyCakes was not about to miss any of this.

The first bag held a small card, a religious painting of Madonna with Child on one side, name and date and prayer on the other. "Hildegarde Felger," read Libby. "That was his mother. It's just the traditional prayer card from her funeral. Lawrence will tell you. Everybody holds onto these, especially for a loved one."

The second bag contained what looked like a store receipt. Libby had a hard time making out its faded print. "My first guess is that it's the receipt for this notebook. Am I seeing the date right? Is it twenty years old?"

"That's what the lab thought," said Grass. "Seems Father Henry didn't write every day. Sometimes he went for long periods without putting anything down."

Libby moved to the next bag and examined a smaller card. "This is from the nursing home where Mrs. Felger ... but wait, 'Alice, Room 309' is ... oh, that's Bernie's mom. He probably gave it to Father. I see now. It's an appointment reminder card. I probably got one for both these ladies—and ten others—from people I plan or planned at one time to visit."

"Anything seem unusual?"

Libby squinted at the card, turning it, trying to get it to reveal more.

She shook her head. "Seems pretty normal to me. Wouldn't have been unusual for Bernie to give it to Father, or for him to have picked it up himself. Guess the receipt and Father's packrat tendencies, and the fact that he didn't write in the diary all the time, makes this stuff seem kind of insignificant. Haphazard at best. The sort of stuff you put in a book you're reading or leave on the counter when you come in the house, then it gets tucked somewhere just to get it out of the way. Out of sight, out of mind."

She took a moment to ponder the diary in her lap. Her mind was not so far away from having worked on her cryptoquote, trying to stay open, trying to let the code review itself instead of imposing her own solutions. "Unless," she said with hopeful expectation, "unless these things marked special places *in* the diary."

Her little lift of excitement didn't get very far.

"We noted all the spots where these things were found," explained Grass, "but their placement seemed insignificant and random." He motioned to Libby, and she picked up the remaining bag.

"What's this? A letter?"

"That's the envelope it came in," Lawrence explained. "The letter itself is on the other side. Do you recognize the handwriting?"

Libby examined the penmanship. Neat. A little flair making it distinct, but not flashy or flamboyant. "Should I?"

"Just asking," said Grass.

"We're not sure who it is," Davis said. "You're the first person we're asking."

"It was hand delivered," observed Libby. "No stamp or address. Just 'To Father Felger.' Evidently a personal note."

Grass gave a wave of permission. "Go ahead and read it. It's short."

Libby turned the bag over and began to read. Suddenly she felt guilty reading someone else's letter, especially one that might have meant something special to Father Henry. "Seems kind of intrusive. Reading Father's private correspondence."

"Privacy goes out the window when you're murdered ... er, popped on the head." Detective Grass fumbled. "Dead."

Grass cleared his throat and coughed lightly while Davis said, "None of this is going any further than your living room, Libby. We're just crossing off things that may or may not be relevant."

It was a reasonable point, and Libby proceeded to read:

Dear Father Henry,

All of my life I have searched for a spiritual home. Today, you and the people of this parish have become that for me.

When I first met you that afternoon BJ showed me around before the Christmas concert, you were sitting quietly in the sacristy praying. You didn't seem to care that we broke in on this sacred time, but instead welcomed me, even though I turned out to be one of those "non-Catholics."

Through our talks—which were always funny, interesting, and challenging—my instruction, your wonderful homilies and personal example, you have lighted for me a path to the God and Community I longed for. No other relationship has meant more to me on this journey of Faith.

Thank you for all you've done and all you are.

Blessings and peace,

Andrew C.

Grass watched Libby reread the note with care. "Do you know who Andrew C. is?"

"Pretty sure it's Andrew Clark," she said, laying the letter on top of the pile of other bagged items. "It's a ... lovely note," she said, touching the words through the plastic. "I can see why Father kept it."

"And who is Andrew Clark?"

"The guy who decorated the church before Daniel."

Grass checked with Davis. "Did you know him?"

Lawrence shook his head. "Before my time. I've only been at St. Hedwig's a couple of years."

"Why would Father Henry keep a note from him?" Grass flipped through his own list of possibilities. "Something *special* about him? Special about this relationship that meant so much to him?"

The innuendo was hardly subtle.

Libby was not surprised by the suggestion of something illicit. As a fifty-plus-year-old unmarried person, all her relationships could be, and often were, considered "suspect." Libby found the limited way people viewed human interactions so confined by social labels that she rarely took offense anymore at the small number of options they could fathom. There were so many wonderful, rich, even intimate, while not physical, connections to neighbors, teachers, renters, church friends, work friends, vets, dental hygienists, librarians.

"No," she said, smiling in a way Grass could not readily

comprehend. "No. I don't think, and I certainly never saw or heard evidence of anything *special*, if you mean sexual or a particular friendship, between Father Henry and Andrew Clark. He was a convert of Father Henry's. Rare as those are these days, I imagine they're always kind of special for a priest."

Grass looked to Davis for clarification.

"Like signing up a good player for your team," he suggested.

"A feather in your cap sort of thing, eh?"

Davis searched for a better analogy. "No, not exactly like that. Not to a priest, I wouldn't think. Certainly not to Father Henry. More like … a …"

"More like adopting a child," said Libby. "Taking someone into your family. They are as happy and grateful, overjoyed, to have found you as you are to welcome them in. Spiritually, you've helped give them a heart transplant. You've saved them."

"You say he was the last decorator. What happened to him?" Grass went for a little levity. "Father Henry eventually tick him off, too?"

Libby didn't hear levity. "He … moved on," she said curtly.

Grass pushed against her prickly reaction. "That doesn't answer my question. Did he …?"

"He died."

Sheer annoyance, thought Grass. "What did he die from?"

"Cancer."

Pursing his lips, Grass leaned back. He was honked off at himself for not being more judicious about the way he questioned this woman. Davis was right. She wasn't stupid. Guarded, but not dumb.

He, Grass, was right, too. Libby knew things that could help the investigation, things she might not even be aware of, but she would clam up fast if she felt the need to be defensive. It was all complicated by the fact that he had to press her like a prime suspect.

"Okay," he said, this time letting a hint of apology float over his words. "We're trying to track down these leads to see if there's anything we can learn that sheds light on Father Henry, his life, and possibly his death."

As fiery as Libby could be, she could also quickly regain control if she sensed an affront had been removed. She wasn't above being helpful. She squeezed BabyCakes's dangling paw and went on with less resistance. "Andrew Clark was a very nice guy. Father liked him, and he was good at his job. He was only here about two years. In the course of that time, he got interested in the Church and eventually joined. Converted. It was all relatively low key."

"And yet," Davis concluded, "Father Henry kept this letter."

Libby concurred with a nod. She held out the pile of bags she'd collected.

Detective Grass took them and set them on the coffee table. "There are a couple of other things I'd like you to read," he said, returning the diary. He pointed to a long passage, and as the living room fell silent, Libby read to herself:

I'm not trusting the Church here. If I leave a base amount to some beneficiaries up front and enough to bury me, with directions to make sure Dunkirk and Calico Two are secure with Maggie, then I'll need to leave the rest, the biggest chunk, in a safe place.

Probably the best is somehow with my true family, no names here, just in case this falls into the wrong hands. If I leave it all with them, they can make sure everything ends up in the right places. That way, those who have been so loving and kind and loyal to me in life—a little needy at times, contrary now and then, but always there for me, making life so much more bearable—will be left in good shape.

Then what should I, how should I, let them know when to turn it over? Some kind of sign. I'll have the Vicar ask something like, "Do you have Father Henry's envelope?" No. Father Felger's file. Kit. Packet—yes. "Do you have Father Henry's packet?" Exactly. They'll know that's the clue; that they can trust the person asking exactly that and hand things over.

Do you have Father Henry's packet?

"Wow," Libby said slowly, taking a minute for this information to register. "So, that's where the money for the chapel is?"

Grass studied her face and tried to remain neutral. "Is that how you read it?"

"I figure that's what the *biggest chunk* refers to."

"What about his *true family*?" asked Davis.

"Normally I'd say it was …" Libby reread the passage and shook her head. "The pronouns are so inconsistent. I can't tell if someone's already got the money or is going to get the money to be taken care of. Not unusual, I suppose, for a diary. Stream of consciousness writing; the person not worried about making sense to anyone else, not concerned about grammar. It's more like he's talking to himself …"

"Libby?" Grass pulled her from her own stream.

When she looked up, she saw the two detectives leaning forward: Davis almost at military attention, Grass anchoring his elbows on his knees, his hands clasped between them. He enunciated very distinctly. "Libby. Do you have Father Henry's packet?"

They were like two teenagers asking their parent for the car, hopeful, expectant, but a little afraid of the answer.

Understanding the gravity of the question, Libby gave a serious and firm "No. I do not." She was truly sorry to disappoint them.

No big deal, thought Grass, placating his disappointment. She's only the first person we've asked.

"Okay," he said. "You don't have the packet. You're not the *true family*?"

"Apparently not."

"Any ideas who might be?"

Some options seemed obvious to Libby; others did not. She picked through the data her mind was presenting. "No doubt, one would start with real family. Blood relatives. The cousins—in town and out."

"And Wayne Nichols. Trust me, they're all on the list."

"Wouldn't they have come forward, though, jumped forward at the reading of the will?" asked Libby. "They all seemed pretty anxious and interested in getting what was theirs. Even better if that included this *biggest chunk*."

Lawrence Davis leaned back and crossed his long, basketball-player legs. "It sounds like you have to use those exact words—*Do you have Father Henry's packet?*—to get them to give it up."

"Kind of Agatha Christie-like," mused Libby. "Didn't know Father Henry was into the mystery thing."

"I think he was more into the protect-my-money thing."

Dash sneezed. Libby bent over and rubbed his ears until they twitched and he fell back asleep. "Maybe they don't know what is in the packet. Maybe Father Henry told them to hold onto it until someone asked the specific question; and once word was out from the reading of the will that there were millions of dollars involved, they might have decided to wait until things settled down. Or just hold out."

Davis ran his hand across the top of his head, down the back, letting it come to rest at the nape of his neck. It looked as if he was already worn out by the search. "This is supposedly someone Father Henry trusted, so I hope not."

Libby tried to picture an envelope, a packet, full of millions of dollars. "That's an insane amount of cash, even in large bills. I wonder if it was in stock certificates or if it's got a key to a box of gold bullion, something other than dollar bills. Like cousin Edward was suggesting."

"Won't know until we find that *true family*."

Grass rearranged the pile of baggies on the coffee table in front of him. "While we're checking out the blood relatives, I have to ask if there's anyone else you can think of who fits this description? A close friend of Father Felger's? I guess the last decorator guy is out. Maybe another convert?"

Libby dug into the years she'd worked side by side with Father Henry, at church, at meetings, all those times just talking in the sacristy. People he mentioned he seemed close to. "He had one or two classmates from the seminary he kept in touch with. The Vicar might know. They weren't from this diocese. As far as I could tell, they were Christmas and birthday card friends more than anything. Once in a while somebody from one of his former parishes would show up. Never seemed like anyone all that special."

"How about this parish? St. Hedwig's?"

"No one comes to mind." She looked over at Davis. "I don't know, Lawrence. You're out in the pews. In the back when Father interacted with parishioners."

"I drew a blank, too. He went out to dinner regularly with one couple. A movie once in a while with a widower usher."

"We'll certainly check all those," Grass said, stepping in, "but I think we're looking for someone he really trusted. Was really connected with."

Libby couldn't tell if he was asking for another name or the confirmation of one he already had in mind. His prodding became more insistent.

"Someone he relied on. Probably saw often."

Did she sense a change in the atmosphere? The questions more goading than inquiring?

Grass continued, "We're back to looking at Father Henry's inner circle. Some of the people in the investigation. The ones with keys to the church. Maybe Father trusted someone who then realized what he or she could gain by getting him out of the way."

"Oh, come on," said Libby. "We're all basically employees. Except Wayne. But who in their right mind would trust him with …"

Grass quit beating around the bush. "Don't you think Father Henry trusted you more than the others?"

"Me?" She didn't want to sound defensive. In fact, she'd come to realize it was often in her best interest not to sound so. "He didn't rely on me any more than say, Maggie. Wayne and Daniel were there all the time. And Bernie. Bernie and I were basically just there for the services."

"It seems as if he counted on you to be there in a more … personal way. Not special, just personal. Like a good friend."

Libby took a deep breath. Very deep. To the count of five. She let it out with enough air and energy that both Dash and BabyCakes went on the alert. She patted them both to reassure them. And herself.

She passed the diary back to Detective Grass. "Look," she said evenly. "I do not have the packet. Trust or no trust, Father Henry did not give it to me."

The detectives glanced at each other. A look passed between them that Libby couldn't miss. She took another deep breath. "Is there something else you're trying to say?"

Grass opened the diary and located the page he wanted. He handed the slim book back to Libby.

"Read this."

Chapter Thirty-Eight

Bowl in the sink; water in the bowl. Bernie ate a dish of oatmeal every morning. It didn't matter if he was hungry or not, it was how the day began.

Bird Hawkins had blabbed to everyone within a hundred miles about finding Father Henry's diary, so Bernie knew the police had it. They were coming over shortly to "ask a few questions." He couldn't think of anything that might be in it that would affect him. He and Henry had been good friends for a long time.

The organist wiped around the sink and counter with a sponge. Another dumb night of tossing and lying awake. He would feel better after he got out and moved around. He looked at the clock above the stove. 9:18. At noon, after the visit by the police, he would deliver Holy Communion to the two homebound parishioners he attended to every Saturday.

He rinsed the sponge.

In the living room, he sat in the brown recliner his dad had loved to watch TV in. Bernie slouched into a comfortable position, then squirmed to pull from his front pants pocket a wooden rosary, a gift from the missions in Brazil in return for the small donation he'd made.

A worrier by nature, Bernie assumed the most catastrophic scenario for his upcoming meeting with the detectives. The thought that what the police were coming to his house for could turn out to have nothing to do with him would never occur to Bernie.

Ever.

~ ~ ~

Saturday mornings belonged to Maggie. She awoke early, naturally, and followed her own impulses. She might go for a walk, read, or do laundry.

This midwinter morning, she took care of the dog and cat, who were both ancient and easy; brewed a cup of coffee, delighted in having cream for it; and sat, her legs tucked up under her on the chintz loveseat, and loved her home.

Maggie lived in an old house in an old, once-glorious neighborhood. Next door had been chopped into apartments. Across the street, a fraternity touted Greek letters in its windows and sucked up all the parking. But in between the houses that narcotic squads monitored and the ones where old folks grew vegetables in the front yard, were places for people like Maggie, people who adored big, lazy porches and leaded-glass transoms.

By nature, Maggie had a good eye and a frugal streak enhanced by her meager income, in addition to a labor-of-love work ethic that scraped old paint tirelessly, re-plastered cracked walls, and outfitted rooms with refurbished antiques from yard sales and pillows she made herself.

Dusting under her coffee cup led to dusting the end table which led to dusting the fireplace mantel. Soon she was going over the hardwood floors and vacuuming area rugs. She deadheaded a lush philodendron and curled its vines up into itself.

"What are you getting all whipped up for?"

Maggie's daughter, Julia, leaned against the living room doorway, floppy pajama bottoms pooling at her bare feet.

"Hi. Good morning," said Maggie.

All tousled like that, Julia looked to Maggie like a toddler who any minute would ask for some juice. But she was a young woman. With a husband probably still asleep in their basement living quarters.

Maggie had always been direct with Julia. "The police are coming this morning. They found Father Henry's diary."

Julia padded over sleepily and draped her arms around her mother's shoulders. It was a gesture she'd inherited from her father's side, not Maggie's more stoic side.

"It's all going to be okay, Mom."

Maggie chewed her lip. "We'll see. Depends on what he wrote."

~ ~ ~

Paul Thomas stood in the doorway to the living room with a glass of cranberry juice and watched Daniel go at the classical piece of music he'd retreated to lately. He didn't stand there long. He wanted to clean up after breakfast before the police arrived, and he knew Daniel's selection was both lonely and lengthy.

~ ~ ~

As the sun made a firm appearance above the rooftops on Apple Street, Detective Grass directed Libby to the page of Father Henry's diary lying open on her lap. "Start in the middle there. Out loud, if you would, please."

Grass sat back; Davis sat forward. Both were alert.

Libby was apprehensive.

Sometimes the tingling ends up with my legs going numb. During the day I'm tripping and bumping into things more. At night it keeps me awake. The new meds are experimental ...

Libby looked up. Her voice was subdued, concerned; as if she had just stepped into the doctor's office. "What's wrong with him?"

This was Lawrence Davis's pastor and friend, too. He answered with compassion. "He had MS."

Libby swallowed. She stared at the diary pages filled with Father Henry's handwriting, handwriting she recognized and could now see was shakier than she remembered it being in the past. There was a small pitch in her stomach. Everything suddenly felt very personal. Father Henry's thoughts privately written in the shadows of St. Hedwig's confessional.

Everything also seemed alive. Father Henry's words flowing across the pages were as if he was sitting in her living room talking, just shooting the breeze, as they had done so many times in the sacristy before a Mass.

... the new meds are experimental. The only side effect is a little dizziness—Lord, I'm starting to walk like Father George! I knew God would get me for making fun of him. If things get bad, okay, when things get bad, maybe I'll ask Libby K. just to push me down the back steps ...

Fireworks exploded in Libby's brain, but she kept reading, glued to every syllable.

... She can call it an accident, say my legs gave out, which they might of their own accord. She'd think of something snappy to say. Dramatic, yet plausible. Do not resuscitate. Yes, I would trust her ...

Detective Grass did not have a great poker face. Good. But not great. A tiny piece of him twitched with "let's see what she does with this."

Libby stared. Dumbfounded. She stared at Lawrence Davis. Stared at Detective Grass. Yes, it was smugness she read on his face.

The fireworks in her brain stopped abruptly; the smoke cleared.

"You're not taking this seriously, are you?" She sounded more confident than she felt, but that alone gave her some balance.

"You tell us," said Grass.

Definitely a little smug.

"First of all," began Libby, a little louder than she wanted. BabyCakes jumped away. "I did not know Father had MS. I'm sorry about that. Sorry he had it and sorry that he didn't think he could ... trust me enough to tell me. And secondly, no, I do not take his comment about pushing him down the steps seriously. It's a joke. Don't you get it?"

"Did he joke a lot about being pushed down the steps? Which, if I may remind you, is exactly how he died. Exactly."

"He never said anything to me—specifically—about being pushed down the stairs. We did joke about dying and being buried. You have to understand, I sing at a lot of funerals. A lot. The topic of death does come up." She turned and appealed to someone she knew better, counted on more as a friend, an ally. "You've been in the sacristy before, Lawrence. You know how flip and crazy the conversations can be."

Lawrence seemed more reluctant to admit it than Libby had hoped for. "Yes, I know," he finally said.

They obviously needed more convincing.

"Look," Libby said, "I always said I wanted to be composted. Organic, environmental, and all that. Father Henry said he had a friend who just wanted to be put in a Hefty garbage bag and set out by the curb. It was all part of kidding around in the sacristy."

The detectives exchanged glances. They said nothing, but the appraising, evaluating, was practically audible, as if some adding machine were tallying up the pros and cons of her explanation.

Lawrence Davis gave the first assessment. "You have to admit, Libby, it looks pretty weird to have Father Henry's murder outlined, exactly, in his diary. And then for it to happen almost exactly that way."

Grass spoke louder than he wanted. "With you already one of the main suspects."

Dash took exception to this. The dog raised his head.

Libby did her own calculating: the key, the left-handedness, the opportunity, the no alibi. She had read enough to know her next move.

She closed the diary and passed it to Detective Grass.

"So," she said, "is this where I ask to see a lawyer?"

Chapter Thirty-Nine

Where Libby Kinder was an active participant, Bernie Fruehauf was passive. Detective Grass had not been called sir so much in his life. Old-school around authority, he surmised. Or old-school fear.

After a flutter of graciousness, Bernie offered the most comfortable chairs to Detective Grass and Detective Davis, no longer referred to as Lawrence. Their host settled on the couch with the geometric design, where he braced himself and picked at its threadbare edges.

A blank look on Bernie's face eventually melted into a confused one, until he finally gathered the courage to ask, "What packet, sir?"

He did not have it, whatever it was, nor did he know who might. *Family* was a literal term for the organist, and even when prodded, he had a hard time coming up with an alternative to the cousins.

"How about another priest?" suggested Grass. "One he might have thought of as a good friend?"

Bernie shook his head slowly. "Not that comes to mind. Sir."

"A classmate? A colleague?"

Bernie's head drifted back and forth again. "Don't get me wrong. Henry got along with the other priests. Same with parishioners. He might go out to dinner once in a while, but he never made it sound like these people were anything special. Even when we traveled, he kept more to himself."

Grass looked around the clean but sterile living room that probably hadn't been redone in seventy years. Old-school frugality. "He was kind of a loner, eh?"

This isn't so bad, thought Bernie. He spoke up. "Henry was an only child like me. Liked his quiet. His own space, as they say today."

This time around, Grass tried to word the question more carefully. "Even loners have *special* friends. Male and female."

Bernie might have lived the life of a good Catholic bachelor, but it was not unconnected to the real world. He, too, was offended by the implication. "Father Henry was a good priest. A holy man. He did not have special friends. Not like that."

Grass took the response as a similar rebuke. Going down the list in his own notebook, he went to the next topic. "Did you know Father Henry was ill?"

The blank look. The confusion.

"How … how do you mean?" Bernie stammered.

Davis was more gentle. "Father Henry had multiple sclerosis."

More confusion. "Are you sure?"

"We checked with his doctors. Yes."

"Oh. My."

"He didn't tell you?" asked Grass.

Involuntarily, Bernie's head slowly shook from side to side, as if it were disconnected and moving all on its own. "No. He didn't tell me."

Grass heard shock; Davis would have called it hurt.

Grass handed one of the plastic baggies to Bernie. It contained the convert's letter. "Maybe Father was close to this guy. Nothing special. Just a good friend," he said.

Bernie read the note, then commented. "A very nice man. But he died a couple of years ago, sir. I don't remember him and Father doing anything more than talking sometimes when they were in church together. He took care of the decorations. Did a really nice job. He and Father Henry would meet in the sacristy and talk when he was taking instructions to become a Catholic. He was a quiet guy, worked a lot, I think. I doubt if he and Father Henry got together for anything more than those instructions."

Bernie identified the prayer card, pausing a moment to softly, sweetly, recall, "Ah, Hildegarde. Father's mother. Always so nice to me."

He shrugged at the sales slip, then took an extra moment turning the nursing home appointment card over in his hand. "This was in Father's diary?" he asked.

Davis observed the note of surprise. Both detectives saw Bernie's hands tremble slightly and heard the catch in his voice. "This was my mother's room number." He looked down. After several moments he added, "We were both very close to our mothers. Both of our parents, I guess."

"Any reason Father Henry would have kept this card?"

More head shaking.

Grass realized he was talking to an old man. Instead of Bernie Fruehauf's home making him appear more at ease in a familiar setting, he looked frail and small, sitting on the old couch amid furnishings from another era.

"Just one last question," said Grass. "If Father Henry would have relied on any one—a priest friend, the Vicar, his relatives, you, someone from the parish—to do something for him, something important, what one or two names come to mind?"

Bernie gave it some thought. "If it was something to do with church business, St. Hedwig's, probably Maggie. Anything else, I'd say Libby Kinder."

~ ~ ~

"Of course, I know what they mean." Maggie returned the baggies to Detective Grass, who stacked them on top of Father Henry's diary on his lap. "They mean he was a packrat. I wish I had a dollar for every appointment or prayer card that man left lying around."

Lawrence Davis chuckled. "He probably wouldn't have disagreed."

A pair of overstuffed chairs flanked a row of windows across the front of the room, one for each detective. Slants of sunshine spiked onto the carpet, where a large, old dog, Hugo, nestled with a large, old cat, Punk; their bellies rising and falling in synchronization.

There was no doubt Maggie Mueller was flip. She was also helpful and direct, but Grass often heard in her replies an undercurrent of disdain, often humorous, sometimes peevish. Seeing her here, in her own home, though, Grass saw a different side of the church secretary. There was a care about her surroundings; attention given to selection, placement, and grouping; while still giving the feeling of hominess. He knew this not of his own accord, but from all the instruction and pointing out of such things by his wife over their almost thirty years of marriage.

Sitting opposite Grass, Davis, who was more astute and observant about such things, came to the same conclusion about Maggie. In addition, he was acutely aware that money did not come easily or abundantly to this household. It was apparent to him, too, that it was not spent frivolously, but on things that were treasured and had meaning.

"All right, you don't have the packet." Grass had worded the question exactly as the diary instructed. "What about this *true family* thing? Nobody, even remotely, comes to mind?"

Maggie folded her arms loosely and took in a thoughtful breath. "Bernie was right. Father was basically a loner. I can't think of many people he connected with on a regular basis, especially these last few years. Out for breakfast, daily Mass, doctors' appointments. Watch TV, nap, brush the cats. A few meetings, never at night. I assume you've checked with his cousins. They always invited Father for holidays, and he went, but the way he groused around beforehand didn't make me think he was all that close to them. Didn't leave them much in his will anyway, that's for sure."

"How about Daniel?" Grass asked, writing briefly in his notebook.

"Daniel Giglia?"

"Yeah. Wasn't he around a lot?"

"That was pretty much an employee/employer relationship, as far as I could tell. I'm sure they respected each other. Father was happy with Daniel's work. But I don't see him taking Daniel and his partner out for a drink."

Lawrence chuckled again, but he left the follow-up to Grass. "Was Daniel's being gay a problem for Father Henry?"

Maggie relaxed into the corner of her chintz loveseat. "To be honest, I'm not sure when that fact actually dawned on him. That Daniel was gay. It's not like Paul Thomas came to church with Daniel. Father Henry saw Daniel as the guy who kept the church looking beautiful. That was important to him. Other things didn't matter. For the most part." As comfortable as she looked, Maggie chose her words carefully. "Eventually, I suppose, it was going to be a problem. Daniel was getting more and more open. It was less easy for Father not to know. Or pretend not to know. As long as he didn't acknowledge it, he didn't have to do anything. Church-wise, that is."

"Like fire him."

"Personally, I find that option despicable." She made direct eye contact with Davis. "Off the record."

"We're in your house," said Davis from the other chair, "not the rectory."

Grass didn't care where they were. "So, how do you keep working at St. Hedwig's, a Catholic Church, if you're not sold on the whole program?"

Maggie laughed out loud. "I don't know any Catholic who's sold on the whole program. Including priests. And if they are, they don't fully understand the program they think they've bought into." She cocked her head at Lawrence and with a good-natured smile threw in, "Just a personal observation."

"Understood."

"For me," Maggie went on, "a lot of the romance went out when I started working for God's Divine Representatives. Although having a mother who dragged us to holy hours, quizzed us until we bit our nervous nails to the quick about the Gospel every Sunday after Mass, and a father who demanded that we be pure and holy in the name of God and then swore at us all the time, well, let's just say it was difficult to weed out the pure and holy from the demanding and oppressive."

Grass found Maggie's combination of businesslike and flip, sometimes playful, attitude appealing. It was less confrontational and erratic than Libby Kinder's. Certainly less trying-to-please than Bernie Fruehauf.

In his line of work, Grass had seen his share of single mothers turn harder and more bitter in circumstances similar to Maggie's; circumstances that required them to stay at a job they might detest because it was the only way to support themselves and their children.

"Must be difficult sometimes," he remarked.

Maggie answered more seriously, but still at ease. "Sometimes."

Grass closed his notebook and picked it up along with Father Henry's diary and the plastic bags. He stood, giving the exit cue to Davis. Maggie followed suit.

As he tucked his red Tartan scarf into his coat, Grass turned to Maggie. "When did you realize he had MS?"

"I didn't know exactly what it was until you just now told me. I'm not sure I noticed much difference until very recently. For years, Father Henry would come home after morning Mass and just veg upstairs, watching TV or going through his World War I stuff. All day if he felt like it. Easy to do at St. Hedwig's.

"If you ask me, being a priest is one of the easiest jobs in the world to do poorly. I don't know how many times he sat across from me in my office, refusing to take phone calls from parishioners who really had problems, really wanted to talk to their pastor and get advice about personal, spiritual, or Church matters. They needed him. At night, he'd let the answering machine take all the calls and then pretend he hadn't gotten them. Left me to clean up after him," she said. "Get furious if he couldn't get out of something that interfered with, as he saw it, his … life."

Apparently there was a treasury of examples for Maggie to choose from.

"He'd call poor, old Father Halberstadt and get him to cover for him—weddings, funerals, confessions—when I think he just didn't feel like doing them. The priest was ancient, but so kind to Father Henry. Never turned him down. Then …" Maggie's eyes narrowed with her topper, "then, when Halberstadt died, Henry couldn't be bothered to go to his funeral."

She realized Lawrence Davis was getting a fuller picture of his pastor than he might have had before. Her tone changed slightly, not quite sympathetic, as she returned to Grass's original question. "But, I could tell when he started bumping into things that something was going on. Times he'd be fasting for a blood test. Thought it might be something like this. He denied it anytime I tried to bring it up. I told him he should get more exercise. Walk more. Eat something other than pasta and pretzels. He could be proud and stubborn and stupid. I think if he could have figured an acceptable way to call it quits, he would have."

"You mean commit suicide?!" Lawrence had a hard time keeping the shock out of his voice. This was a priest, after all, and according to the Church, committing suicide could lock the soul out of heaven and God's presence. For eternity.

Grass, on the other hand, whose God was not so hard-lined, was thinking of someone being put out by the curb in a garbage bag.

Maggie shrugged. "Probably not. But he hated being sick. And if he really had MS and saw the future as a miserable invalid, which he would have been—miserable, I mean—that would have been awful, intolerable for him. For a lot of people, I suppose."

"Is that how you would feel?" asked Grass.

Maggie looked around her house. "I don't know." Her glance noted the dog and cat curled in the sun, framed photos on the tables and shelves. "I have other things to live for. To put up with pain for. I think many priests lead very lonely lives. They act like it's a choice, but often it's the way they learn to cope with having no one. Unless they have family. Or they're partiers. I've worked for that breed, too. Lots of friends. But in the end … maybe God shows up for them."

Davis buttoned his coat and flipped the collar up. "Thanks for your time this morning, Maggie."

As Grass reached the door, he turned once more to his host. "And you're sure you can't think of anybody—mailman, your daughter, a call to the bank or something, someone you talked to or even just saw on the day of the murder?"

The answer was the same firm answer she had delivered every time she'd been asked. "As I said, in the winter, when I don't have to go out for anything and I've got bulletins or end-of-the-month bookkeeping to keep me busy, those days are not unusual."

"Are they gone?" Julia whispered from the kitchen.

Maggie sagged against the heavy front door until the latch caught. She took in a very long breath.

Ducking down as if a bird was loose in the living room, Julia crossed in front of the windows, trying not to be seen by the police getting into their car. "So? What did Father Henry write about you in his diary?" she asked, still squatting next to her mother.

"I annoyed him. A lot."

Julia rolled her eyes and stood up full.

"But. He also thought I was helpful and kind, and the parish couldn't run without me. Oh. And sometimes I made him laugh."

Julia whooped out into the room. "Go, girl! See. I always told you he liked you. And you, you're gonna miss him and you know it. Because he made you laugh, too. Let's celebrate. I'll fix coffee!"

"Is your husband awake?"

Julia rolled her eyes again. "Worked till four. Dead to the world. It's just us two."

The young, pajama-clad woman hooked her arm through her mother's and pulled her toward the kitchen. Playfully, she mussed the top of her mother's head. "I really like this hair."

Maggie pivoted and swung Julia back around to the living room. "Good. Then you won't mind cleaning up the wad of it your cat yorked up next to the bookcase." She smiled and tousled Julia's hair. "I'll make the coffee."

+ + +

Eight to ten inches of snow in her driveway and the poor thing has no garage. Eleven below zero. Said she parked so close to the back door she could slide in and start the car off and on all night so the battery wouldn't give out. In her pajamas and a scarf. Slept in her boots. Both of us laughing now. I told her not to come into work. No one's going to call. In fact, I'd just as soon have no one in the rectory. Everything can wait.

No, she's hell-bent on being here. Got her daughter up to shovel—bet that was a trick—they cleared all twenty-five feet down to the street. She's inside getting dressed when the city plow goes by and leaves a two-foot-high pile across the entrance of her

driveway. I'm in tears by now. She's laughing and spilling her coffee as she tells me the story. Out again—so stubborn—another hour of chipping through that crust of half snow, half ice.

And, in she comes to the office with a helping of homemade beef and noodles besides. She's such a curmudgeon.

They say laughter adds years to your life. I'm putting this down to remind me.

Especially when Maggie drives me crazy.

Chapter Forty

We know you're not related. We're just trying to expand that to a less literal definition of *family*."

Daniel screwed up his face. It made him feel slightly better to think the police might be incompetent. "What does the packet look like?"

"We don't know," answered Detective Grass, now used to not trying to sound apologetic for the lack of description for such an important item.

"An envelope? A box? A folder?"

Grass and Davis, sitting across from Daniel in his living room, agreed they did not know.

"And you don't know what form the booty is in?"

Both heads shook.

Daniel smoothed the striped afghan on the couch next to him and waited. The ball was in their court.

But Paul Thomas felt emboldened to ask his own questions, questions that might take their suspicions in a different direction— away from Daniel. "Am I understanding that whoever has this packet is sitting on a lot of money, or access to a lot of money?"

"Yes."

"Money that only gets realized, set free, with Father Felger's death?" Paul Thomas pursued.

"That's our understanding."

Paul Thomas took his time. He was scared and careful and trying to protect all that was important in his life. "I'm finding all of this a bit confusing. One minute you suggest Daniel had such an adversarial relationship with Father Henry that he threatened to fire Daniel, and Daniel, in retaliation, killed him. Now you want to know if they were so close that Father Henry considered Daniel like family and trusted him with some big fortune?"

To be honest, Grass hadn't expected much from this interview.

He and Davis thanked the two men for their time on a Saturday morning and left.

+   +   +

Probably the best is with my true family ... If I leave it all with them, they can make sure everything ends up in the right places. That way, those who have been so loving and kind and loyal to me in life ... a little needy at times, contrary now and then, but always there for me, making life so much better, will be left in good shape ...

+   +   +

Cousin Phyllis handed Wayne a mug of hot coffee, which matched the other floral mugs around the table. Yellow and white placemats added a cheery note to the breakfast nook, even with the fogged-up windows preventing a view of the sun-sparkled, white winter garden outside. Something sweet from the oven helped, too.

Wayne took the mug and slid in on one side of the booth as Detectives Grass and Davis returned to the chairs they had added at the end of the table. Up until this moment, the detectives had been offered, but refrained from taking, coffee or tea at Libby's, Berne's, Daniel's, and Maggie's. Having coffee at every stop they had scheduled that morning would either slosh their brains or wire them too tight to function. The cousins' interview was the last on the agenda for this particular issue, and the number of people being questioned was large enough to warrant indulging in a cup. Mug.

Both detectives were surprised and pleased to discover Cousin Phyllis capable of making a good, strong brew.

Cousin Ruth, tucked in the corner next to Wayne, pushed the tray of sugar and cream toward him; then smiled coyly as she nudged a plate of fresh butterscotch cookies—her mother's recipe—toward the police guests.

Wayne declined everything but the black coffee in the floral mug, which he set down to cool. "Tell me again, " he said as he unzipped one hooded sweatshirt layered over a second one layered over a flannel shirt. He blew vigorously on chapped hands, then cupped them around his mug. "The diary was in the church?"

Phyllis corrected him in a saccharine, schoolmarmish way. "The confessional."

Wayne gave a slight nod at the clarification. "And what you're saying is the big chunk of money Henry set aside, some for the stupid chapel and the rest for some family member or members who took care of him? Or do you think this family someone has the money and they're only keeping it until … ?"

He was cut off by Ruth, who giggled. "Go ahead, Detective Grass. Ask him."

Phyllis straightened up in her seat. "Yes. Ask him. Ask him the question."

Wayne looked at the two women who appeared to be busting at the seams. They were no less ridiculous than he already thought of them.

Their attempt to hold back did not last, and they soon blurted out with excited exaggeration, "Do you have Father Henry's packet?!"

Wayne recoiled from the blast.

Four faces stared at him as if a magic spell had been cast and they were waiting to see if it took effect.

He said nothing.

Grass focused on the custodian, who continued to look from one person to the next, staring confusedly, then aggravated like someone left out of a joke.

With precise enunciation, Grass repeated the question. Slowly. "Wayne. Do you have Father Henry's packet?"

Wayne looked again at each expectant face. Finally, he reached for his mug. "I don't know what the hell you're talking about."

Visibly deflated, the women sank back in the booth. There was a collective sigh of disappointment, like the air hissing out of several balloons at once.

Although Father Henry had used the term *family*, neither Grass nor Davis believed it was meant to be taken literally, and yet, a sliver of hope that it referred to one of the three people seated before them persisted.

It would have made things so much easier.

"Our understanding," Davis said, "is that that's the phrase whoever has the money will respond to."

Wayne scoffed. "You mean, you say this 'Father Henry's packet' crap, and they hand over all the money?"

Phyllis took a cookie. The consolation prize. "It's neither one of us."

"It's not the cousins in Minnesota," added a crestfallen Ruth, her eyes dropping as she broke off a crisp edge of her own cookie. "You were the last relative on the list."

Phyllis reared up. She would not give up so easily, and she wasn't about to let the wayward Wayne off the hook so easily. "Are you sure you're not hiding something? You spent a lot of time over there at church with Henry. Maybe he had you put the money somewhere. In the church. Just like the diary."

"Me?" Wayne roared back. "I'm hardly the only one over there. What about Daniel Giglia? He's at church all the time, fussing with stuff. Shit, the secretary practically lives there. They say Bernie and Henry go way back. Sounds like family to me."

"But you *are* family," protested Phyllis.

Wayne sneered. "Yeah. We were that close, ol' Henry and me."

Dipping a wedge of cookie into her coffee, Ruth mumbled to herself, "The diary says the person was needy at times. And contrary. That could be you."

Phyllis sniffed and reached for another cookie. "Certainly contrary."

Wayne had found these women silly before, and this morning they had not budged from that assessment. Calmly sipping his coffee, he would not take their bait. "You're just pissed because it isn't you.

After all that sucking up to Henry. All those Christmas dinners."

Taking the bait, however, was Phyllis's forte. "He was family," she barked. "That's right. Family!"

Grass gave a subtle signal to Davis to let the cousins bicker away.

Bicker about who else might qualify as family. About why each of them had the most right to the title. And the money. And why the others did not. The grandfather's fortune shot back onto the agenda along with the inheritance they all thought they deserved more than Henry. In the end, the image of Henry Felger alternated between a generous, funny, dear cousin and a miserable, selfish cleric.

When they started complaining about the money-grubbing Church and the outrageous chapel plan, Grass stepped in.

"It appears we have arrived at a dead end," he said in a decidedly conclusive manner as he folded his notebook shut and slipped it into his pocket. "Detective Davis and I are checking out some of the people not physically related to Father Henry, that you and other folks have suggested might be someone he took into his confidence. Until then, if any of you think of someone or something else that could help us locate this money, please, contact us. Thank you."

In the car, Detective Grass passed his foil-covered paper plate of Cousin Ruth's mother's butterscotch cookies to Detective Davis, who juggled it with his own.

"Just like all family gatherings," remarked Davis, with a bit of a smirk. "Good food; good fights." He looked out the frosty window at Cousin Phyllis's home. "Family being a relative term."

Grass groaned as he started the engine and pulled away. "Are you really making that joke?"

But Davis's thoughts were already miles away. "Of the cousins and Wayne. Libby, Bernie, Maggie, and Daniel—everyone we talked to today," he said reflectively, "which one of them do you think is lying?"

Chapter Forty-One

Once again, there had been no talk of arrests, no don't-leave-town ultimatums. Maybe Grass knew better than Libby did herself that, scheduled as she was to sing at the five o'clock Mass later that same Saturday afternoon, the nine o'clock one the following Sunday morning, and yet another funeral Monday, her sense of duty would keep her firmly tethered to St. Hedwig's.

Thoughts of getting legal advice dropped to the bottom of her to-do list.

At four, Libby arrived and opened the church to a few early and ardent worshipers. At the cantor's podium, she found the roll of black electrical tape she had hurriedly located for the priest with the broken glasses at Father Henry's funeral.

Still in her winter coat and boots, she bounded out the back door and down the outside steps to return it to the basement workshop. And again saw the pile of gift cards in the drawer.

Wayne's drawer.

Wayne's pile of gift cards.

Seeing the cards brought Libby up short. With the funeral and the discovery of the diary, Libby had forgotten about them.

Even though she believed Wayne had taken them from the Storm Relief Fund boxes, she had no proof. They were generic national chain cards. But if he had stolen these, he could have stolen others. Had

Father Henry discovered that and threatened to fire him for it? Or maybe this showed how desperate Wayne was for money, so that even a small inheritance was worth killing for. Maybe he just snapped. Maybe the opportunity just presented itself. Was he dumping the ashes after the funeral, and the thurible was just conveniently in his hand?

No.

Daniel said he did that.

Daniel dumped the ashes.

Muffled voices overhead in the church interrupted Libby's thoughts. She couldn't make out whose they were or what was being said. Having left her keys on the podium, she replaced the electrical tape and hurried upstairs and outside not to be locked out.

"I only left the door open a minute. I had to return something to the basement," she said breathlessly to Bernie, who stood at the top of the back steps. A young priest stood next to him.

"I was also expecting our sub," she got out with a wheeze. "Who must be you." She grinned at the young man. "I'm happy to meet you, but I'd be happier if we went inside where it's warm."

Heat welcomed them into the bride-side sacristy. Libby put out her hand. "Hello. I'm Libby Kinder. Your cantor for the weekend."

"I'm Father Wendell." He met Libby's greeting with a brief graze of a gloved hand.

Father James Wendell was a small man. At first glance, he was very young: hardly any beard and a round, un-weathered face. Untouched, unchallenged, untested. At second glance, he had a preserved look about him: a short, conservative haircut; gold-wire-rimmed glasses from another time period. It wasn't just that this was how he might look when he was old, but that he was already there, and that there would be little change forthcoming.

"Hello, Father Wendell," said Bernie with his usual openness. "If she sings; I'll play. I'm Bernie Fruehauf, the organist here at St. Hedwig's."

"Yes …" The sub gave a considered pause to eye Bernie. "Yes, I was here for Father Felger's funeral. And you, I believe, played at the Men's Christ in the Wilderness Conference last fall."

Bernie was impressed. "You have good eyes—and ears—and a sharp memory."

They chatted as Libby led the trio around to the priest-side sacristy.

"What parish are you from, Father?" asked Bernie.

"I'm working in the Chancery downtown, for the present," Father Wendell said, removing his gloves and his coat. "Hoping for a parish of my own soon. Substituting until then."

He looked around, holding his apparel until Bernie responded to his unspoken request and reached for a coat hanger.

"Wow. The Chancery," said Libby, who missed the interaction, having turned away to snap fresh batteries into the priest's wireless mic. "You must know all the inside scoops. The hub of the Diocese."

"Lots of conversation right now about your priest being murdered. Such a disgr- ... shame." Father Wendell, unhurried, examined the microphone switches. "And apparently by someone in the parish."

It was subtle.

But Libby's ear could pick out that hint of disdain in a clergyman's voice faster than anyone. A reverent, soft-spoken quality did not distract her.

The sub made sure his coat rested squarely on Bernie's hanger. "Also," he went on, his manner smooth, fluid, "a lot of talk about that woman thinking she can be ordained a priest. I assume you've heard about that."

Libby said nothing.

Bernie placed the hanger in the vestment closet. "I guess she found a bishop somewhere to perform this rite."

"An *ex-communicated* bishop." Father Wendell raised his eyebrows slightly above his glasses. "You've heard, Miss Kinder?"

"I have." Her friendliness took a slight hit.

Not Bernie's. "I heard it on national news."

"A lot of good people will be scandalized by a woman being so overtly defiant of Church Law."

There it was—the self-righteous authoritarian note. Libby always wondered if priests had to learn it or if it was just innate to some.

"Even if someone were to attend this charade, this sham, out of curiosity, let's say, they would give scandal to others." Father Wendell laid the battery pack precisely next to the microphone earpiece. "We must pray for them. That they know what is the right thing to do."

Libby had heated up; so she unbuttoned her coat before

proceeding with substitute instructions. "Everything here on the end of the table is ready to set out for Mass. Does it look like there's anything else you'll need?"

Father Wendell judged the cruets of water and wine and the several large, gold chalice-like containers filled with the wafers to be consecrated for Holy Communion. "I don't need all of these ciboriums."

"You might," said Libby. "Our Saturday night Mass is often crowded, especially in the winter. The old people come tonight instead of getting up on cold Sunday mornings."

"Good for the soul to get up on Sunday. Comfort is not the important issue." Overly pleasant with a slight edge.

Libby exchanged glances with Bernie.

"We won't need them," the sub clarified, "because I will be the only one distributing the Sacred Body of Our Lord."

Libby continued as if she were having a reasonable conversation. "We already have several Eucharistic Ministers from the parish designated and scheduled to help."

"Some of them may give out the Precious Blood. The rest will not be involved."

Summarily, Father Wendell began combining the hosts into one main ciborium. He looked up at Bernie. More pleasant words. "Just so you are aware, I'll be singing all the celebrant parts of the Mass, including the entire Eucharistic Prayer and …"

For a priest to sing that much of the Mass was always an option. Most did not indulge. Most were wise enough to know they did not have the voice; the rest declined because of time constraints, if nothing else. After spending most of his last seventy-six years working for the Church, Bernie had been conditioned to be ready for any request made of him by a priest. If he could, he would do anything he was asked. He didn't skip a beat. "Yes, Father."

In those two words, Libby watched the world of the sacristy re-order itself. The patriarchal hierarchy was firmly established; the chain of command and demand made abundantly clear. It was the world she had been raised in. And had hoped had been transformed. She had to physically grip the chair in front of her to keep from losing her bearings.

Bernie was in full compliance. "Would you like me to intone anything for you on the organ?"

"That would be acceptable."

The priest's attention shifted to Libby. "You're cantoring? Will that be from the choir loft?"

"No, I sing from the podium downstairs."

"In the sanctuary or in some other area?" His glance drifted above her. "Is there any chance you will be wearing a covering on your head?"

She gripped the chair harder and forced a smile, forced a lightness that went against her own childhood conditioning. "I don't look good in a hat, Father."

Father Wendell's tone did not change, still pleasant; nor did his determination to get what he wanted. He smiled, too. "I won't require it, but I would, perhaps, recommend a small veil or some other covering for tomorrow. If you're to be in the sanctuary."

Later, Libby would wish she had rebutted the demand by saying that only women in other cultures and other religions or denominations wore head coverings like that. Or in the Third World to demonstrate their subservience. But she knew that wasn't so. Like the Latin Mass, chapel veils were making a comeback in the Catholic Church. She hadn't worn a hat to church since Easters in the 1960s, not counting her stocking cap for warmth.

The best she could get out at the time was, "I don't have anything like that, Father."

His eyes—bright, sharp, focused—behind the shield of his wire-rimmed glasses, did not blink. "Pity. As I said, it's merely a request."

Libby walked with Bernie down the side aisle to the back of church, more to get away from the sacristy and Father Wendell than out of any real need to go. She followed the organist through the swinging oak doors of the side vestibule and veered left when the options were restroom or choir loft, taking comfort in the familiar cadence of their climb up and around inside the spiral staircase.

"I haven't heard the whole Preface sung for a while," he said.

"Probably has a nice, long, fire-and-brimstone, going-to-hell, homily for us," she remarked.

"He sure is old-school."

"Old-school?!" Libby practically shrieked.

The two stepped into the open space of the first chamber of the choir loft. Libby put her hand against the entranceway doorjamb to catch her breath.

"Old-school?" she repeated in a forced whisper, lest she send her displeasure booming out into the church. "He can't be more than thirty years old. He never went to that school! It's not like he's recapturing the Golden Age of his youth. I don't get it."

Bernie yanked at one of the drawers of the metal file cabinet against the wall. "I hope all that other music he wants is in here. Haven't played it for a long time." The drawer bumped forward with a cranky scrape.

Leaving Bernie to his search, Libby walked forward to where she rested her elbows on the smooth oak railing and looked out over the quiet church. The Church where she'd looked to find God all her life. How much of what she found was God and how much was community, friendship, support, and audience was hard to sort out.

This was more grief and upheaval than she had anticipated. She had wrestled a lifetime with blind faith, examined faith, revised faith, hypocritical faith, the whole gamut, including sometimes drawn to chucking it all for no faith.

At this age, in her fifties, she wanted the struggle to be over. Or settled.

It wasn't happening.

"Doesn't surprise me," said Bird Hawkins, pushing a cart of hymnals past Libby on its creaking way to the center aisle downstairs. "Every time I've talked to Father Wendell, he's seemed like a Latin guy, an incense guy, into all the old, heavy, ornate vestments. Can't say it wouldn't be nice once in a while to see all that stuff back again. Like old times."

Libby did not trust herself to have a conversation with Bird Hawkins. Especially on this topic. Besides it ending in an argument— he getting blustery and dogmatic, she angrier and more caustic than persuasive—she knew Bird's big mouth would spread everything she had said to the four corners of the Earth, if not to the downtown police station.

When she reached the steps that led up into the sanctuary, she was met by two young girls rushing from the priest-side sacristy.

"Aren't you serving today, Aisha?"

"The priest in there said he doesn't need us today. Just Nathan."

They dashed off a genuflection, breezed past Libby, and down into the church proper, giggling.

Libby was certain they did not have a clue about what had just happened.

At five o'clock, Father James Wendell processed in and took center stage on the altar. He introduced himself at length and then continued, under the guise of pastoral instruction, to describe and define all the parts of the service as if in front of a congregation of heathens.

Libby's attention drifted back to what Father Wendell had said about the murder of Father Henry ..."by someone in the parish."

It had seemed a pointed and insensitive remark.

Now the sub was talking about the *Confiteor*, saying how beautiful it had been in Latin. In fact, Libby had learned it in Latin. It was beautiful. And mysterious. And utterly remote to most people who rattled off the foreign syllables. She listened to it now being said in English:

I confess to Almighty God
And to you, my brothers and sisters,
That I have greatly sinned,
In my thoughts and in my words,
In what I have done and what I have failed to do
Through my fault,
Through my fault,
Through my most grievous fault ...

Even in Father Wendell's overly-precious recitation, it was a powerful prayer, a simple but thorough acknowledgement of one's wrongdoings. What was that he had said ...? "There's talk of your priest being murdered by someone in the parish."

Someone in the parish. Possibly in the church at this moment?

What would a murderer feel when reciting these words? wondered Libby. How would they feel about what they had done "through their most grievous fault"?

Things were beginning to re-form in Libby's mind, shifting, the perspective changing, refocusing and coming in from a different angle. As she sat quietly at her cantor's podium, apart from the congregation, apart from the celebrant who encouraged the separation, Libby thought of the murder of Father Henry. Not about the fault of the one who had murdered him, but rather, what part was his, Father Henry's, fault. What had *he* done, in his thoughts or in his words to enrage someone so passionately?

At seven forty-eight Saturday night, a guy shot another guy in the parking lot of a neighborhood bar.

Detective Grass overlapped his red Tartan scarf across his chest before pulling his winter coat over it. He kissed his wife, who was settled in with the basketball game they had been watching on TV. He did not bother interrupting his two teens, plugged into friends or video games or homework in their bedrooms.

Going out into the cold night was not something Grass relished, but the distraction it would provide could prove helpful. All afternoon he'd pored over his notes on Father Henry's murder at St. Hedwig's Catholic Church. He had a strong suspicion, but no proof to back it up. Yet.

He tapped absent-mindedly at on his steering wheel, as was his habit. Something in Father Henry's diary stuck with him. Something said at the funeral luncheon, too. And something in all that huff by Bird Hawkins he'd had to wade through.

Experience told him that most murder cases were neither orderly nor sequential, that the further one got into the investigation, the more pieces from early on that might have seemed irrelevant could take on meaning.

Nothing like a nice, uncluttered shooting at a bar to distract him and let things in the other case percolate.

He did, however, have one concern. In close-knit circumstances, like those at St. Hedwig's, where all the suspects were friends, there was the chance that in the complacency that that breeds, they might forget they were dealing with a trapped animal. One who was potentially dangerous.

+ + +

It was easier telling Josh he couldn't do a reading for his sister's wedding than his mother. She's a good woman, a good parishioner, but, as I told her, leaving the Church has its consequences.

He could have made a good priest. Interest. Reverence. Seemingly comfortable with the routine.

Beautiful vestments and those spectacular processions—that's what got me.

Sat next to a guy from Africa at the Conference. Said he became a priest because when he was a kid he watched a priest back home in Uganda anoint his dying grandfather. Thought it was the most wonderful—and holy—experience of his life ... the look of peace and relief on his grandfather's face, the absolute joy and satisfaction the priest got giving such spiritual comfort and the "fallout grace" he called it, for himself, for merely being a witness to this visit orchestrated by and presided over by a loving God.

Loves hospital work, seeing the sick, the dying. Liked working with converts, too. Guess he's got a lot of them in Uganda. I'll take them any day over the sick and needy. Half of them don't even recognize you—just want you to sit in those hot, stuffy little cubicles they call a room. Nursing homes. Everything smells. People in the hallways bleating like hurt animals. They hold your hand, and hold it till you're both sweaty while they ramble and repeat themselves over and over. What do you say?

I know I should be more sympathetic. God knows it will be my turn in that bed soon enough.

Just let me go.

+ + +

It was clear Libby had a love/hate relationship with rules.

In youth, her bone marrow had been infused with their wonderfully concrete lines of demarcation: everything on one side was good and right; everything on the other, bad and wrong. Injected by teachers, Church, and society, it was nice to have a reliable code to expect others to abide by, just as she abided by it herself.

But as she grew older, things didn't seem to go as planned. They became murky.

At first, she thought it was she who was too lax, not compliant enough; and for a long time she strove to comply harder. Was it fervor or obsession?

Then she thought it was others' fault for not toeing the line and thus wreaking havoc on the system. So she worked to re-form them. With limited success.

What began to emerge, was that it was reality that fell short. The binary system was itself flawed. There were exceptions—reasonable, compassionate, natural exceptions—that bore no "fault" at all, but merely were the way things were. The soup wasn't morally good or bad; the soup was just the soup. It tasted good or not, but that wasn't right or wrong. If someone was upset about the sound system, they were just upset, not morally off the mark with their opinion.

And then there was the Duplicitous Truth problem, the Equivocating Postulate, as she discovered that the same rule could be observed in opposite ways—and both ways be right. Or both wrong. Like the debate the city was having about building a casino: a bad thing because it would encourage gambling and people could lose their shirts; a good thing because the revenue would fund the local schools.

Hard enough to live with ambiguity, much less make decisions in all that gray area.

It drove her crazy.

Libby lay in her bed, her oversized socks pulled up to her knees, her flannel nightgown pulled down to meet them. No gap. Dash and BabyCakes were already curled into the warm crooks of her body and breathing steadily.

If Father Henry had begun to close the Church's door to Libby on certain issues, the likes of Father Wendell were slamming it shut. Could he be the new—old—face of St. Hedwig's? Was it time to stop pushing against it? Maybe it was time for a timeout. To listen, unbiased, and let the Universe speak its own Truth to her. Be conscious, pay attention, honor it. Go with Thoreau theologically and simplify, simplify, simplify.

Was Monsignor Jimmy onto something, that it was enough to start with kindness?

It was not in Libby's nature to relax and let things progress in their own time, but instead to sort and search and push for meaning.

It often made for very cold, very sleepless nights.

Chapter Forty-Two

No one needed to get to St. Hedwig's early Sunday morning. A cold wind went to the bone, but there was no snow or ice; so no Wayne was needed. Music was a repeat of the night before, so Bernie had nothing to run through. About eight o'clock, Libby arrived at the back door. She removed one of her crazy-patterned mittens, picked out the freezing metal church key on her ring, and let herself in. Locked the door. Turned off the alarm. Turned on the lights.

She padded down the geometric flooring of the center aisle in her warm boots and unlocked the front doors. Ushers came early. Sometimes so did substitute priests.

Libby was there. She was ready. She did not, however, have a covering on her head.

He took note of it immediately. Libby watched Father Wendell's eyes dart shamelessly to the top of her head. "Good morning, Miss Kinder."

"Good morning, Father." She bolted the back door behind him and worked hard to sound friendly. "I think everything's ready for this morning. The church secretary said you might also be our celebrant for tomorrow's funeral."

"Yes," he said, pulling off his thick gloves and unbuttoning his coat. "Unless something unforeseen comes up, that's the plan."

Libby's plan was to let Father Wendell in and send him over to the priest-side sacristy while she busied herself on the bride-side or out in the main church. Father Wendell accommodated her on this.

Perhaps it was his preference as well, and with no other remarks, he disappeared around the dim hallway to the other side.

Libby was standing in the middle of the bride-side, undecided on a direction, when Lawrence Davis ducked in from out by the altar.

"Thought I saw someone moving around in here."

"Oh, hi, Lawrence," said Libby.

In recent days, Lawrence Davis's appearance had signaled police interrogation and confrontation. This morning, in contrast to coming up against the Church of days gone by and the scrutiny of her head gear, Libby thought him a welcomed face. "Get your lectoring date straight?"

"I did."

"I was just letting Father Wendell in, our sub for the day."

"Another sub? Wonder when they'll assign someone permanently." He lowered his voice. "How is this guy? A potential?"

"He's … okay. If you're the right gender. And have amnesia about what century we live in."

Lawrence chuckled. "An old guy, huh?"

"Can't be over thirty."

Lawrence frowned. "Kind of amazing, isn't it? They want a romanticized Church that never existed. It had some charm, but needed fresh air, as Pope John XXIII said. Dependable, but dogmatic and oppressive at times. I know. I was there. Compassionate? Not so much."

Libby mirrored his frowned. "Where will it go, Lawrence?"

"Where we let it, I suppose." He shrugged. "Where the Spirit takes it, if we're lucky."

Libby looked at the handsome man—Sunday best, his lectoring voice deep, his manner smart yet easy-going. Familiar. Dependable. Maybe that's all anyone really wanted in their church life.

She dropped into one of the chairs by the Formica table and realized how much she had been missing her old ways at St. Hedwig's. Was she romanticizing those as well? The predictability of Father Henry? The camaraderie in the sacristy? The chummy talk? The joy?

Recently the whole church piece felt like duty and obligation and suspicion, instead of joy, not to mention inspiration. It was as if she'd taken a new job and didn't know who to trust.

Libby bent to remove her snow boots and slip on dress shoes. Then she sat up and decided to take a chance. "I found a slew of gift cards in Wayne's workshop downstairs."

True to his training, Lawrence didn't react except for the tiniest lift of one eyebrow.

It was enough to launch Libby into her presentation. "I think he's probably been taking them regularly from the Storm Relief Fund boxes. I know how donations were going up to a certain point and then seemed to drop off. Sharply. I thought it was just the nature of the beast—people giving a lot at the start, then losing interest—but this seemed, I don't know, when I look back, not the same."

"You think Wayne killed Father Henry and stole the cards that day?"

"I know it's pretty circumstantial."

Lawrence smiled. "I see you've picked up more lingo."

Libby returned a weak smile, not feeling particularly confident, lingo notwithstanding. "I know the cards could be from anywhere, anytime."

Lawrence's smiled dropped away. "I didn't mean that in any denigrating way, Libby. You're closer to all this than anyone. And you're observant." He curled his fingers on the back of the chair across from Libby. "I'm curious. If Wayne was already stealing from the boxes, what do you think his motive was for hitting Father Henry over the head for them? Wayne had easy access to the church, could have taken the cards under cover of darkness. Or in broad daylight, if he'd wanted to."

"I wonder if that's why Father Henry got so adamant about emptying the boxes after every Mass," said Libby. "He said he was worried someone might come in off the street. Maybe he suspected— or knew—it was …" Libby's eyes widened. "Maybe he confronted Wayne about it. Maybe there was an argument that day, but it wasn't with Daniel. It was with Wayne. You know Wayne doesn't get along with Daniel. Maybe Wayne said that to throw suspicion on somebody else. If nothing else, it shows how mercenary Wayne is. Makes getting money from the will an even stronger motive."

Libby sat back and rapped her knuckles on the table. She leveled her glance at Lawrence and said dryly, "A more plausible motive than being asked to push a person down the steps because they're ill, when the asked person doesn't even know about it."

"I know this has been unsettling for you, Libby," Lawrence said sympathetically. "It's not fun being accused of murder."

"Unsettling doesn't begin to cover it." Libby picked at a dry cuticle. "I keep feeling these lulls where I forget all this. The murder seems … over there," she said waving a hand at a distant spot. "Not part of my life, not any of my concern. Except that this is my church, such as it is. Father Henry was my pastor. Then boom! You're the only left-handed suspect. Lull. Lull. Then boom! The diary thing." She looked up hopefully. "I don't suppose there was anything about firing someone in there?"

"Not specifically."

Libby chewed at the side of her fingernail. "Are you sure I don't need a lawyer?"

Detective Davis paused just long enough to make Libby uncomfortable. She wanted reassurance. He didn't give it.

They both turned as they heard young voices in the sanctuary and keys jingling at the back door.

Lawrence didn't wait. He moved quickly to lay his hands palm down on the table and lean in close to Libby. "I will only say this: there are certainly others with more incriminating motives. Right now, yours *is* a little thin."

The back door creaked open. Bernie stepped in with a waft of cold air and a look of concern when he saw Detective Davis.

"Oh. My."

Libby switched around, a sudden lift in her voice, one that had been missing so far that morning. "About time, Bernie. We were coming to get you if you didn't show up soon."

The organist pulled off his cap cautiously. "More detective questions this morning?"

"Nope," said Lawrence, straightening up and laughing. "Not on Sundays. Wearing my lector hat today."

Bernie visibly relaxed. "Father Wendell will like that. Won't he, Miss Libby?"

Lawrence looked momentarily puzzled. "Because I'm a guy?"

"That, too," said Libby, standing. "Father Wendell is very fond of hats. Not required, but highly recommended."

"Oh?"

Libby shoved her chair in. "Don't get me started."

Two impish brothers bounded into the sacristy, muttering hellos to the adults as they crossed to the cupboard of altar server outfits.

"Oh, good," said Libby sarcastically. "Servers with all the right parts."

There were two songs on the roster that Libby really liked that morning, and she let them raise her spirits as music always could for her. After an uneventful Mass, Libby walked to the back of church where she inquired about a parishioner's sick husband and accepted a compliment about the beautiful altars from a visitor.

The church cleared out quickly. Bernie closed up the choir loft and left. Libby took the Storm Relief Fund boxes and emptied them of donations in the bride-side sacristy. She waved to Lawrence and the last of the ushers who checked that the doors to the main entrance were locked as they claimed waiting spouses and went out.

She felt better. This was how Sunday mornings were supposed to be: connecting, greeting, singing, praying. Thinking of more than herself and her own small world. Of course, it had helped considerably for Lawrence to say what he'd said.

Alone in the quiet, Libby hummed "A Mighty Fortress" and walked unhurried to the sanctuary then into the priest-side sacristy, where she would get numbers to put up on the hymn board for tomorrow's funeral.

She was surprised to find Father Wendell sitting at one end of the long oak table, prim in his black shirt and stiff white collar. He looks so small, thought Libby. But she knew that was misleading. His hands were cupped inside each other, composed, on top of his breviary prayer book. Like a CEO who had all the power.

"Would you mind staying a minute, Miss Kinder?" he began coolly. Or was it steely? "I'd like to have a few words with you."

She did mind. But Catholic upbringing and social indoctrination, mixed with curiosity, pulled out a chair and she sat down.

"Let me be direct," he said. "I know you're the cantor for that woman's sham ordination."

Libby, too, clasped her hands together on the table before her. Bird Hawkins, she thought, and tried to keep from shaking.

"I bring it up," he continued evenly, almost breezily, as if he might next offer refreshments for their chat. "I bring it up for two reasons. First, I'm aware that a clear and convincing motive for the murder of Father Henry still eludes the police. If Father Henry Felger had known you were participating in this condemnable event—and he no doubt could have heard of it as easily as I—he would most certainly have had to take action. Had he done so, or had he forbid you, perhaps that angered you. A woman. A *liberated* woman, some might call you." His eyes softened, but the accompanying smile came from the corner of his mouth. "Mind you, I'm not saying this did occur, but I feel the police ought to know about it as part of their investigation." He flipped his hands open in a plaintive gesture. "Of course, it may mean nothing. Nor your reputation for blowing up over such matters."

Pure Bird, thought Libby. Pure Bird Hawkins.

Father Wendell was not finished. "While I may be civically concerned about the legal aspect of this, please believe me when I say I am more worried about the spiritual component. About your immortal soul."

More former training, with a dose of fear, kept Libby polite. Only those who had been through the same Catholic boot camp would understand how hard it was to get out the next sentence.

"You know, Father, I appreciate your concern, but I think I'm capable of taking care of my own immortal soul." As Libby pushed away from the table, Father Wendell stood.

His faced darkened. He was saving a soul. This was his vocation, his calling, to bring the sinner back in line to God. He stepped around to her, his casualness replaced with zealous intensity. "There are two weeks until this unholy abomination. You have time to bow out gracefully. They can replace you. I'm asking you to withdraw. Tonight. You will regret it if you stand witness to it." He laid his plan at her feet. "I will be here tomorrow for the funeral. If you have not removed yourself by then," he added with adamant resolve, "I will reconsider telling the police."

Libby stared at him. Her mouth had fallen open. Even long and strict training could not keep the word from spilling out. "Blackmail?"

Father Wendell's eyes grew so large behind his glasses they nearly overtook them. "I prefer to think of it as … providing options."

"You can prefer it, but it is what it is. Father."

The pastoral tone, the figurative patting on the head. "I shall pray for you tonight, Miss Kinder," he said with holy insistence. "I'm giving you a chance to make the right decision." He plucked his black coat from the hanger in the vestment closet and picked up his breviary from the table. "I only mean to encourage you to do the right thing."

An angry woman? Yes. Liberated? Who could tell? But what

came out of Libby's mouth, as she stood there like a second grader, was the unadulterated, peace-at-any-price, don't-offend-anyone, turn-the-other-cheek, all-priests-are-holy line. At best, she hoped for a little sarcasm to shine through.

"As I said, Father, thank you for your concern."

She bolted the door after him.

Boom! The Forbidden Ordination motive.

Chapter Forty-Three

Y ou *thanked* him?!"

To be honest, Libby was as shocked as her niece, once she was away from the sacristy and Father Wendell.

Sunday nights at her sister's were not only meant to be a chance for Libby to trade the quiet joy of singlehood for the chaotic joy of family, but also a distraction from her own cares.

Except this Sunday night.

Except for Father Wendell's blackmail proposal.

"You actually *thanked* him? Seriously?" Caroline's dismay echoed around the table as she spooned out hearty portions of lasagna, the cheese on top stretching from pan to plate like a sloop of wire between two telephone poles. "Why didn't you yell at him?"

"I can't yell at a priest," said Libby

"You yelled at Father Henry."

"I didn't yell at him. I argued with him. True, sometimes loudly."

"You should have told this guy off."

Libby's defense sounded lame, even to her own ears.

Her sister, Jane, however, understood perfectly. "You can't tell a priest off. I'm not saying he had a right to say those things or that Libby shouldn't have stood up for herself, but when you've been conditioned like we were ... Shoot, we weren't allowed to talk to a priest. If you ran into one in the school corridor you were supposed to stop talking and bow, like they were, well, like they were God."

Jane flipped a towel over a basket of hot buttery garlic bread and passed it down the table. That attracted two small great-nephews of Libby's like birds to a feeder, which alerted the others, and the customary banging of the piano ceased for the moment.

The mother of one of the birds handed him a prepared plate. "It doesn't really matter, does it, Aunt Lib? I mean, what he threatened?"

"Of course it matters, Dodo-head." The loving remark came from Caroline's husband, loading a plate for another child at the far end of the table. "This is murder. I don't know why you guys don't think it's a big deal. If this priest calls the police—which he will probably do—no matter what the worm says. It gives the police more reason to nail Libby, who, unfortunately has a lot going against her. They could arrest her, put her in jail; and even if she's innocent, let her rot there for a year until the trial rakes her over the coals and exposes every dark corner of her personal life."

He reached for the salad dressing.

Except for the birds twittering, the room was silent.

Libby took a swallow of water to dislodge the bread stuck in her throat. It was surreal. Sitting and talking like this. Feeling that such catastrophic things were happening and that she, even in the middle of it, had so little control.

Jane's husband, Joe, broke the ice.

Because no one could stand the thought.

Because they felt helpless.

"You will not rot in jail, Lib," he said. "Even on *Law and Order* they would let you out on bail."

The comic relief worked. Everyone laughed and returned to eating lasagna and began offering to chip in money for her bond.

Caroline, not so conditioned as her mother and aunt, persisted. "Why is it so wrong anyway? Singing at this ordination thing?"

Libby was happy to talk about anything but prison. "I'd be giving witness to something the Church doesn't recognize or condone. Forbids, really. Women being ordained. At least at this point in history."

The mother poured milk for one of the birds. "But you're just singing. You're not a witness. Not like a maid of honor."

Now everyone tried to be helpful. "If you were a Catholic florist, could you only deliver to Catholic weddings?"

"No Jewish events?"

"Nothing to the Buddhist Temple?"

"You're right," said Libby, slowly taking her own side. "I'm a professional. I may be a friend, but I'm primarily there as a singer. It doesn't matter if I believe what the woman is doing is right or not."

"Who makes up these rules?" asked Caroline's husband, fixing his own plate of lasagna.

Jane had studied in the old school. "What about scandal? Will they claim that just by being there you're giving scandal?"

"To whom?" Libby's voice rose, both in indignation and to compete with the toddlers' resumed piano recital. "If somebody comes to the event, they're already in favor of it. They're glad to be there. If somebody's scandalized by it, they won't be there. Who will know I'm there?"

This was better than being distracted; this was heartening.

In a sense.

It outlined a defense for the Church issue for Libby. Was it mere justification? No, she wasn't looking for justification. She believed in the ordination. But it was a comeback if anyone asked. If Father Wendell had to be refuted.

And so, the murder piece of the conversation and prison were put in denial, and Libby let lasagna move front and center.

Then dessert.

Sliced strawberries on angel food cake or lemon-lime sherbet in cones. Libby helped deliver the cones to the pianists, who had progressed to "Chopsticks" with the aid of an older sibling.

Conversation at the big table also moved on. Over mugs of hot tea, talk of the latest novel and the price of gasoline replaced sensitive subjects. Eventually, the young and rambunctious wore out; needed, and were given, baths. Toys were put away as Sunday night drew to a close and parents carried their clean and swaddled babes into the cold and dark to cars already warmed up and waiting.

Libby started to help with the dishes, which Jane, as always, reprimanded her for. "Don't bother, Lib," she said, while sorting and wrapping leftovers for care packages to send home.

Ejected from the kitchen, Libby took to wiping down the piano keys, sticky with sherbet. "This is going to need more than a damp cloth," she said. Jane, who had joined her, began wadding up stray napkins. "Although," Libby added, rubbing a large spot, "the lemon-lime color is very chic."

Jane advanced to straightening out the piano books. Then shuffled and straightened them out some more. She paused, finally, and looked at her younger sister.

"Are you okay, Lib?"

Turning from the octave above middle C, Libby read the concern on her sister's face. Having relaxed in the temporary distractions of others, she had once again been lulled. Libby wasn't normally a worrier or easily frightened, but it was beginning to feel as if danger and peril were coming at her from every angle. "It's not like I have a bare lightbulb swinging overhead and a hardboiled detective forcing a confession out of me."

"Doesn't mean it isn't serious," said Jane."

Libby swiped another row of sugary keys. "I keep expecting imminent threats. Someone watching my every move, lurking in the shadows."

Jane clicked her tongue at the drama. "Too many movies, Libby."

"Or at least have the police say, 'click, click, click. Got it. Break in the case. Clues all fell into place, and you're off the hook. Thanks for your help. Sorry to have bothered you.'"

Jane quit straightening books. "You're innocent, Libby. Getting off the hook will happen. It can't take them that long to see through the flimsy evidence against you."

Libby folded over the damp dishrag. "You know what's really driving me crazy? Not that being arrested and rotting in jail isn't a grossly disagreeable thought. Some of those movies have to be legit. But I have this perverse arrogance that thinks I ought to be able to figure out who killed Father Henry and how it happened."

Jane took the rag from Libby. "Nancy Drew revisited?"

"Exactly. Don't you think we read enough of those in grade school to give us an edge?"

~ ~ ~

Libby made room in her refrigerator for the container of lasagna Jane had sent home. Behind her, she heard Dash's toenails click on the tile floor. When she turned, the full welcoming committee had gathered: Dash stretched onto forward paws; BabyCakes sat upright, motionless, except for a cavernous, full-mouth yawn.

"Come on, Dash," she said, reaching for the dog's leash. "Let's go out and be done with it; then we can settle in for the night." She slipped her mittens of many colors back on and looped the leash over them.

"Drat!" She looked down. "What is—ugh. Lasagna." Tomato sauce on the mittens. On the leash.

She started to the basket by the door for a different pair of gloves but decided to clean everything when she got back. "Come on, boy."

The night was glass-shatteringly clear. The edge of the moon was so distinct it looked as if it had been stenciled in and added after the sky had been painted. She and Dash turned at the corner, and in the stillness of a winter Sunday evening, she looked ahead toward the park down several streetlight-lit blocks lined with trees—tall, leafless, stark.

Perfect negative space.

Libby let her eyes play with the landscape, seeing the shape of the black masses of trees, bushes, and houses, then re-focusing to see the shape of the block of light around them.

It was just a feeling.

Below the surface.

As if it had finally been quiet enough in her head to hear the tumblers of a lock beginning to click into place. Given a little time, a little re-focusing of facts, all would fall into place, and the lock would spring open.

Not quite there yet.

If only there would be enough time before other things intervened.

When Libby got home, she barely remembered the walk. Fortunately, Dash knew the way and had brought her safely round to the back door while her mind had been engaged with other concerns.

Reality returned as she set her food-splotched mittens to soaking.

She stared down at Dash's leash in the sink, wiping off a smear of lasagna.

Chapter Forty-Four

It wasn't the light that woke Libby. Clear skies from the night before had succumbed to swollen, gray clouds tumbling in and threatening sleet as temperatures rose, hovering just near freezing.

It wasn't BabyCakes's reveille, insistent mewing and crisscrossing the blanket over Libby's body.

It wasn't the alarm, which she had switched off prematurely.

It wasn't the light. Nor the cat. Nor the alarm.

It was "Chopsticks."

The children's sticky-fingered selection from the piano recital last night at Jane's had crawled into Libby's head early, long before she got out of bed.

Although she had slept, Libby had the feeling that her subconscious, accompanied by the tune, had been working all night; consulting its own notebook; shaking data loose from old conclusions; firing off new suggestions; looking at the shape of things around the shape of things; events around events, converse, inverse, opposite questions. Negative spaces.

Nothing seemed trivial or off limits; everything seemed important.

But "Chopsticks"?

Da-da-da, Da-da-da; De-de-de, De-de-de—dogged her through feeding the pets, eating her own breakfast, and while she tried to warm up her voice for the funeral in an hour or so. The notes fell in sync with brushing her teeth and again with chipping away the layer of frost on her windshield before she buckled up and started out.

The main streets were clear; Monday school bus and business traffic flowing smoothly. The side streets were a different story. Nearing St. Hedwig's, Libby eased up, cautious on the slippery pavement. Also on the lookout for Father Wendell's car.

And Detective Grass's—if he had been signaled by the substitute priest to be around in case Libby insisted on singing at that woman's ordination. Maybe Father Wendell would use the detective's presence as leverage, i.e., blackmail, to get Libby to promise to give up her sinful endeavor.

Would Grass think that Father Henry's knowing this was a possible motive for murder? Would he assemble a pile of small pieces of her puzzle and let one more item seemingly make everything else fit?

Libby tracked a van inching its way down the icy street ahead of her. There would be no stopping quickly, so she slowed to put some distance between her car and the van.

To her right, she caught sight of Mrs. McGrew picking her way up the rectory steps, one hand tight on the railing, with Jonny Kwan on the sidewalk below, doing the dance of alternating his feet in the cold. He was holding her pie carrier and his own casserole dish for the funeral luncheon in a few hours.

Maggie emerged on the rectory porch, her pretty colorful shawl a bright spot on the ominous, gray morning as she met the older lady on the landing. Maggie looked out; Mrs. McGrew swung around, and seeing Libby's car come slowly into view, waved a gloved fist curled around a clump of Parish Hall keys.

Maggie waved, too, but by the time Libby had lifted her eyes to look at her, Maggie had turned away and retreated into the warmth of the rectory.

When Libby tapped her brakes, her own tires refused to grab momentarily, and the short sideways slide of her car jolted her attention back to driving. Between the tenuous road conditions and the anticipation of a possible confrontation with priest and police looming, her whole body had tensed.

She got the car under control and pulled safely into a space in the church's back parking lot. Wayne's rusty truck sat a few spaces away next to Bernie's old car. Obviously, he had not collected his inheritance yet.

Libby was early and a little shaky from the slippery drive. Since either Wayne or Bernie would have opened the church and let in anyone from the funeral home, she allowed herself to pause. The car's heater was sending soothing warm air at her feet and face. She let it blow, leaned her head back and closed her eyes.

Tap. Tap, tap.

Alert!

Libby gave a swipe at the steamed-up driver's side window.

A man.

A blurry man.

A blurry Antonio.

Libby lowered the window.

"Sorry if I scared you, lady," he said, every syllable a frozen puff. "I tried to catch you out by the street, but I was afraid to get in your way when you started to slide." He blew on his hands. No gloves. No coat. "I just wanna tell you something. I don't see you so much in the winter. In the cold, you know?"

"Come on," she said, flipping the lock and tossing Dash's towel to the backseat.

Antonio climbed in. He hunched in the seat and tucked his hands into warm armpits. "Man, it's cold today. They say storms. You got a funeral?"

"Yes, another one." Libby directed half the heater vents in Antonio's direction.

"I tell my wife, mi esposa, all the time how you got things going on over here. She thinks I'm kinda nosy, but I say I just like to see what's going on. It's my church, too, you know?"

"There's certainly been no lack of activity lately, that's for sure."

"Hey, I been wanting to thank you. For helping with my nephew Billy, you know? He's not a bad kid. He gave back all those credit card things he took. He didn't take any money. He's still gotta do some probation work service. My wife says the police, they wouldn't have believed him just by his own words. You know, he's a kid and they don't believe a kid. They kept trying to make him say he killed the Father, you know? He would still be in jail if you hadn't helped stand up for him. So, I told my wife I gotta thank you when I see you next time."

Libby was aware that she had come closer to putting Antonio's nephew in jail than getting him out, but there was no need to go into all the hookah details. "I didn't do that much, Antonio, but I'm glad everything turned out okay for Billy."

Antonio looked out the windshield and regarded St. Hedwig's standing solidly before them. He nodded, his arms and hands rendered useless in their attempt to stay warm, crisscrossing Antonio's chest and tucked away. "Most people in this church are okay," he said. "Most of them, really friendly. Say hi to me every time, you know? That Maggie lady at the priest's house? She's got no husband, does she?"

"No."

"He died. Really young. And Father Henry. I kinda miss him. No matter what, he always said something to me. Waved. Not like that one guy. Looks kinda mean. He killed the Father, you know?"

It almost went right by Libby. Lulled by the drone of the heat blowers and Antonio's rambling evaluation of the church population.

Not a pause. Not a breath. He just plowed on. Libby sat up.

Alert.

"He came out that day Father died. Slipped. I saw him slip. He didn't bother to salt the steps. That's what killed the Father."

Libby didn't know where to break in. She was instantaneously too warm. She turned down the blowers and their noise. But she was also instantaneously wary. Wary of Antonio coming up with his own version of things.

"You saw Father Henry slip?"

"No. That guy who's here a lot. Not the old guy who plays the organ. He's here a lot, too. This guy works here."

Wayne or Daniel? wondered Libby. They were similar in height, but not in build. Daniel was more muscular, confident; Wayne, slender and sulky. But in the winter? From a distance?

"There are actually two guys who work here," said Libby. "Two that come and go a lot. Who were here that day."

"Yeah, I seen them both."

"Was this before or after the funeral?"

"After. I think. First, the nice-looking one."

"Daniel?" Libby guessed.

"I don't know his name. He says hi to me sometimes, too. But he didn't see me. It was kinda raining icy stuff. He had his head down."

"How did you know it was Daniel? The nice-looking one?"

"He wears a black leather coat. They're not very warm, you know? I asked him one time. He says they mostly just look good. Probably why he hurried to his car. Getting out of the cold."

Libby looked at the back steps of the church through the clear circle defrosted for her on her windshield. "Where were you when you saw him?"

"By my car." Antonio twisted in his seat and nodded in the direction of his house across the street. "I bought this little humidifier I was loading up. My wife thought it would make it easier to breathe. Our house gets dry, she thinks. But then she says I can take it back 'cause she thinks it doesn't work like she thought it would, you know? Then she says, 'Come get this box down before you go.' So I go do that. Then when I come back out to my car, I see the other one, the mean-looking one, like he's mad all the time. In a sweatshirt."

Definitely Wayne.

"He pulls the hood up when he comes from that other door." Antonio swiveled around and nodded in the opposite direction. "I don't know where that door goes to."

Libby followed Antonio's glance to the door to the right of the church steps. "That's the church basement," she said. "It's where the furnace and maintenance equipment is."

"Oh. Okay. I see him go in there a lot."

Antonio turned in earnest to Libby. "I tell you, he slipped right there at the bottom of the steps. Had to hold onto the railing. You know if the sidewalk was that slippery, those steps were even worse. He didn't do anything about the ice on those steps. Isn't that his job?" Antonio frowned. This was a man who, by nature, kept an eye out for what needed to be done. "I put salt on my steps." His hands finally escaped to emphasize his point. He let them fall back into his lap. He stared out at the scene of the crime, where the event he could not prevent had occurred. "He should have done that on the church steps," he added quietly, soberly. "But he didn't. You know? That's what killed the Father."

Libby said nothing as she sat next to Antonio, who also said nothing and seemed worn out from recalling the movements of that disturbing day. He had proven to be unknowingly helpless at the time and was equally helpless in the retelling.

Libby tried to pick through Antonio's digressions to glean which were facts and which of those were relevant, hoping to weigh how reliable an observer he was. And if he was, how did the sequence of other events the day of the murder line up accordingly?

She did not believe Father Henry's death was merely a matter of him slipping down the steps left icy and dangerous by a lazy Wayne, although it did add to her distaste of the maintenance man.

She asked, "Did you see the hooded one, Wayne, actually leave?"

"Yeah, 'cause, you know, he drives that old truck. He spun when he came out of the parking lot. I was ready to go to the store with my humidifier for my wife, but I waited till he passed 'cause I don't think he always pays attention. Or doesn't care. Mostly he's getting a cigarette going."

As Libby's brain worked to rearrange the new information, she was aware that she had to ask Antonio as much as she could before he wandered off into his own story.

"Did you ever see Father Henry?"

"No. I left. But when the police let Billy go, they said he was already dead for a while. Billy was still in school. Or at his work in the restaurant. I think the Father came out later and slipped and hit his head, you know, on that sharp railing there."

Libby could see how Antonio had arrived at this explanation. It had a lot of reasonable elements to it. More importantly for Uncle Antonio, whether it was conscious or not, it let Billy off the hook by blaming someone else.

"Did you tell all this to the police?" Libby asked.

"I told them that guy didn't put salt on the steps. That's what killed Father."

"What about seeing the two men leave?"

"I was so scared and mixed up. I didn't remember about them right away, you know?" Antonio gave a pleading look at Libby. "They were going to put him in prison. My nephew. My sister's niño.

When I talked to the police the next time, I told them how I see those guys come and go. But I couldn't say exactly the time." He fiddled with the latch on the glove compartment. He looked away.

"I heard one police say, 'Now he remembers. Convenient.'" Antonio went quiet again. "They don't ask me anymore. When I remember better, I don't tell the police. After all that stuff about my nephew Billy. I'm happy not to talk to them, you know?"

Movement caught Libby and Antonio's attention. Wayne had popped out of the back door of the church and was standing on the landing at the top of the steps. Turtle-like, he pulled his head into his sweatshirt and lit a cigarette.

"I gotta go," said Antonio. He spoke to Libby, but his eyes never left the mean-looking one.

"Me, too," she said and turned off the car.

Antonio lowered his voice, as if Wayne, who, at the sound of the engine stopping, gave a cold stare in their direction, could hear. "I just wanted to tell you, thank you," he said. "You're a good lady."

Antonio ducked behind the car and, watching his footing on the slick walkway, inched his way across the street away from the church. Away from Wayne.

Reaching for her music bag, Libby tried to calm the butterflies taking off in her stomach, disturbed into flight by Antonio's firm belief that it was Wayne who had killed Father Henry, flimsy as his proof appeared to be.

Once on the sidewalk, she heard and felt a familiar grit. She looked down. Salt pellets. Today he puts down salt pellets.

"How's the cantor this lovely morning?" asked Wayne, borderline fawning as he eyed her steadily.

"Good, I hope," replied Libby evenly.

It was beginning to dawn on her that one of the things that disturbed her about Wayne was his erratic behavior. One minute he was wanting to have lunch with her, the next he was sneering at her. Had he always been that way? She wondered if murdering someone unhinged a person so that their actions didn't always seem appropriate or logical.

When she came to the small landing at the top of the steps, instead of moving aside for her, Wayne clasped Libby's arm. It wasn't rough, but it was enough to make her stiffen.

Alert.

"What?"

"Jum-py," he said, almost laughing as he let go but still blocked the door. Was he teasing or jeering? He took a drag of his cigarette and, twisting his mouth, blew the smoke off to the side. "Don't want you downwind of my carcinogenic habit. Not good for the singer's throat. I see you were chatting with the old gossip of the neighborhood."

Libby found her voice. "We were talking about his nephew."

"The little thief?"

How ironic, thought Libby, picturing the pile of gift cards in Wayne's drawer in the church basement.

"I wouldn't get mixed up with that group," he cautioned her. "They're not above lying their way out of things."

She shivered. She was cold. And she was nervous.

"I'd better see if everything's set up for the funeral."

"Relax. Bernie's in there fussing around."

Stay calm, Libby told herself. Sound casual. "Priest not here yet?"

"Nope."

Wayne turned to flick his cigarette into a nearby bush, which gave Libby the chance to start for the door. He did not touch her, but moved again to stop her, and went on as if they were happily shooting the breeze, "Hey, before you go in. The cousins and I were talking. We know you were in thick with Henry. Here all the time. Helping him with whatever. That's cool. I know he asked your opinion on a lot of stuff."

Wherever this was going, Libby did not want to incite the man in front of her. She chose to keep it light. "Well, I'm here for the same reason you are. Just working." She forced a laugh. "And, in case you hadn't noticed, I'm always willing to give my opinion."

She reached for the door handle.

Wayne's hand got there first.

"Just like family?" The smell of cigarettes was overwhelming. "Look, Libby," he said, smiling, almost convincing in his false sincerity, "if there's money to be had, we're not above sharing. Or maybe it all goes through you. Don't you think the Christian thing to do is to give a little to those of us who could really use it? We wouldn't ask for a lot, but what kind of God wants an expensive chapel when the rest of us could have life made a little easier?" He suddenly changed tactics. "The cousins are all set to take you to court if they have to." Wayne, the fox in the henhouse, smiled again. "I could be interested in cutting us both, you and me, a good deal."

There was a low rumble of thunder, harbinger of the predicted storm as temperatures rose. Sleet, not snow, would fall soon. Libby instinctively glanced up at the clouds darkening the sky overhead, an excuse to go in. "Sorry, Wayne. I'm not the *family* you're looking for. The police already asked, and I've got nothing."

Finally, in a moment of resignation, Wayne backed off.

Libby seized the break and went for the inside door, which

unexpectedly fell away under her hand, and she lurched forward.

"Oh! My!" Bernie gave a small shriek. It startled an already jumpy Libby.

"Bernie!" she squealed as she lurched forward through the door.

"Shit!" sputtered Wayne, close behind her. All three bunched inside the back door, which Wayne then slammed shut. "What're you squawking about?"

Bernie was immediately apologetic. "I heard voices and was going to unlock the door. I thought it might be Father Wendell."

Libby and Wayne had barely stepped inside the bride-side sacristy when there was a knock at the door.

Libby swallowed.

Alert.

Get ready, she told herself as she hastened to remember her practiced response about singing at the forbidden ordination of a woman.

Wayne pulled the door open. The bowed head of a black-clad priest bobbed into the sacristy. When he stood up full in the room, Libby had to stifle another shriek.

"Monsignor Jimmy!"

Chapter Forty-Five

Had it been appropriate, Libby would have hugged the old monsignor. The large, gregarious priest unfolded into the room, a head taller than anyone else, even with the slight stoop of his eighty-seven years. He patted down wisps of white hair blown free by the wintry mess he'd come in from and smiled broadly in return for the effusive greeting.

"Good morning, everyone," said Monsignor Jimmy, shaking Wayne's hand, then Libby's. "How's our beautiful singer?" His voice was rich and playful as he acknowledged Bernie. "Bernard. Our beautiful organist."

"What? Oh. I don't know about the beautiful part," said Bernie, just catching up to the priest's quip.

"What brings you to St. Hedwig's on a day like this?" asked Libby. "Friend of the deceased?"

"Didn't know the man," said Monsignor Jimmy, matter-of-factly. "I'm here to say the funeral Mass."

Libby blinked, hoping she had heard correctly. "What happened to Father Wendell?"

Monsignor Jimmy sucked on his upper teeth. "Called late last night. Some appointment he had this morning, a call by the Bishop or something? Anointing of a sick parishioner? Was I available? Yes, I was. Here I am."

Libby figured it must have been an appointment with the Bishop—or the Pope—or a detective—to miss out on confronting her. "How kind of you to come." She meant it more sincerely and in more ways than the priest could have guessed.

"Always happy to help out if I can." The delight in Monsignor Jimmy's eyes clouded over. "I am still just so sorry about Father Henry. The older I get, the longer it seems to take to adjust to these things. Of course, it's always difficult to lose one of my brothers. And this—such a tragedy."

Wayne pushed himself into the conversation, which he'd found banal, as usual. Until he heard the magic word. "Your *brother*?"

Bernie wasn't following as closely as Libby, who cut in to save the good monsignor. "Wayne, don't …"

The old priest sensed clarification was needed. He gave a wide gesture of embracing the group. "As we *all* are brothers and sisters."

Wayne wasn't mollified, discouraged, or deterred in any way. He stood directly before the man. "Do you have Father Henry's packet?"

The words came out so stilted and precise it sounded like Wayne was addressing a genie in a lamp.

"Excuse me?"

Like a pit bull clamped onto its victim, Wayne could not be pulled off. "Do you have Father Henry's packet?" he insisted.

Monsignor Jimmy's bushy eyebrows flew up, then dipped in concern. "I guess the answer is no." His grin and chuckle returned. "I didn't know I needed a password. Heh-heh."

An embarrassed Libby cleared her throat. "Don't pay any attention to Wayne."

Not to be dismissed, Wayne made a show of importance, reaching for charcoal briquettes and readying them in the borrowed thurible sitting on the table with the other funeral paraphernalia for the impending service. He had work to do.

Libby touched the priest's arm. "Come on, Monsignor. Bernie and I will get you set up for the funeral."

The three left Wayne and made their way along the back corridor. Even with the lights on, the storm outside darkened the passage more than ever.

"You didn't wear a coat, Monsignor," commented Libby, once they were in the priest-side sacristy. "Will you be warm enough going to the cemetery?"

"Not to worry," he said, patting his slight paunch. "Plenty of padding."

Libby opened the vestment closet and brought out a gold-and-white funeral chasuble. She looked over at Bernie. "Are you going to the cemetery? You said you kind of knew this guy."

"Me? No. No, I don't think I'll go today."

"No padding on you, Bernard," Monsignor Jimmy teased. "But you've always been kind of scrawny."

Libby pointed out the pertinent liturgy books and microphone switches as she chatted away, still elated from not having to deal with Father Wendell. "There'll be a nice luncheon when you come back, Monsignor. Bernie will hang around for that, won't you?"

Monsignor Jimmy leafed through the lectionary, making sure the long purple ribbon marked the opening prayers. "Last time I was here, Betty, Betty … Anderson's funeral, I believe, I had the best pie of my life."

"Mrs. McGrew's," Libby and Bernie said in unison.

"Pies and soup are her specialties," Libby added. She reassured the priest. "Saw her bringing a pie this morning."

Wayne appeared at the doorway that led out to the sanctuary. Two red-eyed teenagers hung back behind him. "Readers," he said in curt explanation, and then promptly abandoned them.

"Mourners," Libby corrected under her breath. "I'm so sorry," she said, addressing the two young women, sympathy and service overriding her sentiments about Wayne. "Were you related?"

"Uncle," one of them choked out, while the other twisted a tissue to shreds.

Libby gently instructed the nieces about their readings and helped two nephews who had volunteered to be servers; then she turned on the necessary lights and sound system.

Bernie went upstairs and began to play softly, under the subdued conversation in the back of church by the coffin. In the sacristy, Libby helped Monsignor Jimmy with funeral vestments, then took a moment to organize her music at the cantor's podium.

Not many pews from the front, Libby spied Daniel and Paul Thomas. Dark suits. Ties. Surprised and curious, Libby checked the time. She slid into the pew in front of them and gave a questioning shrug.

"Old history teacher," whispered Daniel, hitching a thumb toward

Paul Thomas.

"More than that," added his partner quietly. "He became a good friend. To both of us."

Daniel smiled in agreement. "He was a kind and gentle soul. I guess kids loved him."

Paul Thomas looked around to the casket. "I'm glad they put him in plaid."

This struck all three as humorous, and they worked with difficulty to stifle laughter. Paul Thomas faked a cough and Libby stood, smoothing her navy dress, trying to regain her composure.

As she dodged around one of the huge main pillars, she nearly ran into Don Fleck from the funeral home. He worked like a stealth bomber in a gunmetal gray suit, soundlessly moving up and down, in and around people, pews, coffin, and flowers. Without a word, he handed Libby two white business envelopes.

"Would you give the other one to Bernie? I tried to nab him before he went upstairs, but he didn't look right nor left today. Couldn't catch his eye. All business."

Most funeral homes were reliable and consistent in handling the fees for music at these services, standard fare, but Libby always checked that the names and payments were correct. One for her; one for Bernie. Inside hers … whoa! A hefty bonus. She raised a questioning eye at Don.

He shrugged. "What can I say? One of your fans. Left special instructions: you to sing the 'Ave Maria,' and you and Bernie to get that very generous remuneration."

What could so often be just a job, sometimes became touchingly personal. It was humbling.

Libby looked in the envelope again. "Wow. You just never know, do you?"

"In this business, nothing surprises me," Don said with a wink. "They're all unique." He scanned the church. "Just think. Last week we had your Bishop and enough priests to choke a horse. A week before that, we had police all over the place watching that convicted felon."

A reaction, as sure as if a rubber mallet had hit her in the shin bone, made Libby look up and quickly scan the church herself. Don fleck was right. No police.

No Detective Grass.

Not in plain sight anyway.

Lazarus, again. It was, after all, one of the most read Gospels at Catholic funerals, and Monsignor Jimmy was proclaiming it again today for the plaid-wearing history teacher.

More than anything, Libby had wanted to sit down and contemplate what Antonio had told her earlier. Her body was on automatic pilot; standing, sitting, singing, and reciting as her mind wandered around on its own.

The stained glass windows were drained of color and rattled in the wind that was spitting ice against them. Lantern lights glowed over the small congregation as Monsignor Jimmy preached about the friend of Jesus who had died and was buried while Jesus was away. Lazarus's sisters blamed their Lord, "You could have done something for him if you had been here. You could have done something and you didn't."

The gentle drone of Monsignor Jimmy's voice and Lazarus and Antonio and Father Henry drifted into Libby's distracted state …

She pictured the dead one coming forth. With each step out of the tomb, it became another person; another layer of burial cloth fell away. Up out of her subconscious, a forgotten piece of information showed through, an alibi fell aside, a half-truth was exposed. A shift in focus. What was once background, moved front and center.

By the time Libby stood and began to sing the "Ave Maria" after Communion, she was sure she knew who had killed Father Henry.

Pretty sure.

She had one more piece of information to confirm. To be certain.

And she knew who had it.

She did not, however, relish the idea of the confrontation that obtaining it would force.

Strains of the recessional hymn led priest, servers, casket, pallbearers, family, and friends back to the main entrance of the church.

For Libby, it seemed to take forever.

Incense bathed the procession, swirling inward as the front doors were heaved open to the wind and sleet. Black umbrellas bobbed up and down the church steps, escorts led people to cars flagged by Fleck and Fleck Funeral Home, lined up for the trip to the cemetery.

Out of habit, Libby collected her music and the two white envelopes. Otherwise, every unengaged part of her was assessing who was where, formulating what she had to ask, still trying to fit a few final pieces of the puzzle together.

And time.

How much time did she have?

Just as Monsignor Jimmy returned down the side aisle, Daniel and Paul Thomas, instead of following the procession outside, headed into the sanctuary.

Libby quickly crossed to them. "Not going to the cemetery?" she asked nervously.

Paul Thomas pondered the high ceiling, listening to the sound of sleet badgering the roof. "Not in this stuff."

Monsignor Jimmy approached them. "Sorry to interrupt, Libby, but I forgot to give you a message from Father Wendell. He was quite insistent."

The old priest turned to see the funeral director, like a specter at the front doors, waiting to drive him to the cemetery.

Libby was losing her grip on Daniel and Paul Thomas as they politely deferred to the priest. "Wait," she said anxiously. "I need to ask you something."

"We'll be right here," Daniel called back as he headed into the bride-side sacristy.

Meanwhile Monsignor Jimmy closed his eyes, his face puckered in recall. "Let's see. Verbatim. 'Remind Miss Kinder that Father Henry would have been furious. I *will* call *unless* you have called me *by noon*!'" The old priest's eyes shot open. "Emphasis his."

Oh, great, thought Libby as Monsignor Jimmy broke away in a rush to change out of his vestments. "Grass is probably already on his way," she said out loud. "This will screw up everything."

She started in several different directions, changing her mind at each. Wayne must be dumping the thurible ashes. Or hiding in the basement.

Monsignor Jimmy hustled past her toward the front with a wave.

Upstairs, Bernie was shutting down the organ.

Libby found herself slapping the pay envelopes against her palm as she tried to think things through. It was one thing to know her final goal, but how to make things fall into place? What question did she need to ask first?

Confront and confirm.

She started down the main aisle to the back of church. Hymnals in the pews today. Salt on the steps. Go figure.

One by one, whole sections of lights snapped off, leaving a few lighting the main altar behind her, the choir loft, and only one or two out in the church.

Wayne.

The atmosphere changed.

What had made the church glow and feel inviting on a stormy morning went dim. What had been a gathering of loved ones was now an indifferent skeleton crew locking up. What had been organ and voice raised to comfort, fell to the sound of harsh rain drowning out the clack of Libby's heels on the marble floor.

In one instant, St. Hedwig's had become empty and impersonal.

And frightening.

Libby felt the isolation grip her as she kept walking toward the back, kept looking around. Watching. Thoughts bouncing around in her head.

Confront and confirm.

At the back, she turned to the right and pushed open the thick oak door to the choir loft vestibule.

The restroom door suddenly swung open.

Maggie stood in front of her.

"I knew you'd come back here," she said. "Eventually. Bernie says you always bring his check up to him."

Libby swallowed. "You … you startled me."

Maggie gave Libby a long, cool look. "You figured it out, didn't you?"

Chapter Forty-Six

Keep talking, thought Libby. Get what you need.

Maggie was frozen in the restroom doorway. "When did you know?"

"Just this morning," said Libby. "After you gave Mrs. McGrew the Parish Hall keys on the rectory porch. You turned and waved. But not at me."

Libby couldn't read Maggie's reaction. Defiance? Resignation? Relief?

Maggie pulled the blue and yellow shawl in close around her shoulders. What was she trying to hold in? What was she keeping out?

"You seemed so calm, so … happy, standing by the door," said Libby. "Even with the storm and cold blowing around you. This pretty new shawl. The haircut. Why did you lie?"

For a moment, Maggie appeared to give in, her voice went slack. "I tried not to. But once I started, I couldn't keep things straight. I couldn't remember what I told you or Detective Grass or Mrs. McGrew."

Then Maggie stepped forward.

Instinctively Libby stepped back, bumping against the door in the tiny vestibule.

Maggie's movement and the tone in her voice were aggressive. "What do I have to do to keep you from talking?"

CRASH!

A loud thud from above echoed wildly throughout the vacant church. Then a short, sharp cry from upstairs.

Without waiting, Libby turned and yanked open the door to the choir loft. She rushed, spiraling upward on the century-old stone stairs. Her hand flattened against the cold bare wall for balance, but the faster she climbed, the more her head spun. She could hear Maggie, close behind, taking the same dizzying ascent.

Twenty-eight steps, Libby knew by heart. Around and around; up and up.

At the top, Libby burst onto the wooden floor of the first choir loft chamber, gasping for air. A dingy gray light greeted her. The sound of sleet, muffled in the tunnel-like stairwell, now loudly pelted the windows not more than an arm's length away.

Close on Libby's heels, Maggie tumbled out.

Both women paused, bent over to catch their breath, panting, steadying themselves with hands against the wall after their frantic race up to the loft.

In front of them, unperturbed, stood Bernie.

The metal file cabinet had slammed to the floor, springing loose sheet music and file folders in a shower of paper that had landed mostly in the first chamber, some blown as far as the organ.

Maggie took in the organist, helplessly staring down at the mess. "Are you all right, Bernie?" she asked.

"It wouldn't open," he said plainly. "I kept pulling and pulling. And it wouldn't open." He spoke to the sheets on the floor. "I had to clean out all this old music of mine. I don't really need it anymore."

Clinking glass. Downstairs. Rhythmic thudding. Downstairs.

Attracted to the sound, Bernie walked around to the organ and the choir loft railing; with Libby and Maggie trailing. All three directed their sight to the empty church below.

The almost empty church.

In the sanctuary, Daniel climbed a stepladder, replacing burned out candles, their glass receptacles clanking as old ones were lifted out and new ones were set in.

In the church proper, Wayne collected funeral songbooks from the pews and dropped them unceremoniously on the cart waiting in the main aisle.

Both men, having turned and looked up at the sound of the crashing metal cabinet, noted the people peering, unharmed, over the railing above, and returned to their projects.

"Look at Wayne," said Bernie. "Putting away the hymnals. For a change."

"Creepy Wayne," hissed Maggie under her breath.

Bernie continued to stare down at the men, small and distant.

Then abruptly he turned. "He's the murderer, isn't he, Libby? That's what you said from the beginning." He sounded like a child hoping for a treat.

Libby would not grant the request. She answered firmly. "No, Bernie. He's not."

"I'm sure it's Wayne," said Bernie.

"It has to be," Maggie demanded.

Bernie's eyes squinted in confusion. He looked back out over the loft railing and whispered, "Oh. My. It's Daniel?"

"I didn't think so, at first," Libby began. "I couldn't imagine it. Then, the longer Detective Grass kept pushing in that direction, I had to reconsider. I had to reconsider because Lawrence Davis told me I was high on the list. Because I'm left-handed."

"The killer is left-handed?" For Maggie, it was a question full of wonder.

Bernie studied the man on the stepladder. "Daniel's not left-handed, is he?"

"Neither am I," Maggie declared triumphantly.

Libby shook her head. "No. And neither is Daniel."

She felt like she was juggling balls—the suspects, their motives and alibis, the clues she was sure of, and those still suspended in midair. "I woke up this morning, and all I could hear in my head was "Chopsticks." At first, I thought it was because my nieces' kids were banging it out on the piano last night. Then, I remembered Paul Thomas said he couldn't even play "Chopsticks," but that Daniel was like an octopus when he was at the piano. Ambidextrous."

Bernie muttered, "I didn't know Daniel played the piano."

Libby continued to explain. "During Father Henry's funeral, I watched you play up here, Bernie, and realized you could be ambidextrous, too."

He nodded at Libby. "Anybody could be."

"Well, I'm not!" Maggie protested vehemently.

Glass candle holders rattled downstairs; hymnals thudded onto the cart; rain thrashed outside.

As logically as she could, Libby proceeded. "According to the police, the killer stood above Father Henry on the landing on the back steps of church. Even if someone used their non-dominant hand, they had that position in their favor."

Maggie folded her arms and said with a pouty snarl, "That just puts us back to square one. Another point, like all of us having keys to church, where we all come out with equal strikes against us. Except Wayne's creepy. And he's an ex-con in line for some inheritance. Most likely to succeed, if you ask me."

Then she sighed and looked below. "Of course, Daniel has the best motive."

She stretched her arms out across the railing and said more reluctantly, "I'm sorry he's gay. And that it pisses the Church off that he has a loving partner." She glanced sideways at Libby. "Everybody deserves to have … that …" Her voice trailed off. Then it picked up steam in her argument. "Father Henry was probably going to fire him. Church law is Church Law, he'd say."

Libby looked pointedly at the secretary. "That's exactly what he'd say, isn't it?"

Before Maggie could respond, Libby put up her hand. "Don't worry. I'm in the same boat you are on this one. You were spotted at the Women's Health Clinic; I will be spotted at an unholy singing event. Both of our souls are in jeopardy according to the Church Fathers."

"Bird Hawkins." Maggie spat the name out. She didn't know which was worse—the Church's archaic stance by a bunch of men who knew nothing about women and families and children and marriage … Or the invasion of her privacy by a busybody church gossip.

She had had to make tough decisions in her life. And she had thought about the consequences of her choices; and yes, had even prayed about them; looked outside her own interests and tried to do the best she could. No one else needed to bully her with their "Representative of God" status.

Bernie couldn't keep up. He was tired. He just wanted it all to be over. He had spent his life dedicated to following the Church and the very laws Maggie denounced. Their clarity, their clear-cut imperatives, knowing exactly what to do and how to act had been reassuring. Even when he'd done something wrong, he knew the path to forgiveness. He realized others in the world did not believe as he did, but he was completely mystified by people who supposedly shared his beliefs but then acted so contrary to what the laws prescribed.

"I don't understand," said Bernie. "Are you saying it was Maggie?"

"Wait a minute." Maggie moved in Bernie's direction. "You're the one who plays the organ. You're the one who's ambidextrous."

Libby understood this all too well—the feeling of being trapped, the need to strike back, to accuse anyone just so the accusations pointed to someone else.

Bernie's voice went high and squeaky. "No. We were friends. Henry and I were friends."

Maggie kept at it. "And you don't have an alibi."

Bernie uncharacteristically shouted back. "Do you?!"

The accusation hung in the air.

"Actually," Libby broke in on the dead silence, "Maggie is the only one of us who does."

But it was not relief on Maggie's face. "No. Don't," she stammered.

Libby had to confront her, had to say it, but she did so gently. "It was the copier repairman, wasn't it?"

Maggie turned away, pulling the shawl tighter, pulling her defenses together. "Please, don't."

It was a piece Libby had to confirm. "Mrs. McGrew said that when she left the luncheon—the Webber luncheon—on the day Father Henry was killed, there was a van where she usually parks between the Parish Hall and the rectory. The plumber mentioned it being there in the morning, said what a busy place the neighborhood was. Then Mrs. McGrew had to dodge around the same van at four p.m., when she dropped off the Hall keys. She said it was unlike you to not to come over and check on things or at least be there to lock up after the luncheon."

Maggie chewed her lower lip. She hung her head and let her foot nudge a page of music on the floor. "She put the key in the rectory mailbox," she said. "I don't know what time it was. She's probably right, that it was three or four in the afternoon. You and I both figured Father had to be dead long enough for that soup to freeze." Without looking up, Maggie said, "Why didn't Mrs. McGrew see the body?"

"Because it was so icy," said Libby. "She'd driven over from the Hall to the rectory. It was already dark, and she was anxious to get home. Double-parked by the van, she left her car running while she ran up and dropped the keys in the mailbox on the front porch. Her head was ducked down to avoid the sleet. She never looked up."

An ironic smile crossed Maggie's lips. "You know, he really did come to fix the copier. And he did work on it all morning. We didn't do anything except stuff fliers for the spaghetti dinner in the bulletin. It was just nice to have some human company for a change. Not to have to listen to Father's complaining about how tired he was, how much work he had to do."

"People were dismayed," Libby said, "when you told them you were in the rectory all day with no phone calls. It didn't seem unbelievable to me. I work at home and can go a long time with no contact from anyone. Then, I wondered if you had gone somewhere. Played hooky. Weren't even in the rectory. But Mrs. McGrew made the strongest point. It was unusual, unheard of really, for you not to check on things at the Hall after a luncheon."

"He did have an appointment," said Maggie, a hopeful lift in her tone. "He's been our repairman for almost three years; so it didn't seem that different to have his van parked outside for so long."

"And that's who you waved at this morning," Libby confirmed. "Not at me, but at the van in front of me."

Defiance returned to the secretary's voice as she swung around to Libby. "I don't want him dragged into this. He's innocent. I'm innocent. We're adults, for God's sake. Neither of us is married. We didn't do anything to be ashamed of."

There was more noise downstairs. Indistinct voices or footsteps or hymnals? It was hard to determine over the storm letting loose outside.

Maggie glared at Libby. "What now? You've got my excuse. Damning as it is, it isn't murder. Are we back to Wayne? Weasel Wayne. Trying to get the inheritance no one can conveniently find?"

Libby worked to piece it together as she spoke. "Antonio told me he saw Daniel and Wayne leave on the day of the murder. If he's right, they left pretty much at the time they both said they did. One right after the other. Daniel off to lunch at his house, then to work; Wayne to a one o'clock appointment with the plumber. And when they left, Antonio swears there was no body on the steps."

Maggie wrinkled her brow, perplexed. "So, someone came back?"

Now that she had to say it out loud, Libby wished it wasn't so. "Or someone never left."

It wasn't at all like in the movies. Or in books. He didn't pull out a gun and threaten to take the two women hostage. He didn't try to jump over the railing. Or push Libby over it.

No. None of it.

Bernie merely walked over and began picking up the sheet music on the choir loft floor.

It could have been any day in the last fifty years, him preparing for any number of services he knew practically by heart. Except that the organist's hands—always steady, always nimble and strong—were trembling uncontrollably.

Libby inched in close enough to interrupt any potential flight, but far enough away to let him not feel trapped. She knew Bernie. Or thought she did. She was having a hard time tamping down the eruption of so many new emotions—apprehension, pity, fear. There was more she wanted to know.

Confront and confirm.

She worked to keep her voice low and unthreatening, as if she was still talking to just Bernie, her colleague, her friend. "Mrs. McGrew said she made take-home plates for you and Bird at the Webber funeral luncheon. And you, Bernie, you got a whole pie that had never been put out. What kind? What kind of pie was it, Bernie?"

Kneeling on the floor, Bernie never stopped shuffling and gathering music. He needed no hints about the pie. He remembered immediately. "One of my favorites. Lemon meringue."

Maggie let out a long, slow breath. "The sticky stuff on Father's collar."

Sweet, sticky sherbet on her sister's piano keys, thought Libby. "Chopsticks."

Bernie's voice was flat, his motions mechanical. "I only hit him once."

There. It was out. Not so bad, thought Bernie.

He didn't see Maggie's eyes widen in horror.

Or Libby's lower with precaution.

Maggie couldn't help herself, couldn't contain her shock. She paced along the railing. A million questions flooded her mind. "Why?

When did you …? What the hell were you doing with the thurible?"

Bernie said nothing. He tapped a small pile of music sheets against the floor to straighten them.

Libby hushed Maggie with a quick wave of her hand while she continued to engage Bernie. "It was going to the Latin Mass funeral, wasn't it?"

Bernie nodded, not looking anywhere but at the floor. "They never have what they need over there at St. Bede's, so I always take ours. Henry says it's all right. If we're not using it. It was just there, in my hand."

Maggie tried to follow Libby's lead, to sense Bernie's fragile state. "But why, Bernie? You and Father Henry were friends."

"We *were* friends," he said emphatically. "I told you, Henry and I were friends. All those years. Why didn't he act like a friend? He was so … like it didn't matter." Bernie's voice went flat again, but he was no longer reluctant to talk. His account started slowly, then gained momentum, as if he'd turned the faucet on and was waiting, testing, as the water got hotter and hotter.

"I went back to church after the luncheon," he began. "To get the thurible. I had already put the pie in my car, but my fingers were sticky from carrying it. I knew I got some on the thurible, but I washed it off. And … and the blood. I asked him again if he didn't want to go to Jonny Kwan's son's funeral … visitation. He should have gone. I would have picked him up, driven him in that icy weather. I didn't care, and I would have taken him, because that's what you do. That's what you do for a friend. He said no one would notice. It wouldn't matter to anyone. It wouldn't mean anything. He just wanted to sit in his room. Be comfortable." Bernie's voice went up slightly. "Well, it does matter."

Completely baffled, Maggie paced again. "Jonny Kwan? This is all about Jonny Kwan?"

Libby didn't believe that either. It wasn't enough. It was part of the reason, but … "Was it the principle, Bernie? That Father Henry should have gone to the funeral home?"

"Of course he should have gone. That *is* the principle. Every time it's the principle. Not just Jonny Kwan. Everybody. All those years, everybody asking, everybody expecting their priest to be there. Expecting him to be there. For comfort. For …"

Maggie could not take her eyes off Bernie, still picking up music, as his story rolled out. "We'd better call the police," she said, almost in a whisper. "We know who did this now, even if we don't understand …"

Again Libby put up her hand. Just give him a little more time, she thought. Jonny Kwan was the tip of the iceberg, the catalyst, but what was the rest of it? What was below the surface?

Then, one of the tumblers clicked into place. A piece of the puzzle found its home.

She heard herself say it out loud, even as she was still processing the information that was surfacing. "Room 309. The nursing home appointment card."

Bernie looked up at her, his friend. She understood. She had complained, too.

His eyes pleaded. "For five years, my mother asked me every day. I went to see her every day. And every day when I got up to leave, she only ever asked two things. When are you going to take me home? Please, take me home. It broke my heart. And then. Then she'd ask, when was Father Henry going to come visit her? Every day she asked the same two things. And I asked Henry. Over and over. At first, I just hinted at it. Then, I asked him outright if he would please visit my mother."

It was silent except for the sleet hitting the windows.

As his thoughts unwound, Bernie's voice gained strength. "And he always pretended he didn't hear me. Turned and looked at something else. Or he'd say, 'Maybe another day.' You know me, Libby, I don't like to be pushy. If he didn't want to go, I wasn't going to keep asking."

The muscles in Bernie's jaw twitched. His hands shook the pages they held. His voice was hard. "Then, Jonny Kwan. Such a good man. At church all the time; helping Father. Praying. It was his son. His child."

Suddenly there was a flash of wild anger. "He made me mad!" Bernie clenched the pages so hard his knuckles went white. "He made me mad. He made me so mad. 'It doesn't matter,' he said. And I hit him! I hit him hard! It does matter! It does matter!"

There was fire in Bernie's eyes. The same fire that must have brought his hand up to slap Stanley Webber all those years ago for carving his name in the choir loft railing. The fire that brought his hand up with a thurible against Father Henry.

Not for what he had done, but for what he had failed to do.

Bernie simply folded, slumped against the organ console, and began to weep.

Crumpled music sheets slid to the floor while the organists' hands hid his face. "I'm so sorry," he choked out. "I'm so sorry."

With the sound of the blistering rain, neither Bernie nor the women heard Detective Grass climb the stairs to listen and watch from the first chamber of the choir loft, his gun un-holstered and at the ready.

Libby and Maggie only caught sight of him when he stepped around the tipped-over filing cabinet and came into the main chamber.

Detective Grass did not relax his weapon. He had a murderer in sight, albeit one gone as limp as an exhausted child. As he moved into the room, Grass's eyes darted from person to person, on his guard.

"It's Bernie," said Maggie.

"So it is. I heard it all from over there."

Libby watched Grass lower his gun and holster it before bending to help Bernie to his feet.

"Be gentle," she said.

Bernie's nose was running, his hands were shaking, and his shoulders were collapsed inward. Libby passed him a Kleenex as Grass rattled off Bernie's rights and, in one swift, practiced movement, handcuffed him.

"I'm sorry." The tears began again as Bernie croaked out his words. "I'm so sorry. Why didn't he visit her? Every day. I went. He could have come. Just once. 'When is Father Henry coming to see me?' ... I'm so sorry."

The sound of heavy feet stomping up the steps echoed from the stairwell. Two police officers rushed into the choir loft, guns drawn, followed by Daniel and Wayne, who ventured in tentatively.

Once Wayne realized there was no danger, he regained his arrogance. "Bernie Fruehauf. Who'd have thought you had the guts to do something like this?"

"Leave him alone," Maggie said, moving forward protectively.

"Oh, Bernie," was all Daniel could say.

The two police officers took Bernie by the arms and, without knowing his personality or life, left thick footprints on the music strewn all over the choir loft floor.

Bernie stumbled, still quivering with great, heavy sighs. For the last time, he made his way down and around the spiral staircase of his church home, St. Hedwig's.

Maggie was stunned. She did not want Bernie to be the killer—and over such a seemingly small thing. Yet she could understand his anger and built-up frustration at Father Henry—not for himself but for someone he loved; someone for whom a kind word, a bit of understanding, and a few minutes of time from her priest and pastor could have made a difference.

Libby distracted herself by picking up the trampled music. Maggie joined her.

Wayne clicked his tongue. "Do you think I'm next in line to inherit the car Henry gave to Bernie?"

Daniel stared at him. "You are something else. I can't believe this church ever hired you."

"This church? The Church? Ha." Wayne tossed his head back with a mocking laugh. "The Church has done nothing for me."

"But Father Henry did," said Libby. "He gave you a job."

"We were family," snapped Wayne. "And he owed me."

"Ah, I forgot," Daniel said. "That does explain it."

Let the sniping begin, thought Detective Grass. Not a particularly abnormal reaction to the tensions of the past two weeks.

Libby couldn't resist. "With your colorful history with the police," she pointed out, "he certainly could have overlooked the family angle."

"Oh. That explains even more," remarked Daniel.

Wayne was ready. "Talk about a colorful history. That great Church isn't greeting you and your freaky gay partner with open arms either, is it?"

Daniel had been taunted by the best; Wayne Nichols couldn't hold a candle to them. When the jabs descended to this level, and Daniel found himself joining in and descending to the same, he worked against prolonging the conversation. "I'm going downstairs." He had other things to do.

Maggie stood with her stack of music. At a loss of what to do with them, she finally handed them to Libby. "You're such a joke," she said, looking at Wayne. I'm going back to work." She followed Daniel down the stairs.

Wayne had heard it all, too. "Now, that's the Church I know and love."

"I don't know about the Church," said Libby. "Sometimes you just get what you give."

"Profound," Wayne said and turned to Detective Grass. "I assume you're done harassing the rest of us, now that you've bagged the real murderer."

Grass gave a small shrug. "Consider yourself off the list."

Wayne walked away from the detective and Libby, triumphant, justified. But it was his jaunty footfall, winging around the stairwell, that declared his more immediate and evident emotion: relief.

Chapter Forty-Seven

Detective Grass surveyed the loft. He took in the overturned file cabinet, the music still on the floor, the console of the huge organ, the hundreds of pipes rising toward the high ceiling, and Libby Kinder standing in the middle of it all.

She had figured it out.

He should have been pleased.

First and foremost, as a detective, Grass was satisfied. Father Henry Felger's murderer had not only been caught, but had confessed in front of the detective and other witnesses. He'd been taken into custody with little fuss—no bloodshed, no heroics necessary.

Grass turned to Libby with a cock of his head toward Wayne. "You thought it was him, didn't you?"

"And you thought it was me," Libby shot back.

"That Father Henry believed your soul would be damned to hell for a singing gig did seem like a convincing motive."

Libby rolled her eyes. "I see Father Wendell got ahold of you."

Once again, Grass found himself butting up against Libby's resistance. He didn't think he was being offensive, rather taking the opportunity to explain things, to show how his point of view merited consideration. "Look," he said, "whether you like it or not, you've got a high profile position at St. Hedwig's. Every week people see you as much as they see their priest. No doubt, if Father Henry had gotten wind of you singing at the verboten woman's priest-making thing

…"

"Ordination."

"Ordination. He would have called you on it. Asked you, strongly, not to do it, don't you think? And I have even less doubt that you …" He let his hands splay out in Libby's direction. "… admittedly a woman of strong opinions, would have had words. Argumentative, dissenting, combative …"

"Okay, I get it. I get it."

"… angry words. And if …"

"Yes, *if*," Libby broke in. She struggled to keep argumentation out of her side of the story. Even knowing she was no longer a suspect, no longer in any danger of being blamed for Father Henry's death, she had a hard time staying cool when trying to convince this detective of her own point of view. "*If* Father Henry had known, *if* he'd said something to me, *if* I'd gotten angry."

Sometimes he did admire her spunk, her logic. "But, you see, that is my job—dealing with *ifs*."

Maggie left the church and returned to her office in the rectory to resume her duties as parish secretary. Calico Two obliged her by moving off the Rolodex, so Maggie could find the copier company's phone number.

Paul Thomas met Daniel in the bride-side sacristy. They embraced, with relief that it was finally over. They left out the back door, oblivious to the steady, cold rain that fell.

Downstairs, Wayne, the ex-con and possible pilferer of gift card donations, and all-around contrary and belligerent suspect, paraded down the center aisle of St. Hedwig's like a self-absorbed bride, the center of his own attention. After putting the few leftover funeral accessories away, he veered to the priest-side sanctuary. It was unclear who had dumped the thurible ashes and then hung the borrowed instrument on the hook in the sanctuary, but it was there. Longing for a cigarette, he pulled the hood of his sweatshirt over his head and left a few lights on for Libby to deal with after she finished with the detective. He, too, left out the back door.

Up, over, down. Up, over, down. Detective Grass's right hand swept the contour of the carved oak arch at the end of each pew, like a kid fanning the slats of a picket fence, as he and Libby walked in step down the side aisle on their way toward the sanctuary.

"You were so hot on Wayne's trail. What changed your mind?" Grass asked.

Libby reached for a stray hymnal in a side pew. "I have to admit, I really wanted it to be Wayne." She paused, mid-step. "That's not entirely true. Mostly, I didn't want it to be any one of the rest of us. Not Daniel or Maggie. Not Bernie. And it wasn't just that he was my only alternative." She caught the detective's arm for emphasis. "I really believed it was him. Even though his plumber alibi was pretty solid." Her heels clicked as she started walking again. "Unconsciously, I guess I just kept trying to make the facts fit the picture I'd painted of him."

Grass's hand slowly rounded another pew edge. "Occupational hazard."

Libby smiled weakly. "And here I'd been trying hard to break loose from such confining—and prejudicial—perspectives. Trying to apply all that negative space stuff."

"Excuse me?"

"Just a different way of looking at things. I tried to see the facts not only as individual nuggets, but in context; to see what surrounded the bird as much as the bird itself."

Had he missed something?

"Are you talking about Bird Hawkins?"

Libby laughed. "No. Sorry. As I said, it was just a way of looking at the evidence."

He frowned. "Not a technique I've run across."

"Actually, it's an art term." Libby stopped walking. Holding out her hand, she splayed her fingers across the blue cover of the hymnal. "Mostly when we look at something, all we see is the positive piece—my fingers. But, if you shift your attention to the space around the fingers—the blue in this case, that's the negative space. Instead of constantly looking at each suspect, I tried to look at the space around them. Not just focus on what each of them, each of us, was doing, but what was going on around us."

She looked down at her spread-out fingers and wiggled her index finger. "Father Henry was last seen at the Webber funeral luncheon.

What else was going on there? Who did he talk to? Did he argue with anyone there? Did something else happen?"

She wiggled another finger. "Daniel. He went home, then to work. Did something happen at work? At home? Something with Paul Thomas before he came to church? And so on."

"So, when you wiggled a finger for Bernie, you got how miffed he was about Father Henry not going to Jonny Kwan's son's funeral visitation."

"Eventually. Bernie's immediate surrounding space included what went on before the funeral here, at St. Hedwig's; the Webber luncheon; and the Latin Mass funeral at St. Bede's."

"Our investigation does something similar. Perhaps not as succinctly put. Yours is kind of like doughnuts and doughnut holes."

"You've got it." Libby took a moment and thought about how one thing had led to another. "That also turned me toward purpose."

"As in …?"

"As in, I think we are really creatures of habit. We don't normally do wildly random things. It was a cold day. Most of us only came out for one purpose—the funeral. And there was purpose when we left. Maggie's purpose was to stay put—with the copier repairman. My purpose was to go work on my grants. Daniel, to lunch and work. Wayne, to the plumber's. Bernie, to the luncheon before Kwan's visitation and another service. Father came back to church. Why? For Mrs. McGrew's soup."

The detective completed the list. "And Bernie came back for the thurible."

"Exactly. It wasn't just randomly in somebody's hand. It was there for a purpose."

"The Latin Mass funeral."

"The music director at St. Bede's said Bernie often brought funeral accessories because St. Bede's doesn't have them. It's basically an outlier parish. Not fully staffed or equipped." Libby pulled her hand off the cover. "The other sense of negative space that popped up was the idea of considering not what is there—what you see—but what you don't see—what's not there."

"Kind of Sherlock Holmes-y."

Libby shot a surprised look at Grass. He was human, after all. Maybe she needed to re-evaluate her prejudiced ideas about him, too. "Precisely," she granted. "It wasn't what Maggie did, but what she didn't do. She didn't go over to the Parish Hall to check on things, which was her habit. To lock up and get the keys. I began to flip things around. In the end, it wasn't who cared so little for Father Henry, but who cared so much. Not who was his enemy, but his friend. Not who took and used the thurible, but who had such scruples and guilt that they had to bring it back.

"Of course," she continued, "it was a major shift when Antonio told me not only what he did see—both Wayne and Daniel leaving church when they said they did—but what he did not see—Father's body on the steps at that time. Again, there was no reason for those guys to remain. They went their merry way."

Grass stopped. "What about Maggie? We considered her for a long time; especially with that unlikely alibi of not talking to anyone all day."

"As luck would have it, I realized I'd seen the copier repairman's van in front of me this morning, right before I had the conversation with Antonio; so, all of a sudden, Maggie's story fell into place. Why she was taking no calls. Why she didn't venture out or get concerned about Father not stopping by her office. It wasn't hard to figure out she didn't want to expose this guy or herself, so she kept everything to a minimum. Still, I needed to confront her about it. Fortunately, she met me in the back of church after the funeral, before I had to track her down. Then, I knew."

Libby took a deep breath. "The only person left was Bernie."

They started to walk again.

"I needed to confirm that he'd come back for the thurible. I needed to confront him. I knew he might talk, not necessarily confess. But he would talk to me. If it was true. I couldn't be certain, but assuming Father Wendell might talk to you, which would eliminate my only chance to have the conversation alone with Bernie, I went to him as soon as today's funeral was over. I didn't want to put him through a confrontation that ended up with him having a reasonable explanation. There was always the chance I might have it all wrong. But, like I said, Maggie found me first, so she was there."

As they approached the front of the church and the main altar, they eased their pace. "So," said Libby, another huge sigh blowing out through puffed cheeks, "that's where all that negative space took me."

Grass reflected for a moment in the quiet church. "I guess I'm more sequential. Lining up fact after fact, narrowing things down, tossing things out. Your way seems a little backward, if you don't mind the word."

"Maybe it's because I'm left-handed." She laughed. "Maybe that was a help after all. My non-sequential brain happy to do some of the work." Libby gazed at the main altar rising up high above them. "Early on, I thought how backward and topsy-turvy things seemed. For some of us, it wasn't that Father Henry was breaking Church rules that ticked us off, but that he was keeping them."

Libby wondered how Detective Grass regarded her church, if he regarded it at all—the structure, the magnificence of its size. Whether he was religious or not, he would be able to pick out Jesus, she figured. He might not be so versed, as few outside the Catholic Church are, on the lesser saints, represented abundantly at St. Hedwig's by statues in all the nooks and crannies built into the gothic German architecture. Statues of notoriously reformed sinners stared out from alcoves and niches, their stories of weakness overtaken by holy heroism as familiar to Libby as stories of her own ancestors.

"In the end," she said, "it wasn't what Father Henry did that prompted his murder ..."

"It's what he didn't do," Detective Grass finished for her.

"Yes," said Libby soberly. "What he failed to do. 'Through my fault, through my fault, through my most grievous fault.'"

Chapter Forty-Eight

"You already know?"

Detective Grass yanked off his red Tartan scarf, tossed his coat over the back of his chair, and slapped a file folder on his desk. He'd stopped on his way back from St. Hedwig's only long enough to pick up some chili at a drive-thru. When he first came into the station, it offered welcomed warmth, but that had quickly jumped to stifling.

"How the hell did you find out so fast?"

Detective Lawrence Davis, sitting in a chair across Grass's desk, waited until the detective sat in a huff and pushed aside the fast-food bag before answering. "As usual," he said. He pulled the crease in his pant leg into line. "A little Bird told me."

"I don't understand. Where does Hawkins get his information?"

"Let's see … he plays bingo with the women. Bowls with the men. He's a church usher. No one better informed than ushers at a church. Don't get me wrong, they're all good people and they mean well. Parishioners come really wanting to let the Community know what's happening to whom so you can keep that person and their troubles in your prayers. Could be cancer, could be marriage problems. Apparently, could be murder. He might as well be CIA."

"I still don't get it."

Davis looked at his frazzled colleague and tried to redirect the frustration. "Who all was at the scene?"

Grass mentally set all the characters in the choir loft—Libby,

Maggie, Bernie, Wayne, Daniel, and … It dawned on him. "Two officers. And apparently at least one," he added, "with a big yap."

The detective gave a short snort. "We probably should have just asked Bird Hawkins who the killer was in the first place."

This realization re-ignited Grass's perturbation about the meddling "investigators" of St. Hedwig's Parish. Grass's pride was in getting the facts, sorting things out, and coming to logical conclusions. But he'd always known he didn't have the knack for being where the information lived. Grass didn't believe that Bird Hawkins processed clues and figured things out, merely that Bird had the good fortune to have information dropped in his omnipresent lap.

"That Kinder woman is another one. Not only does information drop in her lap, she's got some built-in radar for it. Like a magnet, evidence flies at her like bits of steel shavings."

"Everyone develops their own method," Davis commented. "You know that. What works for one person doesn't work for another. Libby Kinder was lucky. And on the inside. You know that's a big advantage."

Since this corresponded with Grass's own take on things, he was placated. "True. And if that Antonio guy had been more reliable, told me he'd seen Daniel Giglia and Wayne Nichols leave and not seen the priest lying on the steps, it would have been easy to eliminate them and go for the organist."

Davis leaned back and crossed his legs. "You could have eliminated everyone, and I still wouldn't have thought it was Bernie. People teased him about his temper, but I sure never saw any indication of it, and certainly not to this degree."

Grass pushed the chili bag out of the way and opened the file folder. "Apparently Father Henry's refusing to go to this other funeral …" He consulted the paper in front of him. "Jonny Kwan's son. Some sort of argument, probably the argument Wayne Nichols heard from downstairs—it wasn't Daniel, the decorator guy—an argument about how Father Henry ought to go to it … how it dredged up the memory that the priest wouldn't visit Bernie's mother all those years when she was in the nursing home. He just snapped."

Grass ran a finger down the page of Bernie's confession.

… the thurible was in my hand … Father Henry was on the step below… He laughed, said it didn't matter. I know it wasn't right. But

it made me so mad. Then I hit him.

Davis closed his eyes and inhaled slowly. He was a homicide detective. He dealt with deaths and confessions on a daily basis. But these were people he knew, lives that intermingled with his own. Now, one of those lives was gone and another one was ruined. "It's always so sad," he said, exhaling loudly and clasping his hands together on top of his head. He nodded at the confession. "Ever get anything about the sticky stuff on Father's collar?"

"See. That's another thing." Grass extracted his chili from the bag. He meticulously folded the paper sack and placed the chili carton on top. "Maybe it was all that negative space business. I looked at the facts—sweet, sticky substance on the collar. Lab identifies it. Try to track down its source. Libby, she knew how things at those funeral luncheon's work. The carryout desserts. The lemon meringue pie that's Bernie's favorite that he takes home and has on his fingers when he touches the thurible and gets it on Father Henry's collar." He tore the plastic spoon loose from its wrapper. "I was looking at the doughnut; she was looking at the doughnut hole, the space around the facts. The luncheon, people's habits …"

"Doughnuts?"

Grass waved the reference aside and rolled on. "She knew Maggie had changed her haircut. See, just dumb luck. I could never have uncovered that. I didn't even have access to the doughnut, much less the hole."

Grass stopped what sounded like gibberish even to him. He balled up the wrapper. "She could have let us in the loop."

A low chuckle came from Davis. "If you remember, the loop was around her neck."

Grass pointed his spoon at Davis. "That is a fact. Oh, she's not a bad person either," he conceded, going back to his lunch. "Smart like you said, interesting even. But she's either a driven Type A or obsessive-compulsive." He relaxed and ate a spoonful of chili, careful not to spill any on the folder. "You never believed it was her, did you?"

Davis shook his head slowly. "I never believed it was Bernie."

Before indulging in more chili, Detective Grass straightened the papers before him and placed them squarely in the file folder and closed it. "Per usual, doesn't matter so much how we got here. We got the killer—and the confession." His eyebrows lifted, and he grinned. "And the credit. Always nice to add a high-profile murder—solved— to your resume."

Setting the folder safely out of the chili's harmful way, he suddenly frowned. "And don't you think she had a pretty good idea who the *family* in Father Henry's diary was all along?"

~ ~ ~

She was slight but moved with the certain strength and energy of an athlete, hardly giving evidence of her forty years. Her dark-blonde, naturally curly hair with ringlets, frizzed and blowing carefree, framed a friendly, open face. Periwinkle eyes narrowed as she sized up the unfamiliar man who asked the question. Reassured by the clerical collar, she gave a succinct nod.

The two strangers could have been actors in a play, both of them with memorized dialogue, waiting for their scene. With his entrance, he had said his line—and she had responded on cue.

"Yes," she said with conviction. "Yes, I do."

Glancing over her shoulder, she addressed another woman, younger, nearby. "Take care of Gretchen till I get back, will you, please? I'll only be a minute."

The Vicar waited. Amazed really.

Simple.

It had all been simple: the place was simple, not that he had much experience with such locations; the question simple; and finally, finally, the answer he sought had been simple.

Yes.

The woman returned bearing a large, thick accordion file tied with a bow of brown string.

Simple.

She stood in front of him in the reception area. "I was wondering when someone was going to come for this."

She started to hand the file to the Vicar, then hesitated. Her voice changed, not from a stage direction, but with her own ad lib of sentiment as she looked down at the packet. "I'm sorry Father Henry died. He was a really nice man. And took such good care of the kids." She gave a toothy grin. "That's what he always called them."

The Vicar smiled back. "I'm sure you'll see them again. They're to be well taken care of."

She let the packet go. "He gave very strict orders, you know, about this thing here. Made me keep it locked up in my little safe. 'Don't give it to anybody, no matter what happens,'" she recited, "'unless they use the exact words—Do you have Father Henry's packet?' And, here you are."

"Yes, I am."

The Vicar accepted the folder. He shook the woman's hand, and finding her grip firm and capable, no doubt indicative of her character, he was not surprised Father Henry had entrusted her with so much that was precious to him. "Thank you for taking such good care of everything for Father Henry."

As he reached the door to leave, the woman with the curly hair called after him, "Hey, Father. Can I ask what's in there?"

Literally, no matter where in the world the Vicar would have parked his car, he would have had the same impulse—to snap the locks down on all the doors. He hunched over the accordion file fanned opened before him as pleat after pleat revealed stock certificate after stock certificate, purchased long before the digital world rendered them obsolete. He knew enough about the stock market to comprehend that there was enough money for any kind of chapel Father Henry Felger could have ever wished for. The Vicar was glad, too, that he'd looked in the packet right there in the parking lot. Not only because he wanted to check the value of the bundle before going anywhere, but because it made it possible for him to hand deliver the business-sized envelope he found in the front of it addressed to the woman he had just left. It gave him great pleasure to give the envelope to such a faithful steward. He couldn't see the check amount, but by the shocked look on her face, the blonde curls sent springing as she danced around the room, he was led to believe that Father Henry had acknowledged her faithfulness quite generously.

Chapter Forty-Nine

Dinner at Libby's had been the right idea. The sleet and rain of the day before had turned to all snow overnight. By this evening, streets and sidewalks were cleared, leaving paths through mounds of the fresh snow that made the world look clean and uncluttered. It was still winter, but the rain of yesterday had reminded people that January wouldn't last forever, that it would give way to February, and that would eventually slide into March; there would be an end to this season of cold; and spring would break through.

For the night at hand, Paul Thomas's bean soup with homemade cornbread and Daniel's wine graced the menu. Libby had been inspired to toss together butternut squash, grapes, onions, and fresh sage, all roasted and caramelized for a savory side dish. While she chopped the vegetables in the warm kitchen, Libby's guests poured wine and chatted.

Everyone came in casual jeans and bulky sweaters, their thick socks exposed, having left boots and shoes by the back door, coats and gear dropped on nearby chairs and counters as if they were at a hunting lodge up north, coming in from a formidable day in the wilderness.

A small buffet was soon underway, spread out on the coffee table in the living room Libby had cleared so they could eat by the gas fireplace, crackling and snapping.

BabyCakes was perched along the back of the couch while Dash sat, front and center, poised as usual for any morsels that might come his way.

"I made it with four kinds of beans. And zucchini," boasted Paul Thomas, using a large cup to scoop the hot soup into bowls from a crockpot. "I put zucchini in everything."

Libby raised her glass of wine to him. "You've truly embraced your Midwestern roots."

They all laughed. Which was as nourishing as anything on the table. They passed the cornbread and talked, without suspicion, without pumping or second-guessing, for the first time since Father Henry's death had been labeled a murder.

They were able to examine the events of the past few weeks, talk about how frightened they had been, go over how the investigation had developed, and fill in the blanks of the narrative with curiosity instead of ulterior motives.

Libby detailed her journey through her own investigation—forming hypotheses, tracking down hints and clues, arriving at conclusions; some on the mark, some totally misguided. "Now that I've admitted I did have to seriously think Daniel might be guilty" she said, with some embarrassment, "tell me who you thought was the killer."

Into the awkward silence, Daniel and Paul Thomas blurted, "We thought it was you!"

Libby's fork stopped midair. "Me?! You thought *I* killed Father Henry?"

BabyCakes lifted his head at the shrill rise in Libby's voice; Dash came to her side, tongue out, panting and concerned.

"You had no alibi," explained Paul Thomas.

"And I've heard you argue ..." Daniel said, "well, at least have vigorous, loud disagreements with Father. Not that we all haven't been there."

Libby swallowed her squash and a little of her pride. "Speaking of arguments, we know now that it wasn't you who argued with Father Henry that morning, right?"

"No," Daniel said slowly. "Not that morning."

"Then why were you so mad at work?"

"Wait, you asked at my work?"

Libby gave an apologetic wince. "I was only trying to clear you."

Paul Thomas disregarded his cornbread. "Were you mad at me?"

"You'll know why I was mad," replied Daniel. "The secretary from the AIDS Task Force had called that morning, before I left for church. It's why I went in the first place. I'd completely forgotten about the funeral and was hoping for a little quiet time to … to find a little peace."

Paul Thomas closed his eyes. "Say it wasn't about that minister from Grant Avenue Christian Church." His eyes sprang open, and he turned to direct his words at Libby. "The dear Reverend took it upon himself to scream vitriol at us during the last march. Daniel tried to have a rational conversation with him." Paul Thomas picked up his cornbread and waved it. "I told you not to try that rational stuff."

"Now, he's tracking me down all over town," said Daniel. "Trying to convert me, convince me, rehabilitate me. Scripture me to death."

Paul Thomas buttered his cornbread. "Don't be fooled. Daniel's being nice. Nothing comes out of that man's mouth, Holy Scripture included, that isn't full of hatred."

The more intense Paul Thomas got, the more Daniel aimed for calm. "When I got home for lunch, I saw that he had left a rather strongly worded message on my voicemail. Which I erased."

"How invasive. How awful," said Libby. "See, I should have just asked you," she said sheepishly.

The wine bottle was passed around.

"Although, I can't begin to think what I could have possibly asked Bernie earlier that would have helped." Libby drank more wine, hoping to subdue the shiver flitting across her stomach at the memory of her friend weeping in the organ loft. "I'm not sure he really knew or understood what happened. I think he blocked it all out."

"It's possible," said Daniel. "Possible that no matter what you would have asked Bernie, he wouldn't have been able to go there. The suggestion behind any question, whatever you were driving at, I don't think would have registered."

For a moment, images of Bernie filled everyone's mind. It was still difficult to absorb the way things had turned out.

Libby revisited her own scary days of floundering with questions, of not comprehending what the police were driving at. Or rather, understanding all too well what they had in mind.

"So, you both thought it was me?" she said, wonderment still lacing her words.

"To be honest," Daniel said, "the two of us knew you were going to sing at Deb Draper's ordination."

At Libby's confounded expression, Paul Thomas clicked his tongue. "You must know any gender issue is never far off our screens."

Daniel helped himself to more soup. "It didn't take a detective to figure that if Henry got wind of it, there'd be fireworks. Heck, he went ballistic when I argued against the bloody rampage of the Crusades centuries ago; contemporary women's rights could easily put him over the edge. That is, if he knew. More often, I think he preferred to claim ignorance."

"Ignorance is the operative word," Libby said, taking a second serving of vegetables. "The Church is out to lunch on so many social issues. Not just out of step. I think they're wrong. Sometimes I think if I didn't love singing, I'd be out of there."

"One would have to be out of his mind to stay in a program like that." Paul Thomas stared pointedly at Daniel. "In a place, a group, that hates you. Persecutes you."

"The Church doesn't hate me," Daniel said, with no sign of rancor.

"No, they hate *us*," said Paul Thomas.

Daniel had been over this so many times, with so many people—his parents, priests, his beloved spouse, his God. Himself. "I stay because I believe the Catholic Church is a vessel—not the only one in existence—imperfect as it is, with so many human fingerprints on it, that holds Jesus's energy of love and carries it through time. Love. Of each other. Of the Earth. Of the poor. Yes, I agree, as it has passed through all those years through the hands of all those people, that energy has been, in an effort to contain it, rule it, use it to unholy purpose, sometimes been formalized, codified, even bastardized."

"Paternalized," added Libby.

"Screwed up," said Paul Thomas.

There were short bursts of laughter, then a pause in the conversation. Everyone let their attention be drawn to the fire. The hissing. The light darting about the room like beams of flashlights in the hands of children, jiggle-waving them around.

Dash jumped up and settled next to Libby. She stroked his head, his long dachshund-terrier muzzle burrowing, half buried against her thigh. "Sometimes I think my faith is just an updated reaction to a

Universe that's bigger and more mystifying than we know. Like primitive cultures making up explanations, rules, rituals, myths, all to court a beneficent Being and to ward off the Evil One. Don't you think," she tried to reason, "the more science understands stuff like the biological explanation of why people are gay, the more the Church needs to adjust its thinking?"

"In one way, yes," said Daniel, "but in another, it's not about thinking, about knowing. Love loves. Without credentials, without background checks, without prenups. Progress and advances in science just keep making it clear what and who we're to love; oftentimes the what and who we got caught up in mistakenly believing were the enemy. Gays, Muslims, Jews, Chinese, the other tribe, the other color, the other sex. Organic food. Farm. City. Living my Catholic faith is about trying to extend the boundaries of love. Unfortunately, to be human is to have limited vision.

"Look at all of us," Daniel continued. "Look at this murder. Father Henry failed to extend the boundary of love to Bernie. To Bernie's mother. Such a simple act of kindness. And Bernie. Not just the murder, but long before that, Bernie failed to extend the boundary of love to Father Henry. To grant him his weakness." Daniel laughed. "And look at me. I can hardly be civil to Wayne over dumping incense ashes."

"The core message may be simple," agreed Libby. "Like Monsignor Jimmy told me the other night, it never hurts to start with kindness. But that Church vessel can take you into a labyrinth, a maze of rules and constricting boundaries that can keep it pretty hidden. Camouflaged. Or kept in place by instilling fear. And guilt. To mix a lot of metaphors." Libby's skepticism rose to the top. "And a lot the messengers in the big C Catholic Church suck."

"Well," Daniel said, reaching for another square of cornbread. "I won't argue with you there."

Libby, Namita, and the two dogs walked quietly down the snowy, night-time streets. For Libby, after the rich soup and cornbread dinner, physically moving was a welcomed activity.

"What's up?" asked Namita.

Libby explained everything that had happened of late that fell under that heading. It was a lot.

The explanation sent Libby into silence, whether from exhaustion of replaying and reliving recent events or relief from having it all be over.

"It's so crazy," reflected Namita, "that the motive for this murder was supposed to be some huge social justice issue—gay rights, women's rights—and then it turns out to be a simple, personal grievance."

They walked in the late night darkness, their way dotted with street lamps, past houses gone to bed, houses still awake.

Namita, used to all manner of conversation on such evening strolls, did not shrink from Libby's latest question: "What would you say is the guiding principle of your religious belief?"

"I come with a pretty mixed bag. A combination of Hinduism from my mother, Methodist teachings from my father, and the Unitarianism of my own choosing. I suppose we all lean toward some variation of 'do unto others as you would have them do unto you'— or as the wise minister in Mahabharata says, 'Don't do to others what you wouldn't want done to you.'"

She looked ahead at the night, at once clear and beautiful, cold and unknown. "All my religions are full of beautiful songs and moving prayers, lovely bowing, ceremonies, great literature, but most always they end up at the same place. How about Catholics?"

Libby sucked in the fresh air. "Love God. Love one another as you love yourself. Not too awfully different."

Namita took in the few stars overhead. "I think it's nice so many of us agree. Don't you?"

Chapter Fifty

"The groomer?! The cats' groomer?"

The small conclave of concerned parties hung up their coats, sipped water from glasses put out for them, and settled themselves in the Vicar's office downtown. Wayne, Maggie, Libby, Cousin Phyllis and Cousin Ruth—the beneficiaries from the original reading of Father Henry's will.

Except the Minnesota cousins, who, having been informed, signed away their right to be present. And except Bernie Fruehauf.

Surrounded by bookcases stacked with religious tomes, the Vicar's desk marked one side of the room for business, while the other was defined by an oval coffee table and comfortable chairs, extras having been brought in to accommodate the present number of guests. Wine-colored carpeting set the palette for the generous space, a color picked up in the mats of gold-framed photographs of the current Church hierarchy, from Pope to local Bishop, hanging on one wall.

Sitting in the midst of the group, the Vicar, in his usual black suit and white clerical collar, folded his hands on the accordion folder in his lap.

He did not anticipate a long meeting. He did, however, most assuredly, anticipate the reaction to the news that the groomer was the holder of Father Henry's packet.

Cousin Phyllis, her cloche pulled down securely on her head, was typically vocal. "He put all those stock certificates, all that money, for safekeeping with a pet groomer? How do you know it's all there? That this woman didn't take some of it? All of it?"

Of course, he didn't know. But the Vicar trusted his instincts. On more than one occasion, he'd dealt with the thieving side of humanity, heard the confessions of more than a few dark hearts. They did, indeed, come in all shapes and sizes and occupations. But the woman he had encountered at Happy Paws Pet Grooming had not aroused suspicion or apprehension. In the end, he trusted her as Father Henry had trusted her.

"Like *family*?" Phyllis carried on. "Henry considered a complete stranger who washed those cats *family* when here we are, relatives by blood and circumstance." She was having a hard time keeping anger, humiliation, and the sense of betrayal under control, none of which was approved behavior in front of a priest.

"Excuse me, Vicar," Phyllis said, finding a sweet smile in her bag of expressions. "I always thought we were close. First cousins, as you know. Bad enough, difficult enough, the money is going for a ... a chapel." It was difficult to tell if a snort had escaped or if she had choked on the last word. "All those holiday dinners."

Wayne remained slouched. "Which were just chances to suck up to him with a meal."

"Which you never bothered to come to," she snapped.

Libby didn't need much of this. She shifted in her chair.

Big mistake.

"And, how did you know it was the groomer?" The eyes of the irate cousin bore down on Libby, laser-like across the small space keeping them apart. "Why did you wait so long to tell anyone?"

Practice had made perfect. Libby had already been through this interrogation once, and faced similar aggravation. She answered Phyllis exactly as she had Detective Grass. "I didn't think of the groomer at first." And she hadn't. "All the other possibilities the police suggested were just as good a guess." And they were. "And I did have other things on my mind. Besides, anyone who knew Father Henry well, knew he thought of those cats as his children."

She hadn't meant the last to come out so waspish, but it did. She tried to extend her boundary of love to take in Phyllis's disappointment. To be kind. "I have a dog," she began again. "And he has a groomer. Over the years, we've become very close. She is someone I would trust, in my inner circle, without burdening full-fledged family. I thought it might also be the vet or those old nuns who used to care for the cats when Father Henry took a vacation. Only when I saw my own groomer's appointment on the calendar a few days ago, did it finally click."

"I will miss him."

All eyes switched to Cousin Ruth, who looked as small as the voice that came from her. Even her bright-pink sweater didn't add much to her presence.

Maggie couldn't believe anyone had this point of view. The rectory was quiet without Father Henry. Certainly all the phone calls and small, but numerous, parish decisions fell into her lap. Not really so different, she thought. Just cut out the middleman. The indecisive, procrastinating middleman. It was hard to believe he had followed through on something as considerate as leaving the cats she'd come to love in her care.

Ruth's well-practiced hands folded in her lap as if in prayer. "I also understand perfectly why Henry regarded the groomer like family. I have taken every dog I've owned, and that's many dogs, for many years, to my groomer, Beth. I attended her wedding, and she came to my mother's funeral. When you see someone once a month, consult with them when your vet is stumped or not available, and cries with you when your companion of fifteen or eighteen years passes away—that's a bond. That's family." She gave a slight lift of her chin. "Also. Personally, I think a Felger Chapel will be nice."

Phyllis tipped her head at the cousin seated next to her. "Aren't you angry, I mean, disappointed at not getting more money?"

"Charlie and I are in decent financial shape, praise God. I suppose a little more would have been nice, but we're fine. Besides, it was, always, Henry's money."

Phyllis squared her shoulders. "Grandfather's money." She'd gotten her final dig in.

Wayne had his own axe to grind. "I have no trouble saying it. I'm pissed. Not disappointed. Pissed. I am not fine, and Henry could have made my life easier. Stupid priest. Stupid cats. Thought he was being so charitable by giving me a stupid job."

Maggie didn't skipped a beat. "And, will you be wanting to continue with that stupid job?"

Wayne's fingers twitched, untethered by a cigarette. "I don't know," he spat out. He recovered enough to finish his litany. "Stupid chapel, for Christ's sake. What a friggin' waste."

Phyllis sat up to him. "Maybe people will go in that stupid chapel and pray for your peevish soul."

"My soul can take care of itself."

Here was someone with more self-interest than herself, and it brought Phyllis's moral superiority back in line. "Ruth is right. Maybe a chapel is a good thing. A God good thing. Henry deserves to have it built in his memory. In the family name." She lowered her head. "God rest his soul."

Libby watched them all work themselves back into their long-held beliefs—that Father Henry had been selfish or saintly depending, not on his merits, but on how they perceived the world from their own singular vantage point. Libby had wondered about the money for the chapel, not from the perspective of it not going to her, but that it was not going to build a school or fill a food pantry. On the other hand, she loved St. Hedwig's, the grandness, the beauty and comfort of place it carved out of the everyday world.

"Amen," the Vicar tacked on robustly. "God rest his soul."

He pressed the pleated folder closed and tied it with the thin, brown string. "As I said when I called each of you, this was mostly a courtesy meeting. I wanted you all to know that Father Henry's money had been located and that everything will proceed just as he wished. You are all free to go, save Ms. Mueller, whom I will ask to stay for a few minutes to finalize the care of the cats."

Turning to Maggie, he asked, "Did you bring the figures for food, vet, groo—" He cut himself off, careful not to reignite that discussion.

Maggie quickly handed a manila folder of papers to the Vicar. "Here are the statements and tallies you asked for."

Practiced at bringing meetings to a close, the Vicar stood and said with crisp authority, "Thank you all for coming down to conclude Father Henry's business affairs. I shouldn't have to bother you again."

To be sure, all present were products of parochial school educations. Even Wayne fell in with them. When a priest stood, the class stood, mid-sentence if need be.

They had been dismissed. As were many of their hopes and financial expectations.

With little fanfare, the beneficiaries slipped on their coats. At the door, Wayne turned impulsively and thrust his head between his two relatives. "Hey, Vicar." He was excited, animated. "Now that Bernie

Fruehauf's going to the slammer, can I have Henry's car?"

The Vicar promised to look into it; and then cordially, but firmly, closed the door on all but Maggie.

As the church secretary followed the Vicar to his desk, numbers swirled in her head. She had never totaled the cost of pet care before. The stark realization of what she'd agreed to, on her secretary's salary, with a going-to-college daughter and her husband living at home, had never been so vivid. Vivid, too, were the miserly ways of Father Henry. She begged him in death to at least cover some of the cats' food for a while.

"I must ask you again," the Vicar said, sitting across from Maggie at his desk. "Formally and legally, will you keep both cats? For the rest of their lives?"

Maggie loved them. She barely hesitated. The thought of them going to someone else? No, she was attached. She might have disagreed with her boss on a multitude of things, but on this subject, they were of one mind. "Yes, I will take them."

The Vicar perused the information she'd given him. "It's evident Father Henry took excellent care of his … most important possessions. And this is the total cost of that care for the last calendar year?"

Maggie double-checked the number he pointed to. She swallowed and confirmed it. *Why couldn't Father Henry have gotten strays like my urchins and fed them discount grocery food?*

Tick, tick, tick. Tick, tick. The Vicar tabulated on a small calculator. He quoted as he wrote the check. "To cover their care, monthly grooming, food, necessary veterinary appointments, etc., for the rest of their lives." He looked up to make his little joke. "This should cover all nine of them, should they go that route!"

"With my luck, they'll set records."

"When they pass away," he proceeded, "you are to have them cremated, the ashes buried in Father Henry's plot in the Catholic cemetery."

Maggie wondered if she had heard correctly.

A bit of a smile formed on the Vicar's lips, suppressed immediately by a hand stifling a cough. "Father Henry suggests you do this perhaps under cover of darkness." The Vicar consulted the directive before him. "Any remaining money is yours to keep and do with as you wish. Father Henry notes that you are rather prudent in such matters. In my experience, if you invest some of it, it is quite likely to be sufficient. For both you and the cats."

He handed her the check.

Maggie blinked at it. Several times. Her mouth went dry.

After staring at the check, she looked up, nonplussed, at the Vicar.

His eyebrows went up, and a wide smile brightened his entire face as he closed the folder on his desk. "As I said before, Father Henry took excellent care of the things he cared about, did he not?"

~ ~ ~

After leaving the Vicar's and making a stop at another office downtown, Libby swung by St. Hedwig's, where Maggie, at the door on the rectory porch, waved her to come in.

"That's great," said Libby. "I hope he put some in there to cover your own contribution to their care."

Down the wide staircase padded Dunkirk and Calico Two. Ignoring Libby, the cats followed Maggie, landing on her desk, greeting her with much head butting. She, nuzzling and petting, returned the welcome. "Yes. Yes, he did." She draped her coat on the back of her office chair. "He was … hard to say … generous."

"Hard to say or hard to admit?"

"Hard to believe." Maggie switched on the computer. "What brings you over this way?"

"Thought I'd put up the hymn numbers for the weekend. Daring, in light of Father Henry's superstition, but it's nice not to have to come in early before Mass on Saturday and climb up to the board in my good clothes." She held up several sheets of paper. "I also have to run off the liturgy lineup and notes. For the substitute organist."

At that moment, Libby's words stopped.

Maggie folded her arms and hugged herself tightly. "I know," she said.

"It's like another death," Libby finally choked out. "This will almost be harder for me than losing Father Henry. Bernie and I worked together for so long. Were so used to each other."

"I still can't believe it." The secretary smiled sympathetically and held out her hand. "Here. Let me. I can run it off for you." The smile evolved into a grin. "My copier is working great."

They both laughed.

"Good for you," said Libby. "But, thanks, I need to go into the choir loft anyway …" She struggled to keep a smile on her face. "To pull music and … and maybe straighten things up now that the police are finished. Get things ready, anyway."

Libby scratched each cat's ears and wished them well.

"I'm taking them home tonight," said Maggie. "I'll take Father's pillow for their security blanket."

At the front door, Libby and Maggie stopped and stared out the beveled glass. "You know, Bernie took a good chunk of those Storm Relief gift cards Father was carrying that day," said Libby.

"I thought Antonio's nephew took them."

"He took some, but I never thought they were all accounted for. Bernie told Detective Grass that he felt he was owed them for all he'd done for the Church and the little pay he got. Said he'd seen priests do less than he and get so much more. Something about first-class travel and country club dinners; we can guess who that might be. But typical Bernie. Just like with the thurible, he felt guilty."

"What did he do with them?"

"Gave them all back," said Libby.

Maggie pulled her shawl tighter. "Poor Bernie. He could return the cards and put the thurible on the stand, but he could not bring Father Henry back."

"Bernie, Bernie," said Libby, a puff of breath leaving a circle of fog on the glass. "He must have been frantic. So out of his element." Libby pulled on her crazy-patterned mittens. "Any word yet on our pastoral replacement?"

"No." Maggie's sigh sent a twin circle of fog onto the window glass.

"Anyone you're hoping we get? Or hoping we don't?"

"The first list is short; the second is a mile long." Pausing a moment, Maggie took clear-eyed stock of the prospects. "It's a job. I've been through four pastors so far. I've got solid coping skills. I will say this," she said, stepping aside to open the door for Libby, "I don't need anyone with more cats."

Place was important to Libby. She knew people who happily moved every few years, others who transplanted themselves halfway across the country to experience new cities or new climates. She loved to travel for those same reasons, but she also loved returning home, to look out her solarium window, to walk to the park, to drive over the river into town, to sing at St. Hedwig's.

Even though the feeling of having a firm home base currently eluded her soul.

Lights were not on in the church, and there was not much heat. Nothing she wasn't used to. She kept her coat and crazy mittens on. The shadowy afternoon fit her mood as she sat, quietly, a few rows back in the empty pews of St. Hedwig's. Having lost heart to put up the new hymn numbers, Libby clanked the heavy brass figures she had pulled, one against another.

And she cried.

Cried for Father Henry; cried for Bernie. And, as the poet Blake would have pointed out, she cried, after all, for herself. She cried for the mystery she had helped solve and the mystery in her soul she could not.

Acknowledgments

It seems a wonderful irony that when something is written and comes to fruition (as in being in print), the overwhelming feeling is one of gratitude—to others. Ironic because after all, it's the author, who did most of the work—dreamed up the characters, stewed over the plot, chose the words. And yet after my first stunned joy at seeing the completed piece, my first impulse was to thank and thank and thank. No wonder acceptance speeches go on forever.

Of course, there are those to thank who were directly involved like Mary Jo Zazueta for help in editing the manuscript and designing the front cover, then formatting it all for the Kindle version; Charkiera Smith for the full cover design, interior layout, and formatting the print version.

Yet having thanked them, I became Walt Whitman, keenly and helplessly aware that "I am a part of all that I have met," that I have a debt of gratitude to siblings, parents, teachers, childhood friends, pastors, therapists, neighbors, colleagues, readers.... And not just people I know personally. I feel like thanking people who, even having never met them, have still, through their own art, been beside me all the way: Robert McKee, Julia Cameron, Louise Penny, Vincent Van Gogh, Anne Lamott, Agatha Christie, Annie Dillard, Geneen Roth, Beethoven, Charles Dickens, St. Francis, St. Peter, Emily Dickinson...

And what about all those people who held my hand through this specific project, who sat across from endless cups of coffee and Wendy's baked potatoes, who walked dogs in the rain, and who stayed late and wrinkled after swimming class to listen to plot points and commiserate on the emotional ups-and-downs of writing? Who ordered the best pizza to celebrate minor triumphs along the way and who never tired of asking, "How's it going?"

So the wonderful irony is that for what from the outside appears to be a most solitary endeavor of writing, it turns out, once again, to be proof that we never truly accomplish anything alone.

Thank you.

Made in the USA
Middletown, DE
27 February 2017